Birds of America

Birds of America is the story of a young American student, Peter Levi, an innocent abroad and at home.

In the autumn of 1964, aged nineteen, he arrives in France for a year's study after a bizarre farewell holiday with his mother in a rented historic house in a New England fishing village.

In Paris, like every student there, he suffers from homesickness and loneliness. He also worries about the ethics of using the PX store, and the health of his *Fatshedera* plant and takes the plant for regular walks to give it an airing. He worries too about the ubiquitous *clochards*, and anxiously eyes the young workmen tossing back a quick one at the corner bar. Inevitably, in due course, he falls for a girl – a dauntless vegetarian.

Peter has a stubborn attachment to his other mother, Nature, and to the old America, which once thought itself the New World. He is an egalitarian too and tries to live his daily student life according to Kant's dicta, hoping his will may have the force of natural law. Foreseeably, it results in comedy, mild disasters, ineffectual clashes with the police and other forces of order. Continuously frustrated, he has all the persistence of a weed.

Birds of America is a funny and touching comedy, a *Candide* for the seventies.

also by Mary McCarthy

The Company She Keeps
A Source of Embarrassment
Cast a Cold Eye
The Groves of Academe
A Charmed Life
Sights and Spectacles
Memories of a Catholic Girlhood
Venice Observed
The Stones of Florence
On the Contrary
The Group
Vietnam
Hanoi
The Writing on the Wall

Mary McCarthy

BIRDS OF AMERICA

Weidenfeld and Nicolson
5 Winsley Street London W1

ISBN 0 297 00472 7

Printed in Great Britain by
C. Tinling & Co. Ltd, London and Prescot

'. . . . to attempt to embody the Idea in an example, as one might embody the wise man in a novel, is unseemly . . . for our natural limitations, which persistently interfere with the perfection of the Idea, forbid all illusion about such an attempt . . .'

TO HANNAH

Contents

Winter Visitors

IN the Wild Life Sanctuary, the Great Horned Owl had died. The woman who showed the Palmer Homestead, on the edge of the woods, remembered the event distinctly: he had passed away the winter before last. Peter Levi, a college junior, swallowed this news with a long gulping movement of his prominent Adam's apple; grief and shock choked him. 'You have to expect changes,' he heard her say in a sharp tone, as he turned away from the doorstep, unable to speak. The old witch knew he was blaming her for the knockout punch she had just given him, standing calmly in her white shoes on the doormat that spelled out 'WELCOME,' her hands on her hips. Until she spoke, he had supposed that the owl was still somewhere about, cruising in the woods, a noiseless shadow, hunting his prey. The idea that he could have 'passed away' like any senior citizen had not crossed Peter's mind. Revisiting the great bird in his tall outdoor cage littered with owl pellets of hair, claws, and bones was a treat Peter had been promising himself from the moment he heard from his mother that they were coming back to Rocky Port for the summer; it almost made up to him for the fact that she and his divorced father had agreed that he could not go to Mississipi with the Students for Civil Rights group. His mother, left to herself, might have let him go, but his father, who was more realistic, decided that Peter was too unsure of himself with people to take part in the programme. Peter felt the *babbo*'s criticism was validated by his behaviour this afternoon.

Instead of simply knocking and asking what had happened

to the owl, as he had planned when reconnoitring the house from across the road, he had paid the price of admission (Adults, $.50) and let himself be conducted through the homestead before he dared pop the question and at the last had nearly chickened out, for fear the woman would think he had been *using* her for his own stealthy purposes, which were antagonistic to old panelling and original floorboards. Peter, a philosophy minor, was an adept of the Kantian ethic; he had pledged himself never to treat anyone as a means ('The Other is always an End: thy Maxim,' said a card he carried in his wallet, with his driving licence, vaccination certificate, and membership in SNCC, CORE, and SANE), and yet because of his shyness, which made his approaches circuitous, he repeatedly found himself doing exactly that. It was only a kind of wild loyalty to the owl that had disgorged the question from his lips just as she was about to shut the door. If he did not ask now, he prodded himself, he would *never* find out. It would be no use asking in Rocky Port, where no one knew anything, and he could not come back here to inquire, for that would put his present visit, already suspicious ('Funny a boy your age should be interested in antiques'), in a still more bizarre light. Yet if he did not find out, it would be as if he did not *care* – another horrible sin. When he finally did ask, addressing her on the stoop from an inferior position on the lawn, it was in a casual preppy voice. 'By the way, could you tell me what's become of the Great Horned Owl they used to have over there in the Wild Life Sanctuary?' How could he hope to fight for civil rights in Mississippi when he did not feel he had the *right* to ask a simple question in 'neighbourly' New England? The *babbo* knew best.

Except in the class-room and of people he already knew outside it, Peter loathed asking questions. When he was little, he could not bear to have his mother stop the car and call out to a native for directions. 'They won't *know*, Mother! *Please* go on!' Prevention being the best cure (Peter was fond of adages), at a very early age he became a whiz at map-reading, sitting on her right on a cushion; Peter the Navigator, his stepfather in the back seat used to call him. He had never outgrown the feeling that a quest for information was a series of manoeuvres in a game of espionage. In a library, rather than apply to the librarian, he would loiter about till he discovered where the card catalogues were kept and then trace the book he wanted to its lair through the Dewey Decimal System – Melvil Dewey, on his school lists, figured as a Great American, outranking Eli Whitney and the inventor of the McCormick Reaper. In a museum, he learned how to use the plan posted near the cloakroom while he was still in the first grade and would be tugging his mother towards 'Armour' before she could question a guard. Similarly with a new A & P supermarket, whenever he and his mother moved; he raced about quivering like a magnetic needle till he found the bearings of Tide and tapioca and Grape-Nuts. He could always smoke out the toilets, hers and his, in filling stations and restaurants.

When he was young, the game was easier and more fun, because no one noticed him; a child, he observed, possessed a natural camouflage and could blend into the social landscape – a corollary of Peter Levi's Law that normal adults were not interested in children. But now that he was an adult himself, in all but the right to vote or marry without his parents' consent, he had become suddenly visible, and the surreptitious pursuit of information had become not only much more difficult but also associated with a kind of anguish, whose source was a notion of duty.

This afternoon, for example, when he found the cage in the woods empty and derelict and the wire netting torn, he at once knew that he would have to *do* something about it and he could not tell whether this was the cause of the anger he felt spurt out of him or whether that fury was a pure primary reaction to the fact that the marvellous bird was gone. He had slunk out of the sanctuary and sat down at the entrance under a tree labelled 'Buttonwood', where he noted that a house across the road, set back on a hillock, had a sign on the lawn: 'Open to the Public.' Then he saw the manly course that was open to *him*: inquire of the owl's nearest neighbour. He was scanning the small-paned, brown-shingled redoubt when a curtain twitched in a downstairs window; a counter-spy was watching him. 'Now or never,' he said hoarsely, cawing like the Raven. The word *never* usually got results. Another magic formula, which he used to ward off discouragement after failure, was 'Once more unto the breach, dear friends.' He was inclined to think of himself as a collection of persons who had to be assembled for any initiative.

He ought to have thanked the woman for telling him, but he could not. Still swallowing hard, he bolted across the stubbly lawn to where his motorbike was parked. The screen door slammed. In a minute it opened again. 'Young man! You didn't sign the guest book!' Starting the motor, he pretended not to hear her. This was the only satisfaction he could chalk up for the afternoon. She had not got him to sign! He had spotted the book, open, the moment he entered the homestead and had cunningly diverted her attention with a purchase of postcards, which were now in his jacket pocket. The total expense, including admission to this waste of shame, was $.65. The owl's blood money. Peter, who was thrifty, decided to enter the sum as a reward he had offered for knowledge of the bird's whereabouts. 'I am a propitiatory person,' he chanted, to the tune of his sputtering motor, as he chugged home. He could already hear his mother's cheerful voice, probably emanating from the kitchen, wanting to know if he had seen his friend the owl. The word *friend* stabbed him in the guts; he pictured himself in Mississippi, hanging about a county courthouse or a garage or general store, trying to learn, without directly asking, what had happened to a missing Negro friend. . . . Moreover, he knew that his mother would feel almost as badly as he did when he had to tell her the owl had croaked.

Coming back to Rocky Port, to strengthen his roots before going abroad, was just one radical blow after another, as far as Peter was concerned. 'Guess you'll notice changes,' the village chorus greeted him. Or, in fugue, 'You won't find many changes.' Peter always answered 'Yes' to the first of these challenges and 'No' to the second, wondering why the local *amour propre* should keep twanging so insistently on the theme of change. The changes Peter noticed were not those the storekeepers and the mailman seemed to be alluding to. He was not even aware, till duly admonished, that the Portuguese had built a new Catholic church, replacing the old one, which the Yankees now said had been 'charming'; his mother had had to point out to him the new Sugar 'N' Spice Shop and the new Bait & Lure Shop and the new Corner Cupboard and the Lamplighter and the second art gallery and the hand-lettered signs advertising merchants and realtors that swung on curly iron brackets at the turn-off to the village, replacing the old 'commercial' billboards. He did observe that most of the houses had sprouted little historical notices, bordered in yellow, also hand-lettered and with ampersands and wavy dashes, telling when they had been built and who had lived there or kept a school or a tavern or a marble yard there. The house his mother had rented, painted a dark colonial red, bore the date 1780, and Peleg Turnbull, a ship's chandler, had kept a shop in the front rooms. One of Peter's mother's first actions had been to find a hammer and remove the placard stating this. At once there came a written protest from the landlady, to which his mother answered that this epidemic of historical notices reminded her unpleasantly of the coloured quarantine signs of her childhood: 'Measles,' 'Mumps,' 'Scarlet Fever.' Yellow, she thought, had been measles.

'Quarantined by history,' Peter remarked in his slightly hoarse voice, backing up his mother's stand. But really he was attached to history, provided it stayed still. Now that the point had been called to his attention, he rather missed the old billboards as well as the neon storefront signs. Except in the field of civil rights, he was opposed to progress in any direction, including backwards, which was the direction Rocky Port seemed to be heading in, and wanted everything in the sensuous world to be the same as it had been when he was younger. When he was nearly four years younger: fifteen.

That was when he and his mother had first come to Rocky Port, in the fall, out of season; she had rented a house near the water, in the 'wrong' section of the village, where the

Portuguese lived. From his bedroom window, he used to watch three cormorants that stood on pilings in the cove and he had been counting on seeing them again on his return. He had three sentimental journeys planned: the first to the cormorants, the second to the Great Horned Owl, and the third to a hidden waterfall up in the back country. To date, he had had two disappointments. Number One, the cormorants were gone. The first evening, while his mother was wrenching off the placard, he had hurried down on foot, past the laundress's house, to where they used to live. A single boring gull sat on one of the piles; that was all. He kept coming back to look at different times of day, pretending to be taking a stroll. But it was no use. They were gone. And nobody but he and his mother seemed to be able to recall them.

'You mean gulls, don't you, Peter?' his mother's new friends said. 'No,' he said. 'Not gulls. I *know* gulls.' 'Can he mean the Arctic Tern?' 'He means cormorants,' said his mother. Then at a cocktail party, given at a house on the harbour, he met a retired admiral whose small hawk face he remembered. 'The cormorants? Sure, son,' said the admiral, who came from the South. 'They're nesting now in Labrador. They'll be back in the fall.' 'I won't be here then,' said Peter. In the fall, he would be in Paris, taking his junior year at the Sorbonne. For the first time, he felt sad at the thought. He could not understand, either, how he could have forgotten that cormorants migrated, when he had spent hours in the reference section of the village Free Library, identifying the three black birds, uncertain to start with whether they were the Double Crested Cormorant or the Common Cormorant, which was a lot rarer. He was worried that he might be losing his memory. To cheer himself up, he decided that some fall he could come back here and find them again, when he was through with college and the Army. Maybe on his honeymoon. 'The cormorant's life span?' said the admiral. 'Hell, son, maybe ten, fifteen years. Those three damn birds have been here winters as long as I have. Now let's see. I retired in '58. . . .' It was clear to Peter that the admiral was just gassing to cover up his ignorance; like most people here, he was not interested in getting to the bottom of anything. He began to talk vociferously, waving his short pipe, about the ages attained by ships' parrots, in an argumentative tone that Peter was coming to recognize as the cry of the Rocky Port species, mature, male, which always sounded as if its assertions were about to be contested by another species – foreign or black. Peter felt he would not welcome a heart-to-heart with the admiral on the topic of integration. Yet this chat, he feared, was on his summer calendar, as predictable as Fourth of July fireworks or the appearance of a spring robin on a Rocky Port lawn. Despite that, he rather liked the old man, first for remembering the cormorants, second for remembering him, and third for surviving unchanged from that other year.

That year had a special value for Peter because that year he got the wish he used to make on every baby tooth he put under his pillow to dream on: to live in a little house in New England with his mother by themselves. He had never liked California; he missed the winter. He hated his stepfather's garden in Berkeley, with roses and daffodils and tulips and irises all blooming at the same time, so that there was never anything to look forward to. The only birds that appealed to him there were the humming-birds. He hated the desert; he was convinced that it was the product of some nuclear catastrophe that had befallen an earlier race of scientists. He declined to consider Death Valley a part of Nature. Peter was strongly in favour of Nature, and he was against modern physics for interfering with Her.

His stepfather was in the physics department of the University of California, a very valuable man; he had helped bring heavy water to England from the Continent during the war. Peter had always imagined Hans carrying it in his suitcase through customs. He was a refugee, like Peter's own father. The difference was that Peter's father, who taught history at Wellesley, had left Italy for political reasons and not just because he was Jewish, while Hans might still be pottering in his laboratory in the Fatherland if he had not been born a Jew. Peter's mother was not Jewish. He had heard his aunt say that her sister had a 'thing' about Jews, which he hoped included him. Peter slightly preferred his own father to Hans, but he tried to think that this preference was impersonal, like preferring the seashore to the mountains or breakfast to lunch: he liked the East better than the West, Italy better than Germany, history better than physics. Personally, Hans was genial, and the *babbo* was bad-tempered. Peter always felt wicked when he would place his baby tooth under his pillow, to dream of running away with the fair Rosamund (called 'Rosie' by Hans), and then wake up the next morning to find a silver dollar that he knew Hans had put there. Silver dollars were one item Peter approved of in the West. In the end, when the wish came true, he was quite sorry for Hans, who had agreed to what he called a 'trial separation'. Coming east on the train, four years ago, come September, the gladder Peter was at the thought that he and his mother were alone at last, the sorrier he felt for Hans, who had waved them off at the station.

Four years ago, he was deeply in love with his mother. He was a tall boy with a long nose and gaunt features – the picture of his father at the same age, except for his eyes, which were grey, like hers. He often stared at himself in the mirror, but for the opposite reason from Narcissus; it was *her* eyes he gazed into, captive in his Jewish face. He had known for a long time about the Oedipus complex; his stepfather, teasing, used to call him 'young Oedipus'. But he did not think that, on balance, he would like to sleep with his mother, only to be with her where there were no other people. He was sure that despite what she said she would marry again, and he would have a new set of stepbrothers and stepsisters, probably. All he asked of the gods was a year with her. Already he realized that this year, when he was fifteen, would be the last year of his childhood; at sixteen, he would be a youth and lose his innocence. He had seen it happen to his stepbrothers.

Peter wanted to grow up; he did not plan to be a Peter Pan. But he felt that a halcyon interval was owing him, particularly because of the divorce, which required him to spend the summer with his father, so that only the school year, the darker part, belonged to her. Because of school and 'activities', he hardly ever had her to himself, unless he was sick, and unfortunately he got sick mostly in the summer. When he was little, she used to read to him at bedtime, but now he was too old for that. Holidays – Christmas and Easter – were allocated by Hans to family trips. On weekends, Hans was always home. That was the way the ball bounced. The fact that his mother did not love Hans as much as she did Peter made her always anxious to 'include' him in all their projects. Knowing his mother, Peter often felt that it would have been a lucky break for him if he had been her stepchild, instead of the wormy apple of her eye.

Yet she must have had it in mind all along to 'make it up' to Peter when she was free. Then it would be his turn. Though she was reticent about personal things, Peter guessed there was some sort of promise between them, which involved, on his side, being patient. It did not surprise him when she told him that she and Hans were parting. Each of her marriages, Peter pointed out to her, had lasted seven years – a Biblical span. She had never counted, but he had. Nor had there ever been any question for Peter but that she was living in exile out there in corny California; when the two of them finally cut and ran, it would be back to New England, their real home. The only problem was where.

She put that up to Peter; he could choose, providing it was not an island. He picked Rocky Port. It looked lonely – a thin finger of land pointing out to sea, far from a main highway. She laughed when he showed it to her on the map. 'Define a peninsula, Peter.' A body of land almost entirely surrounded by water, from the Latin *paene insula*, an almost-island. Peter laughed too. Then she protested that they did not know a living soul in the vicinity; nobody she knew had ever been to Rocky Port. But that was how he had plotted it, dismissing Cape Cod, Vermont, commuters' Connecticut, and hesitating over the Massachusetts North Shore, which attracted him but where they would be likely to get visits from the *babbo*. Peter had calculated the driving time from Wellesley to

Ipswich; he was not taking any chances on a renewed romance between his parents.

It worried her that he might not find friends of his own age in such an isolated (there was that word again) village. But this was the last year, Peter explained, that he would *want* to be solitary; next year, he would be interested in girls and parties. Up to now he had always lived in an academic community, even in the summer, because the *babbo* invariably vacationed with a lot of other professors. It was the last year too, he argued, that he would be allowed to be by himself with birds and animals unless he planned to be an ornithologist or a zoologist. A young boy was expected to like animals, but he would have to be forty before he could watch them again without somebody watching *him*. Hearing the desperation in his voice, his mother capitulated. Besides, she had told him he could choose.

In her place, Peter would just have gone there, without further research, but his mother was trying to reform from being a 'hopeless romantic', in the words of her sister. She got the state guidebook out of the college library and looked up Rocky Port; she found the name of a real-estate agent in a directory of realtors and sent off a letter with their specifications, asking about schools and transportation. She signed it 'Rosamund Brown', her own name, which Peter would not have done, even though he was glad that she was giving up Hans's moniker. He would have liked them to live under an alias.

The agent, a Mrs Curtis, wrote back immediately with listings and asked if she were *the* Rosamund Brown; if so, she had some of her records. Peter's mother was a professional musician. 'But my records are all out of print!' she cried. She was always surprised and touched when someone remembered her, because she had not played a recital or in a real concert for years – only for fun with a University chamber group. She had given up the concert stage when Hans was summoned to Berkeley; California was too far from the centre. Peter could tell that she took the realtor's letter as a wonderful, strange omen; she was being recalled to life. For his part, Peter took the omen as bad. If his mother had a fan in Rocky Port, it was no longer virgin territory. The place was probably full of artists and writers and music-lovers generally; he ought to have been put on guard by the elm-shaded streets and the Greek Revival doorways in the photographs in the state guidebook. He was relieved to learn from the agent's second letter that the artistic colony closed their houses early in September.

'I'm afraid you'll find it rather bleak,' Mrs Curtis wrote apologetically. 'After Labour Day, we go "back to Nature". The little house you're interested in is in rather a "slummy" section, but it has a lovely view and you'll be quite by yourselves. There's no television set, I'm afraid, for your son, but there's a good working piano. I realize that isn't the same as a harpsichord, but you can probably "make do". The kitchen is fairly well equipped; I imagine that, like so many of our musical artists, you like to cook wonderful things. Your son can walk to the old Rocky Port high school on the harbour; the grand new consolidated high school on Route 1 isn't finished yet – politics. Do I understand you won't have a car? Would you like me to have the piano tuned?'

His mother, as always, was her own piano-tuner, and they did not have a car, that fall. Both cars had stayed with Hans, which Peter, on the whole, was glad of, for it limited his mother's movements. When his bicycle finally came by Railway Express, with the harpsichord and the clavichord, he mostly left it in the cellar, because she did not have one. Instead, they took walks together, which they had never done in Berkeley. Every clear evening they walked down to the point, past the abandoned lighthouse and the boarded-up whaling museum, to see the sun set; this was their daily contact with the natives, who came in their Fords and Chevrolets for the same reason. It was a local ritual, like the lowering of a flag. They watched the fishing boats come home; the pink sky was full of gulls. Then they would wend their own way back to supper, past the plastics factory and the Doric bank and the Civil War cannon in the square. At home, the cormorants would be standing on their piles, three black silhouettes in the paling light; they never came to the lighthouse point. They never mixed with the other birds – a fact that struck Peter from the beginning.

He decided they were sacred birds, an unholy trinity. Standing on their dark piles in the water, they had an evil, old, Egyptian look; gorged, their black wings spread to dry in the sun, they resembled hieroglyphs or emblems on an escutcheon. In their neck was a pouch that bulged when they had been fishing. They did not swim or float on the surface like other birds but darted through the water in a sinuous, snake-like way. He had never seen them squat or sit. They were always erect, spreadeagled; not sedentary – vigilant. They seldom moved, though they occasionally gave a flap of their wings or a turn of their long serpentine necks. They usually stood facing away, surveying the cove like sentries, or, in profile, commanding the open sea, but sometimes he would come back from some private sleeveless errand to find that they had wheeled about and were facing him in glistening formation. Unlike the shrieking terns and squawking gulls, they did not utter a sound. This stillness and fixity were what made them seem so horribly ancient, Peter thought, as though they preceded time. That and their snaky appearance, which took you back to the age of flying reptiles. Moreover, their soundless habit gave their slightest movement the quality of a pantomime; from his bedroom window, he could pretend he was watching a drama of hieratic gesture.

He did not know why he connected the cormorants with his mother and their flight back to Nature's bosom, but if he could have had a seal ring made (he was still a sealing-wax addict) in memory of that year, it would have been incised with three cormorants – his sign. His mother said they made her think of the three black-cloaked masked Revenges at the end of the first act of *Don Giovanni*: Donna Elvira, Donna Anna, and Don Ottavio. Peter agreed. There was that about them too. Three pouchy pursuers, storers-up of grudges. He wondered about their sex. Were they father, mother, and son? Or three brothers? The last of their race. In one bird book he had read that only a few hundred Common European Cormorants were left in North America. There must be even fewer now than when the book was written. Unless, of course, they were protected.

The Great Horned Owl seemed very old too, nearly extinct, with its immobile dilated pupils and its long nightgown of ruffly feathers. He was exceptionally pale for his species, cruel-looking, and very big. Peter's mother almost thought he must be an Arctic Horned Owl because he was so pale. They had come upon him like an apparition in the chill solitary woods, having discovered the Wild Life Sanctuary in the course of a Saturday walk. The Boy Scouts, they decided, must have marked the trails with visual aids pointing to squirrels, autumn foliage, and owls – ordinary screech owls, not this great tufted tigerish creature. And someone, a very brave Scout, must have captured him and put him in the home-made cage nailed to a tree and labelled '*Bubo Virginianus* – Great Horned Owl'; someone must feed him field mice and whatever other sacrifices he regurgitated in the form of those hairy pellets. But they never met a Scout or any other human being in the sanctuary.

Besides the trails through the woods and the captive owl in his tree-house, it had a log cabin with educational exhibits of pyrites and quartzes and shells and stuffed birds and stuffed animals and butterflies and amusing insects like the Walking Stick. There were wild-flower and fern charts on the walls. It was the kind of place where you would expect to find a custodian to reprimand you or get you to join the Audubon Society, but it was empty except for the taxidermic presences in the glass cabinets. To come on it, swept and garnished, in the woods was spooky, like the story his mother used to tell of the ship *Marie Celeste*, which was found afloat in mid-ocean in apple-pie order, with mess tables set and ovens still warm and not a hand aboard.

Nobody Peter and his mother met in Rocky Port had ever visited the sanctuary or could say who ran it; they thought Peter and his mother were talking about the *bird* sanctuary, which was something different, a desolate state preserve of dunes and marshes and jackpine, where couples went to make love. Mrs Curtis took Peter and his mother there in her car one Sunday morning, and they did not see a single worth-while bird – just beer cans and the remains of campfires. It seemed funny to Peter that there should be *two* sanctuaries in the locality and each, as it were, unaware of the other, like two people that had not been introduced. Mrs Curtis could not explain it. If Peter wanted to find out more about *his* sanctuary, she advised him to sign up at school with a Nature Study group. The manual training teacher was the one to see; he would know all about it. Peter refused the suggestion. He did not want his relationship with Nature organized and managed for him.

Indeed, he liked the mystery surrounding *his* sanctuary and the fact that he and his mother were its only (visible) initiates. Exploring, they found a dark stream, stepping-stones, mallards, a pond. By Christmas, his mother said, the pond would surely freeze over; she promised to buy skates at the hardware store and teach him to skate. They could use the log cabin as a shelter to thaw out their feet. Already a black frost had come; the autumn leaves had fallen, and you could identify the dedicuous trees only by their shapes. With the end of daylight-saving time, the afternoons were shortened; when they left the sanctuary, it was almost night. In the dusk sometimes, from the road home, they would head an ululating cry, and Peter would hoot back. He knew from his reading that Great Horned Owls bred in snow and ice; it worried him that the lonely hooter did not have a mate. The idea occurred to him to let him out of his cage, which would not be hard; his mother, who was fearless of authority, would help him. Selfishly, too, Peter longed to see him fly, just once – the drifting flight the books described, like a big moth coasting overhead.

But then Peter would be *responsible* for the sequel. What if the owl, weakened by captivity, was unequal to liberation? It might starve, left on its own in the woods. Alternatively, the predatory killer, freed, might make a holocaust in the wild-life refuge. Peter thought with anguish of the pine grosbeaks he and his mother had seen, almost tame, in a wild apple tree on Columbus Day; he imagined their rosy bodies all red with gore. A sanctuary was meant to be *safe*. He recognized with a sad Hello the classic conservative arguments as they passed through his head – arguments for not meddling with the *status quo*. A silent shadow, like the shadow of the hunting bird, fell across his happiness. He wished he had never thought of releasing the owl in the first place. Now that the notion of change had glided into his mind, he could not just accept the bird's being there as natural. It had to be *justified*. Perhaps he was simply getting bored, but it no longer gave him much pleasure to engage in a staring match with the barred and striped prisoner – a game that, in any case, his mother deplored. When Armistice Day came, he rejected her offer to bring a picnic to the sanctuary. 'Let's take in a movie,' he said in a sullen voice.

His mother was bewildered; he often hurt her by his unwillingness to explain himself. It would have killed him to tell her that he was depressed by his lack of guts about the owl; she did not even know that he had been weighing the question of setting him free. He loved her too much to confide his weaknesses to her. He preferred discussing hers, which were obvious.

For example, she had gone and bought him a large illustrated *Birds of America*, to replace (in *her* mind) the little blue Peterson guide that had been left behind in Berkeley. Peter was quite happy using the reference section of the Free Library, even if they did not let you take the books home – it was good training for his memory. He enjoyed being resourceful, living off the land, like a hunter, not always having to buy things in a store. Moreover, he considered the gift a placebo. He disapproved of her habit of leaving their possessions behind whenever she got a divorce; she had done the same thing with his father.

He particularly objected to her leaving the phonograph with Hans, who never remembered to change the needle. He and his mother had long arguments about this on the train coming east; he loved arguing with his mother, who was quite intelligent, he used to tell her, for a faculty wife. A house that had a piano would surely have a phonograph, she said, and when she found she was wrong (the real-estate agent, *Peter* said, would have *mentioned* a phonograph), she went and bought a cheap stereo portable. 'Did it *have* to be stereo?' Peter groaned, homesick for their old mono set. He disliked being offered substitutes. At least she had brought along some of their records – those she called 'Peter's', like the Haydn Hunting Horn, which bayed, *he* thought (his mother said no), like a lost hound in the woods, and Handel's Water Music, which bubbled and gurgled. But Peter had not been able to reason her into taking any of the art books or the eleventh edition of the Britannica. 'Hans doesn't want it, Mother. He says it's completely out of date in all the sciences.' 'We'll advertise for another,' she said, soothing. 'If we take it, he'll miss it.'

Peter did not applaud his mother's 'noble' side. Naturally, he would have hated it if she had stuck Hans for alimony, but it would have been a *kindness* to Hans, in Peter's opinion, to take the espresso pots and half the sheets and towels, to speak only of the baser items, instead of borrowing the sheets they were now sleeping on from Mrs Curtis and drinking awful coffee from a dripolator. The least his mother could do for Hans, if she was going to leave him, was to give him some petty cause for grievance, something that would lay her open to criticism in the Faculty Club. Instead, she had been 'perfect', taking only her mother's silver and Peter's baby cup and fork and spoon and every Christmas present Hans had ever given them, naturally – so as not to hurt his feelings – no matter how useless or hard to pack. The result was that it was Hans who was open to criticism, sitting out there with two cars in his garage and cupboards full of china and linen and glasses and kitchen stuff, while she, innocent and good, was 'roughing it' with chipped plates and corny glasses with mottoes and taking the bus to the nearest town twice a week to buy groceries in the supermarket. His mother, he decided, was being so good she was bad, and this worried him.

She must want Hans to feel that an *angel* had left him, which meant, according to Peter, that she wanted Hans to still be in love with her. If she was really eager for Hans to

24

'get over' her, she should show him her worst side. Like letting Peter pinch the old German binoculars that were hanging in the hall closet in Berkeley and that Hans never used because he could not bother to take off his regular glasses.

She claimed that you had to pay for freedom by being ready to give up everything. It was ignoble, she said, to latch onto property, even if it was partly yours. O.K., but every week she bought something that was a duplicate or reasonable facsimile of some article she had left in Berkeley. Like the stereo set or cake racks or an iron griddle for flapjacks. This jarred on Peter morally, as well as on his bump of thrift. To buy the same things over again, even if you needed them, was not his definition of renunciation.

This being alone with her with the leisure to study her faults was a great pleasure to him. Peter loved America, and his mother's shortcomings were exactly those of the country; they could be summed up under the heading of extravagance. That formulation he owed to the *babbo*, who often held forth on the theme to other academics. Puritanism, the *babbo* said, was an extravagance, like Prohibition; Americans were logicians with no idea of limit. Peter's father loved America too – which tended to puzzle Americans, Peter noticed. He always liked to hear the story of his mother's first meeting with his father, at a party in New York towards the end of the war – she was studying musicology then at the Mannes School and working with Landowska. After the party, they walked down Park Avenue, and she said to him 'But what do you like about America?' since most refugees she had met were musicians who were pining for the cafés they had come from. Peter's father thought. 'I like the American birds.' She said this was what had made her fall in love with that dark, scowling man. 'It was such a funny thing to hear. Instead of "I like your tall buildings" or "I like your long-legged women" or "Your democratic institutions". ' 'But what did he mean?' Peter always asked. His mother was not certain. 'Maybe he just meant they were different from the ones he knew.'

Now that he was a full-grown male, Peter thought he

understood the *babbo*'s gambit. With her light-brown hair and grey eyes and rosy skin, his mother was like an American bird – the rose-breasted grosbeak, for instance, modest and vivid. His father had been paying her a compliment. And probably, like a lot of Europeans, he was fed up with what he knew and wanted to meet another human species, which at least would be *different*, like the birds of the New World. '*Mi piaceva il suo candore*,' he said to Peter one summer, as if grudgingly, when Peter was drawing him out. Peter had taken this to mean that the young Rosamund, like the Father of her Country, could not tell a lie. Now that he knew Italian better (he was taking Italian Lit. at college as part of his Romance languages major), he knew that *candore* was the usual word for naïveté.

The *babbo* used to say that Peter's mother was the first girl he met who was what he called a 'real American', meaning a descendant of the old Puritan colonists. To an historian, Peter guessed, that might have been pretty exciting, and the more so because her forebears out in Ohio had taken part in the opening of the West. A Boston deb could have bored the *babbo*, but Peter's mother came from pioneer stock that had settled in Marietta from New England after the Revolutionary War. The fact that she had been very pretty was a point his father did not mention. Nor did he recall having said anything about birds the night he met her. According to him, he had told her that he liked her name: Rosamund Brown. Peter liked her name too; it reminded him of a Thomas Hardy poem she had once set to music and which had a refrain: 'Dear Lizbie Browne'. When he was small, he could not connect 'Brown' with himself; he felt much more like his father than like her, to the extent of always thinking of her as a Gentile. That was why her faults pleased him, like an unfamiliar kind of marking or speckling.

At almost nineteen, he looked on the fair Rosamund with cooler eyes. He loved her still, but he was no longer in love with her. He had become cautious about her, mistrusting her consistent sweetness and unruffled temper. She was too good to be true, he discovered. Like all older people, she betrayed.

Besides her faults were no longer unfamiliar. He recognized them in himself. Her zeal to please had set him a bad example; it had made him placatory. Her scruples in him had become irresolution and an endless picking at himself that was like masturbation – a habit he had not completely outgrown and which seemed to him ignominious, even though both she and the *babbo* had said it was natural in puberty; on that score, he felt, they had given him a wrong steer. Moreover, her good qualities (she was generous, to a fault, he acknowledged dryly) did not inspire imitation. Rather the contrary. Everyone, he had observed, around the fair Rosamund turned into an ogre to protect her from herself. At nineteen, he admired his father for having the strength of his defects (something Peter would never achieve, thanks to her training, alas) and viewed his mother with a kind of ironic sympathy. But when he was fifteen, he was living in a childish world of magic where his mother was the stranger and his captive.

While he was in school, she practised or analysed pieces on the clavichord, working out the fingering; he gathered this was quite hard. She was preparing an all-Elizabethan lecture-recital to go on a tour of colleges. That was how she had got started, when she had left Landowska's master classes. Her field used to be early English music; she talked about it to college audiences and illustrated her talk on the harpsichord. Later on, she gave recitals and played with a group. His aunt told him confidentially that his mother was a better musical scholar than she was a performer. Remembering this, Peter wondered whether she would ever make the grade again. He hoped she knew that that music of olden time was not so much of a novelty as it had been in her day, right after the war. He did not let himself dwell on what would happen to *him* if her tour finally materialized. She could not play at colleges, obviously, during summer vacations, which was the time he would normally be with his father. And if she went away in the school year, who would stay with him? He was too old for a sitter and too young – public opinion would say – to stay by himself; he would not want her to get into trouble with the spcc. Hans would have come in handy, but now there was no Hans.

When he was little, it seemed, before they were divorced from his father, he used to start crying at the sight of the truckers who were coming to take the harpsichord. He had learned that this meant that his mother was going away again. The *babbo* and his nurse could never persuade him that she would come back. Once when he was holding onto the harpsichord's legs, to keep the movers from taking it (he must have been about four, he guessed), his father had picked him up and spanked him hard; he remembered his mother crying, which made his father even angrier. '*Ricatto!*' he shouted. 'Blackmail! The boy must get used to it. He should be glad you are an artist!' Peter's nurse would not tell him what that funny word, *blackmail*, meant; later he heard it quite often and always applied to himself.

When he was little, Peter hated his father for (as he thought) making his mother go away when she did not want to. He did not believe her when she explained that she *liked* having people listen to her music. If she liked it, why did she and his father argue about it? Why did his father yell at him if he disturbed her when she was practising, while *she* was always glad to stop and get him a cookie or an animal cracker? Why had he overheard her, pleading, in his father's study, 'Have pity, Paolo' (the fair Rosamund talked like one of her madrigals when emotional). 'Let me cancel the concert. This is killing me'? He had gone and got his toy gun and pointed it at his father: 'You let my mother stay home!' His mother always said, now, that she was grateful to his father for having made her go on with her concert appearances. He ought to be grateful himself, he guessed, for not having been permitted to tyrannize over his mother. But *would* it have been so bad for him if she had laid off the concert stage for a couple of years, till he was old enough to understand what it was all about?

That fall in Rocky Port, he was reconciled, he thought, to his mother's career for practical reasons. They were living off capital, which he gathered was some sort of sin. If she did not take alimony, she would have to earn some dough. But the day was still far off, he assured himself; it would be months before her programme was ready, at the rate she was going. He had nothing to worry about so long as she was still tinkering with the clavichord. When she started working on the harpsichord, that would mean she was really rehearsing. He knew this because she had told him so. He did not understand much about her instruments, except that you could not do *mains croisées* on the clavichord because it had only one keyboard. But the point of *mains croisées* escaped him. Nor did he follow her when she talked about things like figured basses and *continuo*. He did not regard her seriously as a musician, because she was his mother; besides, the only music he liked much, in his heart, was opera.

He did not mind an instrument like the hunting horn or the trumpet in *The Messiah* ('the trumpet shall sound . . . and we shall be changed'; his mother said that was a musical pun) that made him think of a solo voice. If he had been able to play himself, he would have been a trumpeter. But that would have to wait for his next incarnation. On his eighth birthday, he had learned the awful truth. Kindly Hans gave him a child's violin; Peter found it at his place at breakfast, and he saw from his mother's stricken face that it was a surprise to her too. 'You think he is too young, Rosie?' Hans queried anxiously. The next thing Peter remembered, he was standing by the harpsichord, singing a scale as she struck the notes for him. 'Ach!' said Hans. Hans had not noticed, till then, that Peter was tone-deaf. Or at least, as his mother put it, he did not hear intervals well enough to play the violin. He could be trained, she said, to read music and appreciate it; no one was *really* tone-deaf. He could learn to play the piano, which did not require an ear and would teach him something about music. 'You can have piano lessons for your birthday instead,' she said gaily to Peter. But Peter did not want that. He wanted the little violin, which Hans, an Indian giver, took back to the store. In revenge, he would not listen to the childish music like *Peter and the Wolf* that

Hans brought home to instruct him. When he got interested in opera, he always started the record *after* the overture. He refused to be broadened by going to concerts with Hans and his mother, and though he had recently admitted the horn family to his friendship, he drew the line there. He would not let his mother buy him more Haydn or Handel; he suspected her of using the Hunting Horn and the Water Music as the opening wedge.

Yet sometimes in Rocky Port, when he came home from school, he would hear the clavichord tinkling in her bedroom upstairs and he would shut the front door quietly and listen, imagining that this was a fairy-tale house with the miller's daughter upstairs spinning a room full of gold for the king, her husband. For the first time, he 'got' this courtly music. Before disturbing her, he would fetch some wood and build a fire in the fireplace, making a fanciful design of logs and kindling. He would have liked to get ice and fix her a drink, but she disapproved of children's serving as bartenders to their parents – a custom Hans, who liked his *schnapps*, had tried to introduce on the grounds that it was American.

Of course, it was American, but his mother would not admit it. She had her own notions of what was American, going back to her own childhood. Reading aloud to children in the evening, Fourth of July sparklers and fireworks, Easter-egg hunts, Christmas stockings with an orange in the toe, popcorn and cranberry chains on the Christmas tree, ducking for apples at Hallowe'en, shadow pictures on the walls, lemonade, fresh cider, picnics, treasure hunts, anagrams, checkers, eggs golden-rod, home-made cakes, muffins, popovers, and corn breads, fortune-telling, sweet peas, butterfly nets, narcissus bulbs in pebbles, Trillium, Spring Beauty, arbutus, lady's-slippers, cat's cradles, swings, bicycles, wooden ice-cream freezers, fishing with angleworms, rowing, ice-skating, blueberrying, hymn-singing. Her family had been mostly doctors, judges, and ministers; when she was in grade school, she had learned to play the organ in her grandfather's church. Her first professional performance was substituting for the organist when he was drunk one Whitsunday morning – when he was drunk he always wanted to play 'We Three Kings of Orient Are'.

She was strong for the traditional and whenever she made an innovation, it became part of the tradition, something that had 'always' been. Like chess, which Hans had introduced, or Peter's Monopoly game. On the other hand certain items of Americana were never admitted to the fair Rosamund's canon. They included ketchup, trick-or-treat, square-dancing, sailing, golf, skiing, bridge, and virtually anything in a can. Also Christmas-tree lights and those coloured Christmas-tree balls you bought in boxes. Peter had got her to confess that out in Marietta in her childhood they had had balls and lights on the tree as well as ketchup in the pantry. But he did this only to try her. He too preferred the tree as it had 'always' been, with everything on it edible except the paper chains he cut and pasted and the star he used to make, with her help. He was averse himself to sailing and skiing or at least to the smooth types who went in for them, and she had persuaded him, empirically, that home-made chili sauce was better than the bottled ketchup his peer-groupers poured on their hamburgers, just as she had converted him to the doctrine of the home-made cake by teaching him and his school friends in Berkeley to bake in her kitchen on Saturdays – first a cake made with a mix and then a real one; their mothers, he estimated, had not necessarily thanked her for this proselytizing work. As for being a bartender, back in Berkeley he had accepted the deprivation, agreeing that it was nauseating to see little kids shaking up Martinis for a smirking crowd.

In Rocky Port, with just the two of them, it would have been different, he thought. But he guessed she was bothered by the old Oedipus business there. Somebody had warned her or she had warned herself that she should never let Peter take over the offices of a husband, which meant that he could not make drinks or put out the lights for the night or unlock the house door when they came home from a trip together. He was allowed to set the table and sometimes to help her with the dishes; on Sundays he could make scrambled eggs for their breakfast, because he had always done that; on Saturdays occasionally he could bake a cake – ditto. But if she had a drink before dinner, she did not even like it if he joined her with a Coke. Too connubial, he supposed. After he had done this a few times, she discontinued her nightly Scotch before the fire. That was her way (a sacrifice) of edging out of an awkward situation. Her plight called forth Peter's chivalry. He rescued her, perceiving that she as an adult needed a pleasure that he did not share. Shortly before dinner, after their sunset tryst, he would take a Coke from the icebox and repair with it upstairs to his room. 'Why don't you have a drink, Mother, while I hit the homework?' Thus she knew the coast was clear. He would stay at his desk till he heard her rattling things in the kitchen, which told him that she had had her grog. Then he would come down and lounge in the kitchen doorway, watching her with critical comments while she cooked. It would never occur to her to do as most kids' mothers did and bring her drink to the kitchen.

Her problems in keeping him at a filial distance amused him and made his heart swell with tenderness – the same tenderness he felt for those laborious creatures, birds and animals. Watching her fend him off, he was also reassured for the future. She would never 'encourage' a suitor, if Peter's experience was an index. And yet how had it happened that Hans had subtracted her from his father?

He could always get her goat by calling her by her first name. 'Stop that, Peter! Stop it, this minute!' 'Why should I, Rosamund?' he would say, in a clowning voice. 'Rosamund, give me a reason.' It was as if she were being tickled; she laughed but really she was scared. His mother, he decided, was dressed in a little brief of authority that she was afraid would slip off. She was firm about being treated as his parent and no nonsense. After supper came the Children's Hour; they would sit by the fire and talk. Sometimes she mended. Or they would both read. If the night was clear and still, they would go out and look at the stars. He was teaching her to find the simpler constellations from his old star book – a present from Hans. If it was not a school night, he could vanquish her at chess. At nine-thirty, on school nights, he would start upstairs for his bath. Once he was in bed, she would come and open his window and kiss him good night on the top of his head. After he was asleep, she set the table, he supposed, for breakfast, measured and sifted flour for flapjacks or muffins or whatever, put out the garbage, lowered the thermostat, went around turning out lights, drew a bath. This night self of hers was unknown to him; he never heard her go to bed. In the morning, the first thing he knew, she was shutting his window and opening the curtains to let in the light. Usually, she was dressed and she was always in a good humour, which he was not.

That year, he did not masturbate. He had kicked the habit, temporarily, because of her. It did not seem to him democratic to give himself that solitary bang when she was all alone in her bedroom or downstairs in the kitchen getting things ready for his breakfast. It had been all right, from that point of view, when Hans was around, but it was not all right now. Peter, his family said, was a born Solon on points of equity; the *babbo* never tired of telling a story Peter hoped was apocryphal: about how he had worried about chattel slavery when he was in the first grade and had announced to his teacher that it was 'a good idea, but quite mean'. His fair-mindedness made his mother hope that he would be a judge, like her father. His birthday was under the sign of Libra, and family legend had it that as a child his passion was weighing things on a toy scales, which he toddled around with like an attribute of Justice. 'Peter ponders,' said his mother. One notion he had pondered, while still quite young, was the accepted idea that grownups should work while children played. 'Your work is to grow, my boy,' Hans used to tell him. Peter could never buy that. It was not a just division of labour. Still less could he 'play with himself' when his mother' thanks to him, was not even going to parties. After a while he was not in the mood.

They were living a life of virtue, or so he believed. That year he equated virtue with happiness, still ignorant of Kant's teaching. From a Kantian angle, he now recognized, nearly everything he did or refrained from doing in Rocky Port was outside the moral law, strictly speaking, since he was obeying not Duty but Inclination. Being helpful, chaste, minding his mother was a pleasure in those circumstances, where the well-tuned clavichord gave the pitch; he no longer sighed over his homework, though he missed Hans's help with his algebra. Nor did he groan at getting up in the morning, for his rising was a daily ceremony like the cormorants' toilet, which he could watch from his window while he pulled on his clothes. From his present vantage point, he could confirm that he had been living not just in a fairy-tale but in a paradise, in which his love for his mother coincided with his love of Nature and of the austere New England landscape. That was why he had that sense of homecoming or repatriation. And one of the features of the Earthly Paradise (which made it preferable, in Peter's view, to Heaven) was the absence of others.

Winter was in the air, described by the postman as a cold snap; Peter's favourite stars, the Pleiades, were so clear in the frosty night that he had seen the Lost Pleiad. Yet except for the tradespeople, the postman, and sundry ministers of grace like Mrs Curtis, Peter and his mother still knew no one in Rocky Port. Peter was on terms with his classmates, but he had deliberately made no friends. He did not want to invite anyone home, as though it would break a spell.

He liked to fancy that he and his mother were pioneers, exploring a wilderness unknown to the aborigines. This notion gained support not only from their lack of friends and of a car and a television set but also from the ghostly music of the clavichord, from an American history course he was taking, and from the meals his mother dished up. Having left her cookbooks behind (naturally), she had bought an old Fannie Farmer in the village junkshop. This gave her the idea of cooking American, at which Peter to start with had raised an eyebrow. American in his experience meant steaks spread with charcoal seasoning, frozen corn-on-the-cob, shredded lettuce with 'Russian' dressing, 'Hawaiian' ham and sticky pineapple. In Berkeley, he had been proud of his mother's disdain for the prevailing cookery. For a while there, she had had a game of cooking the foods of the countries Peter was studying in geography or whose stamps he was collecting in his album – his favourites had been black beans (Brazilian) with orange slices and Persian chicken with rose water. For Hans she had made Tafelspitz and German and Austrian desserts and for Peter her old Italian stand-bys, such as green *lasagne al forno* – he used to help her roll out the sheets of *pasta* for it and hang them up in the kitchen like dish towels. In contrast to this, an American diet would be pretty monotonous; he hoped she was not going to ask him to dig a barbecue pit. She told him to wait and see.

Peter waited. They had pot roast and New England boiled dinner and fried chicken and lobsters and scallops and blue-fish and mackerel and scalloped oysters and clam chowder. They had Cape Cod Turkey, which some people said was salmon but his mother thought was baked fresh cod with a stuffing. They had codfish cakes and corned beef hash and red flannel hash and chicken hash (three ways), spoon bread and hominy and Rhode Island jonnycake and country sausage with fried apple rings and Brown Betty and Indian pudding and pandowdy and apple pie and cranberry pie. Before the first black frost, she bought green tomatoes and made jars of pickles. They stole quinces from a bush in the yard of a closed-up captain's house with a widow's walk, and she put up quince jelly. Peter was ready to admit that he had never had it so good.

His mother turned everything she did into a game – with rules, of course. The rules of the Rocky Port kitchen were that every recipe had to come out of Fannie Farmer, had to be made entirely at home from fresh – or dried or salted – ingredients, and had to be, insofar as possible, an invention of the New World. Pennsylvania Dutch dishes were permitted, but *gnocchi*, they sadly agreed, although in Fannie Farmer, did not get under the wire. Noodles but not spaghetti. A dish, his mother decided, did not have its citizenship papers if it had been cooked in America for less than a hundred years – discriminatory legislation, Peter commented.

In case of dispute, Peter was assigned to go to the library after school and look up, for instance, when the Portuguese had first come to America, not counting Magellan: late nineteenth century, imported as cheap labour to work in the cotton mills of New Bedford and the North Atlantic fishing industry. His mother thought she was opposed to progressive education, but in fact she was a natural progressive educator. Because of this cooking bee, he learned about the Irish potato famine, and the '48 revolutions in Germany, and the depressed price of wheat in Sweden in 1886 – a peak year of Swedish immigration into Wisconsin and Minnesota. German Jews had begun coming in large numbers after '48, so that on the length-of-residence principle, as he slyly remarked to his mother, she should be making *gefüllte* fish and matzoth balls. Those dishes, she quickly replied, were not in Fannie Farmer, which proved they had not been assimilated, unlike Irish stew – chauvinism, said Peter, getting a rise.

Mixes, obviously, were out, as well as frozen foods. Canned tomatoes were allowed, because housewives had 'always' put them up, and an unexplained exception was made for canned bouillon. Portuguese bread was allowed, because, his mother said, it belonged to the locality, and it would be stupid to eat store bread under the circumstances. She would make French toast but not 'French' pancakes. Lunches did not count. Peter could have tuna fish with store mayonnaise and Campbell's vegetable soup with the alphabet in it and salami and yoghurt – whatever he wanted. For lunch, his mother usually had bouillon, an apple, and milk.

The game was not as easy as it sounded, since the Rocky Port market leaned heavily on its frozen-food chests, and there were few fresh vegetables to be had, even in the supermarket in the neighbouring town. They had onions and carrots and potatoes and cabbage, red and white, in various forms and leeks and broccoli (which Peter questioned) and beets and squash and spinach (though not the bag kind) and fried and scalloped tomatoes. His mother rang the changes on apples and pears and quinces and dried prunes and apricots; she made ambrosia, using fresh coconut, and 'snows' and soufflés and puddings and cobblers. They had nuts and what the grocer called rat cheese. There was a lobster pound on a wharf just down the street, and Peter learned to boil the lobsters himself; his mother would not hear of his bisecting them alive for broiling, though he guaranteed her that was a more merciful death.

Getting fresh fish was a problem, despite the fishing fleet. It was easier for a gull. Finally his mother found a fisherman who sold her striped bass and mackerel and bluefish and cod-fish and smelts; she waited outside the back door of his house to get it, like contraband, which reminded her of her father's stories of Prohibition and the moonshiners who had stills in the woods and came up before him as a judge in federal court. In the grocery store, she bought salt codfish in funny wooden boxes with a sliding cover that Peter used afterwards for his stone and shell collections. 'When I was a girl, I kept buttons in them,' she remembered.

This made her think of the artistic-button collections housewives used to show at country fairs when she was a girl, and this, in turn, made her think of the oil paintings done on cigarbox covers – views of the Rhine – German farmers gave her great-grandfather, a country doctor. 'In those days, Peter, nobody threw anything away. They tried to think what they could *do* with it or *make* of it. Waste was considered a crime. "It's a crime to throw that away", my grandmother always said. What that really meant was that you were stupid if you couldn't find a use for something. Like burying fish-bones in corn hills when you were planting, the way the Indians used to do. Or making potpourri of old flower petals. Or patchwork quilts. People were conservationists, like Nature.'

Peter could not imagine, she said, what America had been like in those days, at least for the comfortable classes, which included carpenters and house-painters and streetcar con-ductors. Already it had been changing when she was a girl. It had only been in the summers, when she and her sister went to their grandmother's farm, after their mother had died, that she had really seen the old America, which she connected with the speckled foxglove in her grandmother's yard. In the winters, in Marietta, where she had grown up and gone to college, it had not been so different from now. Just the difference between radio and television and between short-play and long-play records. She smiled at Peter for idealizing the days of radio.

But in the war years, she said, America had become more pastoral, more the way it had been in the farmland. That was because of the scarcities. Nobody could get help; the girls were all working in the war plants. You had to do things yourself. Rationing made you economize. People walked again because of the gasoline shortage. Old wood- and coal-stoves came out on account of the lack of fuel oil. Meat and canned goods were going to the Army. She had liked the war years. Peter thought maybe because that was her youth and she had got away from home. She and her sister came to New York in '42 to study at the Mannes School; that same year, she started with Landowska. Peter, who kept relentless tabs on her birthdays, knew that she had been twenty-one then. They had had what she called a dumb-bell apartment – two big rooms with a narrow connecting passage. Back home, their stepmother had planted a Victory Garden, and every week in the summertime huge boxes of vegetables, packed in damp newspapers, arrived by Railway Express – their step-mother was too patriotic to waste fertilizer on flowers, which did not help the war effort. His aunt was impatient with these shipments and wanted to dump them in the garbage. But the fair Rosamund distributed string beans and cucumbers and squashes to everyone they knew; she studied cookbooks and stayed up late in the warm summer nights (that was before air conditioning) pickling and preserving in big crocks and Mason jars. She gave the results as presents or bartered them for sugar coupons. They hitch-hiked to the seashore, where they dug clams and gathered mussels. A painter on Fire Island taught her to mushroom in the pine woods. Her grandfather, the minister, kept bees in the parsonage yard and he sent them fresh honey. Peter was sorry he had not been alive then. The way his mother described it, the war sounded like an idyll. He filed the thought away in the Two-Sides-to-Every-Question compartment.

Excited by her sessions in the Rocky Port kitchen, she told Peter tales of her girlhood, of phosphorescent wood and fire-flies and prodigious snowmen. He heard about her ancestors and the old Northwest Territory, which had been organized in Marietta, the first settlement in the state. He was glad to know that the Ohio Company had prohibited slavery in the territory way back in the eighteenth century. She promised to take him, some day, to Marietta, where he had not been since he was a baby; it had been an Enlightenment capital, full of educators. The streets had been given classical names, such as Sacra Via, which had greatly pleased the *babbo*, who in a fit of enthusiasm had wanted to have Peter christened by his great-grandfather. But his mother said no; a Jew could not do that in the year 1945. Peter was surprised to hear that the old parts of Marietta were in a Classic Revival style that looked in fact a lot like Rocky Port. He had imagined Ohio as an inland California.

His mother – like many musicians, she said – had a re-markable memory, and she never repeated a story, except as an encore, just as, this fall in the kitchen, she never repeated a dish. Peter was keeping score. She had not yet had a failure despite inadequate equipment, which led her to swear some-times, especially when she was making a piecrust, using a wine bottle for a rolling-pin. 'The poor workman blames his tools, Mother,' he would tease her, leaning against the kit-chen door.

They often discussed why they felt so at home in New England. It could not be just the Doric columns and peri-styles and pediments, in his mother's case, or the fact that Peter had been born in South Hadley, Massachusetts – his father had been teaching at Mount Holyoke then. Could there be such a thing as racial memory? But if so, why was that memory selective? Why 'remember' New England rather than Florence or Palestine, neither of which drew Peter at all? Maybe there was a collective American memory

of white meeting-houses and village greens that you acquired
at birth or naturalization. New England was the promised
land, even for those who had left it behind or who had
never seen it, except in the movies. His mother said that
was because New England *looked* like the ideal America
that you studied in civics; it looked republican, with a
small *r*.

Going to school every day, Peter was well aware that he
had not left Berkeley and the Radiation Laboratory totally
behind. It did not need Preparedness Drill to tell him that.
He had only to look at his classmates, many of whom would
leave school at the statutory age of sixteen to go to work in
the plastics factory or at the nearby submarine base. But his
mother had more illusions to shatter. Since she seldom
talked with anyone except an elderly storekeeper, she could
believe she was living in the past. It was a storekeeper who
delivered the blow. The village hardware store did not carry
bean pots.

'How extraordinary, Peter! The man says they don't
make them any more. Do you think that can be true?' She
was always asking him wide-eyed, troubled questions like
that one, to which he could not possibly, at his age, know the
answer; it was a kind of flattery, applied to the male ego.
The only bean pot Peter was familiar with was pictured on
a can. But he saw that for his mother this was a truly upsetting discovery, tantamount to finding that the American
Eagle was extinct. She was even more ruffled when she
returned from her weekly shopping trip with the report that
the two hardware stores in the neighbouring town did not
carry bean pots either. 'Don't get any call for them,' one
shopkeeper had told her. The other said, 'Try the antique
store, lady. Two doors down.' 'Can you imagine that, Peter?
How do you explain it? Why, when we left your father –
how long ago was it?' 'Eight years.' 'Eight years. That isn't
such a long time, is it? Well, eight years ago, every hardware store in New England had bean pots galore. Just the
way they had seeds and onion sets and tomato plants in the
springtime. Do you suppose that if I took the train to

Providence . . .? I could go to the Brown Music Library
while I was there . . .'

'Can't you use a casserole, Mother?' Peter was trying to
be helpful, but his mother looked at him in horror, as if he
were a changeling. 'What a question!' she said. He did not
blame his mother for caring about things like bean pots in
the face of a general indifference; indeed, he loved her for
that. On the other hand, he could not share her sense of
shock and loss, just as he could not respond, except lamely,
when she told him someone he had never known had died.
In the end, Mrs Curtis gave them her bean pot, which she
had been using as a vase for a bouquet of dried grasses.
'You can keep it, my dear, I haven't baked a bean in twenty
years. How nice that you're going to do it for Peter!'

Mrs Curtis herself, an eldritch old person, ate most of her
meals in the Portuguese diner; Peter had often seen her there
when he stopped by for a hamburger. 'We must do something for her, Peter,' his mother repeated. He guessed what
was coming: Thanksgiving. The two of them could not eat
a whole turkey between them; they would have to have
guests or do without. Peter was torn between gluttony and
his reluctance to have company. His mother, he suspected,
would not be satisfied to have just Mrs Curtis. She would
want to ask all her descendants too. He had nothing personal
against Mrs Curtis's descendants; one of her grandchildren,
a girl, he talked to at school occasionally. Nevertheless, his
heart hardened. Mrs Curtis would be bound to ask them
back. She had already been telling Peter about 'a few friends'
in Rocky Port who were dying to meet his mother. He fore-
saw a series of musical evenings.

On the other hand, he was familiar with his mother's attachment to Thanksgiving as a day of bounty. In Berkeley,
every year she had rounded up all the lonely hearts available
on the campus – plus a wheel or two (the fair Rosamund was
transparent), so that no one would suddenly glance around
the groaning board and ask himself what they all had in
common. As long as he could remember, wherever he and
his mother lived, there had been company present when she

struck up the hymn 'We are *Gather together* to *ask* the Lord's *Blessing*', which she said was an old Dutch resistance tune from the time of William the Silent. Adjuring himself not to be selfish, Peter hit on a compromise. 'Why don't we ask Aunt Millie to come up from New York with her brood?'

His mother was touched by the suggestion; she knew that Peter did not particularly care for her sister. Her delight made Peter ashamed. Was she all that lonely? Maybe she was just eager to show their new household to somebody; women were like that. He found that he himself was rather looking forward to taking his cousins for a walk in the sanctuary and showing them the cormorants on their piles. 'It is not good that man should be alone,' Mrs Curtis had hissed at him the other day in the library.

Nature rewarded Peter for thinking of his mother. Two days before Thanksgiving, an apple tree in the yard across the street uncannily burst into bloom. Although a confirmed atheist, he could not help seeing this as a blessing conferred especially on their household; the Lord was making a covenant with Peter the Levite. The blossoming tree was Aaron's Rod – what else? – the sign that the Lord had picked Aaron to be high priest of Israel and set him apart, with the tribe of Levi, from the others. Aaron's Rod, if Peter recalled right, had put out almond blossoms overnight; the Lord was a craftsman who worked with local materials – almonds in the desert, apples here. It occurred to Peter that this was only the latest of a series of rather broad hints that he and his mother had been led to Rocky Port to work out a special destiny. He was too modest to suppose that he was the Messiah, but he might be a precursor, a sort of pilot-project in the wilderness. He did not confide the thought in his mother, who, after all, was a Gentile and outside the Law. But he knew that she was marvelling too.

The house across the street was boarded up for the winter, like the other shuttered houses on the water; out of season, no one passed this way except the mailman and the newsboy on his bicycle, delivering the morning paper, and now it was barely light when the folded paper was pitched onto the porch. So that the mystery of the flowering apple tree, like that of the owl and the cormorants, was being enacted just for the two of them, in Nature's private code. The mailman, when he passed – bringing a Thanksgiving card with a turkey on it from Hans to Peter – could offer no explanation. He had never heard tell of an apple tree in these parts blooming at Thanksgiving; he guessed it was a Freak of Nature. 'Radio says snow,' he added, and, sure enough, on Thanksgiving Day, while they were all at table, with Millicent's husband carving, the promised snow came. The whole family rushed to the window. Across the way, snow-flakes were gently falling on the tender green leaves, rose-red buds and pink-and-white shivering blossoms. 'Quite a production,' said Millie in her ironical tones.

'Hey, kids,' she ordered, 'go and get your cameras. Did you put in colour film?' Peter groaned to himself. He watched with savage hate while his cousins stole the apple tree with their clicking Kodaks. 'Have you got it?' said his aunt. His cousins had it in their little black boxes. The graceless meal resumed. Peter's uncle put a drumstick on Peter's plate. With her eyes, his mother warned him not to say he preferred white meat. Later that afternoon, just before dusk, someone tapped Hello on the window. It was Mrs Curtis and all her family come to see the apple tree. His mother had *shared* the secret. The fire was burning in the hearth; outside, it was still snowing. 'Ask them in,' commanded Millie. 'Peter, go open the door.'

In a minute, the little house was full of windbreakers, scarves, and galoshes. Millie's husband was in the kitchen, mixing drinks. Peter's Coca-Cola supply was decimated. He was sent upstairs for his Monopoly set. His chessboard, where he had been working out a chess problem, was commandeered by his uncle to play with Mrs Curtis's son-in-law, who did not know any better than to open with the King's Rook pawn. Peter's fire was relaid, with the logs placed upward, tepee style. And his mother stood smiling on the scene, murmuring with her sister, whom an evil day – which answered to the name of Peter Levi – had brought to Rocky Port.

His aunt, who was older than his mother, took pride in her ability to 'size up' situations; she had the brusque, brutal air of a person detailed to cut Gordian knots. All through the day, she had been interrogating Peter about himself, his mother, and their relations with the Rocky Port community. She had established that Hans still wrote to his mother and that his mother probably answered. Her dry blue eye had inventoried the house, checking off the chessmen, the prism that hung in Peter's window, Handel's *Messiah* on the phonograph, the bird book, the star book, the tree book, the bean pot, the music of his mother's clavichord, the clothes in his mother's closet. At table she had noted the home-made cranberry jelly moulded in the shape of a heart (there were duplicate tin hearts in Berkeley and in the *babbo's* kitchen in Wellesley), the corn bread and walnut stuffing, the green tomato pickle, the mincemeat tarts with home-made vanilla ice cream that Peter had been stirring every half hour in the refrigerator trays. She had learned that the turkey was a fresh-killed local bird and how much his mother had paid for it. She had taken stock of the cormorants and assessed the woodpile. It was as though these separate items 'hung together' in some derisory pattern, like a stitched sampler – Rosamund's folly.

From time to time, she wagged her Clairol-tinted head confidentially at Peter, in token of despair – as when she ascertained that his mother had *walked* to the turkey farm to pick out the bird – and his aunt Millie was such a consummate spectator that he felt himself pulled into a box seat beside her, watching their private life – his and his mother's – unfold, with the embarrassed sense that it was, as Millie would say, a 'performance'. Not real, footlit, with stage snow outside and stagey food on the table, against a painted backdrop of old-time New England seascape. With shame, he saw himself through her eyes as conned by his mother into a storybook romance, which they lived on a daily basis – he licked his lips, mortified to admit it – and not just when they had company. The fact that his mother made his breakfast every morning instead of simply leaving corn flakes and frozen fruit juice and chocolate milk for him, became a hideous confession as his aunt sweated it out of him. He was guilty of being less average than his cousins, and that was his wicked mother's fault.

Peter could well see that his aunt, behind a façade of good nature, was jealous of her sister. His mother was a musician, while Millie worked for a music publisher. When they were girls, his mother had been feckless and dreamy, and Millie had been the practical one, but now his mother had a passion for work, and Millie was shrewd and lazy. His mother had a glowing girlish skin, which she scrubbed with soap and water, disobeying her sister's warnings, while Millie's creamed skin sagged. Most of all, Peter guessed, his aunt was jealous of his mother's 'hold' on himself, which she could not reproduce on her own uninteresting progeny. But jealousy had made her watchful, and Peter, a veteran observer, his mother's privileged critic, could not help responding to the prose in his aunt's view of them. What were they doing here anyway, playing house together, a growing boy and a woman nearly forty, who was old enough to be his mother? Millie's common sense was the Tempter in the Garden. He fell. 'Peter, go open the door.' What could he do but obey?

She had come in the nick of time to set things right; that was what she plainly thought. Aunt Millie always acted like that, whenever she paid a visit – as though her coming was providential. With her tinted hair, she reminded Peter rather of King Arthur's trouble-making sister, Queen Morgan le Fay. A fairy-tale needed a bad fairy; he ought to have considered that before. She had arrived tugging at her girdle and waving her stout wand of disenchantment. And when she left, everything was blighted. 'You feel gloomy because you ate too much, Peter,' his mother told him as he helped her wipe a mountain of dishes. But Peter knew he was not wrong. The next morning, the apple blossoms were blasted, and the tree, he was afraid, would never get up the strength to bloom again in the spring. He blamed this on his aunt and he was not the only one. 'You brought winter with you,' Mrs Curtis had shot at Millie, like a sudden accusation, after her second drink. Thanksgiving, as Peter saw it, had been his last day of grace. After that, he paid his debt to society. The following week, they went to dinner at Mrs Curtis's house. They began to meet people. Thanks to Millie, the sluices opened, and Rocky Port rushed in.

Yet the reality did not live up to Peter's forebodings, which alarmed him, as though his early-warning system had been misled by a flight of birds. Unless he was softening up, their new acquaintances were not a threat. Behind their fanlight doorways was a fog of amnesia, induced, he thought, by alcohol, which flowed in Lethean streams from the liquor store. The worst thing they did was repeat themselves, playing the same dulled record; for years, nobody had bothered to change their needle. They did not have the energy to get up a musical evening. The admiral, who did crewelwork, and his wife, who painted china, were the most strenuous members of the community.

The men drove about in their cars, dressed like hunters or trappers, in boots and mackinaws and fur caps, to visit their frozen-food lockers. Their wives offered Peter's mother lifts to go marketing and invited Peter to view television. The few men in his mother's age-group were already paired off, and their cars would be recognized if they tried to take her to the bird sanctuary and make a pass. There was no danger here that Peter could see. Being a musician, his mother could not hit the bottle. True to her promise, she bought them skates; when it snowed again, their own footprints and the tracks of birds and animals were the only trails leading in and out of the still woods. Peter's uneasiness subsided; he let her go out to dinner without him and did not lie awake listening for her step on the porch. One afternoon, as he was coming home from school, he thought he heard the *harpsichord* playing, but when he opened the door, the music had stopped. His mother was talking on the telephone, and he guessed he might have been mistaken.

They arranged to go to Millie's for Christmas, so that they did not have their tree. Now that they were acquainted in Rocky Port, his mother said, they would never be allowed to

have Christmas by themselves. It would be considered unfriendly. Peter did not argue; he accepted the lesser evil and
besides he would not mind seeing New York, he thought.
But it would have been fun to chop down their own tree in
the woods. He found it queer to think that for the first time
since he was a baby he would not be popping corn over the
fire and watching her string those chains, like red and white
beads, of popcorn and cranberries alternating, that festooned
her lap and trailed over the carpet, while the long white
thread in her needle turned pink from the cranberry juice.
He would not be helping her gild walnuts or make ginger-
bread men, putting in the raisins for the face and buttons
himself. He pictured last Christmas in Berkeley and felt
homesick, unexpectedly, for Hans, heavy-footed on a ladder,
hanging candy canes on the green branches. He was acquiring
a distrust for holidays.

Christmas Eve, on Riverside Drive, he hung up his sock
with his cousins. Millie's tree had balls and lights and
nothing edible on it at all – not even a gold-wrapped chocolate coin. They were lucky, he told his mother, it was not
dyed. From his aunt and uncle, he received – guess what? –
a camera; his aunt's presents were always pointed, like the
baseball mitt she had once sent him, to tell his mother that
he should take an interest in athletics. From the fair Rosamund he got a pair of field glasses, which was what he had
been fearing. He would rather have bought them himself,
second hand, in a pawnshop; his mother was not good at
picking out articles like bird books and field glasses – her
idea was to get the most expensive. She also gave him a seal
ring with the head of some Greek worthy, tickets to *Carmen*
at the opera, and *The Seasons* by Haydn.

On Christmas Day, there was a party. Millie had invited
some of his mother's old gang: her agent, the chamber group
she used to play with, the head of a record company. *E cosi
via*; his aunt did not need to explain the principle of the
party to Peter – he got it. She was master-minding her
sister's comeback. His mother had a new dress, and Millie
took her around and made her talk to all the people who could

'do something' for her; there was a man from the State Department in charge of cultural exchanges and an old society lady who gave recitals at her house. Peter, who helped make drinks, got sick on Martinis and was taken to the bathroom by a friendly woman who said she used to be his mother's page-turner. He retched most of the night, and his aunt philosophically put a basin by his bed; it was time he stopped being babied, she told his mother, who wanted to call a doctor with a stomach pump. When they finally got back to Rocky Port, there was New Year's Eve and New Year's Day eggnog. Then at midyears, he failed his higher algebra.

On receipt of the news, the *babbo* drove down from Wellesley and talked gloomily about college boards. As a pedagogue, he was hipped on college admissions statistics. 'You ought to have looked into the schools before coming here,' he said sharply. 'I talked to your sister. She tells me the boy is not even getting Latin now.' It was true, the Rocky Port high school did not give Latin; Peter's aunt had wormed this out of him during Thanksgiving dinner. 'He will never get into Harvard now,' the *babbo* said tragically. He sounded very angry with his mother. It was just like old times, Peter thought, listening from his bedroom. The *babbo* had already been annoyed with her, it transpired, for leaving Hans and coming here. Why could she not have waited another year, till Peter had finished algebra? 'I find it very upsetting to have you back here in New England,' he grumbled, slightly lowering his voice. Peter's mother ignored this. 'New England has been good for Peter. He feels at home here. You always said he was a zoophile. It's extraordinary what he's learned this fall about Nature.'

'Nature!' the *babbo* shouted. 'Nature! Don't be a goddamn fool! Nature is an anachronism. Does the boy have companions of his own age? Your sister tells me that he has not made a single friend. Can he qualify for any college from this high school? Or do you expect him to join the labour force at seventeen? When you are serious, we may begin talking again.' Peter's mother remained silent. His father burst out,

'And what will he do when you go on tour? Have you thought of that?'

Upstairs at his desk, Peter pricked up his ears for his mother's answer. But he could only catch the word 'problem'; her voice had sunk too low. 'You have not thought,' he heard his father sum up. 'That is like you, *cara mia*. A creature of impulse. But don't forget that I am paying the boy's bills.' This was tough on his mother. She hated being reminded that his father was contributing to his support – which seemed perfectly just to Peter but not to her, because she had left his father. 'What do you want me to do, Paolo? I've taken this house for a year. Do you suppose, if I could find a tutor . . . ? He really has a very good mind.' He heard his father's step; the door to the living room was closed softly. One of the *babbo*'s principles was that a child should never be praised in his own hearing.

So that before he knew it, they had shanghaied him into boarding-school without even asking his consent. When Peter was summoned downstairs, it had already been decided. His father knew a school that specialized in 'the boy of uneven attainments,' that is, the boy who had failed one or two subjects. It was not far from Wellesley. While his mother made tea, his father telephoned to the headmaster to find out if there was a vacant place and when he learned that there was, he ordered Peter to pack. His mother served tea, not making conversation, from shame, Peter knew, and because she was afraid that if she talked she would cry. She just looked at him across his father like somebody trying to exchange signals over the head of a guard. He knew her excuse: that the divorce decree gave his father control over his education. Finally, she spoke up. Peter would have to have a haircut and name-tapes on his clothes; he could not go, just like that. But his father was being a man of action – the old '*cosa fatta capo ha*' stuff. If Peter drove back with him tonight, he would be able to start the new term tomorrow; his mother could see about name-tapes and things of that kind later. If he needed further outfitting in a hurry, the *babbo* could take him to Boston one afternoon after classes.

It was dark when they drove off; they were going to have dinner on the road. His father would not even let his mother fix them supper. 'But when will I see him again?' Peter's mother cried out in the doorway, as though she had not taken in, until that minute, what was happening. 'Go in the house!' his father yelled. 'You will catch cold.' 'Yes, go in the house, Mother,' Peter said, with pity. It was not her fault he had failed algebra; he had brought this on himself. 'At least put on a coat.' But she stood there, clasping her chest, under the wan porch-light till his father impatiently promised to arrange for Peter to come home soon on a weekend, providing the headmaster gave a good report of him. She must not come to the school, which would upset Peter; the *babbo* would drive over himself every Sunday to take him out to lunch and check on his progress.

Peter waved farewell to his mother; he blew a kiss, which probably she could not see. He thought of her alone with the tea dishes and the preparations for the supper he would never eat. 'Tell the cormorants I'll be seeing them!' As his father let out the clutch, it came to him that in fact he had not seen those three fishy characters for several days. Maybe longer. Or could it be that he had ceased to notice them—which meant that, without knowing it, he no longer cared? No wonder his father had come, like black retribution, to take him away.

In school, he tried not to brood about his mother. If he acted unhappy, they would probably not let him go home till Easter. He signed up for the chess team and appeared on the hockey field. At night, he wrote her short amusing letters and sealed them with his seal ring. The only animal at school, aside from a few chickens, was the headmaster's dachshund, to which he gave perfunctory pats whenever their paths crossed. The headmaster said he was making a good adjustment.

On Lincoln's Birthday, which that year made a long weekend, he was allowed to go home. His mother came to fetch him, driving Mrs Curtis's car. It was a beautiful bright blue morning. She had brought a picnic lunch and Peter's field glasses, which he had forgotten. On the way back to Rocky Port, they stopped to eat in a glen up in the back country where they had never been. That was the day they found the waterfall, using a geodetic map Mrs Curtis had left in the glove compartment. Peter circled the spot on the map, so that they would be able to locate it again when he came home for Easter.

But then, in the car, his mother broke the news. *She was giving up the house in Rocky Port.* The man from the State Department (Peter remembered?) that she had met at Millie's Christmas party was going to send her abroad with a chamber-music group. Their regular harpsichordist had had an automobile accident. His mother would have to be in New York to rehearse with them and Mrs Curtis had been very understanding and helpful about finding another tenant to finish out the lease. By a lucky coincidence, a house had burned down in Rocky Port just the other night, and the owners were looking for a place to live while they rebuilt it. It made an ideal arrangement. So that at Easter-time ('Think of it, Peter!') she would be in Rome, playing, and he could fly over and be with her for his spring vacation. The *babbo* had agreed.

Grimly, Peter recognized another of the fair Rosamund's substitutes. It struck him that his being in boarding-school just now was a great convenience for his mother. As she babbled on, flushed and excited, he felt himself turn into *another person* – possibly a man, if they were made of stone. Cruelly, he wondered how long, exactly, she had known about this tour. 'When did you get the invite, Mother?' 'Oh, just the other day. Last week.' He watched her cheek redden, as if she guessed what he was thinking. 'I thought I wouldn't write you about it but save it to tell you when you came.' He stared at the road. 'Who set the fire?' he inquired. 'What fire?' 'The house that burned down so *opportunely*,' he said with an acid smile.

Her hands, in leather and chamois driving-gloves, tightened on the wheel. For a moment, he relented. ' "I suspect Mrs Curtis in the verandah with the kitchen matches," ' he proposed lightly, alluding to their old game of Clue. She patted his bony knee. 'You don't mind, do you, Peter? I thought since you were in school anyway ... And Easter isn't so far off. I thought you'd *like* to go to Rome. After all, you've never been abroad.' 'That means we'll never come back to Rocky Port, doesn't it, Mother?' 'I don't know, Peter. How can I say? Maybe in the summertime.' 'But I'll be with *babbo* then.' 'Not all the time. Now that you're in school it wouldn't be fair for him to have you the whole summer. We'll have to divide you.' 'In what proportions?' he said coldly.

He studied his mother's profile. A tear trembled in her eye. If he were on a jury, he might give her the benefit of the doubt. Probably it was true that she had just got the official invitation. But wasn't it likely – more than likely – that she had been sounded out, some time back, through her sister? Maybe on Christmas Day even, while they slugged him with Martinis. Then his father's visit would have been a charade enacted for his consumption. If he had not failed algebra, they would have found some other pretext. Once they had him in school, they could do what they wanted. If he ran away, the headmaster would have him tracked with bloodhounds, which had already happened to another kid.

He endeavoured to reason with himself. Had his mother ever lied to him before? The stone man answered cynically: not that he *knew* of. He felt his sanity totter. If the fair Rosamund was false, then his whole life, up to now, was a deception, and if she was not false, he was batty. He found himself wondering about the other harpsichordist's automobile 'accident'. Did his mother have an alibi? He giggled sardonically to himself.

His mother's head turned quickly in his direction. 'Pay attention to the road, Mother.' Supposing he were to take her, step by step, over the history of the offer, demanding times and places. 'Was it mentioned to you at Christmas, Mother? Think back. Take your time.' But what if she confessed? He would not want to hear it. And actually the details did not matter. What mattered was that she was *glad* he was in boarding-school, so that she was free to go to Europe. And he was not glad; that was the difference between them. Maybe she had not arranged to put him there; maybe she was on the level. But now that it had come about, she was profiting. All she cared about, he thought with contempt, was that her conscience should be clear.

In their house, everything looked strange. Her instruments were gone, and there was a large blue trunk open in the living room; she had bought it at the junk shop and painted it. His shirts and socks and underwear were packed, with name-tapes sewed on them; she was giving him the stereo set, to take back to school with him, and the records she called his, which now, he noted, included *Don Giovanni*, *The Messiah*, and one of her own old recordings that was a present to her from Mrs Curtis. In the kitchen, she had live lobsters waiting for him to cook.

He went up to his room. The prism was no longer in his window, and all his books had been packed. The white linen window curtains and white crinkly bedspread had been sent to the laundress. He looked out at the cove. It was low tide. Some gulls were squawking around the slimy piles. Standing at his window, he felt no curiosity about the absence of the cormorants, just as he felt no curiosity about what his mother, downstairs, was whipping up for dessert. He could ask her when she had seen them last but he doubted whether she had troubled to keep track of them after he had gone. She liked birds but she was not really interested in them.

He was curious about something else. He went to the head of the stairway. 'Tell me, Mother,' he called out, 'did the headmaster know you were going to Europe?' 'Yes,' she called back. He did not know why *this* should be such a body blow, considering everything. He ought to have sensed it was strange that they would let him go home after only eleven days of captivity; he should have asked himself the reason for this mark of favour. Now he knew.

Four years later, as a hoary ghost going on nineteen, he had amnestied his parents for putting him in boarding-school.

Within their limitations, they had been right. If he had stayed at Rocky Port High, he could never have made a half-way good college; he saw that. Of course, it had solved all his mother's problems to have him in school, but she would not have done it for that motive. Not she. If the offer had come *before* his father's visit, she would have fought off the suggestion of boarding-school like a person refusing to listen to temptation. But a temptation was something attractive; that, for Peter, was the sad part. Though his mother had been sorry when he had been carted off, it was because a sort of promise had been broken, and she always hated that. But she regretted it for *him*, not for herself. As the *babbo* kept telling him, 'You must not forget, your mother has her own life.'

Yet from his present perspective, he could recognize that his parents had done the natural thing, being what they were. His mother's departure for Europe and his own departure for school had been on Nature's schedule for the sub-species they belonged to – white, middle-income intelligentsia. His parents had been responding to a deep instinctual drive of their class, for which he forgave them as individuals, his father somewhat more than his mother. At this late date too, he at last understood why the cormorants had failed to materialize on that February weekend to receive his Hail and Farewell. He was probably right in thinking that he had not seen them since some time during exam week, towards the end of January. There was a natural explanation. They had simply migrated south when the thermometer dropped and had doubtless been living in New Jersey.

The Battle of Rocky Port

PETER's mother had warned him that Rocky Port might be different after four years. For that matter, he was different himself, and so was she. Three years ago, in the fall, she had married again – an art historian this time, a Gentile from Massachusetts, a nice guy. He was divorced, with three little kids, who lived mostly with their mother, like Hans's offspring. Peter had met him in Rome, when he went over that Easter, and guessed immediately that 'Bob' would be his new stepfather. Bob had a grant to do a book on Mannerism, and he took Peter and his mother to see a great many churches, which Peter quite liked, to his surprise, for he did not like the word *Mannerism*. But the churches he liked best, it turned out, were by a madman called Borromini and were baroque.

He was resigned to his mother's marrying, since he was in school. He was not a dog in the manger but more like the fox and the grapes. Now he divided his summers between his parents; his father had finally bought a house on Cape Cod, and his mother and stepfather tended to spend their summers in Europe. Last summer, they had taken a house near Perugia, and Peter had studied for a while at the University, in the school for *Stranieri*. It had been very hot; the level of the courses had been low, and he would have preferred to be with his father on the Cape. There was not much Nature in Italy; the peasants had shot most of the bird population, and Peter missed the American brooks, ponds, and woods. What he had liked chiefly in Umbria were the black-eyed milk-white oxen, which made him think of Io after she had been turned into a cow.

'Why can't we go back to Rocky Port?' he asked every year when summer plans were discussed. His new stepbrothers and stepsister used to copy him. 'Why can't we go to Rocky Port?' Now his demand, so long on file, had suddenly been acceded to, and he knew the reasons. To cushion the blow about Mississippi and to give him a good memory of America, which he could take with him to Europe, where he would be on his own for the first time. His mother had sacrificed her Italian summer to be with him; his stepfather was in Siena for six weeks, working. So that once again he and his mother were alone with her instruments, and he found he was glad.

This year, they had a car, as well as his motorbike. Their old house had been sold to some middle-class types and painted another colour. The 'historic' house they were now renting was on the best street, shaded by elms and maples. It had four original fireplaces, a hedge that Peter had to clip, and two bathrooms. In short, like most Americans, except the poor, they had got richer in the interim. To Peter's slight astonishment, his mother had made a success. She had played behind the Iron Curtain and in India and Japan and South America – everywhere but Africa, in fact. Her records were in the college music shop, with her picture on the cover in a low-necked dress, and his roommate, a music addict, had asked him for her autograph. His stepfather, who taught at NYU, was a recognized authority on Mannerism, which had been 'in' for several years now. He lectured, authenticated, published, and he was always getting grants and fellowships for research and travel. There was nothing wrong with this that Peter could put his finger on; a society that starved art and artists would not, he guessed, be preferable. His mother was making an effort to live as she had always done – only somewhat better. Except when she was in Europe, she still did her own housework; she would not travel first class, unless the government was paying for it. She mended and sewed and gave lessons, free, to young musicians. She did not mind playing *continuo* with a group whose work she respected, and every now and then she gave a benefit to help refugees from Franco or for some other worthwhile cause. She was an easy target for composers who dedicated pieces to her, which she then had to perform. Everyone, especially her sister, told her she was doing too much – a thing she liked to hear. But in fact, to Peter, who refrained from saying it, both she and Bob seemed tired. He believed her when she said she was looking forward to Rocky Port as a respite from seeing people. This summer, with his help, she was going to be anti-social.

That ought not to be hard, Peter thought. Right away, of course, they were invited to cocktail parties and they went. His mother said that if you accepted the first invitation and stayed just a short time, people would be satisfied to leave you alone – you had done your duty. Besides, she was curious about the artistic colony Mrs Curtis had mentioned who were alleged to spend their summers here. But this was one of the changes that had to be expected, apparently. Museum directors, *New Yorker* contributors, Metropolitan Opera songsters, fashion photographers, makers of woodcuts, food-writers, *Reader's Digest* editors were extinct in the area, though their names were still mentioned, as on a village honour roll, like the World War II tablet opposite the Portuguese church. Some, it appeared, had died at an unstated date; others had been divorced or just 'gone away'. Those who still owned houses – chiefly Victorian churches that had been turned into studios or dwellings – rented them for high prices and were living in Rome or on a Greek island.

By contrast, the phantom crew Peter and his mother had met four years ago was still in evidence, more or less intact, beaming on his mother: 'Well, hello, Stranger!' Their number had been increased by new recruits. The great change in Rocky Port, it seemed, was the multiplication of what were now known as All-Year-Rounders. 'Are you Summer or All-Year-Rounder?' Peter was asked, in no idle tones, as he made his maiden appearance at a Rocky Port function. If you answered 'Summer,' he discovered, you were supposed to say it with a sigh. The All-Year-Rounders did not welcome summer people, except as proselytes. 'Come on, boy, get your pretty mother to buy some property here. Rocky Port needs you.' ' "Uncle Sam needs you," ' Peter muttered, lifting an eyebrow. 'Maybe they don't like it here,' a woman suggested, tittering. 'What have we got to offer?' 'Oh, we like it,' said Peter hurriedly. 'But my mother has to be in New York. Because of her music. And my stepfather teaches there.' 'You're never too young to retire and start living,' a man interposed. 'Look at me.' Peter looked. The man, though the worse for drink, did not appear to be more than forty; he was wearing a pair of flowered Bermuda shorts. 'He used to run a coal-mine,' a deep-voiced woman who ran the bookshop explained to Peter. 'Came up here on a yacht and fell in love with the place. Never went back. People here have more leisure to do the things they really enjoy. *Cultiver leur jardin.* They want to get out of the rat-race.'

He had never heard this expression actually used before, except by teen-age cynics, but it was common, he found, among the Rocky Port *gratin.* According to themselves, they were all escaping from the rat-race. 'Poor Jack has to go back to the rat-race,' a young woman who used to be a model sighed, of her husband, a lawyer for breakfast foods. Fortunately there was now a regular air service to New York, and a new motorway had been built, cutting the driving time by fifteen minutes.

Peter was startled to meet this kind of American on the native soil – the kind he had seen in Europe and instinctively disbelieved in: women who said 'wee wee' and were on the prowl for 'the little girls' room', corporation executives with corporations who were either going to vote for Goldwater or considered him 'too extreme', couples with cruisers and sea-skis who were belligerent about 'Veetnam', couples who announced 'We're three-Martini men, ourselves', couples who served drinks in glasses marked 'Wood Alcohol – Your Poison'. In Europe, his mother used to say that this kind of American was manufactured for export only; you never saw them at home. But here they were in Rocky Port, assembled for shipping. 'My husband and I spend every winter in Positano.' It was his first contact, he realized, with the American bourgeoisie *in situ*.

'Stay away from them. They're Birchers,' a voice hissed in his ear at his second cocktail party. It was Mrs Curtis, tapping on his elbow, to detach him from an elderly couple he had just been introduced to. 'Sorry?' 'Birchers,' she repeated impatiently. 'The John Birch Society.' 'Oh.' He stared at the harmless-looking pair who had been offering to bring him together with their granddaughter; they lived in the house on the water where the apple tree had blossomed – he had been going to tell them about it, in case they didn't know. 'Is there really a branch of John Birch here?' he whispered, to Mrs Curtis; he had pictured them mostly out West, like bad men in a movie, wearing Stetson hats. 'Ha ha,' she answered darkly, shaking her small round head with its white Dutch bangs. 'Where do they meet?' 'No one knows. They're underground.' Inwardly, Peter scoffed. He did not want to believe in a hidden network of reactionaries; that was McCarthyism in reverse, he felt. 'But if they're underground, how can you be sure who is or who isn't a member? I mean, do you have any evidence, Mrs Curtis? Those people I was talking to, they didn't sound like crackpots. Maybe they're just regular Republicans.' 'They have their private atom shelter. Stocked with French wines. At the bottom of their garden.' She nodded her white head, with determination, three times. After this, Peter was ashamed that whenever he saw the elderly couple, arm in arm, approaching, he crossed to the other side of the street.

Having seen the lay of the land socially, his mother decided that they ought to take expeditions, get to know the geography better. She went to the county seat and bought a surveyor's map, which she turned over to Peter. The first thing they were going to do was find the waterfall again and swim in the pool at its foot; she loved icy water. But the map, Peter discovered, though printed last year, was already an historical curio. The new highway construction had altered everything; the map bore only a dreamlike relation to the bulldozed countryside. Road numbers had changed, and the old Indian trail, which he had counted on to get his bearings, had melted into the motorway. He could see the waterfall distinctly in his mind's eye. You followed the Indian trail, which was a secondary road, to the edge of a state forest; then you turned left, going by a lake or a reservoir, till you got to the glen. There the road became impassable, but you saw blue blazes painted on trees and leading into the woods. You parked and started hiking. He remembered the spot exactly; a jay had flashed by. Eventually you came to a slippery walk with a rusty iron railing that led up to the waterfall. Beside the dark pool at its bottom there had been an overturned blue canoe. But now, with the roads changed and leaves on the trees, everything looked different. New little houses had toadstooled; they passed a trailer camp. They drove about in circles, misled by landmarks that appeared to be familiar. They stopped to listen, thinking they heard the sound of rapids. They argued. Peter suggested climbing a tree, as in the jungle. Finally his mother said they must give up and ask Mrs Curtis if she still had the map Peter had marked. But Mrs Curtis had junked her old maps when the motorway approached; like many elderly people, she was a new broom. The cobwebs were in her memory. She had no recollection of a waterfall up in that neck of the woods. 'You must mean Pierce's Mills. There's an old mill-dam there, with a falls. Used to be a cheese factory too.' 'We've seen Pierce's Mills,' his mother said. 'That's a *village*, Ellen. This is a *forest*.' 'You don't mean the old granite quarry?' His mother looked at Peter. Why remind Mrs Curtis that it was she who had told them about the waterfall in the first place?

They tried again, twice more. They found a Boy Scout camp on a lake; they found a reservoir. They found a remote village called Green's Falls. But the glen was lost. The waterfall was lost. His mother kept stopping the car at every cross-roads and asking, but no one could help her.

She took the loss of the waterfall harder than the owl's death or the absence of the cormorants. After all, she said, waterfalls did not die or migrate in the normal course of Nature. She felt it as a deliberate blow at her sanity. To console her, Peter suggested blueberrying. Back in the Free Library, he had been reading the old state guidebook, done by the WPA before he was born, and been amused by descriptions of the roadside flower-stands tended by farm wives and of happy urchins selling blueberries from house to house. The flower-stands were no more, but there must still be blueberries in the thin, second-growth woods. In the stores, you could buy only big tasteless cultivated blueberries shipped from Maine. Instead of just setting out on their own with pails and saucepans, his mother had to inquire where the best blueberry patches were. They were in copperhead country, she was told. She would not go and 'she would not let Peter go either. He accepted her veto, just as he had accepted the veto on Mississippi, having pondered the problem of the rights of parents. Until he was twenty-one, his life did not belong to him; he owed it, in fact, to his parents. He did not have the right to risk it without their consent, as long as they were reasonable. If he died at nineteen from a copperhead bite, he would feel awful for his mother, especially since the *babbo* would say it was her fault. And the fact that he would be dead and not able to stand up for her would make him more reprehensible. Anyway, blueberrying without her would not have been much fun.

In recompense, they picked water lilies from a slightly noisome pond. Peter watched baseball games on the village diamond. One day, they drove across the state border to a herb farm, where she bought herbal teas and plants of perfumed mints and geraniums to put in their window boxes and where they saw a humming-bird and a lot of goldfinches. Another day, picking pink mallows in the marshes, they saw a flight of Snowy Egrets or immature Little Blue Herons – without his field glasses, he could not be sure which.

Summer had brought to light a beach club and a golf course, both of which had always been here, it transpired. There was a drive on among his mother's acquaintances to put them up for membership in the club. Four years ago, they could never have made it, because the board had been 'stuffy' about Jews. 'Nobody named Levi would have even been considered. No matter who your mother was.' 'The Virgin Mary was a Levi,' Peter remarked stiffly. It irritated him to have to listen to briefings about discrimination, which inevitably had a smug tone, whether the speaker was for excluding Jews or not. 'Really? Isn't that fascinating? I must make a note of that. Just in case some of the old fogeys try to blackball you.' But that, it seemed, was unlikely, if they had the right sponsors; the club had been integrating. Last year a lovely Jewish family had finally been accepted and were able to swim and play tennis there, though of course they had their own tennis court and their own heated swimming pool, thermostatically controlled, which they had built before they had been let in. The club had come 'a long way' in a very short time; only two years ago, a Jewish boy, brought as a guest, had been asked to leave the dance floor by the club president. 'Is the same guy still president?' Peter wanted to know. Well, in fact, yes; Rome was not built in a day. But Peter and his mother would not have to worry if they brought Jewish house guests for a swim; no one would say a word. The club might be a bore for his mother, but it would be Peter's chance to get to know the young people. There were dances every Saturday night and movies on Wednesday. Peter could swim and play tennis and perhaps even sail, if some of the youngsters with boats would take him on as crew. Thursday was barbecue night; his mother might like to bring steaks or hamburgers and cook out on the beach over the communal fire with the others, which would smooth Peter's path . . .

Peter's interest in this proposition was nil. There was a perfectly good public beach down at the point. Every evening, just before sunset, he and his mother swam there; he would dive from the raft with his former classmates, most of whom were working in a war plant, having been deferred by the Army. From the raft, he could watch the natives – who were not the same as the All-Year-Rounders – assemble in their cars to watch the sun set. Then he and his mother would drive home, wrapped in beach towels, to change. He would light a fire and pour them each a glass of sherry. At such times, he was happy.

He accepted the fact that he would not get to know any girls this summer; the club recruiters had been right on this point. If he did not belong to the club, he would not meet the local younger set, short of nodding to them at parties. Occasionally, on the beach, he would strike up a conversation with girls he had known in high school, who were working in the plastics factory or clerking in a store; quite a few were married and had a baby. But these proletarian girls had even less allure for him than the girls in pony-tails driving Volkswagens. They were not interested in civil rights, even to argue against them. They simply did not care what happened to the Negro. It was not their fault; they had not had his opportunities. The civil-rights fight, he recognized, was a luxury for most of the whites who engaged in it; his classmates who had gone to Mississippi had had their fares and expenses paid by their families, just as though they were going on field period. If he was free (as he hoped) from prejudice, unlike his contemporaries on the raft, this was owing largely to his parents, who in turn had had 'advantages'. He was trying to think clearly this summer, before going abroad, about himself and his country. The native girls on the beach would have been glad, evidently, to 'date' him, because he was from 'away', but he could not date a girl who was not interested in civil rights – which meant, in practice, a girl who had not been to Smith or Wellesley or Swarthmore or Antioch or some other upper-middle-class school. If he had gone to Mississippi, it would have been the same; the Negro girls he might have gone around with, like the ones he used to see last winter, would have belonged to a 'leader group' – otherwise, they would not be in the civil-rights movement. Their fathers would be mostly ministers and doctors and teachers and musicians, just like his own parents. Sexually, he was pretty much a prisoner of his class, and he wondered if it would have been different had he stayed in Rocky Port High. Maybe he would not be still a virgin.

Right now, he was content to stay home nights with his mother, reading and working on his French; he could quite well wait for mid-August to see girls, when he would go to his father on the Cape. And he did not feel he was missing anything if she went out to dinner by herself.

Whenever she went out to dinner, she returned despondent. It was not the people so much (she had found a few she liked), as what she had to eat. Four years ago – she remembered distinctly – a meal had begun with soup or oysters or lobster cocktail or an avocado with Roquefort dressing. *Something.* But now, it seemed, after large basins of Martinis-on-the-rocks (a drink she had considered parvenu, as opposed to the classic Martini), you sat right down to the main course or it was served to you on your lap. Nobody alluded to the vanished first course; it was like a relation that had died and could not be mentioned. 'How do you account for that, Peter? Do you suppose it died a lingering death? Or did it happen all of a sudden, like a stroke?' 'Probably a mercy killing,' said Peter. 'Why don't you ask somebody, Mother, if you really want to know?' 'How can I? Who would I ask? It would have to be someone who still served it, and I seem to be the only one.' 'You'd better lay off it yourself, Mother.' 'Why?' she said, indignant. 'We've always had a first course. Why should I change? They have just as much time for cooking as I have, these women. More.' 'That's just the point, Mother,' he groaned.

Peter hated it when she sent him around to borrow muffin tins or cake racks or a flour sifter. Nobody had them; nobody used them any more. 'You don't get the picture, Mother. You're out of touch. Americans have stopped cooking. You embarrass them.' 'Nonsense. In New York, all my friends cook.' ' "New York is not America," Mother. Old adage.' In the very first days, she had drawn attention to herself by giving Mrs Curtis a list of things that were missing in their kitchen that she considered *essential*, underlining the word, such as pie tins and a breadboard. There was practically nothing in the cupboards, she said, but drinking equipment. Their landlady, a Goldwater stalwart, had taken offence;

she refused to supply any more kitchen stuff unless his mother restored the historical notice to the house front. The situation was deadlocked. His mother said that a house without a griddle or a strainer, not to mention pie tins and so on, had no claim to an historical placard. She refused to buy the equipment herself, on the ground that the house had been rented 'furnished', except for linen and silver. In the end, Mrs Curtis, who still liked his mother, took up a collection from people's attics. The arrival of these items was watched by their red-faced landlady from her house across the street. Peter's mother considered this a triumph, but to his mind it was a draw.

His mother's kitchen-shower included a number of items she had not asked for; e.g., a butter churn, a preserving kettle, and an old wooden ice-cream freezer with a rusty crank. His mother lit up. She was going to make ice cream at once, in their back-yard, for Mrs Curtis's grandchildren; Peter could crank. She found rock salt in the hardware store. The owner was curious as to what she planned to do with it; folks here used it winters, to melt the ice on their sidewalks. She explained. That night, she had a note from the landlady, protesting the use of rock salt in her garden – which was just a flagged terrace without a blade of grass to be damaged, as his mother pointed out in her reply.

The contest between the two had become a sort of sporting event, watched by the community with a certain impartiality of which Peter felt his mother was not wholly aware. The liberals were for his mother, because she was a novelty in the Rocky Port summer scene and was furnishing amusement at no cost except to herself. The Old Guard was for the landlady, because his mother was an interloper who played an outlandish instrument under the stage name of 'Brown', though it was known on good authority that she had been born Rosie Bronsky on the Lower East Side. But on the issues, it ought to have been the other way around. His mother's sympathizers, Peter noticed, were not rushing to follow her example, and among the landlady's supporters there were probably a few old ladies who could still wield a rolling-pin. Be that as it might, his mother was the only avowed reactionary in cooking in Rocky Port, and this was bound, Peter feared, to make her unpopular even among her chums in the end.

She made a share-cropping deal with Mrs Curtis, to harvest her currants. She and Peter were going to pick the currants, make jelly out of them, and give Mrs Curtis half. Four years ago, his mother had bought jelly glasses in the grocery store. Now, the storekeeper shook his grey head emphatically. 'Don't get any call for them.' It was the bean-pot motif, developed. With jelly glasses, naturally, paraffin had gone. And Mason jars with rubbers. 'Haven't had a call for them in years, ma'am. Don't know as they make 'em any more. Guess you notice changes.' 'Yes, I do,' said Peter's mother coldly. 'It's not his fault,' Peter whispered, excruciated.

She was going to make jelly, she said, gritting her teeth, if she had to buy store jelly and dump it down the sink, to use the jars. The thought of this waste sickened Peter; he would rather have gone scavenging in the town dump for old mayonnaise containers. Fortunately, jelly glasses and paraffin were found at the county seat – the glasses covered with dust and cobwebs like some vintage wine.

Then she decided to make watermelon pickle, saving up the rinds in huge quantities in the kitchen, using every available pan and cover to keep the flies off. Peter, who had never heard of this delicacy, could not believe the result was going to be worth the trouble. She bought screw-top jars and procured the magic ingredient – calcium oxide – from a druggist ten miles off. 'Mind if I ask what you want it for, lady?' the druggist said. Peter's mother froze. 'Why? Is it poison?' 'No, 'tain't that. I was just wondering. Haven't had a call —' 'I know,' she said. 'I'm going to make watermelon pickle.' The druggist smacked his lips. 'That's a real old-timer. Hadn't thought of that . . .' 'I'll give you a jar,' said Peter's mother, with her usual impulsiveness, moved to spread the gospel.

The fisherman they used to go to had moved to Florida, and she could not find fish anywhere that was not filleted, though a number of quaint shingled fish shops with sawdust on the floor had opened in the area, selling 'real New England clam chowder' in cans, bottled Tartare sauce, lobsters, cooked, to take home, lobster meat, and canned Chalet Suzanne lobster bisque; in the supermarkets, the fish was frozen. The only fresh fish on the whole coast seemed to be pale, boneless, skinless flounder, 'ready to fry'. 'There are other fish in the sea,' she commented. 'What happens to them?' The clerk in the fish shop was offended. 'Couldn't tell you that, ma'am.' 'Am I wrong,' she demanded, 'to want a whole fresh fish – with head and bones – on the seashore? Is that asking too much?' 'Don't get any call —' Peter's mother put her hands to her ears.

She could not get a fowl from the butcher – only roasters and fryers and chicken-in-parts. 'Folks here don't make soup like they used to. Don't have the time for it. Guess we're kind of spoiled,' the butcher summed up, with a complacent grey grin, twiddling his thumbs in his apron. 'You are,' she retorted.

'Maybe *you're* spoiled, Mother. Only a few rich people with cooks can afford the kind of food you like.' '*I* like!' she exclaimed. 'What about you, Peter? Anyway, the things you can't find here are the cheap things. Like smelts and cod. A fowl is cheaper than a roasting chicken, and you get soup from it too. Then you can make something with the leftovers the next day. Why, the cook we had in Umbria could get three meals for four people out of a hen. I admire that. Economy is a contact with reality, Peter. I love reality. I hope you always will too.' Her light voice trembled with seriousness. She meant what she said, deeply, but he could not help trying to calculate how much she had spent on gasoline scouring the countryside for jelly glasses.

Anyway, it was not just food, she said. What about buttons? She could not buy a button for Peter's shirt at the village notions store, which was full of New England souvenir items, such as whaling ships in bottles. 'Button man hasn't been through in a coon's age,' said the stout woman behind the counter. 'Don't you think you *ought* to stock buttons?'

Peter's mother said earnestly, putting it on a moral plane. 'Supposing I didn't have a car to drive to the nearest town to get them? Or I couldn't afford the bus fare? What would I do?' 'Search me,' said the woman.

Peter was worried. He wished his stepfather would come home. People in the stores had begun to stare, nudgingly, at his mother, and not because she was pretty or famous. She was looking older this summer, and most people in the stores did not know or care that she was *the* Rosamund Brown. It might have been different if she had ever played on television. He offered to do the marketing for her, to take her out of the public eye. Then he saw for himself what she meant. It was unnerving to cross out item after item on the lists that she gave him – not available. And he made a discovery of his own that shocked him: he was unable to buy plain yoghourt, one of his favourite foods. He could choose between prune and strawberry. The clerk in the Portuguese market, which he patronized in preference to the Yankee market when he did the shopping himself, explained to him that plain yoghourt was a 'slow mover'. That, in two words, was the trouble. He and his mother were wedded to slow movers.

'Is a country store just a distribution point?' she exclaimed. 'In that case, it would be better to have socialism. State stores, like in Poland and Hungary.' Peter frowned. His mother, ever since she had played behind the Iron Curtain, sounded as if she was getting soft on Communism. In politics he took after his father, who was still a mainstay of the anti-Communist left. 'We still have political freedom,' he reminded her. 'I wonder,' she replied, 'what political freedom means here now. Take this election, Peter. Hasn't it come down to a choice between prune and strawberry?'

Peter laughed hoarsely. She was right in a way. 'Still, Mother, you do think it's important that Goldwater should be defeated?' She sighed. 'I suppose so. Still, I'd like to be able to vote for Norman Thomas, the way we did in the old days. Or Darlington Hoopes! Now the Socialists aren't even on the ballot.' Peter nodded. The good old days! He remembered starting the second grade festooned with Darlington

Hoopes buttons that he had made his mother procure for him at Socialist Party headquarters in Boston – she had not been able to find them in Holyoke. But he did not encourage her political nostalgia. In November, she might write in Norman Thomas and throw away her vote. Since he was too young to vote himself, he had to trust her to do it for him. It seemed to him that the issues were more important these days than when the Socialists had been running.

Sometimes she divined ahead of time, when she was making her list, that some product like buckwheat flour was going to be unobtainable and she would leave it to Peter to choose between Aunt Jemima and nothing. But sometimes she was rocked back on her heels. He came home one morning to tell her that salt codfish in those wooden boxes with the sliding covers was not to be found – what should he do? 'Did you ask, Peter?' 'I looked. It isn't there.' 'Impossible!' She struck a violent blow on the harpsichord. 'I'll go myself. Probably they've changed the packaging. When will you get over being so shy, Peter?' He loped along beside her down the main street. She waited her turn at the check-out counter and put the question. A peculiar expression crossed the Yankee storekeeper's face – something between a twinge of guilt and a smirk of satisfaction. Peter's mother closed her eyes. 'Don't tell me.' 'Yep! They ain't making that any more. That is "a thing of the past", ma'am.' He rubbed his hands on his apron. 'I can sell you frozen codfish cakes, ready to fry – very tasty. Of course, you pay a mite more; you have to expect that.' 'It's not the same,' she said, her voice quivering. She leaned over the counter, staring at the grocer like his mercantile conscience. 'You realize it's not the same, don't you?' 'Oh, I wouldn't say that, ma'am. No, I wouldn't say that. You put on some ketchup and you won't notice a mite of difference.'

'Give up the fight, Mother.' The news that tapioca, except in instant form, was 'a thing of the past,' too, made him feel old, a weary Rip Van Winkle returned from a drive-in bowling alley. In this sinister summer of race riots, church-burnings, civil-rights workers vanishing in Mississippi, in

New York, a cop, off duty, shooting to kill at a Negro kid, the fact that tapioca, his old love, had kicked the bucket ought not to matter. Yet if he said that to his mother, she felt he was abandoning her.

It disturbed him to see her so irritated by everything. He had always thought of her as equable. He could not accuse her of being a superficial person, but it was at least arguable, he thought, that she was reading too much into the minutiae. She acted as if the difference between sliced bread and unsliced was the difference between wrong and right. He wondered if she was getting near the menopause. For the first time in her life that Peter could remember, she had begun – what an irony! – to have cooking failures. Not when they were alone, but when they had company. And being what she was, she had to apologize. 'Just serve it, Mother. Don't say anything. They'll never know.' Glumly, he watched her trying to turn her battle with Rocky Port into a game, laughing at her misadventures and writing with amusement about them to his stepfather – letters she sometimes let Peter read. It sounded funny when you read about it. Yet he feared that – also for the first time in her life – she did not see herself as others saw her.

For himself, he invented a different game – taking the Goldwater stickers off people's cars. He worked at night, selecting his target before dark came. He burned the trophies in the fireplace when his mother was out; if he told her what he was doing, she would be bound to boast about it, and he would find himself fleeing from Rocky Port with a price on his head – intimidating voters, which he hoped he was doing, was a federal crime. His most daring exploit was getting the huge streamer off the bumper of their landlady's Buick. She kept it parked under a street light directly across the way, a few feet from a downstairs front bedroom where she slept, according to her own testimony, with a shotgun by her side. He needed a confederate to engage her on the telephone in the back hall while he did the job. 'Hell, son,' said the admiral. 'I'd have done the same thing at your age. Down South, I was a Republican before I could shave, which was like being a card-carrying Communist. Now, with this race business, I'm kind of leaning toward Goldwater myself. Guess I'm part of the white backlash.' He agreed to act as a decoy, however, and got his wife to invite Peter's mother to a lecture to keep her out of the way. He and Peter set their watches together and worked out a code for Peter to signal with a flashlight when the deed was done. Failing Goldwater stickers, Peter removed 'Ausable Chasm' and 'Desert of Maine' from the bumpers of passing tourists.

These puerile activities gave direction, of a sort, to his summer and led him to make friends with the admiral, who had lost a son in the war. He was the only older WASP Peter knew, except his mother, who still had some pioneer spirit. The old man was disgruntled with the modern world, and, in view of his Tennessee origins, Peter could almost forgive him for being prejudiced against Negroes (which the admiral denied), because he was prejudiced against so many other groups and persons, regardless of race, creed, or colour – e.g., social workers, J. Edgar Hoover, and the CIA. Peter was hoping to influence him, before the summer was over, to stay at home, come November, rather than vote for Goldwater; he was one of the mass of 'Undecideds' who were a headache to pollsters and political scientists. Peter could sympathize with a pollster who got the admiral in his sampling. He himself had just about decided to class him as a visceral fascist when he learned that the old man and his wife and Mrs Curtis constituted the local chapter of a Ban-the-Bomb organization.

The admiral, known as 'Reb' for rebel – his sobriquet at Annapolis – had a hammock and a telescope on his back porch, from which he viewed the stars. He knew the coast well – the many islands, islets, points, coves, harbours, inlets, salt marshes – and the shore and sea birds. He was a student of the hurricanes that came this way in the fall. Before he had had his heart attack, two years back, he had been vociferous at town meetings. Now he puttered about, smoking his pipe, doing crewelwork, helping his wife with her Gift Shop, slyly drinking snorts of whiskey, and making horrible curries.

What pleased Peter in the admiral was that he resembled the element he had lived in – salty, shifty, protean, like the Old Man of the Sea. He was the only All-Year-Rounder whose former occupation you could guess after a short conversation. He had a small, mean mouth, a hoarse sea bird's voice, and was reputed to be violent when drinking.

The admiral boasted of being unwelcome at the beach club, which had only let him in, he said, because it was 'traditional' to accept naval officers. The word *tradition* was often heard at Rocky Port cocktail parties, usually on the lips of a woman with blue hair or a fat man in Polynesian shorts. The village was protecting its traditions, Peter was repeatedly told, as though Rocky Port were a sanctuary full of banded birds threatened with extirpation. He wondered what had been handed down to these people that they thought they were safeguarding – besides money. There was nothing distinctive about Rocky Port's institutions or way of life, unless it was the frequency of gift shops selling 'gourmet' foods, outsize pepper mills, 'amusing' aprons and chef's costumes, bar equipment, and frozen croissants, 'just like in France'. 'Taking in each other's washing,' the admiral declared. Probably they deserved credit for maintaining their houses and keeping the streets swept. The fact remained that Rocky Port was a museum and, like all museums, Peter's mother said, best when it was all-but-empty and you could hear your footfalls echo. They should never have come back in season.

Still, there was one traditional event, everyone told them, that capped the summer and was unique to Rocky Port; you would not see anything like it at Watch Hill or Weekapaug or Saunderstown. This was the annual celebration of the Battle of Rocky Port, where the British had been defeated in the War of 1812. It was a two-day affair in which the whole community participated, man, woman, and child – a typical old-time New England jamboree. Normally, Peter would have gone to his father in mid-August, but his departure was postponed for the sake of this celebration, which the *babbo*, as an educator, could hardly deny him. It began the fifteenth of

August with an Historic Houses and Gardens tour, under Garden Club auspices, that drew crowds from as far away as Providence. Next morning, there was a parade, led by the Portuguese Holy Ghost Club, which had a brass band; that afternoon, there was a fair on the village green for the benefit of the town churches and charities, with games, ponies, a cake sale, rummage, a sale of second-hand books, and stands of vegetables, flowers, and fruits.

This was the sort of event his mother rose to. If the locals had had any sense, Peter thought, they would have put her on the programme committee. She would have been happy to tell fortunes, look up old martial airs and arrange them for the band, contribute a button collection – cutting them off her own clothes, if necessary; she would have organized a needle-work contest, made pinwheels, donated jars of pickles and jelly, helped sew costumes, put Peter to work painting mints with vegetable colours. It was a disappointment that she was only asked to bake a cake for the cake sale to benefit the Free Library. 'Can't I make a pot of beans for one of the other charities? And a freezer of ice cream?' she said to Mrs Curtis, who had come to sign her up for the cake. 'I'd love to, wouldn't I, Peter?'

'I know you would,' said Mrs Curtis, patting his mother's hand. 'But it won't be necessary, my dear.' The ice-cream concession, she explained, was given to a commercial company – the same people who handled the sale of Coca-Cola and hot dogs. 'I don't understand,' said Peter's mother. 'You can still use some home-made ice cream. Peach, I thought. And baked beans have become a sort of novelty. What are the other women making?' Mrs Curtis looked sideways at Peter; some bad news, he surmised, was going to be broken to his mother. 'It's like this, Rosamund. The company won't sell hot dogs and ice cream for us unless they have the exclusive concession. Doesn't pay them unless they handle all the refreshments. Our charities farm out the stands to them on a percentage basis.' 'You mean that's *all*? Commercial ice cream and hot dogs?'

'And cakes to take home. That's the way it is.' Mrs Curtis

turned to Peter. 'I was afraid she was going to take it hard. It's kind of a shock at first. Why, I remember the time when we used to have potato salads and chicken potpies and clam pies. Rice salad, lobster salad, marcaroni salad. Yes, and baked beans and home-made ice cream. Peppermint was a great seller. Boston brown bread. Oatmeal bread. Datebread. Always a lot of baked goods. You can get women to bake when they won't do anything else. Point of pride with them. Sex, I've always thought. Getting a rise out of the batter.'

'How long has this been going on?' Peter's mother interrupted. 'Well, it's quite some time now. Seems to me the Red Cross started it, with the store hot dogs. Somebody had a relative with Howard Johnson's, it might have been. They came in with their stoves and their frankfurters and rolls and then they cleaned up after themselves. Saved a lot of trouble. The other organizations caught on – the Visiting Nurse and the Community Fund. Pretty soon we were all doing it. Sort of a trend. In the old days, people rushed around the first thing after the parade to get that one's chicken pie or the other one's lobster salad. Then when you ran out, the ones who came late were sore. Felt they'd been cheated. Old Mrs Drysdale, up in the big house, used to send down a pot of bouillabaisse every year, made by her French chef. Always caused bad blood. This way, it's more democratic. The Catholic church was the last to fall into line. They had their own refreshments stand up till '63. Oh, let me tell you, the priest cracked the whip over those women! A real Simon Legree, that one was. Preached against Adlai because he was a divorced man. And they followed him like sheep. It was "Mrs Rodriguez, you'll make your Parker House rolls," and "Mrs Santos, you'll make your Southern fried chicken" – no excuses accepted. But the Church couldn't hold out forever, with the tide running the other way. Pope John, you know.'

Peter and his mother eyed each other sadly. She cleared her throat. 'What kind of cake should I make, Ellen?' 'Whatever your heart desires, dear. Chocolate's always safe. My husband used to like a marble cake. I guess I don't have to tell you not to use a mix.' His mother brightened. 'Is that a rule? How nice!' 'We have the Catholics to thank for it,' Mrs Curtis said. "Nix on Mixes," Father Cassidy – that's the new one – told the women, right from the pulpit. Threatened them with the confessional. Those priests like to eat.' 'Are the Papists running the fair?' Peter wanted to know. 'If they won't use mixes,' said Mrs Curtis, 'we've got to keep in line with them. We don't want them to sell their cakes ahead of ours, do we?'

'Why just cakes?' said Peter. 'Why not pies? You ought to diversify.' 'A good pie is hard to make,' said Mrs Curtis. 'They say it's a lost art.' 'You can't even buy pastry flour in the grocery store,' put in Peter's mother. 'Can't you?' said Mrs Curtis absently. 'Well, times change. There's talk every year of cutting out the cake sale, as more trouble than it's worth. A lot would give the money and more not to have the oven on in this hot weather. But the majority clings to it. We get people coming every year just for the cake sale. It's traditional.'

' "Let them eat cake," ' said Peter. He tried to imagine the contented masses on the village green. 'What games do they have?' 'Well, we used to have archery. Broad jump. Potato races. Weightlifting. But now it's pretty standardized. Mostly throwing rings over the necks of Coca-Cola bottles at ten cents a throw. You win one of those dolls. That's all a concession too. The men come from outside and give us a cut of what they make. Times past, there was one that brought a shooting-gallery, with ducks. But it comes to the same thing if you just throw rings at bottles.'

When Mrs Curtis had gone, Peter's mother said that the fair sounded rather commercialized. Perhaps they had better not expect too much of it. He was too old to ride a pony and if he wanted a hot dog he could go to the diner. She did hope he would enjoy the parade and the Historic Houses and Gardens tour. Or would he rather skip the whole thing and go, as originally planned, to his father on the Cape?

The offer went to his heart. He could not accept it. If he walked out on Rocky Port now, he would be walking out on her and her foundering values. Even if his presence embarrassed her, he had to go down with the ship.

She knew that old houses did not greatly interest him, that he disliked crowds and would probably feel self-conscious standing in line to view flower-arrangements done by Garden Club ladies, although he liked *her* flowers and botany and had giant plants crawling around his college room. But he knew how much she was looking forward to the garden tour, having been deprived of a garden herself this summer. The yard in back of their house was all flagged, with no place for flower beds – only for garden furniture and a 'service area' containing garbage cans. Less maintenance, the landlady stated, and it made a nice setting for cocktails. All summer his mother had been picking wild flowers for their parlour in the woods and marshes, and Peter could understand her enthusiasm at the prospect of seeing what she called 'real' flowers growing in beds and borders. Remembering the acres of armour and miles of mummies she had traversed with him when he was little, he made a resolution not to be bored; it was no good resolving not to *act* bored, as he had learned in Italy.

Those old New England gardens could be marvellous, she told him, especially in seaports. You discovered rare plants and shrubs that ships' captains had brought home from the Orient. Flowers that were in Shakespeare and Keats and that must have travelled from England in the form of roots, slips, bulbs, and cuttings, with the early settlers. Old-fashioned roses. White double narcissus and poppies that bloomed every year on Memorial Day. Spicebush, lemon lilies, a kind of Persian lilac that smelled of Necco Wafers. A plant called Beauty Bush and one called Sensitive Plant that winced when you touched it. Old Ladies' flowers like heliotrope and verbena and pinks. Hollyhocks, self-seeded, against white picket fences. A great deal of honeysuckle, privet and box. Sundials, arbours, trellises, an occasional gazebo. Dogs' gravestones. It was a pity that the tour was so late in the season; most of the perennials, except phlox, would be finished. But the annuals ought to be particularly brilliant.

Something in the sea air or light brought out the colours of zinnias and pale lemon African marigolds. She only hoped there would not be too many dahlias.

On the morning of the great day, she was up early, wearing a pink linen dress. She told Peter to put on his seersucker suit and shine his shoes. At nine, the sky clouded over. A few drops of rain fell. The mailman reassured her. 'Radio says fair. Paper says fair. That rain don't mean a thing. It's just the weather.' At eleven, in fact, it stopped raining. His mother put on a large straw hat, and they took their places in line, outside the first house on the tour. Their landlady, who was an officer of the Garden Club, was selling tickets. 'I'm going to *speak*,' whispered Peter's mother. 'Lovely day, after all, Mrs Hills,' she said pleasantly. The landlady sold them two tickets, which would also entitle them to tea later in the day. 'Did you lock up after you?' she said curtly, making change. 'I never lock up,' said Peter's mother. 'Well, I'm warning you. Strangers in town.' 'But a stranger is just someone you don't know, Mrs Hills,' his mother said, in a friendly tone. 'And don't want to,' retorted the landlady, handing her a programme. 'You get another element these days. Riffraff from the towns. Only come to rubberneck. Never known what it was to own beautiful things and take care of them.' 'My son can go home and lock up, if you're really concerned,' said his mother, who was evidently determined not to spoil the day by a dispute.

When he returned, his mother was studying the programme, printed in red and blue type on thick white paper and decorated with an American flag rippling in the breeze. 'A Stroll into the Past' was the title. Peter counted the stars in the flag; there were sixteen, which he supposed was historically justified – his father would know. On the back of the programme was a little map of the village; each 'open' house had a number. Peter scrutinized it. In their old neighbourhood, he noted some small letters: *a*, *b*, and *c*. 'Portugee gardens,' he heard Mrs Hills explain to a pair of out-of-towners. 'Houses aren't shown.' She pointed to the bottom of the programme, where there was a section headed

'Gardens Open'. They belonged to a Mr Antone Silvia, a Mrs Rose Santos, and a Mrs Mary Lacerda.

He and his mother began the tour with 'a typical sea captain's house of an early time'. Two hostesses were directing traffic through the small, rather dark rooms. Visitors dressed in their best clothes jostled each other to stare at highboys, lowboys, duck-footed tables, carpets, china cabinets, silver, pewter, ancestral portraits, faded family photographs, keepsakes, which were exciting more curiosity than the flower-arrangements tagged with red and blue ribbons and the architectural features described in the programme. 'Please don't touch!' a voice rapped out from time to time, as someone fingered the china or looked for the hallmark on the silver. Peter was surprised by the number of middle-aged men in the throng. It was hot, and there was a strong smell of furniture polish, overlaying a slight mouldy smell of old upholstery. Someone had forgotten to take down the Christmas mistletoe in the parlour doorway. 'Tacky,' was his mother's verdict. While she lined up to look at the flower-arrangements, he tried to take an interest in the books on the library shelves. The most recent acquisitions he could find were Winston Churchill's war memoirs and *Peyton Place*. His mother beckoned. 'Let's go.' In the garden, there was less congestion. They looked around. 'Has there been a drought or something?' Peter wondered aloud. The only evidence of gardening he noted was a compost heap. 'Ssh!' said his mother, peering at the programme. 'Come, let's find "Aunt Mary Chase's roses". It says here they were planted during the Civil War.' They followed a flagged walk that led, past some bushes, to a "service area". They retraced their steps. His mother asked someone. 'There!' A spindly rose with two faded blooms was leaning against a trellis. She swallowed her disappointment. 'What a shame it's so late in the season! Those old varieties of roses never do much after June. It looks as if these people' – she glanced again at the programme – 'had rather let their garden go. But in spring it must be lovely, don't you think so, Peter? Look, they had peonies and lilies of the valley. And that must be iris.' 'Where?' said Peter. She indicated some yellow foliage. 'They ought to separate them,' she said absently. 'Those are violets,' she went on, tapping a leaf with her foot. 'Probably just ordinary wood violets. Oh, see the quinces!'

'Come on, Mother.' He led the way out. They tried 'a fine example of a prosperous shipowner's dwelling'. Peter found Winston Churchill's war memoirs, *The Carpetbaggers*, and the bound files of the *National Geographic*. 'But there aren't any *flowers;*' his mother whispered, in the garden. She exaggerated, but not greatly, It was the same all along the line. Here and there, shrubs and hardy perennials were still gamely blooming, survivors of another era, like Longfellow's *Poems*, which they discovered propping up a small-paned window. Hydrangeas, phlox, Funkia, yucca – his mother named them off. Lilac bushes, indestructible, stood in the dooryards, surrounded by suckers. You could infer from latticework where a rose arbour had been and make out designs faintly traced by decimated box. Raised oblongs in the arid lawns, like graves, testified to former flower beds. 'That must have been a strawberry patch!' his mother cried, pointing. She found some old yellow roses. But there was hardly an annual or a biennial to be seen, except in the yards of the Portuguese section, where zinnias and dahlias were growing in uncontrolled abundance, like the children of the poor. Elsewhere, as Peter commented, old Mother Nature seemed to have taken the pill.

His own mother kept apologizing. 'I'm sorry, Peter.' 'Why? It's not your fault.' She cheered up slightly in Gardens *a*, *b*, and *c*, which were attached to two-storey frame tenement dwellings. Mr Antone Silvia had potted red geraniums and white ruffled petunias and transplanted ferns from the wood. Mrs Santos had scattered seeds of every kind broadcast: cockscombs, zinnias, kitchen herbs, dahlias, cosmos, calendulas, marigolds, asters – a riot, remarked Peter, of bloom. Mrs Lacerda had roses and dahlias. 'The darling Portuguese!' they heard a young woman in tight turquoise pants exclaim to her companion in Mr Silvia's small grassy plot. 'They have a green thumb but no taste. Don't you love them? Red, white, and green – you can *see* Tony thinking out his colours. I always make a pilgrimage to Mrs Lacerda's funny garden, and she brings me a rose in her hot little hand. It was such a clever idea to have them in the Garden Club. We were afraid they'd notice the difference between their gardens and ours. Not at all, my dear. Totally unaware of it.'

Peter's mother's laugh made the young woman jump. 'Take it easy, Mother.' She had attracted attention by a display of mirth back in one of the houses when he ventured the theory that the reason they did not see more flowers growing was that they had all been picked for the flower-arrangements. Other visitors listened while she gaily read aloud from the programme: 'An arrangement of flowers and/or foliage in an old tea-caddy or canister.' 'A doorstep arrangement of wild flowers and/or foliage in a stoneware container.' 'An arrangement of roadside material featuring one or more seashells.' He did not see what was so funny, and neither did the rest of the auditory. 'Well, come and look, Peter.' Then the light broke.

Tea-caddies, ironstone tureens, Lowestoft dishes, sea-shells, and (naturally) bean pots were filled with 'wild material', which, translated from Garden Club parlance, meant weeds. Among them, Peter recognized some old friends. Cattails from the marshes, Queen Anne's lace, beach peas, Black-eyed Susan, Bouncing Bet. His mother said it had been like that in every house so far. He decided to start keeping a tally. According to his final count, the commonest 'flower' in this unusual flower show was Queen Anne's lace. Bouncing Bet scored second – 'so versatile,' he heard a woman say. There was also a multitude of field and beach grasses unknown by name to him but which belonged, his mother said coldly, on a hay-fever chart. Here and there, combined with this wild material, were a few roses and/or blue hydrangeas, some stalks of delphinium, a gladiolus. The visitors filing through seemed lost in admiration. 'Look at that, will you, sweetheart,' an earnest man in a yachting blazer said to his wife. 'It shows what you can do with just one rose.'

The Battle of Rocky Port

An exception was the contest set by their landlady: 'An arrangement of red, white, and blue flowers in an old pewter container. CHAIRMAN: Mrs Frances B. Hills.' The prize-winners here had used conventional flowers like larkspurs and petunias. His mother said this must be because few weeds came in patriotic colours. Yet there were murmurs of dissatisfaction among the viewers; some argued that 'Honourable Mention', who had used Queen Anne's lace, field asters, and devil's-paintbrush (which to Peter's eye was orange), ought to have had first prize. A man stood up for the awards. 'To me, they look bright and colourful.' 'Floristy,' his wife told him. And that indeed was the case. The scandal reached Peter and his mother at the diner, where they were eating their lunch. 'You folks hear what happened?' said the waitress. It was all over town: the first- and second-prize winners in Mrs Hills's contest had been disqualified; they had bought their material from a florist in Westerly. The truck had been seen delivering.

At tea at the house of the Garden Club president, Peter and his mother, in search of a friendly face, found the admiral chuckling to himself on the terrace overlooking the harbour. 'They've confessed,' he said. 'Been asked to resign from the Garden Club. If Frances Hills had her way, they'd be stood in the pillory. "Collapse of public morality." ' He munched at a thawed frozen sandwich from the Corner Cupboard and spat out a sliver of ice. 'Seems as though they could make a sandwich at home.' 'Did you *see* the flower-arrangements, Reb?' The admiral nodded. 'Did the whole tour. Paid good money for it. Only flowers worth seeing came from the florist.' He sourly recalled the days at the War College when he had grown giant dahlias. 'They'll have instant flowers next.' 'A weed is an instant flower,' Peter's mother pointed out. The admiral chortled. 'The country's going to hell, sweetheart. Fellow came the other day, tried to sell me an atom-bomb shelter made of compressed marble dust. Claimed it was a new industry, helping unemployment in the area. The Great Society! I tell you. I'm swinging more and more to Goldwater.'

Peter's mother started to argue. 'Goldwater is *worse*, Reb. Look at his foreign policy. And he runs a *department store*. At least Johnson taught school.' Peter took his mother's empty teacup and glided towards the dining room. The admiral sounded like a fascist, and his mother sounded like a Communist, and they were the two people he liked in Rocky Port. Mrs Curtis in his view was too fey to count politically. He approached the tea table, where Mrs Hills was pouring. 'Young man, why don't you wait and let other people be served before you? This is the third time you've been through the line. Don't you get enough to eat at home?' Peter replied non-violently. 'It's for my mother.'

He went back to the terrace and reported the exchange. The admiral laughed. 'Steer clear of her, son. She's kind of inflamed today. Having that happen at her contest. Never at her best anyway in an election year.' He turned to Peter's mother. 'You know, the other night somebody took the Goldwater streamer off her car. I think she suspects young Peter here.' He winked at Peter. 'Why, that's the most unjust thing! Why should she suspect Peter?' She set her cup down, as though to take action. Peter met the admiral's eyes, slightly hooded, like a hawk's. The old man shook his head. He gently pulled Peter's mother to her seat. 'Let be, honey. Let's you and I go on discussing politics. Now I voted for Adlai in '52 and again in '56. I never liked Ike . . .' Peter wondered whether the admiral was too old to make passes. And if he made a pass, should the fair Rosamund yield if he promised to vote for Johnson?

The next morning, before the parade, a policeman came to their door. Their landlady wanted the historical notice put back on the house front immediately, before the parade started. With so many visitors in town, interested in historic houses, Peter's mother, she claimed, was depreciating the value of her property. 'Says she gave you a written request to nail the sign up where it was more than a month ago.' Peter's mother took a stand in the doorway. 'I'm sorry, but I've rented this house, and there's nothing in the lease that requires me to carry advertising on it.' The policeman rubbed his foot on the Welcome mat. 'Come on, lady. Mrs Hills has the law on her side. Selectmen say every old house in Rocky Port township has to have one of those boards.' 'If she has the law on her side, let her sue me. Excuse me, officer; I'm busy.' She started to turn away; in fact, she was making seven-minute frosting for her cake for the fair.

'Not so fast there, lady,' said the policeman. 'I'm talking to you.' She pushed open the screen door impatiently and came out on to the doorstep. The policeman backed up, bumping into Peter, who had been watering the herbal geraniums in the window boxes. Some water from the watering-can spilled on to the policeman's uniform. A little crowd was gathering under the elms and maples: tourists hung with cameras and a few paraders in period costumes with muskets. Because of the parade, the street had been cleared of motor traffic. In front of the Holy Ghost Club, the band was tuning up. 'Selectmen say —' repeated the police-man in a louder voice. 'Is that a town ordinance, officer?' Peter heard his own voice croak.

Mindful of his civil-rights training, he was making a simple request for information; that was what you did when met by a sheriff and his deputies at the county line. 'Pipe down, Buster,' the cop said. Behind him, Peter saw a tourist hold up a light meter. 'My son asked you a question,' said his mother, as the camera clicked. 'And his name is not Buster.' 'That's enough out of you too, lady.' The band struck up 'Yankee Doodle'. 'Come on, Missus, let's have a little co-operation. I got a parade to handle. I give you five minutes to put that board back.'

That was a tactical mistake, Peter estimated. His mother could not hammer the placard back with all these clowns watching her. Across the street, he observed their landlady surveying the scene from her bedroom window. 'Or let Buster do it,' emended the cop. Peter looked to his mother for guidance. In his opinion, it would be wiser to comply. The cop was flustered and ignorant, probably, of the law – something he would be unwilling to betray in front of so many witnesses. You were supposed to see your opponent as a human being and avoid making him look foolish in public. 'Why don't you go in the house and talk it over, Mother? Maybe you can come to an agreement.' 'I'm afraid that's out of the question,' she said coolly. 'There isn't any board. I burned it.' Peter gulped. It was her bridges she had just burned; the sign was stored in the basement. 'I used it for kindling. By mistake.' She smiled defiantly. The cop could see she was lying – she seemed to want him to. 'Did you report this careless destruction of property?' 'No.' 'Why not?' 'It slipped my mind.' The cop sighed. 'Lady, I'm going to have to ask you to walk along to the police station.'

'I'm sorry, I'm frosting a cake.' In the crowd, someone laughed. 'Don't give me that,' the cop said. 'Step along now.' 'Have you got a warrant?' Peter asked quietly. The cop's eyes narrowed. 'Let's see your draft card, Buddy.' Peter slowly put down the watering-can, balancing it on the window box. The cop prodded him with a finger. 'Let's see that draft card!' 'Don't you touch him!' his mother cried. Another policeman elbowed his way through the onlookers. 'What's going on here? Clear the street, folks. You're holding up the parade.' Encouraged by the reinforcement, the first cop gripped Peter's arm. 'All right, you! Let's have it!' Before he could restrain her, his mother picked up the watering-can, which was still half full, and poured the contents over the cop. 'I advise you to cool off,' she said between her teeth.

Owing to these events, they missed the parade as well as the fair on the green. They were in the village jail, waiting to be charged with disorderly conduct, resisting arrest, and assaulting a police officer. An elderly attendant locked Peter in a cell, while someone went to fetch the matron to lock up his mother. They had not been booked because there was no one to book them; the police force was busy supervising the festivities. There was no one in jail but the two of them – not even a cockroach. In the distance he heard the band. Finally it stopped and was replaced by a loud-speaker. He knew that lunch-time must have come because he was hungry – they had taken away his wristwatch when they searched him.

The jail fare proved to be hamburgers from the Portuguese diner, with plenty of ketchup, delivered by Margery, the waitress, Peter's old friend, who, it transpired, moonlighted as matron in the lockup. She let herself into his cell, handed him his tray, lit a cigarette, and combed out her beehive hairdo. 'I remembered how you liked them – rare, and I made your mother's rare too.' What she had not remembered was that they preferred mustard, and Peter was relieved to glean that his mother had not said so. 'Gee, thanks, Margery; I mean . . .' He hesitated, unsure of how to address her in their changed relationship.

'Go ahead, call me Marge,' she said. 'I can get you seconds, if you want.' He wondered what he should do about tipping her; they had taken away his money too. 'Don't give it a thought, Pete. It's a pleasure. Anyway, the town pays my time here, and it makes a change. Don't happen often that they send for me. We rarely get a woman in jail. Last one was a murderess. Police caught her, where she was hiding out in Rocky Port. She was wanted in Hartford for an axe-murder. Geez, Pete, it come as a shock to me to see your mother here. A lady like her. You never know these days, do you? Nobody told me. Just "You're wanted as matron, Marge." I didn't even have time to slip off my apron.'

'Neither did my mother,' Peter remarked dryly. Margery nodded. 'You don't have to tell me. Geez, Pete, I had to search her. Right down to her panties and hose. A lady like her. Just the same as a hooker. But like I told her, the law says I have to do it. I can't go against the law.' 'You mustn't buy that,' said Peter. 'If anybody feels a law is unjust, he ought to disobey it.' 'You mean like Prohibition?' Peter had not thought of the analogy. 'Actually, I was thinking of seg-regation. Or marching without a permit. I didn't mean it was unjust that you had to search my mother.' 'I was just doing my job,' Margery retorted. 'Like I told her. But, God, it broke my heart. Skin like a baby, she has. Geez, Pete, what are things coming to?'

Peter did not know. Though he could not nurse his mother's wrongs with the same woeful relish as the jail matron, he agreed that she did not belong in 'a place like this' – as Margery kept calling it, shaking her head. In fact, his cell, which slept four, had a toilet and a window box filled with white and purple petunias. Conditions were pretty good. Nevertheless, it shocked him to think of his mother, who was very modest, being stripped by a wardress. He asked himself what was the difference between Margery and a hospital nurse – his mother would be stripped in a hospital as a matter of course. The evident difference was that in a hospital his mother would be a private patient. What was biting Margery was that his mother was getting the common-criminal treatment, while statistically she was an uncommon criminal. It seemed to be otherwise with him. His age, he assumed, made his being in a place like this appear more natural.

While Margery went to fetch his dessert, he pursued his thoughts. Whatever others might feel, he regarded his own presence here as wholly unnatural – fantastic. He could not believe that Peter Levi was in jail in good old Rocky Port. Down South, it would have been different: you went there knowing that you might be arrested; you went to bear witness. Just as the *babbo*, who had done time in Mussolini's prisons, had felt that he 'belonged' there because he opposed fascism. You belonged in a place where you had chosen to be. But this morning's adventure had had a horrible, unreal, automated character from the outset. For one thing, it had all happened so fast, like a car accident. One minute he was peacefully watering the geraniums and the next he was aiming a feeble left at a policeman's jaw. His reason felt aggrieved; what had happened did not make sense in the general scheme. It was like that time, last fall on the Cape, when he had swum out too far and lost his wind: the thought that he might be drowning, all alone in the unfriendly ocean, while his family was sunning on the beach, had appeared to him as a sort of gross insult – the last straw, really. He asked himself now whether this stubborn sense of personal im-

munity, like the sense of personal immortality, was a bourgeois trait.

Another point was needling him. '*A lady like her.*' He
confessed that it had gratified him to hear Margery say it. He
was glad that somebody in this madhouse recognized that his
mother was gently bred, a gentle person. But what would
Margery say of Mrs Hills, who was not a hooker either, if she
landed in the clink? Did Margery know the difference
between his mother and Mrs Hills or was she just evincing
class prejudice? In that case he ought to have corrected her
instead of silently consenting. As an egalitarian, he ought to
be repelled by the survival of feudal notions among the
'lower orders'; yet in his heart he had been humbly thanking
Margery for not confusing his mother with an axe-murderess
from Hartford. This meant, he guessed, that he was uncertain
of his own values and needed a friendly waitress to confirm
them. But maybe in a democracy that was the way it should
be; his mother was a 'lady' by Margery's consent.

The afternoon went by. Solitary confinement, he discovered, did not promote a Socratic dialogue with yourself. You
got bored. He practised the conjugation of French irregular
verbs, sang his favourite arias to himself ('*Se vuol ballare,
signor contino*'), and endeavoured to guess the time from the
length of the shadows cast by the bars on his floor. He supposed he had the right to ask for a lawyer and make one
telephone call but he felt no inclination to exercise those
rights. Sooner or later, he and his mother would be sprung.
No doubt their friends outside were working on that now.
The syrup for his mother's frosting must have boiled away
on the stove. Had anybody turned off the gas?

'So you're in the brig, son.' Peter was dozing when the
admiral was admitted to his cell. He had brought Peter's
pyjamas, bathrobe, and toothbrush, and a stack of magazines.
'Am I going to have to stay here all *night*?' Peter cried out,
forgetting to think of his mother. 'Isn't anybody posting bail
or anything? Listen, sir, tomorrow I have to go to my father.'
The admiral soothed him. He and Mrs Curtis had been to
see a lawyer, who had called up a judge at the county seat.

They could not be released on bail until they had been charged before a magistrate. He delved into his old black satchel and brought out a thermos of Martinis and some cake, wrapped in foil, from the fair. 'Here's something to brush your teeth with. You can eat the cake later.' He poured Peter a Martini into the thermos top.

'Here's how it is, son. The judge and the lawyer-fellow say to go slow. The lawyer's in there now, talking to your mother. His advice is not to insist on being charged. Doesn't do, in a little place like Rocky Port, to stand up on your hind legs and yell for your legal rights.' 'Amen,' said Peter. The old man looked at him shrewdly. 'From what I hear, your trouble, son, was that you thought you were down South.' 'I guess that's true.' 'Down South,' said the admiral, 'with all this agitation, the sheriff knows the law. All the fine print. Has to, if he's going to use it against you. The police up here haven't had the opportunity. Never come up against any civil-rights workers.' Peter laughed feebly. 'Still, even up here, they must know about habeas corpus,' he objected. 'Sure,' said the admiral. 'After twenty-four hours, the lawyer can get a writ. But it won't come to that. Point is to give the police a chance to think it over. The chief of police won't be happy when he finds he has a celebrity in the brig. Once your mother's charged, she's likely to have to stand trial. Papers will get hold of it, and the police won't want to drop the case, because that'd make it look as if they were in the wrong. She could turn around and sue them for false arrest. None of that would do Rocky Port any good, or your mother either. When an artist gets to fighting with the police, the scuttlebutt always is they've been drinking. Kind of a natural conclusion, in my experience. Bottoms up, boy.' Peter downed the Martini.

The admiral refilled his cup. 'After supper, the judge is coming over for the fireworks. He'll have a session with the chief of police. But that'll be kind of late. Fireworks don't start till ten o'clock.' 'Fireworks?' said Peter wanly. Nobody had told him that the annual celebration ended with a fireworks display. 'Looks as if you'd have to miss them. But you'll be a free man in the morning. The judge will appreciate it if your mother sends him one of her albums. Chief of police maybe too.' 'The payola,' muttered Peter.

The admiral weighed anchor after watching Peter finish the second Martini, which he did not really want. He looked at the cartoons in the *New Yorker* and could not get the point of the jokes. A mood of bitter dissatisfaction took hold of him, which he declined to blame on the wormwood he had consumed. He was nauseated by society. It occurred to him that the old man had tried to get him drunk on purpose so as to keep him from insisting on his right to a trial. His mother, he assumed, was taking the lawyer's advice, and he was angry that he had not been consulted. They *ought* to stand trial, he considered. The charges were true. And what was their defence? That a policeman had called him 'Buster' and asked for his draft card. He laughed sullenly to himself. If there was any justice in Rocky Port, they should be lucky to get off with a suspended sentence.

He tried to get his thoughts in order. Naturally, he was opposed to cops' throwing their weight around. But that was how they were. And if that was how they were, they ought to be consistent, handing it out equally to the famous and the infamous. He did not think there was any clause in the Constitution that entitled a citizen not to be called 'Buster'. That, apparently, was a privilege. He was free to resent the way the cop talked to a person he considered nobody, a weedy member of the draft pool, but the cop, in fact, had a duty not to know *who he was*. Peter was ashamed of his mother for letting them talk her into taking advantage of her celebrity and ashamed of the admiral for bringing liquor into his cell and breaking the rules – it was against Kant's teaching to pretend to be a law unto yourself. His mother's celebrity, as a matter of fact, was exactly what had got them into trouble; she was used to being flattered by people like Margery who 'knew' she played the harp. If the cop had 'known' that, he would have handled her with deference, which in turn would have satisfied her ego. So that in some depressing way the whole thing boiled down to a misunderstanding, which the cop would probably pay for.

The old jailer came and took away his dinner tray. Night fell. Peter put on his pyjamas and brushed his teeth with some salt he had saved from his dinner. He washed. These familiar night-time actions made him lonely for his mother. He remembered how she used to tuck him in when he was little, tell him his story, and bring him his glass of water. All at once, he felt contrite. He should never have made her come back to Rocky Port. He took back his harsh judgments. Obviously, a celebrity was in a position to demand courtesy from the law; she would have been wrong if she had not made an example of herself. A cop ought to fear that every nobody was a possible somebody or had a relation who was. This one would think twice before calling the next kid 'Buster' or 'buddy', even a kid from the wrong side of town – as Margery said, you never knew these days. Forgiving all his enemies, he fell asleep.

He had forgotten where he was when he heard someone unlocking his door. The jailer beckoned. 'You want to see the fireworks?' He led Peter down the corridor and up some stairs, out to the back of the jail, where there was a raised porch with some rocking-chairs. His mother was already there, in a dressing-gown and mules, smoking a cigarette with Margery. She hugged him. 'Isn't this fun? We're having an adventure, Peter.' He sighed. That was her way, when he was little, of characterizing some gruesome mishap, such as running out of gas in the desert ten miles from the nearest ghost town. They watched the rockets and the Roman candles. His mother was happy, giving little cries of pleasure as the fireworks bloomed, like big flowers in the sky, and groaning when they fizzled, until the jailer cautioned her not to make a noise.

Peter realized that he was happy too. He and his mother were jailbirds, like Thoreau. True, they were getting preferential treatment, but probably Thoreau had got preferential treatment too. Small worries crossed his mind. He had left his motorbike in the back-yard, with the gate unlocked; he hoped nobody would steal it. His father might be angry if

he was late arriving at the Cape; he was never one to listen
to an excuse. But Peter could not get really alarmed. He felt
safe, with his mother, in this clapboarded jail; it had a cosy,
small-town Yankee atmosphere. Quite near at hand, he
heard an owl hoot. His mother whispered that the fireworks
were *exceptionally* good. 'They don't change much,' said the
jailer. 'Ain't much new you can do with a rocket or a Roman
candle.' They were lucky, he added, to have a box seat.
'Couldn't have picked a better night, ma'am, you and the
boy, for getting yourselves in-carcerated. This town-jail
porch is the ideal spot' – he pronounced it EYEDEEL, with
equal stresses – 'for watching the fireworks down there on
the point.' The rocking-chairs, which had held so many cops'
bottoms, creaked.

To Be a Pilgrim

DURING his first weeks as a student in Paris, Peter moved several times. The Embassy had given him a list of approved French families that took boarders, but he did not want to live with a French family. For the moment, he did not want to shack up with an American family either and baby-sit in exchange for his room and board, though this idea appealed to him more; he liked children. But if he stayed with Americans, he would never improve his French.

Until he landed at Le Havre, he considered himself fluent in French. Against his parents' advice, he had brought his motorbike, refusing to be separated from it, as though, said his mother, it were the fleet of firetrucks he had slept with as a child. Owing to the motorbike, he had travelled by boat, whereas the other students in his group were travelling by charter plane. On the voyage, every day he had gone down to the hold to visit his trusty old steed, which, thanks to the New York Mafia, had a broken headlight, like a blind cyclop's eye. According to his well-laid plans, he would be reunited with it on the dock and speed off for Paris, checking his suitcases and book bag through on the train: a two-pronged assault on the capital. On the boat (an American bottom; Peter was supporting the dollar), the baggage master had assured him that all he would have to do, after seeing the bike through the customs, would be to gas up on the pier and take off. On the pier he would find an agent to handle the shipping of his baggage, but Peter distrusted agents; his travel motto was Do-it-yourself. He had his route mapped; his first stop was going to be Rouen, to inspect the remains of the cathedral and the church of St-Maclou – he had decided to be interested in art this year.

But on the dock the French scored their first victory over Peter Levi, famed linguist. He heard himself say *'De Le Havre'*, instead of *'Du Havre'*, to the porter he had hired to guard his motorbike while he took his bags to *Expéditions*, and immediately his forces were thrown into confusion. He was routed by an enemy tactic he came to know well: they lay patiently in ambush, waiting for you to make a mistake; then they sprang. Confident of the difficulty of their terrain, they could afford to let you forge ahead for a paragraph without offering any resistance – time was on their side. As soon as those two little words (*'De Le'*) plopped from his lips, everything changed, as though, *knowing better*, he had pronounced a sort of negative password.

The porter, who only a minute before had been chiming, *'Oui, monsieur'* and *'Parfaitement,'* suddenly shifted to sign language. The burden of his pantomime seemed to be that Peter should surrender his trusty steed to another porter while the first one carried his bags. Resigning himself to a double tip, Peter agreed. *'On est en France, Pierre,'* he said to himself. But you could not buy off this enemy (there ended the second lesson); not even money spoke to the French.

Before his eyes, the motorbike was seized and wheeled away while his captive bags were hustled off in another direction – towards the boat train, he realized, gulping. He stood swallowing his saliva, uncertain which to trail. The porter with the suitcases turned around and beckoned angrily with his head for Peter to follow. All at once, Peter grasped their manoeuvre. They were trying to put him on the boat train! He ran after his suitcases; the motorbike had vanished into the madding crowd on the platform. *'Essayez de comprendre, monsieur,'* he pleaded, catching up with the original porter. *'Je vais à Paris en vélomoteur. Je ne voyage pas avec le train.'*

The man halted. 'Ticket!' he shouted in English, bringing his face close to Peter's, so that it was impossible not to smell the morning wine on his breath. Peter launched an appeal to himself for a little calm. He spoke as slowly as he could, putting a pause after each word like a language-teaching tape. *'Je n'ai pas de billet. Je vais à Paris en vélomoteur. Rendez-moi mes baggages, s'il vous plaît.'* 'Ticket! Ticket!' repeated the porter peremptorily. Some Americans at the train window looked down at Peter and smiled. He was dressed for the road in leather helmet, leather jacket, khaki pants; strapped to his back was a canvas pack containing his pyjamas, clean underwear, shaving stuff, toothbrush, goggles, Band-Aids, the green Michelin guide to Normandy, road maps, the *Plan de Paris*, candy bars for energy, and a French-English pocket dictionary. 'He wants to see your ticket,' a woman called out from the train.

At that moment, an ally appeared on the platform, smoking a small cigar – a young salesman of pharmaceuticals who used to drop in, slumming, at the tourist-class bar. 'What's your problem?' he said in a thin, snappy voice; he was a blond former druggist from Berkeley who made the trip, cabin class, twice a year on business. Peter explained. He wanted to send his *baggage* by train and get his *motorbike* back. The salesman summoned a man from Cook's. The verdict was that Peter's baggage could not travel unaccompanied on the boat train. 'But I can send it by express or freight, surely?' Did Peter have an address in Paris where it could be delivered? Peter's only address was 'Care of American Express,' and he hesitated to say this in front of the man from Cook's. 'Better hop on the train,' said the salesman. 'Play it their way.' 'But my motorbike!' The motorbike was already in the baggage car (where else?). The porter claimed this was what the gentleman wanted. *'Mais je vous ai dit cinq fois, monsieur —'* Peter started to expostulate. The salesman cut in. 'Give him his check for the bike,' he said to the porter. 'And get a move on with those bags. The train's due out of here in five minutes. Find him an empty place. Second class. Do you want the smoking or the non-smoking?' 'I don't care,' said Peter. 'Non-smoking, I guess.' To Peter's surprise, the porter dug. He complained, in French, that all the places on the train were reserved. 'Baloney!' said the salesman to the porter. 'There's plenty of seats down the line.' He patted Peter's arm. 'You're all set now. See you soon. And let me give you a little guidance. Never try to speak French to these froggies, even if you know how. They lose their respect for you.'

Unstrapping his pack in the compartment, Peter compared this advice with the advice he had received from his father, which was never under any circumstances let a French person trap you into speaking English – they lost their respect for you. Pensively, he took off his helmet and felt in his pocket to make sure his bicycle clips were still there.

Once the train got moving, Peter was filled with gloom. The auspices looked bad. Not only had his project been frustrated and his mount shot from under him, but he had suffered a failure of nerve in the face of French civilization. The fact was, there still would have been time, probably, to get his motorbike off the train. Instead, he had let the salesman arrange the terms of his capitulation and had actually felt grateful to him. The reason was not far to seek. He had been afraid of being left by himself on the pier, in the midst of all those French, trying to do something unconventional like express his stuff to Paris. He guessed he had had an attack of agoraphobia, which was as common as the trots, they said, among American tourists. To tell the awful truth, he now wished he had travelled with a group.

He had been expecting to meet some fellow-students in tourist class, but there were only a few married Fulbrights with babies, who were not interested in a kid his age. The only other student he found on the boat was a Wellesley girl in first class who had graduated last June, a former pupil of the *babbo*'s; unfortunately, she had got off at Cobh. Most students, nowadays, the purser told him, travelled by air, unless they came with their parents. The word *nowadays* after Rocky Port, was poison to Peter; it made him feel like the Last Rose of Summer blooming wanly on D deck.

Staring out of the window at the vanishing oil refineries of Le Havre, Peter wished he knew where he stood about being an anachronism. On the one hand, he admired Don Quixote, who had replaced Sir Pellias the Gentle Knight as his hero when he had to 'outgrow' King Arthur and the Companions of the Round Table and the nightly story he told himself of marrying the Damsel Parcenet. At college he had done a paper on the role of Rosinante in Cervantes' thought for his gen ed course, and he had named his motorbike Rosinante as a pious act. He had bought it, second hand, with his savings freshman year, at a time when others were getting sports cars, and he had brought it to Europe, he supposed, because everybody at home made fun of his attachment to it and of the curious (they said) idea he had that somebody might steal it – according to his father, it was its own best insurance against theft. On the other hand, unlike some of his classmates, he could not swallow Burke and neo-conservatism or Plato's Philosopher King; nor could he wear waistcoats and grow an Edwardian moustache. He was a weirdie without conviction, cast in the part by others, just as, in school plays, he always got the clown's bells, because of his long nose and reedy build; his first year in boarding-school, they had made him be Jaques in *As You Like It*, 'weeping and commenting upon the sobbing deer'. Shakespeare was coarsely punning, their English teacher explained: a 'jakes' was the Elizabethan word for toilet, like 'john' today in girls' schools, and Monsieur Jakes (guffaws) was a 'wet blanket'. Peter had never told his mother that for a while the kids there used to call him Jakes ('Jakes, have you been to the john?'), though he had not been really picked on for some reason – quite mysterious, considering that he hated athletics and that boys at that age were beasts.

At college, there was a Peter Levi myth, a girl on the Cape who had a brother in his class told the *babbo*. He was regarded as a master of one-upmanship, it seemed, and he even had imitators, when the last thing he craved was to start a fashion. His roommate freshman year, a shallow character who owned a Porsche, had congratulated him warmly on the motorbike, telling him that it was a 'great' ploy. It was not a ploy, of course. His aunt Millie had been nearer the mark when she

said the motorbike was his mother's punishment for not
having got him a dog when he was little. He had given it a
new paint job (Mahogany) this summer in his father's barn
on the Cape and he often bought it presents: a padlock, a
rear-view mirror, a bicycle pump, wicker side-baskets. He
knew they were presents because he never spent any money
on himself if he could help it – the bicycle clips were his
father's contribution. And it was true too that he was loyal
to the motorbike because it was old and unsteady; he would
not have felt the same towards it if it had been new, any more
than he would have wanted a pure-bred puppy; it was old
dog-eared dogs he used to follow on the street and try to
pat. He had once brought a stray mutt home, but Hans, who
had asthma, was allergic to dog hair, and when they could not
find the owner, it had to be taken to the pound. Maybe the
motorbike was Peter's animal helper, but if so, that was
something he tried to keep dark. He had been ashamed of
visiting it so often on the voyage and, just now, when he
hurried back to the baggage care to check up on it, he had
been ashamed to meet the salesman checking up on his cases
of samples.

He ought to despise himself, he knew, for worrying all the
time that the bike might be stolen. He hated hearing Americans talk about being robbed and gypped abroad. His roommate freshman year, whose parents had a villa at Antibes,
used to assure him that every beggar in Europe was a mil-
lionaire; it was a known fact, he claimed, and only suckers
gave them money. This maniac travelled with his currency
in his shoes. Other kids Peter had met when he was in Italy
were always insisting that they had had their traveller's
cheques stolen in some place like Harry's Bar in Venice; they
hid their money under their mattress or the rug and were
constantly counting it to see whether the chambermaid had
taken any. Or they were fighting with a taxi driver because
they did not realize that the night rate was different from
what they paid in the daytime. They got these ideas from
their bourgeois parents, obviously.

Peter's parents had erred, he thought, in the opposite

direction. They had drilled into him the principle that to accuse a servant or a cleaning-woman of stealing from you (or breaking your toys) was just about the worst thing you could do. On this they were in perfect accord. If Peter came to his father crying 'Somebody took my ball,' his father would shake him and shout *'L'hai persa! L'hai persa!'* In fact, he had not been allowed to think that *anyone* stole, except professional robbers in masks. His mother just laughed when he told her there was a kleptomaniac in his dormitory in school. He had tried to be grateful for this training when he compared it with what his schoolmates were getting, but there were times, especially at school, when he felt his parents had lived too sheltered a life. After all, he used to remind them, there *was* such a thing as theft; the stork did not carry dollar bills away in its beak. Now he saw their point. It was worse to be suspicious than to be robbed. He would not want to live with an insane person like his ex-roommate as his constant companion, and your constant companion, alas, was yourself.

Still, he could not help worrying about the motorbike. That was different, he told himself, from worrying about a bank roll. Property was theft, his parents were always quoting, to get his goat – his mother had copied it from his father, who used to be an anarchist before he settled down. Now even his stepfather said it. But if one of them had listened sympathetically, instead of scoffing at his worries, he might not have this complex now. In a sense, it was their fault. Peter chewed his lip. He had caught himself trying to pass the buck. What was biting him now had nothing to do with his parents. He was angry with himself for having betrayed a kind of promise he had made to the motorbike, to ride it through thick and thin to Paris.

Peter was alone in the compartment, though some hand baggage was piled on the racks; doubtless, whoever owned it was fraternizing. Outside in the corridor he could hear Americans talking. Their favourite sport, he had observed, was confiding their itineraries in detail. 'Then we fly with sas to Copenhagen, where we got the ferry to Malmö and pick up a Volvo. . . .' 'Frank leaves his medical congress and

meets me in Seville, where we join a tour for three days. . . .'
'We rent a Citroën *deux-chevaux* in Paris and drive it to
Zurich. There we turn it in and get the Lufthansa flight to
Munich. . . .' 'In England we buy a Morris Minor and take
it back on the boat with us. We spend one night in Bath and
another at the Mitre in Oxford. Harold's cousin married an
English girl; they have three lovely children.' The voices,
whoever they belonged to, were always middle-aged and
pursy. Peter had noticed this on the boat. He wondered what
Americans had talked about before they became the Affluent
Society.

It had not been a lively crossing. Of his cabin-mates, one
was a native-born federal employee from Washington who
gave him a play-by-play preview of his hoteling, one was a
Persian who spoke no English, and the third was an elderly
Polish racist from Chicago who was booked from Paris on
LOT to visit his daughter near Poznan. Over his nightly beer
in the bar, Peter listened to stenographers and receptionists
talk to each other and to the barman; he learned where they
had bought what they were wearing and how much they had
paid for it, what movies had been shown on their previous
crossings and who had played in them, their European
programmes with arrival and departure times and identification of carriers. The girl from Wellesley had invited him up
to first class, which he had expected to be more glamorous.
But the only difference he could see was that the people there
wore more jewellery and had different hours in the swimming
pool. The conversations were just the same: exercises in total
recall of the travel graph. When Peter was unable to pinpoint
his movements on his earlier trips to Europe, he felt apolo-
getic, just as he did when he admitted that he did not know
where he would be staying in Paris. It sounded like a ploy.

The train was now in open country. He saw cows and big
barns and apple orchards and, for the first time in his life,
mistletoe actually growing, great springy balls of it, which he
first took for giant birds' nests perched on the apple branches.
His spirits brightened. He was in druid territory, and he
looked around hopefully for oak groves. His favourite Norse

god, Balder the Beautiful an Apollonian figure, had been
slain by an arrow made of mistletoe wood from the sacred
oak. He jumped up and got down his book bag and took out
the French tree book, a present from his stepfather – *Arbres
et arbustes de nos forêts et de nos jardins*. He found *le gui*, but
only its picture and its Latin name. Then he remembered.
There was a Latin proverb about it. Mistletoe was a pest
carried by the missel-thrush in its turds. The orchards that
flashed by, hung with these strange, shiny, pagan ornaments,
might be dying. He could not see any apples on a lot of the
trees – a troubling allegory, he decided. Nevertheless, he was
so excited by the marvel that he opened the door of his compartment and signalled to two girls who were standing in the
corridor. 'Mistletoe!' he said. 'Look!' The girls looked. 'Oh,
yeah, yeah. Well, whaddya know! Thanks for telling us. Say,
have you heard when this train gets to Paris?'

They had not really seen it, Peter thought. They had just
said Yes to be polite. Like the Rocky Porters, they were not
curious. If they had been interested, he would have showed
it to them in the tree book and explained about the turds. But
it was not worth the effort. He hoisted the book bag back
onto the rack. 'These are my people,' he said to himself with
a sort of pang. In a few days, probably, he would be homesick
for these flat or furry voices.

Being an American, he was coming to think, was like being
Jewish, only worse: you recognized 'your people' everywhere in their Great Diaspora and you were mortified by
them and mortified by being mortified; you were drawn to
them, sorry for them, amused by them, nauseated by them.
Not only that. They spotted you as one of them, infallibly,
just as Jews could always spot other Jews, even when they
had had their noses fixed and changed their names. On the
boat, for the sake of privacy, he had been playing Peter the
Hermit, his nose in a French book, his feet in espadrilles, and
his upper half in a striped Italian jersey his stepfather had
brought back from a market stall in Siena; in the swimming
pool, when raked by somebody's toenails, he said '*Oh,
pardon!*' or '*Scusi!*' according to his mood. The Americans

were not fooled. 'You're an American, aren't you? That's what I told my girl friend. This English fellow thought you were French.' In the lounge before dinner he played chess in French with the Persian, who knew the French names of the moves and pieces, and the little kids who drifted up to watch the game were soon calling out to each other, 'Say, this guy's an American! Let's be on his side!' It was no good trying to speed them on their way with '*Via, bambini,*' or '*Foutez le camp.*' For them, he was as American as Mom's macaroni or a Swedish meatball.

It was worse than being Jewish, Peter felt, in the sense that nobody was excluding you and you made your own ghettoes around Army bases and in 'exclusive' hotels abroad, eating your own version of kosher like his table-mates on the boat, who were always clamouring for ketchup and suspecting their steak of being underdone, or like the dinner-jacketed clowns in first class who had to have sour cream and chives on their Great Big Baked Potato and acted martyred if the meat they were getting was only us Choice instead of us Prime. Being a Jew gave you a history of martyrdom that at least was old and dignified. If you were a Jew, you were 'one of the chosen', while an American was just a Philistine. Jews were told by non-Jews that they should be proud of their heritage, steeped in tradition, et cetera; that was one of the mixed blessings of being Jewish. But nobody told an American how great it was to be him. You could not be proud of being an American, not any more. Peter took his mother's word for it that you could when she was young. Now, even the insensitive type, like the pharmaceuticals salesman, was bluffing when he put out the Stars and Stripes. On the boat, every American Peter met asked the same question – in lowered tones – when they heard he was going to Paris as a student: 'Aren't you afraid of anti-Americanism?' Peter could not figure out why they treated this query as a top secret, looking around to make sure nobody heard them ask it.

He had resolved not to think about anti-Americanism while in Paris. The fear that people might be prejudiced against him was not one of his weaknesses. Some of the students in his group had been asked by a sociologist to collect instances of discrimination against them as Americans, but nobody had asked him to do that, fortunately. If they had, he would have given them a blast. As though anti-Americanism were a disease, like anti-Semitism, that could be studied scientifically by some government agency. These kids were actually going to be paid for finking on waiters and landladies – like getting a bounty from the state if you sent in muskrat skins.

Peter did not blame the French or anyone else for not liking America after what had been happening last summer while he sat getting a tan in Rocky Port. Just being white, he thought, did not make him guilty, but it was one strike against him, like original sin, which was not your fault and yet had to be paid for – he had been sending contributions from his allowance to CORE and SNCC and he would have mowed lawns in Rocky Port and donated the proceeds if anybody had had a lawn left to mow instead of a flagged terrace or what they called 'ground cover'. He was not a civil-rights hero; on the other hand, to be fair to himself, he was not a racist murderer, and he felt a sympathy for his country that had to look at itself in this ugly mirror every night on television.

The *babbo* had given him a good briefing on this, in his study on the Cape, the day before the boat sailed. Peter trusted his father when he said that America was not going fascist; his father did not even think Goldwater was a fascist – the historical conditions for fascism were not present. This meant that it was all right still to register with your draft board and have a passport and defend your country in argument when some French egghead tried to tell you that all Americans were conformists or that university education was restricted to 'the Pullman class'. His father was worried about America this summer but he felt there was hope. He said Peter should not be too much influenced by his mother's pessimism. It was a mistake to think that Communism was better because it did not have a television culture; that only meant that Communism was backward, and a television culture, when it came, would be much worse in a totalitarian state, where dissent was not possible. Peter was relieved to hear this view put forward; his own faith in America had been shaken by Rocky Port, which the *babbo* dismissed – too easily, perhaps, not having spent the summer there. 'Your mother always liked those old resorts. Snug harbours. It is no good crawling back into the American womb. It has had a hysterectomy.' He laughed. Peter looked at him. 'Be serious, *babbo*,' he said plaintively.

Maybe it was childish, but Peter wanted to give his country a hand abroad. Of course, there was nothing he could do that would wipe out the civil-rights murders in Mississippi and the bombings and church-burnings and assorted atrocities. In fact, if he realized his plan of being a model student, kind and courteous to all, far from straightening the French out about the US, he would really be deceiving them as to what a lot of Americans, maybe the majority, were like. The thought of serving as a sort of whitewash had been preying on his mind; he could never have confided it in anyone but his father, because it sounded conceited.

The *babbo* nodded. He said the scruple was typical of the Anglo-Saxon mercantile conscience, always fearful of giving a false impression to the foreign buyer. 'You are like my students at Holyoke when I first came there – all those pretty girls wearing big glasses. "You mustn't get the idea the average American thinks the way I do, Professor Levi." ' It was not up to Peter to worry about whether he was truly representative. At best, as a quality export, he might create a little good will for his country, which was badly in need of it. Peter was right to take his mission seriously; he and his young friends had an important role to play abroad. He must not be ashamed, for America, because he was a minority: five just men would have saved Sodom, if Lot had been able to find them. The main thing was to be himself; if Peter were true to himself, nobody could be misled, for nobody could suppose that such an unusual boy was a standard American product. ' "To thine own self be true . . . thou canst not then be false to any man" ,' Peter had muttered, pleased and confused by the compliment. Every father, he guessed, was a Polonius when he sent a son abroad. He wondered whether he himself was a prig, like Laertes, who had probably been anxious to counter the rotten reputation of Denmark with the Parisians of his day.

In hard fact, Peter was less apprehensive about anti-Americanism among the French than about anti-Americanism in himself. Ever since he had left the native shores, he had been having violent bouts of it, followed by bouts of remorse. It was a thing, like malaria in the tropics, that you caught abroad, evidently; at home, he was drawn to the man on the street or behind the gasoline pump. He would have thought that by this time – it was his third trip to Europe – he would have built up immunities to the bug. But it was not so. Halfway to Paris, in an already weakened condition, he had a bad attack. The other occupants of his compartment returned – three stout old ladies in crêpe blouses and woollen skirts who were part of a tour of retired grade-school teachers from the Middle West. Peter had seen them on the boat tied up in those orange life-jackets during lifeboat drill. The rest of the tour, he now gleaned, was in the adjoining compartment with their tour director, who had met them at Le Havre. They had never been in Europe before and already they were beefing.

Peter tried not to listen; he unpacked the *Plan de Paris* and started to chart his course from the station to the Left Bank. But he could not help hearing what they were discussing. One of them had broken her bridge that morning on a toasted English muffin. She was the stocky, white-haired one, resembling a bulldog, in a blue blouse, with a silver-and-turquoise brooch, looking like a Navajo trophy brought back from the Southwest. She had saved the remains of the English muffin – a hardened leathery criminal – as evidence against the steamship company.

Peter felt thankful that no Asian or African student was sitting in his place. He believed in the American public-school system and he had a good memory of the older women who had taught him fractions and long division and *Ivanhoe*;

he had liked them nearly as well as old female librarians and much better than most professors and masters in private schools. But now his point of view seemed to have suffered a sea-change. The voices of the trio were loud and argumentative. *Of course* Miss Lewis was entitled to compensation, it was her *duty* to teach the steamship line a lesson, the whole tour was behind her, et cetera. As for their tour director, they could *not* understand that man's attitude. He might have taken a *little* interest, out of common courtesy; he might have *looked* at the bridge, to see if it could be soldered together, instead of acting as if it would bite him. That was what he was paid for. That was what they paid him for, wasn't it? They could visit museums and churches without his help. Their travel agent ought to have told them he was one of those Hungarian refugees, not even French, more of a glorified guide than a real tour director; a real tour director was supposed to be *handy*.

The old woman fished in her purse and pulled out something wrapped in Kleenex. Peter had a horrid view of the bridge – some yellowish teeth and very pink gums, backed with metal and with little metal hooks at either end. One of the hooks was broken, and three of the teeth had come out; they were wrapped in a separate piece of Kleenex. The exhibit passed from hand to hand. On request, the old woman opened her mouth wide, divulging some grisly stumps, and fitted the appliance into place, while her companions, in turn, peered at the result. All three acted as if Peter were not there. One of them, who had bifocals, grey hair, big pearl earrings, and a grey blouse, suddenly clicked her tongue. 'I wonder now . . . I've got some Fasteeth in my beauty case.' While Peter watched, she reassembled the denture, sprinkling it with some white powder – a fixative, he supposed – which she shook from a little blue can onto the artificial gums. 'Try that, Miss Lewis. Put your denture back in, dear, and grit your teeth. Let it set for a couple of minutes.'

Resuming her seat, she 'included' Peter with a tap on the knee. 'You're an American boy, aren't you? That's what we thought. "An American boy is sitting in our compartment,"

I told Miss Lewis. "We won't have to stand on ceremony with him." ' Peter groaned to himself; between Americans abroad, there could be no secrets, apparently. 'It isn't the first time he's seen a lady's denture, I bet.' This was the third teacher, a red-faced jolly one, with popping eyes, like big Bing cherries; she wore a pink blouse and a lot of pink glass jewellery – probably she had taught the first grade. She gave Peter a wink, as though false teeth were part of a woman's mystery, like knickers or bloomers or whatever they wore where she came from. 'As a matter of fact, it is,' Peter said hoarsely. Then he feared he had given offence. 'There was a poet who came to college to give a reading,' he volunteered. 'His false teeth kept whistling, and he yanked them out and dropped them in the glass of water on the lectern. The audience gave him a great hand. But I wasn't there. I was in the infirmary.' 'My! Isn't that interesting? Was he one of those modern poets?' 'Yes,' said Peter.

'You can open now, Miss Lewis.' The old woman unclenched her jaws. 'There!' said the grey-haired teacher. 'She won't be able to eat, of course. But cosmetically it's more attractive, isn't it?' She took out a pocket mirror. 'Smile, dear!' There was a clink of china and metal as the denture fell, rattling, against the patient's lower teeth. Peter gagged sympathetically; he was afraid she was going to swallow it. He heard a choking noise. But she reached in and grabbed it in time. 'Drat!' she said, as the loose teeth scattered on the floor. Peter got up and chased them for her on his hands and knees. 'Your pearls, madam,' he said with an awkward bow, trying to lighten what he felt must be a dark moment for a woman, even an old woman. Down on the dirty floor, he had put himself in her place. It was no joke to break your teeth on your first day in Europe. It was no joke to be old and crumbling like masonry.

'I've got the name of a French dentist,' he offered. 'Maybe he could help you out. I'm going to him eventually to get my teeth cleaned. Our family dentist in New York recommended him.' 'I want an American dentist, young man. Isn't it aggravating that our tour director doesn't know one? You'd think he'd know a thing like that. He's paid to know a thing like that.' She salivated angrily as she spoke; her toothless upper gums spat.

'You see,' smiled the grey-haired teacher in bifocals, 'Miss Lewis doesn't want some mercenary French dentist to go and make her a whole new bridge. That's a long job, and we only have the week in Paris. She wants this bridge soldered together temporarily, to get her through the trip. But if she goes to one of these French dentists, chances are, as soon as he sees she's an American, he'll try to take advantage of her.'

'Do you have any evidence for that statement?' Peter was tempted to ask, but he let the missionary opportunity pass, not, he hoped, from cowardice, but because he had made a rule recently not to bait people who were too old to change. Instead, he remained stiffly silent. 'Well!' said the jolly one. '*I*'m the lucky girl! I brought along a spare plate. My daughter warned me. The bread in Europe is so *chewy*, she said. My son-in-law lost a gold inlay on their last trip, and the food kept packing in. "Mamma," my daughter told me, "you go and get Dr Edwards to copy your old plate in plastic." It's wonderful what they can do with plastic. Just feel how light that is.' Another toothsome exhibit, wrapped in gauze, made the rounds.

Peter averted his eyes. He sat hunched in his corner – Peter Levi, noted misanthrope. He did not even have the recourse of looking out the window; he had given up his usurped seat when the teachers came in. If he went out to stretch his legs in the corridor, it might be taken as a snub – despite appearances, Americans were sensitive. He listened while the retired educators kicked around the proposition that people over here took such *poor* care of their teeth; the school children did not get milk; they were not taught dental hygiene; there was no fluoridation programme; and the wine they drank gave you tartar. No wonder dentists here were still in the dark ages. To Peter, this did not follow. He would expect countries with *bad* teeth to have *good* dentists. Like America.

He decided to give them a shock. 'My father used to think all Americans had false teeth,' he blurted out. 'You know, like movie stars. My father's Italian,' he added lamely. The teachers laughed. 'Isn't that typical? The ideas these folks get about us!' Peter did not join in the merriment, though he had to admit that at home when the *babbo* told the story it was as a joke on himself. 'I hope,' said the grey-haired one severely, 'you're going to try to give your relatives over here a better picture of the us. You talk like you were American-born. Is this your first trip to Europe?' 'No,' said Peter curtly, feeling that he had dealt out enough information. Then he repented. 'It's my first trip to France. I mean, except for a couple of days at St-Tropez when I was younger, I drove up from Italy with my family, and we took the boat at Cannes. The *Cristoforo Colombo*. But I've never been in Paris before.'

Indeed, he had never arrived alone in a big foreign city before; someone had always met him. The sense of the difference hit him. No one would be waving to him from the platform, as the train pulled in. No one would hug him, crying 'Peter!' No one would waft him off in a cab to a hotel, pointing out monuments on the way. No one in fact would know he was there.

If these old teachers did away with him, it would be quite a while before he was missed. Only his faithful motorbike would be waiting for him in the station, unclaimed. When his parents did not hear from him, eventually they would cable the Embassy, but by that time the trail would be cold. His heart lurched at the thought that for the first time in his life he did not count, i.e., nobody was counting him; he was nobody's chicken. Not even God's because there was no God. If a universal roll call were decreed tomorrow, there would be nobody to mark Peter Levi 'Absent'. This meant that *pro tem* there was no Peter Levi, except in his own mind. It was a creepy idea, like solipsism in philosophy. He would only begin to be real again when he had an address and people started checking up on him.

But supposing when he arrived he could not find a place to stay? Foolishly, as he now felt, he had not listened to his

parents and made a hotel reservation. He had wanted to be
free to do a little touring en route if the spirit moved him; on
the map he had marked a place called St-Wandrille, near
Rouen, where there was an old Benedictine abbey – some
Catholic convert had told him the monks there took pilgrims
for the night. He liked the pious notion of being a pilgrim,
sleeping in a monk's cell and hearing them chant the plainsong when he woke up with the birds. He saw himself in
some old woodcut, with a humble scallop shell – his dinner
plate – and a pointed pilgrim hat with another tiny scallop
shell on the crown, hitting the trail of Saint Jacques. Or as a
young knight in home-made wattled armour like Sir Percival
of Gales (the darling son of his poor widowed mother), seeking shelter from a kindly hermit. Or crossing the Seine on a
rude ferry; he had checked a *bac* on the map near the abbey
and pictured the rustic ferryman, a giant Christopher, pushing off with his solitary passenger for the other shore. But
now the sense of adventure, which he had opposed to his
parents' prudence, had abandoned him. Unhorsed, he did
not feel errant. Instead, the responsibility of finding a hotel
room in an unknown city weighed on him like some vile duty
he would like to shirk.

'I suppose you spoke Italian in your home.' They were
questioning him again. 'When did your folks come to America?' 'My father came during the war,' Peter answered shortly; he was too dejected to pick up the conversational ball.
Besides, if these old educators could not figure out from that
datum that his father was an anti-fascist exile, he was not
going to tell them. Let them think his father was a Wop
immigrant instead of a Wop emigrant – who cared?

In any case, maybe he should have said 'My father's an
Italian Jew,' just in case there were anti-Semites present.
People of Jewish 'extraction' (the word reminded him of the
Rocky Port kitchen with flannel jelly bags dripping in concert) ought to be willing to declare themselves, but Peter often
forgot. What he disliked about being Peter Levi was that
there was so much to explain. He almost wished he had been
born Pinkus Levy in Flatbush – a self-evident proposition.

Technically, he was an Italo-American on his father's side, which would not have been so bad if his father had been what was meant by an Italo-American, instead of being a professor and a Jew, which would not have been so bad either if he had been what was meant by a Jew, instead of being, primarily, an Italian, since his part of the Levi family (a Triestine outfit) had been assimilated in Florence for generations, and, growing up in a Catholic country, the *babbo* had a lot more in common with the Jesuits, whom he hated, than with a rabbi, whom he knew nothing about.

As a Jew, Peter was a farce; the proof was that nobody had ever given him a rough time on that account. He was grateful to his last name for saving him the labour of telling people he was Jewish; on the other hand, like many labour-saving devices, such as dishwashers, it made almost more work in the end. There was no easy way to get it across that he was only a half-Jew. He could not send out announcements saying that his mother was a Christian or wear half a yellow star on his coat-lapel. In other times or climes, he would have had no worries on this score: under the Nuremberg Laws, he would have counted as a Jew, while in Israel he would count as a Christian, since what mattered to them was your mother – he did not know how he would fare in the Arab states.

Maybe it was not important anyway to set the record straight. To point out that you were 'only' half-Jewish although your name was Levi made you feel like a recreant. Yet it was part of being an American that, once you got started, you felt impelled to tell all the people all the truth all the time. His college tutor, a stupid Freudian, had advised his mother that Peter had an 'identity problem'. But *he* was quite clear who he was; the problem was whether it was necessary to clear up other people. His tragedy, he had decided, was that his every move in this domain seemed to require a lengthy gloss, e.g., in his school, which was trying to be liberal, he was told that he could be excused from the headmaster's course in Christian religion – a low blow to Peter because he was quite interested in Christian religion. When he said No, thanks, he would like to take the course, his attitude seemed natural to him but not, he discovered, to the headmaster or to the other kids, who thought he must be nuts to go to a class he could get out of. The headmaster made him write out his reasons for taking the course and did not accept that being an atheist was a valid one, till he heard from the *babbo* about all the dominies on the fair Rosamund's side. From the kids' point of view, Peter was practically a scab. They envied a certain Weinstein, who was allowed Yom Kippur and Rosh Hashanaoff, and a Catholic kid named Ryan, who even got excused from chapel. Peter would have been glad to belong to some religion that got you out of athletics, but he enjoyed chapel – it was the only peaceful moment in the school day. Looking back, he concluded that taking Christian religion must have been his first innocent ploy.

One of the attractions of Europe for him was that he would not have to go into all this with the native population. In Europe, you did not have to have antecedents if you came from the New World. You were an American, and that was it.

'Does your mamma make the real spaghetti?' the jolly teacher wondered. 'Spaghetti with meat sauce!' She sighed. 'Out in Kansas we don't get the real Italian food. My daughter told me it isn't the same at all.' 'My mother usually makes it plain,' Peter replied cautiously. 'With just butter and cheese.' The three women turned a joint suspicious stare on him. 'Yes,' he said. 'You'd be surprised. A lot of Italians eat it that way. You watch when you're in a restaurant. What they like is the *pasta*. Your daughter probably had it *alla bolognese*. Or *al ragù*. Sometimes my mother makes it with *pesto*. Like "mortar and pestle". That's Genoese. You take basil and parsley and garlic and pine nuts and cheese and pound them in a mortar with olive oil. It's green.' He ground to a halt, reminded of Peter Levi's Paradox: most people did not care to be taught what they did not already know; it made them feel ignorant.

'Well, live and learn! What else does your mother make? Those pizza pies?' Peter hedged. 'She's got a pretty big repertory.' A little bird with an olive branch in its beak was telling him to avoid Italian words and phrases since he could not avoid pronouncing them correctly. 'A few years ago, when we lived in New England, she had a jag of cooking American.'

'Isn't that nice now?' They softened. 'I guess she was trying to please you. Give you the same as your friends had, in *their* homes. You must have a very smart mother.' 'Yes, I have,' said Peter, drawing a deep breath. He seemed to have been elected 'It' in a game of Twenty Questions that would end in their finally discovering that their modest train companion was the son of Rosamund Brown, the famous harpsichordist. Whom they would never have heard of. But that was not the point. The point was, if he did not give them a clue or two, he would be meanly concealing information that these women, as his fellow-Americans, were somehow entitled to, even though, when they got it, they would feel disappointed – all that work for nothing. Having a celebrity in your family gave you an unfair advantage over people who did not guess you had a celebrity in your family. If the teachers were to find out afterward that he had had this ace in the hole, they would think he had been laughing up his sleeve at them. In common decency, he ought to help them out. If it had been a real game of Twenty Questions, at this juncture he could have given them a weary hint: 'Look, you haven't *asked* me if my mother is Italian.'

'Where did you attend high school?' The grey-haired one rapped out the demand. 'In Massachusetts.' Peter hedged again; he felt embarrassed to admit that he had gone to a private school. 'I mean, that's where I graduated.' Then he mumbled the names of his previous schools: Rocky Port High, junior high at Berkeley. 'Your folks moved a lot,' the teacher commented. 'It's a wonder you weren't put back a class.' Old Miss Lewis nodded. 'Always hard on a transfer.' 'Have you got lots of brothers and sisters at home?' asked the jolly teacher kindly.

'Well, yes and no.' Peter licked his lips. 'My parents are divorced.' Though divorce was common as measles in the us, he could feel himself turning red. 'So that I have quite a few stepbrothers and -sisters. And a half-brother and -sister on my father's side. But I'm my mother's only child.' Of all the facts about himself, this business of divorce and step-parents was the one that, for some reason, he hated most to talk about. But of course it had to be the one that came out most naturally in the course of a casual conversation. If you were under twenty-one, oldsters always asked you if you had brothers and sisters; it made them feel benevolent.

As he had feared, silence followed his revelation. Probably the teachers were pitying him for his 'broken' home. In fairness to his parents, he ought to explain that he *liked* the net effect of serial monogamy: being an only child and still having a flock of kids around of whom he did not have to be jealous, as he would have been, certainly, if his parents had gone on breeding together when he was little. But the average American, he had noticed, looked sceptical when he said he approved of divorce for parents: they seemed to think he had been indoctrinated. He decided to pipe down. If he went on talking, he would be bound to disclose that his mother had been divorced *twice*.

There was still an hour to fill in before the train got to Paris. Outside in the corridor, two transistor radios were playing. Peter would have been glad to read or sleep or practise his French argot, but the teachers obviously felt they could not let the conversation die at the point it had reached. 'My!' said the jolly one. 'You've got a lot of books there! Are you over here to study?' Peter answered that he was taking his junior year at the Sorbonne, under a super-vised programme; lots of colleges had them. Someone, he reflected, could make a fortune with a small, battery-powered tape-recorder, designed for travel, that would play back standard answers when asked a standard question, such as 'Will you be taking your courses in French?' 'How big is the Sorbonne campus?' 'Will you live in a dormitory?' 'Do they have fraternities and sororities?'

'Of course you've got a place to stay in Paris.' Peter swal-lowed. 'No, I haven't. My plans are sort of fluid.' He laughed weakly. 'I thought I'd just cruise around and find a cheap hotel room. Back home, you could sign up to live with a French family, but I couldn't see me doing that.' The teachers stiffened. 'Don't you know that Paris is *jammed* at this time of year? Our travel agent says there isn't a *bed*. Why, our tour has had its reservations for months! What were your folks thinking of, not to get you a hotel room?'

'My mother wanted to. She kept telling me Paris was crowded. But I wouldn't let her. I . . .' The argument he had given his mother was that he was not sure, exactly, when he would get to Paris. But that, he recalled with a jolt, was ancient history now. Incredibly, he had nearly forgotten the premise of his reasoning: the cherished idea of visiting Normandy en route. For a minute, his guard had been down. If he had not caught himself in time, it would have all come out about the motorbike and his defeat at the hands of those porters. The very thought of being *here*, penned up with these nosy old women, when he might have been *there* in solitary splendour, musing in a cathedral like Henry Adams, made his throat tighten. It was as though his plans had died young and he was travelling with their coffin. No one, he resolved, was going to prise out of him this unspeakable chapter in his history – not even his mother, when he wrote to her tonight.

The teachers were waiting. He cleared his throat. 'Well, you see, I've got a principle. About not being forehanded. A lot of this compulsive planning, if you get what I mean, is just a way of trying to stay ahead of the next guy. Be smart and reserve in advance so that when some dumb guy shows up, you've got the priority. I mean, it's O.K. probably for older people – people your age – and women with little babies, but for somebody my age it's repulsive. Either there are enough rooms to go around, so why bother with all the early-birding? Or there aren't enough rooms to go around, so why not take your chances with the rest of humanity? Let the other guy be first. Live dangerously.'

'Well, young man,' observed old Miss Lewis with unexpected force, 'you talk like a real American. It's nice to meet a boy these days that doesn't expect to have everything done *for* him, from cradle to grave. Not afraid to rough it, are you? Did you learn that in your Scout troop?' 'Well, no,' said Peter. 'I never was a Scout. As a matter of fact, I got it from my father, probably. He used to be a philosophical anarchist. They believe in mutual aid. There's a whole book, very interesting, by Prince Kropotkin, about mutual aid in the animal world. And they think that nobody really owns any- thing as long as there's a scarcity. I mean, take the jacket I'm wearing. I treat it as if it were mine, but it doesn't really belong to me as long as somebody else doesn't have a jacket. I just sort of have it on loan. It's the same with a hotel room.'

The grey-haired teacher looked at him sharply through the upper half of her bifocals. 'Out West, where we come from, there's a fair share of mutual aid. We call it being neighbourly. In Kansas, you could sleep in a barn or a hayfield. Or in most folks' spare bedroom. Folks are pretty nice, that way, to strangers. But Paris isn't Kansas – from what I hear anyway.' Peter grinned. 'Yeah, I've heard that too.' 'So what will you do, if you don't find a hotel room? Have you considered that?'

Peter had been considering it. 'They say you can get arrested and spend the night in jail.' He gave another weak laugh. 'Actually, that isn't as bad as you might think. My mother and I spent the night in jail this summer. Of course that was back in New England.' 'Speeding,' nodded the jolly teacher. 'Those state troopers in New England are something fierce, my daughter says.' Cravenly, Peter decided to let this pass. 'My mother says that in London if you can't get a place to sleep, you just go to the police station, and they lock you up for the night. Only you have to get up early. In Paris, I could sleep under a bridge. With the *clochards*. Those are the French bums. But I guess they might not accept me. They have a pretty tight organization. I wouldn't mind being a wandering scholar. Like in the Middle Ages. They were sort of intellectual tramps.'

'Oh. We thought you were dressed kind of funny. That pack and all. Miss Lewis thought she saw you with a motor- cycle back there on the pier.' 'Must have been two other guys, ha ha,' Peter said. His resistance stiffened. He was not going to feed their hungry curiosity. Anyway, it was not a motorcycle. If they did not know the difference, *tant pis* for them. 'We thought maybe you might be one of those Beatniks you hear about.' Peter was slightly offended. 'I don't smoke pot, if that's what you mean. And the Beats usually have beards.' 'That's what I said, girls!' exclaimed the jolly teacher. 'And they don't wash either. I said, this young fellow washes. And he's had his hair cut not too long ago.' Peter flinched. 'Samson Agonistes,' he muttered.

The teachers ignored him. 'Back home,' said the jolly one, 'he could go to the Travellers Aid in the depot. But I don't guess they have that over here.' 'The Y? Time was, a young fellow could always get a room there for a dollar. Is there a Y in Paris, I wonder? What about a church group? Young man, are your folks Catholic or what?' Peter gulped. Here was his opportunity. 'I guess they're "what". My father is a Jew. But he doesn't have any religion.' 'We're Methodist Episcopal ourselves,' said the grey-haired teacher briskly. 'But to us you're a fellow-American, regardless of creed or colour. Why, we may have a Jew for president if Barry gets in.' There was a silence. She gazed out of the window and clicked her tongue. 'Wouldn't you know it? It's raining. Our first day in France. Now how are you going to look for a room in a downpour like that?' Peter glanced at the streaming windowpanes.

'Please,' he said, 'let's drop the subject, if you don't mind. I'll be O.K. This is just a shower. I can wait in the station till it blows over.' Their worrying was contagious. He was starting to panic. He reminded himself that he and his mother and his stepfather had arrived in St-Tropez that time without a reservation and he had said they would find rooms and they had. But maybe that had been a fluke. He thought sickly of the population explosion. According to the Wellesley girl, three thousand US juniors were slated to hit Paris this fall. She claimed to have read it in a magazine.

The teachers consulted in undertones. Bifocals put an end to the caucus. 'Young man, we've been thinking. We have a nice clean hotel near the station. Our travel agent back home swears by it. We've each of us got a good-sized room to ourselves. Two of us could double up for the night and let you have the spare room. That'll give you a chance to look around.'

Peter's Adam's apple bobbed. 'Golly!' he said warmly. 'Golly, that's nice of you!' It was true, what refugees like his father said: Americans were a kind people. Peter tried to imagine any European he knew, starting with the *babbo*, being glad to sleep two to a bed so that a college kid who was dressed kind of funny would have a place to lay his head. But Americans were like that, especially the ones from the heartland. His mother might do it, coming from Marietta. Still, she was relatively young. It was harder, Peter knew, for old people, who were generally poor sleepers, to share a room. The cockles of his heart moved. O brave new world! As he used to tell his mother, you should not judge a book by its cover.

At the same time, a cynic inside him warned him to take it easy. He could not figure himself joining a tour of old grade-school teachers from Kansas or wherever. That was the catch: the helping-hand kind of American was usually not the kind you wanted to see a great deal of, abroad or at home. And they were the kind that would not take No for an answer. If he refused, the teachers would assume it was because he was bashful or afraid of putting them out and keep pressing him till he agreed.

'It's awfully kind of you —' 'Not at all. Not at all.' They smiled, showing gums and dentures. 'We Americans have to stick together.' But that was not it. They were doing themselves an injustice. If he were a foreigner, they would be just as determined to help him out. Like a lot of people, they were embarrassed by doing a good deed and felt they had to find a lousy reason for it.

'Well, thanks,' he said. 'But the thing is, I have to be on the other side of town. Near the Sorbonne. Tomorrow I have to register and all that. You know, buy books for my courses and check in with my professors. Stuff like that.' He was aware that this did not sound convincing; he could have used a few lessons from the *babbo*, who was a master of invention when the need arose. 'Well, then, why not leave that pack and those grips of yours at our hotel for the time being? You can go out and scout around then. If you find a room, well and good. If you don't, we're glad to accommodate.'

Peter did not point out that he could check his bags at the station. He sought a more gracious argument. 'I thought I'd park my stuff with the other students in my group. They got here yesterday by plane, and we're supposed to sort of keep in touch. I would have come on the plane with them, but my mother doesn't like me to fly.' He had hit the right note. 'Well, why didn't you say so? The way you were talking, we pictured you as all alone in the big city. If your friends are here already . . .' He was free. There was no way they could ever find out that his group's charter flight was not due to arrive for a week. Even if it crashed and they read about it in the paper, they would have no reason to associate it with Peter.

He was appalled by his line of thought. Accepting the loss of his classmates, like a giant pawn sacrifice, if only he could be safe in his corner. As soon as he got to Paris, he would turn over a new leaf. They were now in the suburbs. Fifteen more minutes, he reckoned. He went to the toilet. Coming back, he found the teachers buttoning up their coats. They had taken down their hand baggage. As his eye travelled upward to inventory his effects, he became aware of his leather helmet, where he had tossed it on the rack. He froze. It seemed hardly possible that the teachers could have failed to see it while taking down their stuff. The chin strap was dangling through the spokes on the rack. His mind raced. How could he explain what this distinctive piece of headgear was doing there, if they were to ask him, which they might do any minute? He was carrying it for a friend? He wore it to protect his ears because of a mastoid operation? 'Never apologize, never explain,' he muttered to himself. But whoever said that had never been subjected to several hours' direct questioning by a team of elementary-school teachers. Admit the truth? That would entail further explanations: he would have to say *why* he had disclaimed possession of a motorcycle. And in fact his reasons for doing so now escaped him. Maybe he was a psychopath and just getting to know himself, removed from the context of home and school. The helmet stared at him. He tried looking the other way in the hope that it would become invisible. Finally a feeble answer suggested itself. 'I guess somebody must have left it there,' he could hear himself croak, in his mind's ear. 'That guy you saw on the pier. Maybe I'd better take it to the Lost and Found.' Somewhere outside a cock ought to be crowing. But now that he was prepared, the three Norns did not call on him. They were pinning on corsages of sweet peas that somebody had sent them to the dock at Le Havre. Still, they appeared friendly. They smiled. Maybe they had not noticed the helmet after all.

Gratitude made him remorseful. They had offered him their bed. In the light of that, his own secretiveness and mumbling reserve looked shady. He had been acting like a miser, hoarding his gold. He was unable to *give*. Too late, he recognized that he ought to have accepted their invitation. At least left his bags with them while he went around looking for a hotel. Even now he could volunteer to take the old lady to the dentist. In his place, Don Quixote would have jumped at the opportunity. But Peter felt too embarrassed. If Miss Lewis had been disguised as a beggar-woman or a ragged refugee, it might have been different, he told himself. Anyhow, he would have plenty of other chances to be a model American, once he was in Paris and free of his compatriots.

But of course he was not free, as he quickly discovered in the station. He was trapped by all the lies he had told. He had been assuming that it would be simple to lose his train-companions in the howling mob on the platform. But he took the extra precaution of letting them get off first, while he lingered in the compartment, pretending to be strapping on his pack. As a final safety measure, he stowed the helmet, *pro tem*, in his book bag. As soon as the coast was clear, he would get a porter to take his bags ahead to the checkroom and hurry down the line himself to claim his motorbike. Once his bags were checked, he would speed off on his motorbike to look for a hotel room. The chances of the teachers' seeing him, from the top of some tourist bus, were one in several million. And even if they saw him, they would not be able to make a positive identification – a cycling outfit made you look like a hundred other guys.

Reassuring himself, he counted up to fifty and then peered out of the window. At the rear of the train, outside the baggage car, the teachers were gathered, with the rest of their tour and their tour director, supervising the unloading of their suitcases. There seemed to be an argument. He quickly withdrew his head. He decided to count up to a hundred. Sweat broke out on his forehead; he was wilting in his leather jacket. He craned his neck out of the window again. A motorbike was being lifted off the train. The teachers were coming his way. Ducking, Peter urged himself to be patient. No one could steal the motorbike as long as he was here watching.

The crowd on the platform was thinning. From his coign of vantage, effaced against the wall, he saw the teachers go by. He stood up and breathed easier. In only another minute, they would have disappeared through the gate. Unless they stopped to talk to somebody they knew. He was alone on the train, he presumed. And now he discovered fresh grounds for alarm. What if the train backed out of the station with him aboard? The car he was in gave a jolt. *'Descendez, monsieur. Descendez!'* a train official called out from below. *'Vous êtes à Paris.'* 'This is the end of the line, buddy,' an American voice said. Peter slung his book bag around his neck. He adjusted his pack, picked up his suitcases, and limply descended from the train. His patience had been rewarded: there was no sign of the teachers. Nor, he became aware, of his motorbike. Outside the baggage car, the platform was empty, and the baggage-car doors were shut. The unthinkable had finally happened.

As if in a dream, he heard himself shouting. *'Au voleur!'* Words he could not have imagined himself uttering and which yet sounded strangely familiar, as though he had read them in a story or a play – which he had, he recognized several hours later: it was the shriek of poor old Harpagon, the local Shylock – Stop, thief! Nobody answered him; they stared and shrugged. He moderated his pitch. *'On m'a volé mon vélomoteur!'* Tears and perspiration were running down his face. Suddenly the train official and several porters all talked at once. *'A la douane, monsieur; Vous le retrouverez à la douane. Il faut passer par la douane.'* They were pointing at some vehicles that had been whizzing past, loaded with trunks, crates, and suitcases. He descried a wheel and a bit of mahogany fender. *'Voilà votre vélomoteur!'*

Peter blinked. He still did not understand. Where were they taking it? *'A la douane!'* repeated the train official impatiently. 'Customs!' 'You have to go through customs,' an American voice said. 'There's a big hall in the station where you wait for your baggage. Then an inspector comes and looks at it.' 'But I've already *been* through customs. At Le Havre. *Monsieur! J'ai dédouané déja – au Havre.'* It was the same story. They refused to listen. 'You went through *immigration* at Le Havre,' the American said. 'This is customs.' Peter shook his head stubbornly. He knew what he had done. Finally he dug. Customs for boat-train passengers was in Paris. He was a boat-train passenger. Q.E.D. Sighing, he repaired to the customs hall, which was still milling with angry people. Someone's baggage was being searched – the Persian. 'They're looking for hashish,' he heard a woman say. He retired to a corner and sat down on his big suitcase to wait his turn.

Soon he heard voices he knew. 'Hoo hoo! Hoo hoo!' They were still around. The whole tour had spotted him and was heading in his direction. 'Here we are! Are you having an *awful* time getting one of those inspectors? My! We've been here for hours, seems like. You just come right along with us. Our tour director will help you. Here, Mr Kormendi, will you get that man to mark the young man's bags too?' Before Peter knew it, he had gone through customs a second time. 'Now what you need is a taxicab. Mr Kormendi will show you where you stand in line for one. We're going to walk, ourselves. Our hotel is just across the way. Here, Mr Kormendi, tell that porter to come back and take the young man's

bags to the taxi line.' Peter said he was planning to go by
subway. 'I have to economize.' 'Well, let Mr Kormendi
show you where you get it. He might as well make himself
useful.' Peter started to say that this would be too much
trouble, when the tour director, a tall fat man with protruding
teeth, resembling a hare, interposed in a guttural accent.
The young gentleman would not be permitted in the Métro
with so much baggage. If the ladies wished, he would be glad
to accompany their young friend to the taxi queue.

Peter drew a deep breath. Across the hall, the motorbike
was standing. On its fender was a chalk mark made by the
inspector this morning at Le Havre, which meant that it
would be easy, he supposed, for anyone to walk off with it.
If he allowed himself to be put in a taxi, he would never see
it again probably. 'Excuse me a minute,' he pleaded. 'I think
I see somebody I know.' And in fact his sweat-drenched eyes
had caught sight of the pharmaceuticals salesman, like a
natty mirage, proceeding towards the exit with a porter and
his cases of samples. 'Hi!' called Peter. 'Why, hi there!' said
the pharmaceuticals salesman. 'I was wondering what had
happened to you.' He stared at Peter and the conclave of
teachers. 'Say, you look kind of white!' 'Can you give me a
lift?' said Peter quickly. 'To the Left Bank.' As the salesman
told him afterwards, he could see right away that Peter was
on the verge of fainting; having been a druggist, he was
familiar with the signs: glassy eyes, cheesy colour, profuse
sweating. He did not ask any questions. 'Why, sure,' he
said. 'Sure. I've got a car meeting me. Happy to drop you
anywhere you want to go.' He tipped his hat to the teachers.
Peter gave a feeble wave of the hand in their direction. 'Thanks
again. Don't let me keep you any longer. I've met this friend.'

Half an hour later, he was in a Caddy '62. In his wallet was
a check for the motorbike, which had been left in the *consigne*
at the station, and he was being deposited at a hotel on the
Bank that catered to the American Air Force. While he waited
in the station bar, munching a ham sandwich and drinking a
restorative cognac, the salesman had fixed it up for him. It
had only taken a couple of phone calls. There was an Air

Force general, it seemed, that he had helped out once with some penicillin for a base in the south of France. The general was glad to return the favour. This hotel, which was not too far from the Sorbonne, was reserved for the military in transit and their families. Civilians not connected with the service were not supposed to stay there. But if you knew somebody, they could usually find you a slot.

Peter listened wanly. He had tacked from Scylla to Charybdis and he no longer cared. When the salesman had said that he knew a cheap hotel on the Left Bank, he had omitted to specify what kind of hotel it was. A man of action, he shot off to telephone, while Peter, the man of reflection, was left to await results. When he reappeared making the V-for-Victory sign, it was too late to jib. The starch had gone out of Peter. He allowed his liberator to check the motorbike ('Take my advice and sell it; it'll always be a headache') and 'fill him in' about the hotel they were bound for without experiencing any special surprise. It was not the Ritz, said the salesman, but the room should be fairly clean, and you did not have to tip. He was going to pass for the general's wife's nephew. He must be sure to remember that when he checked in with the sergeant at the desk.

From the back seat of the Cadillac, Peter looked out of the rain-splashed window. This was Paris. Tonight – 'to make it legal' – he and the salesman were going to have a drink at the Crillon with the general. Later, after dinner, they might go on to the Lido. Peter did not protest. He had stopped protesting. He was floating, like a human shipwreck, on a tide of good will. It was no use fighting against it. If he could only hold out long enough, the tide would recede and leave him to his own resources. All he had to do was avoid further entanglements. The virtue, he argued, of a military hotel was that they would kick him out after a couple of nights. Meanwhile, in the words of the salesman, the tab would be minimal. He would be able to take a shower and maybe, he told himself, crossing his fingers, the sergeant would let him keep his motorbike in the cellar. He wondered where his family had ever got the idea he was obstinate.

Epistle from
Mother Carey's Chicken

33 rue Monsieur le Prince
Paris 6ème
1 Brumaire, CLXXIII

Dear Ma:
I have finally found an apartment. It's on the fifth floor
(American sixth), which is good exercise for me. One room,
'furnished', plus a separate jakes and a sort of bird bath. I've
bought a student lamp, which helps. It has a radiator, but the
heat hasn't come on yet; the furnace is in the landlady's
apartment, and she doesn't feel the cold. She has let me have
some sheets and a so-called blanket, which I took to the
cleaner's. Still, it's better than those hotels I've been staying
in. Did I write you from the one where they had six Japanese
acrobats sleeping on the floor in the room next to me? Con-
tortionists, I assume.

I'm glad to be on my own, making my bed and sweeping.
It's good to do a little physical work, and you feel less lonely
in your own place, with your stuff unpacked. Also, I never
could solve the tipping problem. That was the good part of
that military hotel on the rue Littré. But in those other flea-
bags, where the *service* was *compris* theoretically in the price
of the room, I was constantly on the horns of the dilemma. I
mean, being an American and getting money from home, I
felt I ought to tip the chambermaid even if the other inhabitants didn't. 'From each according to his abilities.' You
know. But then I figured that if I tipped, it was scabbing on
the others, who didn't have the dough. Being *prepotente*,
the rich American youth. Buying the red carpet. And if I

crossed the chambermaid's palm, I did get more service, I found out. In one hotel, every time I started to go to the communal toilet, down the hall, she would rush ahead of me – '*Un instant, monsieur*' – and clean it with one of those filthy hard-rubber brushes they have, all caked with excrement, and when I thanked her, she backed out, curtseying: '*A votre service, monsieur.*' It was on account of that I moved. It got so I was lurking in my room, waiting for her to leave the floor so that I wouldn't get this special treatment I seemed to be paying for. If the other inhabitants had to use a dirty, stinking toilet, why should I be the exception? In fact, it was her job to clean the toilet.

On the other hand, when I didn't tip, I felt like a cheapskate. Because of the way I've been brought up, I guess. It's all your fault (ha ha). I tried asking myself what Kant would do in my position: 'Behave as if thy maxim could be a universal law'. If my maxim was not to tip because the next guy didn't, that would be pretty hard on the chambermaids of Paris, I decided. So, if he was true to his philosophy, Kant would tip. Of course he didn't have to face the issue, never leaving Königsberg. But you could also argue that tipping made it tough on the non-tipper (which I could produce some empirical evidence for), and therefore Kant might be against it. If I understand him, he is saying that an action should be judged by its implications, i.e., if everybody did what you are doing, what would the world be like? Well, a world in which every student gave a five-franc gratuity weekly to the woman who cleaned his room would be O.K., but what about a world in which every *other* student did it? Maybe the categorical imperative is not the best guide for Americans abroad. When you think of it, the rule of thumb about tipping is just the opposite of Kant: watch what everybody else does and do the same.

I never could make up my mind whether tipping or not tipping was more cowardly in the circumstances. Maybe any action becomes cowardly once you stop to reason about it. Conscience doth make cowards of us all, eh *mamma mia*? If you start an argument with yourself, that makes two people at least, and when you have two people, one of them starts appeasing the other.

Anyway, I've found this apartment. It will only cost 30,000 old francs a month, plus the utilities (there's a gas hot-water heater over the bathtub) and a small donation to the concierge at New Year's. The place has its drawbacks, but it's a lot better than the *chambres de bonne* a lot of kids rent in the mansards of old buildings. You ought to see those rooms, like a series of dog-houses under the eaves, where the maids used to be kept. No heat or running water, the usual foul toilet in the hall, and a common tap with a rusty basin underneath where you go to fill your pitcher and empty your slops. No bathtub or *bidet* on the whole floor; I guess they expected the maids to be dirty. The advantage is that, being high up, you generally have a nice view, through a slanting skylight. There are whole families – mostly Spaniards and Algerians – living in some of those holes.

It's an education, looking for an apartment. Quite a few French families want to rent you a room where you share a bathroom and toilet with them and maybe have the use of the kitchen to make your morning coffee. They call it an apartment. You waste a lot of time that way, answering ads. They won't admit on the telephone that the place doesn't have a separate entrance – *une seule clef*. At first I didn't know how to say that and if I said *une seule porte* – like *una porta sola* – they'd say, '*Oui, oui, monsieur, une seule porte.*' Even when they get the idea, they pretend to be surprised, as though a separate entrance was something unheard of and the only reason you could want one was to give orgies or sell your body to French queers.

I got my present pad through the grapevine. The desk clerk at my last hotel knew about it and told the owner I was *per bene*. The putative heating is included in the rent, and there's a two-burner hot plate and a few chipped dishes and a coffeepot. I can wash the dishes in the bathtub. The only thing is, there isn't much light. It looks out on a shaft that goes down to what they call a *courette*, where the garbage cans are kept. But I'll be here mostly in the evenings and anyway the days are getting shorter, as the landlady pointed out. I.e., when I get up in the morning and come back in the afternoon it will be dark outside anyhow. She had fixed the place up for her son, who was a student; hence the amenities. There are even some home-made bookshelves. It is on a landing, up a few steps from the service entrance of her own apartment. I have to use the service stairs.

At night, the big main door on the ground floor is locked at ten o'clock. If I come in after that, I ring for the concierge to push a button that opens the door. The signal is six short rings; otherwise, she won't open, in case I might be a *clochard* or a burglar. The Parisians spend a lot of time worrying about burglars and prowlers. In those hotels I was staying in, the chambermaid, on receiving a tip, would immediately start warning me about the other denizens – they stole. '*Méfiez-vous, monsieur.*' I was urged to be sure to lock my door when I was inside and to put my watch and money under my pillow while I was sleeping. I found this quite unpleasant. It made me look at anybody I passed on the stairs with a sort of smutty curiosity, as though they might have it 'in them' to be a thief. Like wondering whether a woman you see waiting on a corner could be a prostitute. The French are a suspicious people.

But in fact there's a lot of theft in those Left Bank flops. You would be surprised. In one place I was staying – on the rue St André des Arts – a kid had his typewriter taken, a new Olivetti. It turned out that it wasn't even his; he'd borrowed it from a girl friend who typed manuscripts for a living. He reported it to the police, but they just shrugged. Too common an occurrence in that precinct. The way this kid, who was Dutch, reconstructed it, somebody must have lifted his key from the board downstairs, while the desk clerk was elsewhere (half the time in those hotels there's nobody at the desk; you have to ring a hand-bell to get somebody to come), and gone up to his room and helped himself. The Dutchman wanted the police to search all the rooms; he reasoned that it had to be someone in the hotel, who had heard him typing. But the police told him that whoever stole the typewriter

would have gone out and sold it right away. They even implied, when he started making a scene, that he might have
sold it himself and then reported that he had been robbed.

Then I heard about a Swedish *au pair* girl, in that same
hotel, who left her gold watch in the communal bathroom in
the soap-dish; when she missed it, ten minutes later, it was
gone. An American girl found her crying on the stairs and
went with her to the police station. 'My golden watch!' she
kept saying. You'd think that thieves, being hard up themselves, would have a fellow-feeling; I mean, steal from people
who could afford it. But of course people who can afford it
stay in hotels where the clientele is 'above' stealing watches
and typewriters. I guess the world is a vicious circle.

I think I will like Paris better now that I'm no longer a
member of its floating population, which can be fairly sordid.
The food, at my age level, is fairly sordid too. There are a
few *foyers* with a table d'hôte, for students, that are not so
bad, but they're crowded and when the novelty wears off
they're not a great improvement on eating in commons at
home, except that you can have wine. The bread and croissants are great, of course, but the French don't know how to
make a sandwich. And I miss salads and orange juice and
tuna fish. They hardly ever serve vegetables, except French
fries. There's nothing here to compare with the spinach in
the Automat, for instance. And I miss the stand-up bars in
Italy, where you can have a healthy snack and a *cappuccino*.
What I like best in the restaurants here is the *crudités*, but
you can't sit down and order *crudités* and a glass of milk; you
have to be force-fed with the entire menu. Sometimes I just
have a dozen *praires* (which are cheaper than oysters),
standing up, on the street, for lunch.

I've started doing my own cooking, with a vegetable binge.
No icebox, needless to say, in this apartment, but that doesn't
matter with the present room temperature. Besides, the
French, like the Italians, only buy what they need for one
day. I had a shock, though, yesterday, when I went to do my
marketing at the Marché Buci – that big outdoor market,
near the Odéon. At one stall, I asked for a carrot, and the

type refused to sell me one. He said I had to buy a kilo. Like you, dearest Ma, I started to argue. I wanted to know why. How it would damage him to sell me one carrot or one apple or one pear. I explained that I didn't have an icebox and that I was just one person. '*Ça ne me regarde pas,*' he growled. Finally we compromised on a pound. That's quite a lot of carrots for a single man. While he was weighing them, I got into conversation with an Italian, who had been watching me and smiling – very nice, about the *babbo*'s age, an intellectual. He said that in Italy not only would they sell you one carrot but divide it in four. According to him, this only proved that Italy is a poor country, while France is a rich country. I said the Italians had more heart than the French, even if they gyp you sometimes. The French *grudge* gypping you, Mother. Maybe, I said, people in poor countries had more heart than people in rich countries. After all, Poverty used to be represented as a virtue. I hadn't noticed any statues of Poverty on French churches.

By the way, did you know that most of the statues on the churches here had their heads chopped off? In the French Revolution. And in the Wars of Religion, this Italian told me. But he agreed that Dame Poverty was not seen as a Virtue in France, which he seemed to think was a good thing.

After I had bought a pound of carrots, three cucumbers, a pound of tomatoes, a pound of onions, and a huge cooked beet, we went to a café around the corner, near the statue of Danton, and continued the discussion. He thought it was funny that an American should idealize poverty, and when I told him that in America you could buy one carrot even in a supermarket, he seemed sceptical. Perhaps in the Negro sections, he said. No, I said, anywhere. It was a free country; you could buy as much or as little as you wanted. I had to admit, though, that as far as I knew you couldn't buy one cigarette at a time, the way you can in Italy. And I realize now I ought to have mentioned those carrots in plastic bags, which sort of bear out his point. It's odd they slipped my mind.

Anyway, he explained that in Paris you could buy a single carrot or onion or lemon in a *grocery store*. That's different from a market. Only in a grocery store you pay more than you would pay if you bought the carrot at the market. But since you can't, the point is academic. I said maybe students who lived in the quarter could get up a pool to buy a kilo a day of vegetables and fruit at the market and then divide it up. Take turns doing the shopping. He said I was defining a co-operative.

It sank me to learn that I'm too small an economic unit to take part in the French way of life. I love those street markets – so colourful – and I'd counted on haunting them every day after school with my *filet*. What's the point of being in Europe if you have to line up in a grocery store, which is usually part of a chain, just like at home? This Italian said not to be discouraged: I could still buy fish and meat and cheeses at those market stalls, and in time, if they got to know me, the vegetable- and fruit-sellers might relent; I could become '*l'américain du Marché Buci*'.

When we parted, he asked me to come around to his place some evening for dinner; he has kids but much younger than me. If I go (I'm supposed to call him, since I have no phone), it will be the first time I've been in a French household, except that he isn't French. He left Italy under Mussolini, like the *babbo*, and his wife is Russian.

Unfortunately, I haven't made many contacts here. In my course in French civilization, we're all foreigners, obviously. The only student I've had any real talks with is a Norwegian named Dag, who is a sort of Marxist troll. He wants me to go to Poland with him during Christmas vacation. There are some Smith girls I met at a place called Reid Hall where they have supplementary classes, in English, but they stick pretty much together. I asked one to go rowing with me the other day on the lake in the Bois de Boulogne, but her afternoons are all sewed up with her peer group doing art appreciation at the Louvre. On Saturdays and Sundays the lake is too crowded.

I don't see how anybody gets to know any French students,

unless they have a letter of introduction. I've tried going to cafés where they're said to hang out, but they're mostly full of Americans who have heard the same rumour. And if they aren't full of Americans nobody will talk to me. I've actually gone as far as asking for a light. The place to find French students is at the movies. They seem to spend all their time there.

That reminds me. Did you know that you're supposed to tip the usher in a French movie house? I didn't know and got hissed at by the woman the other day when I went to see an Antonioni flick. All the students in the vicinity stopped necking and turned to ogle me as I stumbled into my seat. I gather I was being called a '*sale américain*,' but if she knew I was an American, she might have enlightened me about the local customs. It must happen all the time with foreigners. But I suppose that's what makes her mad. Usually when I'm in some place like a stand-up coffee bar, I watch what the other customers do and follow their example, but in a movie house you're literally in the dark. This little incident wrecked the film for me. I hardly saw Monica Vitti because of the rage I was in. The picture was half over before I finally grasped what I'd done that was so horrible. Then it was too late to rectify it – at least without getting stared at some more. Besides, I couldn't see how much the other customers were giving. In case you want to know, it's a franc on the Champs-Elysées and fifty centimes in the little places. The clerk at my hotel told me.

At home I never thought I was much of a conformist. But I now see that I was without knowing it. I did what everybody else did without being aware I was copying them. Here I *mind* being different. Being abroad makes you conscious of the whole imitative side of human behaviour. The ape in man. The tourists have it better. I don't sneer any more when I see them being carted around in those double-decker buses with earphones on their ears. I envy them. They've all told each other who they are and where they come from, and to the French they're part of the landscape, like the Tour Eiffel – nobody notices them, except other tourists. Here nobody knows who I am, as a person, which is all right with me, but I can't fade into the foliage either. If I still had Aunt Millie's camera and were willing to carry it, it might make me invisible to the French. Just another tourist. It occurs to me that that's why, unconsciously, the men are all draped with cameras and light meters and the old women have their glasses slung around their necks – to show they belong to the species, tourist, which allows them to disappear as individuals.

You were right. I haven't used the motorbike much. Last Sunday, I took a run out to Senlis, to look at the church, which is older than Notre-Dame. I think I like Gothic, at least here in France. It reminds me of the forests these people came out of – druidical. The church in Senlis has a greenish light, as if you were in a sacred wood, with stone boughs meeting overhead in the bosky side aisles and the deambulatory – all that interlacing and those bent perspectives. They treat stone as if it was pliant, like branches. And the choir is a sort of clearing in the forest. While I was there, to complete the illusion, a swallow flew through.

The other afternoon I took the Métro and a bus and went to see St-Denis, which is the first important Gothic in France, right in the middle of a working-class suburb. Unfortunately, I picked the wrong day, so that I couldn't see the choir, where the kings of France are buried; I didn't mind missing them, but the choir is the original Gothic of the Abbé Suger. Probably Bob knows about him. Next Sunday I'm going to Chartres, but I'll break down and take the train, I guess. It's easier than riding Rosinante through the Sunday traffic. That would be quixotic.

Everybody I meet advises me to sell the motorbike. For one thing, it constitutes a parking problem. They don't have parking places for two-wheeled vehicles, the way they do in Rome and Perugia. Which I guess is another proof that France is a rich country, while Italy is a poor country. And if you park it by the kerb you can get a ticket. For the last couple of weeks it's been left in the court of an apartment house near that military hotel, where there's a concierge whose dog I've made friends with. But I can't keep it there indefinitely; being out in the open isn't doing the new paint job any good. I hardly ever ride it in Paris, except to go to the Bois, rowing, to keep myself in shape, and that time I wrote you about, when I went chestnutting in the Parc de St-Cloud. I'd been hoping the concierge in my apartment building would let me park it in the cellar, but it turns out that the cellar is divided up into individual *caves*, locked and padlocked, that belong to the individual tenants, and I'm not entitled to one. Anyway, they're very damp; you can't even store a suitcase in them without its growing whiskers.

If I knew somebody who had a house in the country, I could store it with them for the winter. But I don't. That salesman who helped me out said I should advertise it for sale at the px. The general could fix it up that I could post a notice on the bulletin board. Maybe if I did that, I could find it a good home. By the way, the general said his wife could get me anything I wanted at the px: cigarettes, liquor, canned stuff. It appears that she could even get me a typewriter for one-third less than you have to pay (I quote) stateside. They had me to dinner with their teenage daughter.

What do you think about the ethics of using the px? I don't mean for liquor or cigarettes. But it might be nice to have some tuna fish and peanut butter. And they carry Danish milk there. I can resist the edibles, though. What really tempts me is the idea of a typewriter. And possibly a steam-iron to press my clothes. The px store is supposed to be for the military and Embassy personnel only; you have to have a card to get in. But the general says the regulations are aimed at preventing px-buying for resale, which is unfair to the local economy. I wouldn't be hurting the local economy if I bought a typewriter at the px because I wouldn't get a typewriter at all unless I got it there. Which I guess proves that I don't *need* a typewriter. The same with the iron. I can worry along without them. Which presumably answers my question.

I think *you* would be against buying stuff at the px because you wouldn't want to be the kind of person who loaded up at the px. I agree there's something *antipatico* in the idea. When I went to the general's apartment for dinner, I got a taste of px-living. We had a big canned American ham, which the general carved with an electric slicer; it was baked with Dole's pineapple and brown sugar and with it were canned potato balls and frozen peas and lima beans, followed by American vanilla ice cream and Hershey's chocolate sauce and FFV cookies. They thought I might be homesick, they said. Before dinner, I had a shot of Jack Daniel and afterwards Maxwell House coffee, made in an electric percolator, and chocolate mints. The wife kept announcing the brand names, like those butlers you see in the movies calling out the names of the guests. After dinner, we listened to Rock'n Roll on their hi-fi set. And they showed me all over the apartment; the kitchen was like an appliances salesroom or an ad for Revere Copper. They even get their light bulbs from the px.

They feel that having all this junk around is a political act; they're a sort of showcase of the American way of life for the general's French colleagues at SHAPE or wherever he is. The wives, said Mrs General, would give their *eyeteeth* for her out-size General Motors Frigidaire, not to mention her pop-up toaster, her electric knife-sharpener and can-opener, her washing machine and dryer, her floor-waxer, et cetera. I blushed for her when she said that, but possibly she's right. Possibly the locals do envy them their easy access to all these goodies, symbolized by the px card. What shocked me was learning that even little kids have px cards. Their daughter has had one practically from the time she could walk.

Do you remember that Navy wife we knew in Berkeley who kept asking you whether you didn't want to share a big double-breasted turkey with her? She used to get them at the Commissary somewhere in the Bay Area. I remember you saying coldly that it sounded like a double-breasted suit. She was always after you to get on the gravy train with her and she was hurt when you always refused.

The same way you would never buy anything at a discount house, though you liked Sears, Roebuck. I used to ask you what was the difference, and you said that buying at Sears,

Roebuck was economical but buying at a discount house was greedy. But I think you liked Sears, Roebuck because it was traditional; your grandmother had 'always' bought lawn-mowers and sprinklers there. Sears, Roebuck, to you, was the 'old' America where people had lawns and wore mail-order underwear in the winter. If you'll excuse me for saying so (I've been examining the roots of my thinking lately), you confuse the ethical and the aesthetic. Of course you may be right, in a sense. When Kant asks what would the world be like if everyone stole, that may be at bottom an aesthetic question. What would the world *look* like?

I'd like to talk this over with somebody, but who? When I first studied the categorical imperative. I thought, like a lot of laymen, that it was the same as the Golden Rule. Don't steal from your neighbour because you wouldn't want him to steal from you. But the motive there is selfish. Sort of an imaginary deal or bargain; how would *I* feel if somebody stole *my* pocket-book? I'm projecting my petty self-interest outward. The categorical imperative is purer, like a theorem in geometry. Presented with the question of Should I steal or Why shouldn't I steal, Kant tells me to contemplate a world of thieves disinterestedly and accept it or reject it. If I reject it, that means that I don't care for the overall picture, regardless of where I might figure in it. But then, you might say, ethics boils down to a question of taste. Only, with Kant taste isn't relative. He assumes that everybody, the thief included, would reject the picture of a world in which everybody stole. Because the picture is self-contradictory. He was trying, in fact, to take the taste out of ethics, to base ethics on a universal agreement that would spring from a common recognition of what is evident. The way philosophers have always been trying to take the taste out of aesthetics.

Pragmatically, nearly everybody, at least in the Western world, agrees that the Parthenon is beautiful. It isn't a question of taste, like Mannerism, for instance, which you can get to like, the way you do olives. Kant's ethics, as I see it, is a beautiful structure, based on a law of harmony and inner consistency, that in its way resembles the Parthenon,

while yours, Mother, if you'll excuse me, is more like olives.
Caviare to the general. Your ethics is based on *style*, which
never has to give a consistent reason why it is the way it is.
And if an outsider looks for the reason, it is likely to be
historical: I mean that somebody like Louis xiv introduced
a certain shape of armchair, which a select few can recognize.
Purely contingent.

You shudder at the thought of a double-breasted turkey because a single-breasted turkey is classical. Your style would
be compromised if you joined the herd around the px-trough.
But you can't persuade anyone else to abstain unless they love
you and want to be like you. You saw that in Rocky Port. In
your way, you are an exemplary person, but the common
man can't imitate you, although you think he ought to. It's as
if Mozart said to Salieri, 'Why not be like me?'

You are an accident, Mother, which for some reason you
don't want to recognize. Let's say a happy accident. But you
can't legislate. That's your great weakness, and you know
it. You want your whim or prejudice to be a universal
law. Maybe all artists are like that; they feel they are the *end*
of some teleological chain. I'm coming to the conclusion that
art is incompatible with democracy. If I want to be a demo-
crat, it's an awful handicap to be the son of an artist. I will
have to reject you, if I can, because – to put it bluntly – you
are a snob. Without wanting to be one. You can't help it.

For instance, you don't really want to vote for Johnson, because, you say, he is 'common'. Doesn't that show that your
whole way of looking at things is permeated by archaic caste
notions? If I argue that Harry Truman was common, you say
no, he was ordinary – a fine distinction. I guess an ordinary
person is a common person you approve of. Then you say you
don't like Johnson's face; it's crafty. Well, I just looked that
word up in the dictionary. It comes from craft, the artisan's
skill at twisting his material. Which proves how we still
despise the artisan, the guy who had to work with his hands.

It isn't just you. Our whole vocabulary is rotten with feudal
distinctions. Look at *villain* or *clown*. Those were just words
for peasants. Then think about 'O what a rogue and peasant

slave am I!' Do you know what *rogue* meant? A beggar. Being a prince, Hamlet couldn't think of any worse things to call himself. And Hamlet is an ethical person. The vocabulary of ethics, once you start to think about it, is more foul and retrograde than any other kind of talk. We say an action is low or base or mean or boorish, which are all synonyms for vulgar, i.e., characteristic of the common people. As opposed to noble, gentle, kind, meaning aristocratic. And people who don't use these terms – at least in their own minds – for the most part haven't even entered the realm of the ethical. They don't give a damn whether an action is noble or ignoble, princely or beggarly; they live for their gross desires. There's no vocabulary for a democratic ethics; even words like *free* or *frank*, which you would think were sort of yeomen words, actually meant belonging to the ruling class. I suppose in Russia *proletarian* is still a term of praise, but the proletariat there – in theory – *is* the ruling class. Why can't we find words to express a classless ideal? Do you remember, when I was about six, an old Russian Social Revolutionary came to see the *babbo*? He had just escaped from somewhere, maybe Siberia or a DP camp, and he said, 'I would like to make a little money. In the most dignified and democratic way possible.' This made you both laugh a lot, and the *babbo* used to tell it as a story, but I couldn't see what was funny about it. In fact, Mother, what *was* so funny? Unless you were just laughing at him for his ignorance of the ways of the capitalist world. I would like to meet that man now.

It seems to me that if my generation is serious it will have to reform language. Get rid of its hoary increment of prejudice. Like those French Jacobins chopping off the heads of statues. Around Paris, they've been restored, I read in the guidebook, by Viollet-le-Duc. On Notre Dame, for instance, you have to look twice to see that the kings of Judah on the façade are just plastic-surgery paste-ups. But outside of Paris, they say, you get the full effect – rows of headless bodies on the church fronts. I saw some the other day in the Louvre. A massacre. This gory gallery made more impression on me than practically anything I've seen. Apostles and saints reduced to stumps. Or bunches of drapery. I never grasped before what the French Revolution meant. An Italian – even a half-Italian and a half-Jew like me – can't help feeling revolted by these hacked-up groups in defenceless stone. It goes against the grain. My balls ached in sympathy. For Mother Church, I guess, and her poor bleeding trunk. What a change to wander into the peaceful Italian rooms, where nobody had harmed a hair of that boy Baptist's head! I love Donatello. Italians, unlike the French, are still a *family*. Maybe because they weren't ever a nation. Or because they inherited the Roman *pietas*, which was reverence for ancestors. I will have to mull that over. But I felt it very strongly with this Italian yesterday – as if he were my long-lost uncle. And I gather he reciprocated. The funny thing is, he is a half-Jew too – a tall guy, slightly bald, looks like a patriarch. His name is Bonfante. But his mother, believe it or not, was a Levi. No connection, apparently. She came from Ancona.

We talked about the Terror, and he advised me to read a book by Salvemini, on the conditions that led up to the French Revolution; he is going to lend it to me. I told him I thought the French had a *faible* for decapitation. After all, their patron saint is Saint Denis, who was beheaded, and you keep seeing statues of him carrying his head in his hands like a jack-o'-lantern. An anticipation of the guillotine. Bonfante said the guillotine was just a rationalization of an old inefficient process. I said that applied to the gas chambers, and he had to admit I was right.

But afterwards I thought that maybe those French mobs had been logical in wrecking the symbols of the old régime. Those decapitated statues shook my democratic complacency; whoever did that meant business. Only they didn't go far enough. They should have chopped off the head of language while they were at it. That was the point, of course, of changing the names of the days and months and starting the calendar over. But they needed a bigger purge; no more *ci-devant* words. Only words that pointed to something like *tree* or *house*. Is that the idea behind English linguistic philosophy? I guess you wouldn't know. Instead of devouring

its own children, the Revolution should have killed off its
parents. They would have had to abolish all past literature and
art, including the *lumières*. Grinning Voltaire *and* the Holy
Virgin. Possibly music too – all those masses and madrigals
and stately minuets. Smash the pianos and harpsichords,
unstring the violins. Into the cannon foundry with the
knightly trumpets.

Naturally, this might have been offensive to me if I had
been alive then – after all, I hate to lop off the head of a
dandelion. But if it had been done in 1789, possibly I'd be able
to think clearly today. I feel awfully confused now, as though
my mind were a pool that looked transparent till I started
stirring up its muddy depths with a stick. This could be the
effect of being away from home and becoming a 'rootless
cosmopolitan'. I've never felt before like a foreign particle.
And since I haven't anybody congenial to talk to, I am talking
to myself. Tonight is the first chance I've had to *sfogarmi*, to
get rid of that bottled-up feeling. Don't show this letter to
anyone. Please.

You know, you and the *babbo* always said I was an egalitarian. That used to embarrass me, but it's true. I've got this
bug about equality. And now I'm in the place where the
whole thing started, where you see *Liberté, Egalité, Fraternité*
frowning at you in gold letters from the faces of public buildings. They even have it on the fronts of *churches*, sometimes
stencilled and sometimes cut right into the stone. As though
some kid had gone wild with a rubber stamp that it got for its
birthday. The handwriting on the wall, only it's printed in
big Roman letters. This must go back to the Revolution,
when the churches were turned into powder-magazines or
temples of Reason or Glory. Funny that in all these years
nobody erased it; I wonder if the Germans tried during the
Occupation. Out, damned spot. You would think the guidebooks would have a word to say about this revolutionary
slogan, which hits every tourist in the eye, but they pass it
over in silence, just as if it was one of those obscene graffiti
you see in the Métro. OAS or A BAS LES JUIFS.

I've decided that may be why the Parisians are so sullen

and why they drink. They thought of equality first. My theory is that equality is a sort of poison; once it got into the human bloodstream, nobody could eliminate it. It just stayed there, corroding us. I mean, it might have been better if nobody had ever thought of it in the first place. But they did, and once they did, it should have been thought *through*. Which never happened.

When you consider that mankind lived for centuries without this idea's ever seriously entering anybody's mind! It never occurred to Socrates or Plato or any of the old philosophers. The idea of *everybody*'s being equal, not just Athenians or free men. You could say it occurred to slaves and people like the Ciompi in Florence; naturally it would. But it didn't get into the thinking of the people *on top*, the reasoners and legislators. Not till the eighteenth century. Yet you couldn't say that Socrates or Pericles was stupid or a blind supporter of an oligarchy. The idea of equality was like that play about the man who came to dinner. It was 'entertained', and then we were in the soup. Pardon the unintentional pun.

Equality, of course, is that spectre Marx was talking about, the spectre of Communism, which is still stalking around, haunting the globe, without ever having been *embodied* anywhere. It's still two-thirds of a ghost. At home, in spite of the Constitution, we don't have real political equality, and the Russians don't have real economic equality – far from it. One would lead to the other, logically, or so people suspect: that's why the white Southerners are afraid to give the Negro the vote; the next thing he would be asking for would be a decent job. And if the Russian workers got consumer goods, they would soon be asking for the vote.

I have made a discovery. Mother! Whenever in history, equality appeared on the agenda, it was exported somewhere else, like an undesirable. In the eighteenth century, when the idea began travelling around Europe, it was shipped off to the New World, where there was more room. But pretty soon, as the East got crowded, equality became sort of smelly and was sent out West, in a covered wagon, to the wide-open spaces, so that back home people could forget about it for a while. In your generation, Roosevelt made a few gestures in the direction of equality, until World War II came along and took priority. In my generation, the idea has drifted South and joined the civil-rights movement, where it's stirring up trouble. So a new move is indicated, on the principle of 'Keep moving, buddy'. Maybe into space, if there isn't another world war. Space will be the new frontier, full of homesteaders: opportunity beckons, enlist in space. But the problem will arise there too; the colonists on Mars or the moon will want equal rights with the world or a universal one-hour week or something. Then there may be another migration, into the Milky Way. But finally humanity will have to face the spectre, unless it decides to commit suicide instead, which it might. We may agree to blow ourselves up, like a man who knows he's suffering from an incurable disease.

If the race would try equality once, then we might find out that it worked. Let everybody keep hands off and give it a fair chance. Which the French Revolution never had. Or the Russian. Not even dear old Castro. And if we found out that it didn't work, O.K. We would stop being *haunted* by it.

Let me give you a little parable. In olden times a man who lived in a big house and wore a fur coat felt superior to a ragged man who lived in a hovel. And the reason was simple: a tautology. He felt superior *because* he lived in a big house and wore a fur coat. That was all there was to it. If he was charitable, like Good King Wenceslas (your favourite Bohemian), he could take a few sticks to the peasant in his hovel at Christmastime. But Good King Wenceslas was a *saint*, and besides it was *Christmas*. And, being a saint, he didn't doubt the justice that had put him in his palace and the other in his forest hut. That was where God had assigned them, for some unfathomable reason, and the difference in their degree made the poor man grateful for the king's goodness. Inequality was natural on this earth, though there might be some surprises in Heaven.

Today, though, King Wenceslas would feel guilty because he lived in a palace. It would prey on his mind. If he was a reactionary, he would think he had to justify his accommodation by showing that he had the *right* to them, that he was superior, either by birth or by get-up-and-go to the peasant down the road. He could argue that there was no use turning his palace over to the peasant, who would only wreck it, keep the coal in the bathtub, etc. In short, he would have to find some social doctrine or 'law' that entitled him to be where he was. Appeal to some imaginary tribunal that would *award* him the palace.

If King Wenceslas today was a liberal, with the peasants solidly behind him, he might become president, like Kennedy, and his wife could make the White House more palatial and have artists, like you, Mother, to perform. As long as he was on the peasant's side, he could feel O.K., relatively, about retaining the palace and furs. And the more royal and dynastic he was, the more, probably, he would argue that Society needs Symbols, etc. A liberal King Wenceslas, strangely enough, seems to sleep better than his reactionary uncle.

But nobody today really feels comfortable inside his own skin. The poor feel guilty for being poor, and the rich feel guilty for being rich. The poor are afraid that it's not an accident that they are poor but that there is something ghastly wrong with them, while the rich are afraid that it *is* an accident that they are rich. The over-developed countries feel guilty toward the under-developed countries, and the under-developed countries feel ashamed of standing in line for a handout. You can measure the change in King Wenceslas, thinking by the fact that a hundred years ago a country was *proud* of being rich. I guess no country was ever proud of being poor. Unless a masochistic country like Poland or Ireland?

Last winter, while I was working for civil rights, I worried about being a guilty white liberal. Today I'm not so much bothered by that. I have it in a better perspective. Aside from the fact of not being able to help being white, I have come to the conclusion that working for civil rights is a good thing in itself, even if I do it to bribe my conscience. A lot of the churches and abbeys in France wouldn't have been built if kings and nobles hadn't been trying to purge themselves of blood-guilt. Hospitals too. I send part of my allowance to civil-rights causes, which lets me stay on the sidelines or in the cheering section. If a person feels guilty, it's better to pay a recompense. Be your own redeemer. Take our friend the admiral. If he sent a few guilt-dollars to the NAACP or the Urban League or the Brotherhood of Sleeping Car Porters, he would be a lot easier in his mind. He acts so defiant because he's secretly ashamed of his/our treatment of the Negro. He knows he's wrong. It strikes me that our whole country is secretly ashamed, for being rich and white, and this may make us dangerous.

Possibly I ought to feel ashamed myself, because I'm not giving my whole time to civil rights, though I claim to believe in it. But I don't look for excuses for being here studying in Paris. That's a decision I've made, a conscious act of my will, and I notice that I don't repine much over anything I've done *consciously* – you have to accept the choices of your will in a sporting spirit. *Cosa fatta capo ha*, as the *babbo* says.

What is biting me here in Paris is something different: *being who I am* at this juncture in history. I sense myself as irrelevant to practically everything: this room, this street, this city, this world, this universe. Except to you and Bob and the *babbo*. I'm just an epiphenomenon of your joint history – a wandering footnote. It's only in connection with you people, who formed me, that I make a semblance of sense.

You remember how in King Arthur everybody keeps saying to an errant knight, 'Tell me thy name and thy condition.' Whereupon he tells, and they search his wounds and give him a bath of tepid water. It would be nice to be errant in a storybook where your fellow-knights recognize you when you say who you are. I am slightly attracted to that Smith girl I mentioned because she can place me, like somebody looking in a file: her cousin used to spend the summer in Rocky Port, and her mother met you once in New York, *è cosi via*. In fact, she's quite boring and middle-class, though pretty; she actually said, 'It's a small world, isn't it?' But when I'm around her, I feel slightly more real. She knows my name and my condition.

You may think I'm wandering from the theme of equality. But I'm not. A person has to assume, especially if he's study- ing philosophy, that he has a common world with the rest of humanity. Not just the common world of sense data and a common receiving apparatus but a common *inner* world – his mind, which he uses like a laboratory to conduct experi- ments. As soon as you start to philosophize, you predicate a common world. A basically democratic world, in which Socrates and the slave boy, obeying the command of reason, arrive at the same conclusion. There can't be such a thing as an aristocratic philosophy; once philosophy starts getting exclusive, like neo-Platonism, it turns into a cult, with secret doctrines and initiates.

Then, bang, here in Paris, I see how really isolated I am. Not only don't I share a language (my French is lousy, to my great surprise) with most of the people I see, or a social back- ground, or a political outlook, but we don't have in common the most elementary rules of conduct that I thought were shared by our whole sub-species. In a minute I will tell you what I mean. Those cheesy hotels. Perhaps dormitory life should have prepared me for the shock. But I must have been lucky in school and college. No, Mother, I don't mean steal- ing or homosexuality. Do you know why I *had* to get an apartment? Why I had to retreat into my present private world? Something I've already spoken of. Those communal toilets.

It started in that military hotel. Every morning when I went to move my bowels, after waiting my turn, I found the bowl all smeared and streaked with excrement. Sometimes the previous user hadn't bothered to flush it at all; there would be those turds in the bowl and a smell, naturally. I would flush and open the window to air the place out before sitting down; the seat was often still warm from the bottom of the last guy who had defecated. It made me nauseous, but I said to myself that these were Air Force men: maybe you had to expect that they would have been toughened up, living in barracks.

But when I moved, it was the same. There were the same

oily streaks of evil-smelling shit on the porcelain; sometimes the bowl would be all splashed, even the underside of the toilet seat would be splashed, because the last occupant had had diarrhoea. You know; the Paris trots. If it turned out that I only had to pee (squeamishness was making me constipated) I would find myself in a quandary: whether to carefully clean off the filth with that rubber brush and wash the underside of the toilet seat with wet toilet paper or just to pee and flush and walk out. Well, I never could bring myself to accept the second alternative. I *had* to clean up for the next person. Even though I felt there was something degrading about stooping, literally, to do it. And the smell would make me gag, unless I held my breath. How did you ever stand it, Mother, washing my diapers? I remember (or did you tell me?) that when I had done Number Two, you always washed them out yourself before sending them to the diaper service. I wonder if everyone did. And, if I recall, it was years before I was housebroken.

Anyway, while laving the 'lavatory', far from giving myself a merit badge for public service, I felt furtive. What would anyone think if they found me? Actually once a girl did find me, swabbing away with toilet paper; in that hotel, the john door didn't bolt. She hastily withdrew. At least she couldn't know that it was somebody else's shit I was laboriously removing. That was what I told myself when I met her afterwards in the hall.

I couldn't understand why I should have this complex about being caught in the act. Was I afraid of what a wig-picker might say? Or embarrassed at being a Boy Scout? I tried to examine my motives. Was I cleaning up somebody else's shit for fear that the next person would think it was mine? There might be an element of that, I admitted. But if I had been promised that nobody would see me issuing from that toilet, I could still have cleaned it. I would have cleaned it if I knew that the hotel was going to be demolished five minutes later by a hydrogen bomb.

Of course, Mother, I could have left it for the chambermaid. Or rung the bell and asked her to do it. One morning, in the hotel on the rue de la Harpe, while I was hovering in my room, waiting for the coast to be clear, I heard someone go into the toilet and then come right out again, banging the door; resolute steps marched to the hall telephone, and a voice, speaking good French, told the management to send somebody up instantly to clean the toilet on the fifth floor, it was filthy, disgusting ... Probably the whole floor was listening, and pretty soon the chambermaid came running. I fell in love, abjectly (and maybe I wasn't the only one), with the owner of that voice – it was a woman, that was all I ever knew. She must have checked out that same day.

But I could never have emulated her. Lack of courage, I suppose. Plus the feeling that I would rather be a menial myself than assume that some other menial should take work like that in her stride. That was why it disgusted me that that chambermaid I mentioned should leap to the task with alacrity just because I had tipped her. At that point I had the right to think that if she could do it for me, why not for everybody?

The worst of those hotels, though, was realizing that some of my predecessors on the hot seat had been girls and women. That killed me. Knowing *that* about them. I would see a plump little Irish girl come tripping out of the toilet and go in and find her excrement waiting in the bowl, practically steaming, like horse turds. In my last hotel there was an old Englishwoman on my floor that the desk clerk said was a writer; I used to hear her typing sometimes in her room. If I saw her returning from the jakes, I would turn around and postpone answering the call of Nature, so that I wouldn't have to follow her in and compromise her dignity. It was compromised enough, I felt, by her having to run the gauntlet every morning to attend to her needs: between 8 AM and 9.30 AM, in that circuit, every door on the corridor is stealthily ajar, and the inhabitant is crouched like a runner to make the dash down the hall when he hears the chain pulled.

Actually it got so I was using the toilet in American Express every time I went for my mail, and urinals on the street and in cafés. I developed a horror of identifying the faeces I was finding every morning in the bowl; I preferred them to remain anonymous. Finding pubic hairs in the communal bathtub never bothered me particularly.

If this is the way things are, Mother, how am I going to be able to take the Army? I don't mind latrines, which are sort of natural. What's horrible to me is the combination of (relatively) modern plumbing and beastly squalor. But animals are more dainty. They hide their turds whenever they can. Except herd animals like cows and sheep. Well, horses. But that was what I kept thinking: how much more fastidious animals were. I remembered how I used to say that I preferred animals to people, which worried you.

Don't imagine that I was living on some Parisian skid row. Or in some of the Beat hotels, which at least might have been amusing. All my places were on the fringe of respectability. The clientele was mainly students who looked as if they came from middle-class families, where presumably you're taught not to be physically offensive to others. The way you taught me. You taught me so long ago that I feel as if I'd always known instinctively to clean the toilet after myself, i.e., to look and see if it was necessary. Something I did automatically, without thinking about it, like brushing my teeth in the morning or using a handkerchief or a Kleenex when I had to blow my nose.

After a while, I began to speculate about my fellow-residents. So far as I could tell from the evidence, the majority either didn't mind leaving traces of themselves or else didn't notice. They just went in, did their business, and exited, pulling the chain, without waiting to see whether the water flushed. But how was it possible not to notice the traces of the guy before you and, noticing, not to react? Could humanity be divided into people who noticed and people who didn't? If so, there was no common world.

That thought really depressed me. If there was no agreement on a primary matter like that, then it was useless to look for agreement on 'higher' principles. And I couldn't help feeling moral about it – judging my predecessors in the toilet in a highly unfavourable way. A shitty lot. I was glad I was different from them. I mean, that there was *somebody* around that had a better standard of communal living and that that somebody happened to be me. But if I really believed in equality, why was I glad to be the exception? I ought to feel sad and in fact I did – both at the same time.

I guessed I had finally found what was making me so furtive about my one-man sanitation drive – it was undemocratic. I actually began to worry that the guy or girl who came after me, finding the toilet practically sparkling and a fresh breeze blowing in, would resent the implied criticism of the prevailing mores. On the other hand, I hoped I was starting a trend. Like you, Ma. You're always hoping people will copy you, giving them little object-lessons. You think you're not but you are. Along this line, I went to the Prisunic and bought a can of spray deodorizer; at that point I was staying in a hotel where the facilities had no window. I left it beside the toilet, and somebody stole it. What for?

In reality some of the other denizens did get irritated with me. Because I took so long. They would bang on the door or rattle the knob. But flushing and then waiting for the tank to refill and then flushing again takes a little while; with those old toilets, you can't hurry it. Not to mention the actual cleaning and airing. Then I would weigh the need of the person outside against my own desire to do the job right. Some days there would be layers of faeces, like geological deposits – the bottom one hard and dry and scaly and practically impossible to scrape off without Babo or Dutch Cleanser, which naturally were not supplied. If I was feeling energetic and nobody was waiting to get in, I would clean the brush too, to the best of my ability.

Do you think I could be slightly deranged? It was as if all those rituals were a sort of apology on my part to the rest of the world. An apology for being what I am, the kind of young pharisee whose mother has taught him to clean the toilet. As though I was willing to *slave* for my values to excuse myself for holding them. Yes. It occurs to me that I must have got this from you. Which is why I feel I can harangue you on this malodorous theme.

But maybe it was not such a bad thing, finally, my initiation. Like the bishop washing the feet of twelve selected paupers from the Old Men's Home – do you remember, we saw that in a little town outside Rome at Easter four years ago? A lesson in humility. Only that was rather a token performance; the old men's feet, we noticed, were clean to start with. The trouble with me is that I check my helpful impulses – giving up my seat in the Métro, for instance – when I notice that nobody else does it. My greatest weakness is the fear of appearing ridiculous. Or is that just because I am young? If I saw an old man painstakingly cleaning the toilet, I would respect him for it. Maybe my bug about equality is just the shame of being different. I will have to think about that.

Dear Ma, I am getting sleepy. Forgive this gloomy epistle. I've omitted the things I like in Paris. Above all, the sky. It's always in motion, with clouds racing across it, which is exhilarating, a real Olympian combat. You hardly ever see that at home. Or in Italy. When I'm depressed, I climb up to the Pantheon and look at the sky.

How is the *babbo*, by the way? Have you heard from him? He keeps writing me with anxious offers of advice and help. Telling me to look up people he used to know twenty years ago. As if I could. One of his suggestions was that I should call Malraux. To get him to talk to my professors. And he sends me the names of cheap restaurants that no longer exist. One thing, according to him, that I must be sure to do while I am here is have an affair with a Frenchwoman . . .

Much love to Bob. Are there any art books he would like me to get him? How is the campaign going? Dag and I are going to watch the election on TV at a café. I think the French would secretly like Goldwater to get in – to prove that America is the way they imagine it.

Love to you, Mother, from your errant son,

Pierrot le Fou

Greek Fire

PETER was taking his plant for a walk. This morning the sun was out, for a change, and he was cutting his class. He carried it, swaying, in its pot down the flight of steps, his private companionway, that led from the rue Monsieur-le-Prince to the rue Antoine-Dubois – a mew populated by cats where Brigitte Bardot had lived in *La Verité*. He was a past master of short cuts as well as circuitous ways; though he had not yet travelled by sewer, he liked to pretend that some implacable Javert was trailing him. He came out onto the boulevard St Germain, greeted the statue of Danton, and stopped to look in the windows of the bookshops selling medical textbooks, coloured anatomical charts, and dangling cardboard skeletons.

This uninviting merchandise exercised a gruesome attraction on Peter, who, if he could believe his family, was a known hypochondriac. The quarter where he had elected to live was dominated by the dark carcass of the old Ecole de Médicine, around which, like suckers, had sprung up a commerce in surgical equipment, wheel chairs, orthopaedic pulleys, sputum basins, artificial limbs, as well as these bookstores containing yellowing treatises on every disease he could imagine himself catching, including *le grand mal*. The main School of Medicine had moved to a modern building on the rue Jacob, which was why he seldom saw students around here – only an occasional browser leafing through dusty textbooks; it was as if his whole neighbourhood had been put up in formaldehyde, like gallstones or those crusty corns and giant bunions he sometimes studied in the half-curtained window of a corn-cutter over near the Carrefour Bac.

At the traffic light, he decided to turn up the rue de Tour-non, his favourite street, and walk on the sunny side; there were too many hurrying pedestrians on the boulevard St Germain, making it hard for him to clear a path for the tall plant with its crowning glory of pale new leaves unfurling like little umbrellas. It was a member of the ivy family, as you could tell from its name – Fatshedera – although, unlike the English clan, it did not creep or clamber but stood up-right. He had bought it at Les Halles on a Friday afternoon; at five o'clock the public was let into the weekly potted-plant market, after the florists had made their selections. It pleased him that in Paris there was a 'day' for every kind of thing, as in the first chapter of Genesis: Friday at Les Halles for potted plants and Tuesday for cut flowers, Sunday morning, on the quai aux Fleurs, for birds; there was even a dog market somewhere on Wednesdays. The Parisian apportionment of the week made him think of Italy, where articles of consump-tion were grouped, amusingly, into families resembling riddles, as, for example, the family that included salt, matches, stamps, and tobacco (bought from the *tabaccaio*) or the chicken family that included eggs, rabbits, and mushrooms; his father liked to remember a store in Rome that carried pork in the winter and straw hats in the summer.

The plant-seller had warned Peter that the Fatshedera did not like too much light – which should have made it an ideal tenant for his apartment. But after a month's residence there, looking out on the air shaft, it had grown long, leggy, and despondent, like its master. Its growth was all tending up-ward, to the crown, like that of trees in the jungle. The leaves at the base were falling off, one by one, and though he had been carefully irritating the stem at the base to promote new sideward growth, it had been ignoring this prodding on his part and just kept getting taller, weed-like, till he had finally had this idea of taking it for walks, once or twice a week, depending on the weather. It did not seem to mind draughts, and the outdoor temperature on a sunny day in late November was not appreciably colder than the indoor

temperature *chez* him. He thought he was beginning to note
signs of gratitude in the invalid for the trouble he was
taking; a little bump near the base where he had been poking
it with his knife seemed about to produce a stalk or pedicel,
and there was a detectable return of chlorophyll, like a green
flush to the cheeks of the shut-ins. He spoke to it persuasively
– sometimes out loud – urging it to grow. So far, he had
resisted giving it a shot of fertilizer, because a mildewed
American manual he had acquired on the *quais* – *How to
Care for Your House Plants* – cautioned against giving fertilizer except to 'healthy subjects'. That would be like giving a
gourmet dinner to a starving person – the old parable of the
talents.

How to Care for Your House Plants was full of housewifely
pointers that appealed to his frugality, like the column he
used to enjoy in the Rocky Port weekly *Sentinel* where readers
exchanged recipes for removing berry stains from clothing
and keeping squirrels out of the bird-feeding tray. He wondered what dull adventures it had had before coming to lodge
on his bookshelf: had it travelled from Montclair to Stuttgart
to Châteauroux in the trunk of some Army wife, along with
The Joy of Cooking, 'Getting the Most out of Your Waring
Blendor', 'How to Use Your Singer', and instructions, with
diagram, for carving the Thanksgiving turkey? Obedient to
its recommendations, he had started some dish-gardens in
his Stygian lair from dried lentils, slices of carrots, and
grapefruit pips, setting them out in saucers under his student
lamp, equipped with a seventy-five-watt bulb – his landlady
had confiscated the 150-watt-bulb he had put in originally.
Every day he moved the positions of the saucers, so that
they would share the light equally, determined not to show
partiality in the vegetable kingdom, though already he preferred the lacy carrot. These dish-gardens reminded him of
the primary grades; the avocado and grapefruit plants on the
broad window-sill the class used to water, the acorns he used
to hoard, and the interesting fear (which his mother had
finally scouted) that a cherry stone he had swallowed would
turn into a tree branching out of his mouth.

All children, he guessed, were natural misers and sorcerers; the progeny of his new friends, the Bonfantes, were impressed and delighted by his dish-gardens when he invited them to tea in his apartment. He promised to start them some in their kitchen window from bits of carrots and the eyes of potatoes, and he entrusted them with a sprouting garlic clove, with instructions to keep it in their clothes-closet and gradually bring it out to the light; in the spring, it would have little white bell-like flowers – he did not see why garlic, though not specifically mentioned in *How to Care etc.*, should not act like any other bulb. They wanted to know whether this was American, like the jack-o'-lantern he had made them at Hallowe'en, and Peter said it was. He was the first live American boy Irène and Gianni had ever seen, and they asked him many questions, such as: was it true that Americans ate with their feet on the table? Their conception of America was a blend of Wild West and asphalt jungle, and they listened with doubtful wonder to the stories Peter told of white wooden houses, ponds, waterfalls, skating, clamming, ice-cream freezers, blueberries, corn-on-the-cob – one of his mother's rules for telling stories to children, which she had learned as a child from her father, was always to put in something good to eat.

If he was going to keep up his strength, he felt he had to keep in close touch with his other mother, Nature, while abroad, and, overcoming his shyness, he had asked the young woman at the Embassy in charge of student exchanges whether there was anything like a bird-watching group in Paris. To his surprise, when he returned she had the answer typed out on a sheet of paper: he could join a group called *Les jeunes ornithologistes de France*, which met alternate Sundays for field trips during the fall and winter at a Métro or railroad station. Last Sunday at 10 AM, Peter had been on hand with his field glasses and the *Guide des oiseaux de l'Europe* at the meeting-place – a Métro station near the park of les Buttes-Chaumont, which was a part of Paris strange to him, beyond the Gare du Nord. He waited, studying the subway riders as they mounted the stone steps, and trying to decide, from their markings and plumage, whether they could be young ornithologists. He was on the verge of speaking to a youth in a red hunter's cap who was hanging about the entrance too until he bethought himself of flashing the bird book, spy-wise, as a signal – no reaction. When the group finally appeared, of course they were unmistakable because of their field glasses and hiking boots. Peter was disappointed that there were only five, all males, and all but one quite old; he had been hoping for a Papagena among them, but few girls, even at home, cared about watching birds.

Nevertheless, he had enjoyed the morning, in the grey northern light of the park, which consisted mainly of steep bare rocks, the buttes it was named for, and was traversed by a cindery railroad track. Not a good place to see birds, he would have thought, except sparrows. It was a sparse, scrubby working-class park without amenities – only a little artificial lake, drained for the winter, and a non-functioning artificial waterfall. Yet he had ten new birds listed in his notebook when he boarded the Métro home – one uncommon. It was his first experience of going on a bird walk with a group, and he recognized that, compared with these briskly striding, sharp-eyed Frenchmen, he was no ornithologist. He was always the last to descry a feathered friend, even an easy one like the *rouge-gorge*, the American robin's plump red-breasted little cousin. He kept losing his place in the bird book while trying to correlate the picture with the description; when he actually identified a bird – a tit, for instance – he could not find it in the index, where it was listed, naturally, under *Mésanges*. If he got his field glasses focused on a *pic-épeiche*, or woodpecker, in flight, the group would be closing in on an *accenteur mouchet*, or hedge sparrow, lurking in a thicket. All this bore out the *babbo*'s theory that Peter did not have the makings of a real naturalist – he only liked Nature, which was not the same thing.

He tried to follow the *ornithologistes*' talk. Today's expedition, he gleaned, was not to look at birds for fun, the way *he* conceived it, but to verify a scientific suspicion. They were agreeing that a park like les Buttes-Chaumont, on the edge of industrial Paris, had turned into a first-rate bird station. Migrating birds were stopping off more and more in the city as the city spread; they were seeing certain birds this morning that had not been sighted in Paris in fifty years. The idea gave Peter a ray of hope: one of the side-benefits of megalopolis would be that if you lived long enough you could see flocks of evening grosbeaks in the Christmas tree at Rockefeller Centre. Every cloud had a silver lining. As the old haunts of birds were transformed into sinister housing developments, linked by murderous highways, the city would become an aviary.

At noon, the bird men had gone home to their Sunday dinners, and with them – a strange fact – the interesting birds vanished too, which seemed to show that Nature, like any performer, was dependent on her audience. Huddled in his sheepskin-lined jacket, Peter sat on a bench, eating a sandwich he had made – a cynosure for common sparrows. With his Swiss pocket-knife he providently cut some moss to take back to the Bonfante children as a nest for their sprouting garlic clove; he had been worried about finding them some suitable organic material that would hold moisture without becoming waterlogged. On the whole, he felt content. In his wallet was a receipt for a year's dues – ten francs – that he had forked out at his own insistence to the group's bald-headed leader, which would entitle him to receive regular notices of field trips and slide lectures. Because it was already late November, they had not wanted to accept Peter's money. He could be their guest, they said, for the last two field trips of the year; Sunday after next, they were meeting at the Gare Montparnasse, to go to Trappes and study some waterfowl on the ponds. He could join, if he was still interested, in January, after the holidays. But Peter had persisted.

After they had gone, he took out the receipt and looked at it. It was dated January, 1965 – next year. So he had been their guest after all. The rush of warmth to his heart made him realize that this was about the first time he had had occasion to feel grateful to a French person. In fact, the *ornithologistes* seemed to belong to a different race from the

French he had been running up against on his daily beat. They had been helping him out all morning, silently indicating birds to him, finding him the right page in his book, supplying the English name of a bird when they knew it, pausing for him to catch up if he fell behind – Peter on his solitary bird walks had been in the habit of stationing himself in ambush and waiting, whereas these men strode ahead purposefully, as though on a military patrol. They acted as a unit, rapidly collating their data; there was no disagreement as to what they saw – as though no possibility of confusion could exist – and nobody tried to see *more* birds quicker than the next man, which had been Peter's tendency when in company with the fair Rosamund, who, he feared, had sometimes let him see birds ahead of her, thus admitting a competition between them.

Munching a Golden apple, he had a glimpse of a great International of peaceful naturalists, to whom technological change was only interesting insofar as it affected the habits of another species. Being a Sunday ornithologist could put you at one with the universe, since whatever happened was bound to produce data, and *any* data were bound, by definition, to be interesting to a specialist. The sight of all those 'winter visitors' from the finch and thrush families here in Paris had greatly excited the old *ornithologistes*, as well as the young kid with them, but seeing crows or nothing would have excited them too. If science were still a matter of observing and classifying ancient orders of beings – some of them, like the woodpeckers, already observed by Aristotle – he would like science, Peter thought. Maybe he might have 'found himself' if he had been born in old Linnaeus' time; everything seemed bent on demonstrating that he had come into the world too late. He remembered Hans telling some inoffensive botanist at the Thanksgiving feast that the descriptive sciences belonged to the age of the curio cabinet: taxonomy, useful in its day, had no place in the curriculum of a modern university, where biology and genetics were acting *on* Nature, like modern physics and chemistry, disturbing its inmost processes, forcing it to answer questions, smashing its resistance. Suiting the action to the word, Hans had banged thunderously on the dinner table, upsetting the gravy and spilling several glasses of Napa Valley wine.

Peter, aged circa thirteen, had not wholly followed the dispute; he had thought taxonomy was taxidermy and supposed that Hans was inveighing against cabinets of stuffed birds and animals. But he had understood his stepfather's general drift and felt a quivering sympathy for mute, innocent matter, pummelled and interrogated by Hans and his fellow-scientists, whom he pictured as a sort of Gestapo. His resentment of physics had immediately embraced biology, not to mention genetics and every 'improved' seed strain developed by an Iowa hybridist from some monstrous mutant. He wondered what the plant world had looked like before all this unnatural marrying and crossing had begun – doubtless better, though his mother possibly had a point when she said that experiment ought to have halted with the invention of the hybrid tearose; up to then, she approved. She was always trying to draw the line, her personal high-water mark, across the history of achievement and avoid being a total reactionary: in the home, she said, a good place to stop would have been with the flush toilet and the vacuum cleaner. In front of Peter, she did not add Tampax, but he had heard her say it to her sister.

Ornithology, he now concluded, must be one of the few descriptive sciences extant. You simply watched birds and did not try to change them biologically. At least he had never heard of anybody crossing a nightingale with a parrot. Birds in nature were left to themselves, apart from human interference. The most you might do was band them or coax them to show themselves, with birdhouses and trick devices like the humming-bird feeder. He had had one in Berkeley and he now asked himself whether even that decoy had not trespassed a limit; feeding a humming-bird from a tube containing two parts water and one part sugar was possibly habit-forming. What he liked about birds and animals, moths and stars, was precisely their remoteness from himself, their independence and solitariness. He loathed the satellite hanging like a suspended baseball in the night-time sky – *il pallone americano*, the Italians in Perugia used to call it, when he was at the school for *Stranieri*. The satellite was a foreigner too, butting in on the celestial landscape. Furthermore, it had a boring orbit, like American tourists abroad, while the real stars and planets turned and wheeled in the patterns men had named after gods, animals, and utensils.

Plants were different. People had been 'cultivating' them, like acquaintances, from earliest times, feeding them and caring for them in gardens, so that they had become attached to the human family, as though they were pets or livestock. His present stepfather had copied out a sentence for his mother last summer from a book he had been reading in Siena on Byzantine aesthetics: 'Mortal man was put into the world to be the husbandman of immortal plants.' That summed up the relation quite well, Peter reflected this morning, as he gave his dependent plant its airing: he had been allotted the duty of caring for the Fatshedera, which, barring accidents, should outlive him – so far as he knew, only annuals and biennials in the plant world died a 'natural' death.

His mother might say he had no business to try to keep a plant in his apartment. Certainly the Fatshedera would have been happier in nature, wherever it basically came from – the Far East, he supposed. But he could not set it free, for it would die if he abandoned it. He was responsible for it, though no Plant Welfare League would intervene if he were to neglect it. Besides, it was making a minuscule contribution to the air of Paris. He had read an article in the *Figaro* on air pollution (some doctor had taken a rat from the laboratory and exposed it on the roof of the Opera House; it was dead in twenty-five minutes), which said that Parisians could help by growing plants on their balconies and window ledges; by inhaling carbon dioxide and exhaling oxygen, they acted as air cleansers. Whenever Peter took his tall Fatshedera walking, he felt there was an exchange of benefits; in return for the light it received, it purified the atmosphere like a filter. He did not mind the centaurish figure he cut – half-man, half-vegetable – as he strolled along, the plant overtopping his head; often when he performed an *action*, he noticed, he lost his fear of visibility; it was as though he disappeared into the gest.

He examined a printer's window on the rue de Tournon. Printing, as a trade, attracted him; bookbinding too – there was a bookbinder he liked to watch working on the rue de Condé. He had been thinking a lot lately about what he would do with himself when he was through with college and the Army. He was sure he did not want to become an academic, though that was where his language major was leading him – straight into teaching, unless he took the State Department exams for the foreign service. He would have liked to have been a consul in Persia a hundred years ago, studying the native flora and fauna and Oriental religions and writing long reports home on the shah's court intrigues, but he could not see himself in a modern office building issuing visas, promoting us foreign policy and the interests of Standard Oil, and rotating back in two years to Washington for reassignment – in the old days you were consul for twenty years or for life. His ideal career choice would be an occupation that kept him outdoors, like archaeologist or forester or explorer, yet everything in his background was pushing him to be some sort of scribe, if not a pharisee. His father said these were daydreams and not vocational drives: if Peter were serious about wanting to spend his life in the open air, he would have enrolled in a School of Forestry or worked as a logger one summer or dug up Etruscan remains . . . The *babbo*, Peter had to admit, was a shrewder prophet than his mother, who fondly saw him in a tropical helmet or excavating the skeleton of some Mycenaean warrior when she did not see him arguing before the Supreme Court.

His vocational aptitudes were an old bone of contention between his parents. To his mother, every schoolboy 'interest' – especially when she did not share it – was proof of a wonderful talent to be fostered: for ornithology, ichthyology, entomology, astronomy; she let him bring home a series of chameleons from the circus to roam about the premises, in case he might be gifted for herpetology. To his father, who disliked meeting eels, escapees from Peter's leaky aquarium, on his way downstairs to breakfast, all these hobbies were only an excuse for squandering money; he had vetoed the idea of an aviary, to be constructed in his back-yard on the Cape as a summer project for Peter – if the boy cared about ornithology, he pointed out, he would have been dissecting the dead birds he found during school vacations, instead of giving them funerals.

In Paris, Peter had been dreaming of becoming a binder or a printer, though these trades not only kept you indoors but were probably worse for your health than teaching in a class-room, where at least you were on your feet all day in front of a blackboard. He would have enjoyed operating a clandestine press in the *maquis* and showering the country with broad-sides and leaflets, but there was no Resistance any more except in uncongenial places like the Vietnamese mangrove swamps, and in the US you could not become a printer unless you had an uncle or a father who belonged to the printers' union.

He turned right into the rue de Vaugirard, passed the Senate, and decided against going into the Luxembourg Garden today. Instead, he headed towards the rue de Rennes, where there was a café frequented by some Swedish girls who went to the Alliance Française. As he approached, he heard strange noises – the sound of rhythmic chanting, mixed with honking – coming from the rue de Rennes. He hurried on. At the corner he saw what he took at first to be a parade and he wondered whether today could be a national holiday that he had failed to hear about. All along the wide street, householders were lined up on their balconies, some with brooms and dusters, watching a procession of young people marching abreast and chanting; they were carrying broad streamers and placards with slogans written on them that he could not make out. The traffic on the street had stopped; buses and cars were blowing their horns. Simul-taneously with Peter's arrival, a police car appeared at the intersection, and some gendarmes descended in a body, wearing dark-blue capes that swirled as they moved, giving the scene a festive look. Peter realized that he was witnessing a demonstration, such as he had read about in history.

More gendarmes were running up the rue de Rennes, rounding the corner by the municipal pawnshop and blowing their whistles. Ahead of them came a second wave of marchers, shouting and singing. Moving to the kerb, Peter made out what was written on one of the billowing streamers. He felt slightly let down. It was only a student demonstration for better housing at the Cité Universitaire. The police were trying to break it up. He could hear them growling at the demonstrators, who laughed and jeered back. Behind Peter, in the glass-enclosed terrace of the corner café, people were standing on chairs to get a better view. At the far end of the street, near the Montparnasse station, he could see still more police, alighting from a Black Maria, and he grasped the strategy: they were trying to hem the students in.

The crowd on the sidewalk was augmenting; those behind were beginning to shove. A very tall blond boy in a turtle-necked sweater and tight grey thin jacket edged in next to him on the kerb; Peter was starting to be concerned for the safety of his plant. '*C'est beau, hein?*' said the boy, surveying the spectacle. The police had moved in on the marchers, in salients, swinging their capes. Mentally, Peter compared this airy ballet to the behaviour of the police at home, hitting out with nightsticks; for the first time, he approved thoroughly of the French. They had made an art of it, he decided, as he watched a line of students break and scatter as the graceful capes descended. In these fall manoeuvres between youth and authority, the forces were evenly matched, the students having the advantage of numbers and the police, like matadors, that of dexterity. If he had had two free hands, he would have applauded. He slightly lowered his plant, so as not to obstruct the view for those in his rear.

As he did so he heard a discordant sound of disapproval or derision, like the American raspberry; a policeman on the pavement whirled around and stared at Peter and his neighbour, whose face wore a sleepy, ironical smile, like that of a large pale cat. In a moment, the sound was repeated, and again the policeman whirled; the tall boy's drooping eyelid winked enigmatically at Peter – he was a strange-looking person, with high cheekbones, a snub nose, and colourless beetling eyebrows that seemed to express perplexity. Peter, who liked to play the game of guessing nationalities, decided that he could not be French. A Russian, maybe, whose father worked at the Soviet Embassy? Then the boy spoke, in a slow, plaintive voice. 'Jan Makowski. University of Chicago, Student of Oriental languages. Pleased to meet you.' He had a strong demotic Middle Western accent. Peter introduced himself. 'I thought you were Russian,' he said. Makowski stuck out his lower lip, as though considering the accusation. 'I'm of Polish origin,' he said stiffly. 'Born in Warsaw. My old man "chose freedom" when I was a kid. I went to grammar school for a while here, but he couldn't make it in France; we just about starved. Now he teaches political science at Chicago. Full professor.' 'Same here!' cried Peter. 'I mean my father's a professor and he used to be a refugee.' Makowski did not appear to find this an especially striking coincidence. 'This is great, isn't it?' Peter continued, looking around him. 'Compared to those Cossacks back home, I mean. This is more like a game. Everybody here is having a ball.'

'You think so?' Peter followed the other's frowning, derisory gaze. The line of students, with the streamers had reformed. The *flics* charged them, striking right and left with their capes. A line of blood appeared on the cheek of one of the students; a second student fell to the ground. Peter could see no sign of a weapon and he looked at his neighbour, who stood with folded arms, for enlightenment. The police struck again. Then Peter understood. There was lead in those pretty blue capes; he had read about that somewhere, he now recalled, disgusted at his own simplicity. The students were counter-attacking, ducking the flailing capes. He could distinguish three principal battlepoints in the confusion. Makowski nudged him. They watched a boy aim a kick at a cop's balls; the cop caught his foot and swung him around by the leg, then let him drop. There was blood on the street.

Behind Peter a woman was calling shame on the police. A flower-pot came hurtling down from a high balcony – possibly by accident. Two policemen rushed into the building. Peter's hand tightened on his own clay pot; he selected a target – a tall red-haired gendarme who would make an easy mark. Then wiser counsel – if that was what it was – prevailed; his grip relaxed, and he started to get the shakes. His hands were sweaty. He might have killed a man a few seconds ago – the cop or even a student. 'Peter Levi, Murderer.' The thought was strange to him and not unimpressive, though scary. He glanced curiously at Makowski, judicious, with curled lower lip, by his side, a mere scowling spectator. Nobody but Peter himself seemed to be particularly *involved* with what was going on. Clerks in their bright blue *blouses de travail* had left their counters and lined up on the sidewalk to watch; concierges, with their mutts, were standing in their doorways; shopkeepers, concerned for their property, were pulling down their iron blinds.

The students broke and began to run, pursued by the police. A youth was passed, headlong, from cop to cop, and deposited in a Black Maria that had pulled up on the corner, just beyond a flower-cart, at the Métro entrance. The police were working fast. '*Nazi!*' yelled someone behind Peter at a *flic* who was tripping a student. Two *flics* pushed past Peter and seized the offender, a young kid of about sixteen. When he resisted, they slugged him. '*Nazi!*' '*Nazi!*' Peter turned his head but he could not locate where the voice or voices in a funny falsetto were coming from. People were looking in his direction; he asked himself whether his plant could be acting as an aerial. Then he noticed that Makowski was slightly moving his lips. A ventriloquist! He wondered whether the Pole was crazy, playing a trick like that in a crowd, where he could get innocent bystanders arrested. 'Cut it out,' he muttered.

Now the demonstrators were darting through the throng, wherever they could find an opening, dropping their streamers and placards as they fled into the side streets, into the Métro, into the Magasins Réunis up the block. And instead of just letting them go, the police were hunting them down, aided by embattled concierges and their shrilly barking dogs. They were piling everybody they could catch into the Black Marias. Hungry for prey, then began to grab foreign students coming out of the Alliance Française, youths coming up from the Métro and blinking with surprise in the sunlight. As far as Peter could tell, their idea was to arrest anything that moved in the area between the ages of sixteen and twenty-five. He supposed that he and Makowski owed their immunity to the fact that they were stationary.

What shocked him, as an American, was that the demonstrators, once captured, showed no signs of civic resentment. They did not go limp, like civil-rights workers, but hopped into the paddy-wagons without further protest; it was as if they had been tagged in a game of Prisoners' Base. In the paddy-wagon on the corner, the majority were laughing and clowning; two were playing cards; one, with a bloody kerchief tied around his head, was reading a book. Only the Nordic types from the Alliance Française were giving their captors an argument, which appeared to amuse the French kids, as though being a foreigner and falsely arrested was funny.

Detestation for all and sundry was making Peter nauseous. The Rights of Man were being violated, in the most elementary way, in broad daylight, before the eyes of literally hundreds of citizens, and nobody was raising a finger to help. At home, if this had happened around Columbia, say, there would be dozens of volunteer witnesses telling the cops to lay off, threatening to call up the mayor or their congressman or the Civil Liberties Union; at home, citizens were aware that there *was* such a thing as the Constitution. It came to Peter that he and Makowski, having watched the whole disgusting business from the sidelines, could *do* something about it. They could write a letter to the *Monde*, as *témoins oculaires*, and if the *Monde* would not publish it, they could take it to the *Herald Tribune*. Or they could go to court and testify in the students' defence, assuming there was a trial or some sort of hearing; he was ready to swear that the demonstration had been completely peaceful until the police had used violence to break it up and he could swear too that several of the kids now in custody had not been among the marchers – the police had just arbitrarily seized them and roughed them up when they resisted. His heart thumping with excitement, he carefully memorized the features of two of the most vicious cops, so as to be able to make a positive identification. At the same time, his shyness made him hesitant of approaching the group in the Black Maria, to promise his support, as though a wall of glass separated him on the sidewalk from them, a few feet away, as though he would be *intruding*. A weird kind of politeness was gluing him to the spot. He put the question to Makowski. 'Maybe we should give these guys our names and addresses.'

But Makowski did not agree. He thought it was a lot of shit that he and Peter had a duty to offer themselves as witnesses. 'Of course the *flics* are sadists. *C'est leur métier*. The French take that for granted. You can't squeal about "police brutality" in a court here. Everybody would think you were a fink.' His voice took on a note of whining, offended logic, as though Peter's proposal caused him physical pain. 'Besides, you're a "guest of France". Remember? You don't interfere in a family quarrel unless you want your head busted. These French kids would spit on us if we stuck our noses in. They know how the system works: if they behave themselves and keep their mouths shut, the cops will hold them a few hours and then let them go. It's *entendu* that they don't start yelling for a lawyer or claiming the cops have hurt them.' With foreign students, it was more serious; foreigners were forbidden to take part in political activity. 'Those dumb Swedes and Germans in the *panier à salade* don't dig it but they're about to be deported.' 'Deported?' Peter gulped. Of course, said Makowski; it happened all the time. The foreigners in the lettuce-basket were just unlucky. If you were a foreigner and got picked up in one of these *bagarres*, you were automatically thrown out of the country.

Peter was incredulous. 'Thrown out of the country?' he scoffed. 'Without a hearing or anything? But these guys from

the Alliance Française have an alibi. They can *prove* they
were in class when the march was going on. You're nuts!'
But Makowski only laughed. He indicated two blond be-
spectacled giants whose heavy boots and white wool socks
were protruding from the Black Maria. 'Twenty-four hours
to leave the country!' 'Just like that?' cried Peter, who was
starting to be convinced. A craven fear for his own tenure on
the rue Monsieur-le-Prince entered his bones; in his mind, he
slowly tore up the letter he had been writing to the *Monde* and
consigned it to the ash can of history. 'Just like that,' said
Makowski. 'They relieve you of your passport, and you get
it back at the airport. I tell you, it happens all the time. That's
why I kept my cool just now. It gives me kicks to bait the
police, but France has other things to offer me, and I want to
stay a while longer. You know?' Peter supposed he meant
women. Feebly, he continued to argue, unwilling to submit
to the dictatorship of Makowski's view of things, which,
Peter clearly saw, would deprive him of his freedom of action.
If you want to be your own master, his father used to say,
always be surprised by evil; never anticipate it. Then he
thought of his Norwegian friend, Dag. 'I couldn't figure out
what had become of him. We had a date to watch the election on TV, and he never turned up. His landlady claimed
he'd gone back to Norway. Finally I heard a rumour he'd
been deported. He was great on attending rallies at the
Mutualité. I guess that's what got him. Poor guy.'

Makowski was unsympathetic. He knew Dag's type – a
law-abiding Scandinavian. They made the big mistake of
always carrying their passport and their *carte de séjour*. In-
voluntarily, Peter's hand flew to his jacket pocket to make
sure his were still there. 'Mistake?' 'That only makes it
easier for the police to deport you,' Makowski pointed out.
He had a whole theory based on his discovery that the French
were a lazy people. 'If a *flic* asks me for my passport and I
hand it over, I simplify his job. He passes it on to his boss,
and they rubber-stamp me out of the country like a piece of
second-class mail. But if I tell them my passport's at home,
they have to figure out what to do next. Send me to get it

and trust me to come back? They're not that dumb. Or send an *agent* with me to where I live, which is probably six flights up in some crummy *mansarde*? Nine times out of ten, they'll weigh the headaches involved against the relative ease of just letting me go, with a warning to watch it in the future.'

Peter listened with amazement to the wily Pole's exposition, which sounded irrefutable, like so many statements coming from the East. This was quite different stuff from what they told you at the Embassy, where they advised you to stay glued to your documents and to carry a card in your wallet saying 'I AM PETER LEVI. IN CASE OF ACCIDENT NOTI-FY . . .' etc. – a creepy self-advertisement that Peter up to now had been incapable of penning, even as an exercise in calligraphy. Yet he wondered how his companion, whose age he estimated at twenty, could know so much more than seasoned American officials. A tendency to boastfulness was becoming more and more evident in Makowski, as Peter, his foil, became meeker and meeker; it was an effect, he noticed, that he seemed to have on people. He was ashamed to think of the mole-like life he had been leading: since he had left his hotel, nobody ever asked *him* for his passport, except when he was cashing a traveller's cheque at American Express – something Makowski, he supposed, would not be caught dead doing. 'Number One, they're lazy,' his mentor continued. 'Number Two, they're interested only in their next meal. If you put those two facts together, you've got this country in the hollow of your hand.' He scowled at the distant clock on the Montparnasse station. 'Have you noticed – there are hardly any clocks in this town? They hate to give away the time, free.' Peter laughed. He had made the same observation himself. 'Ten past twelve,' said Makowski. 'The fun here is over. In five minutes, the *flics* will be knocking off for lunch, and Allee-Allee-Out's-in-Free.' Appearances bore him out. The Black Marias at either end of the block were still waiting, with open doors, and Peter could still hear an occasional far-off police whistle shrill all by itself like Roland's horn, but the householders on the rue de Rennes had retired from their balconies, shutting their French windows. On the street the traffic was running normally again, the curious crowds had dispersed, and noontime lines were forming at the bakeries. The two cops on the corner were stamping their feet and looking at their watches. Peter's own feet were cold. 'You want to have a beer in the café here?' he suggested.

But Makowski was late already for a date with a girl at the Flore. 'Why not join us? We can pick up another chick.' Peter was strongly tempted, but he had his plant to take home; he could almost feel it shivering in the autumn wind. Besides, in some crazy way, he felt he *owed* it to the group in the Black Maria not to leave the scene while they remained in duress, able to watch him depart. *Somebody* had to hang around, just as a matter of courtesy. 'Maybe later,' he said. 'If you're still there.'

Makowski loped off to the bus-stop. Too late, Peter realized that he had forgotten to ask him for his address, which meant, he guessed, that he was gone beyond recall. He was not sure how much he really liked the Pole, but obviously they had something in common as hyphenated Americans of an uncommon kind: *accidentals*, they would be called in the bird book. A ninety-five was coming. He watched Makowski get on, not waiting his turn, of course, but charging past a line of people that had been standing there patiently. Peter was spared the pain of grimly noting their reactions, for just then a small dark student came darting out of a building chased by a concierge with a broom. Peter recognized one of the leaders of the march. His pursuer, an aged Nemesis, was screaming for the police to apprehend him: he had been hiding in the service stairway, she panted, and he had done p.p. – '*Oui, il a fait pipi dans mon escalier de service!*' Immediately, a new throng materialized, laughing and passing the word along, as the boy dodged into a doorway. What floor, a joker demanded. '*Le sixieme, monsieur,*' she answered with dignity, resting on her broom and regaining her breath; the gendarmes advanced. '*Il n'était pas pressé,*' an old man in a tweed overcoat said, winking, to Peter. '*Il n'était pas pressé, hein?*' the old man repeated, to a workman in an overall.

More people came, pushing and shoving, and the criminal profited from the confusion to race out, zigzag adroitly between them, and spring with a bound on to the bus, which had started to move as the traffic light turned green; the ticket-taker, like a trained confederate, had quickly released the chain barring entrance to the platform. The boy ducked into the interior of the bus.

The police were slow in reacting; they stood as if mystified on the sidewalk, evidently not grasping where their quarry had got to. Then whistles blew. The cop on the next corner waved to the bus to halt. Peter ground his teeth. It was a tricky intersection, where three streets met – what the Romans called a *trivium* – an ill-omened juncture. And there were cops, all of a sudden, on every corner. From where he stood, he was unable to see exactly what happened next, but in a minute the forces of order were dragging the tall Pole to the lettuce-basket.

At first, Peter was simply stunned. It seemed plain to him that everyone except the stupid police must see that they had got the wrong boy. Yet no one moved to interfere. The concierge of the violated building stood nodding with satisfaction as Makowski was tossed into the paddy-wagon. A wild conjecture passed through Peter's head: could Makowski be doing a Sydney Carton? The Poles were alleged to be quixotic. In any case he decided to wait till the bus had crossed the boulevard Raspail, bearing the small demonstrator to safety. Then he counted twenty and approached a gendarme. To his surprise, he did not feel his customary worry about making mistakes in French; the words came out as though memorized ahead of time from a phrase book for the emergency, and in the back of his mind he recalled with interest the saying of Kant: the moral will operates in man with the force of a natural law.

'*Pardon, monsieur l'agent; je peux témoigner poir mon compatriote. Il n'a pris aucune part dans la manifestation. Il ne s'est pas caché dans l'immeuble de madame. Il était a coté de moi, tout le temps, sur la chaussée, en simple spectateur. Et il ne resemble en aucun détail au jeune homme que vous cherchiez.*'

The gendarme he was addressing had been joined by two others. Silence. They seemed to be waiting for Peter to continue. But he had stated the facts: Makowski had been standing next to him on the sidewalk during the entire demonstration; he did not bear the slightest resemblance to the suspect they were after. '*C'est tout,*' he added hoarsely. '*Croyez-moi.*' The kids in the Black Maria had slid forward to listen. Makowski was smiling strangely. Peter became aware that he had said 'pavement' when he meant 'sidewalk'. '*Je veux dire le trottoir.*' Without warning, he had started to tremble violently; he saw the Fatshedera quaking in his hand and realized that he was having an attack of stage fright. It was like the time he had played Jaques in school and had had to lean against a tree in the Forest of Arden and all the scenery shook. He had not grasped at first why the audience of boys and parents was laughing – '*Sembrava un bosco di pioppi tremoli,*' was his father's comment: 'A Forest of Aspens'. It came to him now that all these people were staring at him dumbstruck because he looked weird with his tall companion-plant; the cops probably thought he was a 'case'.

'*Demandez aux autres si vous ne me croyez pas,*' he cried, getting angry. '*Tout le monde ici peut confirmer que je dis la vérité!*' He was not the sole witness to the fact that Makowski had not budged from the kerb; there were the flower-seller on the corner and the newspaper-vendor in her tarpaulin shelter – courtesy *France-Soir* – and the butchers in their bloody aprons. They had all been standing there like stage extras or a speechless chorus, contributing local colour. '*Qu'il parle bien le français!*' a voice murmured behind him. Peter disregarded the flattery. He was going to insist that the cops take his testimony. '*Voici mon passeport et ma carte de séjour!*'

A shower of membership cards, guarantees, and certificates fell to the pavement as he searched wildly in his wallet for his *carte de séjour*, which to his chagrin was not in his passport; he hugged his plant awkwardly to his body to free a hand. Bystanders picked them up and restored them to him; a young lame girl offered to hold the Fatshedera:

'*Quelle belle plante!*' The senior gendarme, who seemed to be a sergeant, took the documents and slowly looked them over, frowning at the membership in the *Jeunes Ornithologistes de France*. '*Qu'est-ce que c'est que ça?*' He found the *carte de séjour* folded into the yellow health certificate. He studied it. Then he tapped all the documents into a neat pile and handed them back, together with Peter's passport. '*Bon. Merci, monsieur. Tout est en règle,*' he said. '*Allons-y!*' he shouted to the driver of the Black Maria. The motor started. Peter gasped. They were not going to release Makowski! Apparently he was supposed to count himself lucky that they were letting *him* go free. He gave an inarticulate howl of despair.

Behind him, someone coughed noisily. He heard a hoarse, deep female voice. '*Il a raison, messieurs. L'américain vous dit la vérité. L'autre n'y était pour rien. Qu'est que vous faîtes là? C'est une honte.*' It was *les Journaux* in her leather apron and thick sweaters. Peter had always bought *The Times* and *Tribune* from her when he lived in the hotel on the rue Littré; *ô juste ciel*, she recognized him! He felt a lump in his throat. He had *made* it; he was finally 'accepted' by old Marianne, *la France*. And now other 'popular' voices were joining in, muttering and grumbling, *les Fleurs*, a window-washer, an old lady with a cane. '*Soyez raisonnables! Qu'est-ce que cela vous fout? Après tout! Un peu de calme! Ce sont des enfants!*'

The police sergeant appeared to reflect. His subordinates were watching him. '*Vos papiers!*' he said to Makowski. And of course Makowski did not have any. '*Et alors?*' said the policeman sharply. That settled it. This was France, after all (the Embassy was right), and, regardless of any specific charge, not having your papers was prima-facie evidence that you were up to no good. The attitude of the bystanders confirmed this. '*Il n'a pas ses papiers. Zut!*' A collective shrug disposed of the Pole, whose broad face had assumed a plaintive, aggrieved, innocent expression, as though he could not dig what this fuss was all about. You would think he was some hayseed who had never heard of a travel document.

Peter himself experienced an appreciable drop in sympathy. What a clown!

The doors of the Black Maria were shutting on the heap of sprawling kids. Peter's conscience jabbed him. 'Makowski!' he yelled. 'Jan! Don't worry! I'll go tell the Embassy. Right away, I promise.' 'Stay out of this, Peter Pan!' the Pole's voice answered rudely, adding an obscenity that made Peter hope that these French did not understand English. He fell back a step, feeling his neck turn red. It came to him that, insanely, Makowski held him *responsible*. Doubtless he had counted on the *vérification d'identité* taking place later, in relative privacy, at the station-house or wherever, when the cops had had their lunch and were in a good humour. But now it was *public knowledge* that he had been picked up without any papers.

Peter declined to swallow Makowski's tales of mass deportations; that could not happen to American citizens, he felt sure. But in the face of those closed black doors, his confidence was eroding. The tumbril's engine started. He realized that he did not even know where they were taking Makowski now. The spectators on the corner would not commit themselves. '*Sais pas.*' '*Ah, non, monsieur, je ne saurais pas vous le dire.*' '*Peut-être à Beaujon?*' '*C'est pas mon affaire. Demandez aux gendarmes.*' But Peter – the old story, he guessed – felt a horrible diffidence about asking the *flics* outright. The window-washer came to his rescue. '*C'est pas la peine, mon gars. Ils ne le disent jamais. La police, vous savez . . .*'

The Black Maria's motor was still idling. Once it bore Makowski off, Peter might never be able to find him in the maze of French bureaucracy. With sudden resolution, he banged on the door. A policeman stuck his head out. Peter asked if he could accompany his friend, as a witness. '*C'est pas un taxi, monsieur,*' the policeman retorted, slamming the doors. In the interior, Peter could hear raucous laughter. '*Alors, arrêtez-moi!*' he shouted. '*Foutez-moi la paix,*' came the grumbling reply.

It was typical of the French that if you asked them to arrest you, they would not help you out. In his fury, he thought of a ruse. All he had to do was open his mouth and say '*Nazi!*' and every *flic* in the *quartier* would spring on him. He would not even have to say it very loud. He swallowed several times in preparation. At home, among his peer group, he could speak lightly of the cops as fascists, but now, to his astonishment, his vocal cords felt paralysed. As in a nightmare, his mouth opened and closed. No sound came out. Yet it was not from fear, as far as he could determine, but from a profound lack of inclination.

His father was always giving people the drill if they used the term *fascist* when, according to him, they should have used *conservative* or *repressive* or just *brutal*: if you kept throwing that term around, like the boy crying 'Wolf', as an expression of simple dislike, you would be unable to recognize real fascism when and if it came. Peter could not recall all the 'objective criteria' that the *babbo* said had to be present to justify a diagnosis of fascism but he felt certain the French police would not qualify.

Yet there was more to it than that – some squirming aversion in *him*, related maybe to delicacy. Actually, he was unable to imagine circumstances in which he would find it easy to call *anybody* a Nazi, including Hitler probably. If you called Hitler a Nazi, he would not mind, obviously, so what would be the use?

A *flic* in a blue cape had emerged from the corner café, where presumably he had been telephoning or answering a call of Nature. He barked out an order to the driver. Peter heard the clash of gears. It would be hopeless to chase after the police wagon. Even if it had to stop for the traffic light at the next corner, he would be incapable of keeping up for more than a block, hampered as he was by his plant. Then in the distance he sighted a taxi coming up the rue de Rennes. He dashed into the street to flag it down, foreseeing, as he waved, that the driver might decline to follow the *panier à salade*; they loved telling you No. Closing his eyes, he recited one of his magic formulas: 'Perseverance, dear my lord, keeps honour bright.' '*Attention!*' someone called.

The police wagon shot backward. Peter jumped out of the

way. His heel struck the kerb behind him; his ankle turned,
and his long bony foot got caught in an opening in the gutter.
He lost his balance, tried to right himself, throwing out his
arms. The Fatshedera was sliding from the crook of his elbow.
Endeavouring to catch it, he fell. As he did, a ringing, explosive sound reached his ears, seeming far away; it was the clay
pot shattering on the pavement. Somebody was helping him
up. They were asking if he was hurt. He stole a glance
around. Moist black dirt and reddish shards and slivers of the
pot were scattered all over the street and sidewalk; the plant
was lying in the gutter with its whitish root system exposed.
Les Fleurs carefully picked it up and wrapped it in a newspaper. '*Tenez, monsieur.*' She handed it to him. He thanked
her. She meant well, he assumed. But he had seen the crown
of pale new leaves lying a yard away, like a severed head, near
the Métro entrance. Some passer-by had already stepped on
it, leaving a green smear on the sidewalk.

The Black Maria, naturally, had made its getaway, after
putting him *hors de combat*. If Peter had not leapt aside,
would the hit-and-run driver at the wheel have jammed on
the brakes in time? According to Dag, a lot of 'traffic accidents' were really engineered by the Deuxième Bureau. If
the cops killed a person while giving him the third degree,
they just stretched the body out on the *autoroute* on Sunday
and called it a highway death. Shaking, Peter sat down on the
top step of the Métro entrance and buried his head in his
hands. His ankle hurt, and pulling down his sock, he found
blood where he had scraped it. Maybe he would get blood
poisoning and croak. He ought to find a pharmacy and buy
some Mercurochrome, but at this hour they would all be
closed probably. The butchers had taken in the meat, and the
fruit and vegetable merchants along the rue Notre-Dame-des-
Champs were covering their produce. *Les Journaux* was bend-
ing over him, wondering if he was all right. He got to his feet.
'*Votre plante,*' she reminded him. He picked it up. In his
mind, he mimicked his mother's consoling voice: 'Never
mind. We'll get another, Peter.' Aloud, he cried out 'No!'

While he was sitting there, nursing his ankle, a vile temptation had visited him, whose source was that artful Eve, his parent. There was an amusing plant he had read about in his manual, known as Dumb Cane, a member of the Dieffen-bachia species; the stem, when chewed, paralysed the tongue. If he were to whip over to Les Halles this afternoon and look for one . . .? Today, as it chanced, was Friday. He thrust the thought from him. He would have no more plants in his Stygian kingdom, no substitutes, successors, or duplicates, and as for the Fatshedera, he would not take it home for decent burial: he would junk old Fats here at the scene of its decapitation – good riddance. Yet a last trace of humanity remained, he was sorry to perceive, in his hardened heart. He could not perform the committal in plain view of *les Fleurs*, whose stubby chilblained hands had wrapped the grisly trunk in *France-Dimanche*: she would be sorry for her trouble. He would have to wait till he found another trash-basket.

Actually, he disposed of it on American soil, in a waste-basket at the Embassy, where he went to report Makowski's arrest to a bureaucrat in the consular section who could not have cared less. 'If you students take part in street demonstrations, there's nothing we can do to help you. It's strictly against regulations for American citizens to meddle in French politics.' 'He *wasn't* taking part in a demonstration,' Peter protested. 'You just wrote that down yourself in your notes. He was standing on the kerb, next to me.' The official frowned over his notes. 'Ah yes, so you said. I see it here. Well, all I can tell you is the next time you see a march or a demonstration, walk rapidly in the opposite direction. Don't linger there to gawp. For one thing, you may get hurt. A few years ago, during one of their protest rallies, some bystanders were crushed to death in a Métro entrance. Luckily there were no Americans among them.'

Silence followed. The man fiddled with some papers on his desk. 'You mean you won't do *anything*?' Peter said finally. 'Is that the Embassy's policy?' 'Consular policy,' the man corrected, 'is opposed to taking unnecessary action. Your friend's case isn't as unfamiliar to us as you appear to think.

Ordinarily the French police hold these people a few hours, to teach them a lesson, and then let them go.' 'Yeah,' said Peter. 'I've heard that too. But I've also heard that they deport foreign students they pick up, just like that, without a trial or investigation or anything. Actually, it happened to a friend of mine.' 'An American?' 'Well, no.' 'Just as I thought. It's rare,' he went on in a musing tone, 'that they deport an American unless he's been up to some mischief. Odd as it seems, they discriminate, if anything, in our favour. One of those little diplomatic mysteries. It may have something to do with the balance of payments. Every one of you students, you realize, who stays here getting money from home and spending it is hurting the dollar.'

From the wall, the photo of Lyndon B. Johnson looked at Peter with eyes of reproach. The official leaned across the desk. 'And are you sure that this Makowski is a naturalized citizen of the United States?' 'I'm not *sure*. I only met him this morning. But he talked like an American.' 'Didn't you see his passport?' 'That was the whole trouble! I *explained* to you. They were just going to let him go when it turned out he'd left his passport at home.' 'He didn't describe it specifically as an American passport?' Peter sighed. 'No. Why would he? Imagine anybody saying "I left my US passport at home this morning." I mean, that would imply you had several passports.'

'I'm not here to engage in semantics with you. And under the circumstances, I don't see how we can help you. We can't intervene without more information than you've been able to furnish. You have no idea of the number of inquiries we get about you students. Usually from parents, wanting us to find out why Bobby hasn't written. If we called the police and the hospitals about every Tom, Dick, and Harry, we'd have no time left for normal consular business.' He got up. 'Run along now. If your friend doesn't turn up in a day or two, come back and see me. That's the best I can offer.'

'Great!' said Peter bitterly. 'You haven't understood the point. I don't know his address. So how can I tell if he turns up or not?' 'You can find him at the Sorbonne, I suppose.'

'He's not at the Sorbonne. He's at the Institute of Oriental Languages. And tomorrow is *Saturday*. The Embassy will be closed. By Monday he might have been deported. They give you twenty-four hours to leave the country.'

His hoarse voice broke. Some secretaries looked up. In a minute, he supposed, they would call the Marine guard to remove him from the chair to which he remained glued, feeling too weak and dejected to dislodge himself. He remembered that he had not eaten since morning. Then the man reached in his pocket and spoke in a kindlier tone. 'I tell you what you do. Here's a *jeton*. There's a pay phone in the corridor, by the cashier's window. Call the Commissariat of the *arrondissement* where this *bagarre* took place and ask if they're holding your friend. The Commissariats are listed in the front matter of the telephone book. Then come back and tell me the result.'

'There won't be any result,' said Peter, getting reluctantly to his feet. 'You don't know the French, sir, the way a student does. It'll just be a waste of a *jeton*. Can you figure me trying to spell Makowski to some half-crocked police sergeant? "Marie Anatol Kléber Oscar Washington Suzanne Kléber Irma"?' He gave a hollow laugh. 'If *you'd* call, it would be different. They *listen* to somebody with authority.' 'On your way,' said the man. 'Right through those doors.'

It was just as Peter had prophesied. 'They hung up on me,' he reported back. 'I think they recognized my voice.' For the first time, the official cracked a smile. He chuckled. 'Oh, Jesus!' he said. Still overcome by merriment, he pointed to the chair, and Peter obediently sank down. He failed to get the joke, but it did not matter. He knew he had crossed the Rubicon. He watched the man pick up the telephone. '*Monsieur Dupuy, s'il vous plaît ... Bon, j'attends. ... Allo, Jacques? C'est nous encore. Pas mal. Et vous-même? Oui, c'est ça. Une petite bagarre. Comme d'habitude. Vous êtes au courant? Un certain Makowski, étudiant ...*'. He doodled on a pad. '*Ah, bon, bon, merci. A la prochaine fois, Jacques.*' Jan Makowski, naturalized US citizen, born in Poland, had been released at 3.50 PM after verification of his papers.

Peter guessed Makowski had scored after all. He left the Embassy in a good mood. In the end, the vice-consul (he had given Peter his card) had seemed glad that somebody had prodded him into being somewhat nicer than he customarily was. It was funny how people never remembered the well-known fact that virtue was its own reward but had to keep discovering it as a novelty. In the garden, he paused to pay homage to the seated statue of Ben Franklin in his wide bronze rumpled coat. He liked the patron saint of inventors sitting mildly amid the ornamental shrubbery. He looked home-made, like the funny Stars and Stripes still waving over the Embassy's portal. Some English ivy was climbing up his pedestal.

Peter took the lay of the land. Outside the gate, two gendarmes were walking up and down. In the driveway, a chauffeur sat at the wheel of a big black Embassy car. But nobody was paying attention to Peter in the gathering winter dusk. He advanced stealthily toward the statue, taking his time. With his trusty pocket knife, he cut some long shoots of ivy. When one of the gendarmes glanced his way, he had already stored the booty in his sheepskin-lined jacket; the heart-shaped leaves of the Fatshedera's creeping cousin were nestling in his bosom. *Hedera helix* rooted easily in water, and then you could plant it in earth. Satisfied by this act of vandalism committed on us property, he sped toward the Métro station. The idea that a new resident of his apartment had been acquired free of charge and at some slight personal risk compensated him for the passing of the old one. Life had to go on. Actually, in the place of one sickly specimen, he could have a whole lusty tribe, in pots, trained on strings to climb up his walls – and turn his room into a bower. Offering his second-class ticket to be punched by the ticket-taker, he felt like Prometheus, with a gift of green fire. The punishment, he expected, would come later, in the guise of a *crise de foie* induced by the unhealthy French diet.

Round Table, with the Damsel Parcenet

A haruspex peering into the entrails of the sacrificed traditional bird would have warned one Petrus Levi to
beware of divisive controversy on the feast of Thanksgiving.
Holidays, as he ought to know, were unlucky for him anyway.
Instead of obeying the summons to partake of turkey 'n'
trimmings with the other waifs assembled by the general's
wife, he would have done better to stay home with the door
bolted holding no communications. Holidays brought out
the worst in everybody; the Last Supper, terminating with
the Agony in the Garden, was par for the course. As they
handed over their coats to the Spanish maid in the vestibule
of the general's pad in Neuilly, the motley crew viewed each
other with a natural suspicion. Besides the male strays,
readily identifiable in their unwonted ties and sports jackets,
there were a functionary from the Embassy and his family
who had inescapably put the finger on Peter in the close
confinement of the elevator ('I guess we all want the fifth,
don't we?'), a tall fresh-faced girl with long American feet,
an Air Force wife minus a husband, and some middle-aged
French reactionaries, military, with their unattractive daughter, who were supposed to be getting a free glimpse of real
American hospitality. After the vast repast, preceded by
bourbon and laced with sparkling Vouvray, they all had to go
and play softball in the Bois.

There were fourteen at table, which led Peter to speculate
that one of their number had been recruited at the last
minute to take the jinx off. The general normally was a fairly
affable guy, with a white fat baby face, black eyebrows, and

a peculiar haircut, shaved on the sides and standing up on top
in short black bristles, which made him look like a convict.
He was attached to NATO, Peter gleaned today, and was an
expert on supply and procurement. His wife, named Letitia
(pronounced Leteetia by her husband), was small, Southern,
and friendly. 'Can I sweeten your drink, honey?' was her
usual soft refrain. None of the guests, it appeared, had met
each other before, and some were meeting the host for the
first time. His daughter led them up. 'Dad, this is Jay
Williams. Dad, this is Roberta Scott.' 'Good to know you,
Jay. Good to know you, Roberta. Glad to have you with us.'
Peter he greeted by his last name, which perhaps indicated
a promotion. 'How's it going, Levi? Have you sold that
motorbike yet?'

If this had been an All-American get-together, conversation might have found its natural level, albeit low. But during
the cocktail period, just as people were starting to relax,
daughter Jean, prodded by the Frenchwoman, initiated a tour
of the art in the apartment from which, like lifeboat drill,
nobody was excused. Freighted with drinks and cigarettes,
searching furtively for ashtrays or frankly using a trouser-cuff
or the wall-to-wall carpeting, the straggling troops inspected
Korean graphics and Puerto Rican oils, Japanese ivories,
Taiwan scrolls, Spanish fans, German beer steins, Italian
majolica, hanging on the walls or installed in cabinets with
interior lighting – the general, needless to say, had served in
all those places on the US defence perimeter and enjoyed a
perfect recollection of the circumstances of each purchase,
with emphasis, naturally, on the haggling.

Then, at table, his wife actually *explained* the principle of
Thanksgiving to the French. 'It isn't a social event with us,
you see. It isn't exactly a family event either, like Christmas,
which I always think should be for the children. It's the day
when we Americans – oh, help me, Chuck – as we thank
God for our blessings try to gather under our roof some of
our fellow-countrymen who might be lonely or homesick.
And all over the world, Americans are sitting down to the
same meal the Pilgrims ate: turkey and fixings, giblet gravy,

creamed onions, mashed turnips or rutabagas. .... Why, I'd
feel like a heretic if I served duck or Rock Cornish. Though I
was reading the menus in the *Herald Tribune* –' 'The stranger
at the gate,' interrupted the general. 'Yes, thank you, Chuck!
I was coming to that. We always make sure to have some
foreign guests with us. Last year, when we were back home
at the Academy, we had this lovely Japanese couple.' 'It's
just a harvest festival, isn't it?' Peter said, tired of feeling like
the Hundred Neediest Cases reduced to capsule form. As
far as he could see, what was happening was that Americans
were giving loud thanks for being Americans, and, as the
hostess said, this was going on all over the world concurrently
– allowing for the time difference; the orgy had not yet
started in New York.

To Peter, slightly drunk, the meal seemed like a grotesque
parody of his mother's annual bounty. The general's wife had
the same idea as his mother, only his mother was more refined about it. Identifying with the French couple – whom
he disliked on sight – he could not help seeing it as a gross
and stupid debauch. Yet 'Leteetia' was a perfectly nice
woman, according to her lights. She had made that awful
speech like a nervous recitation; maybe service wives abroad
got directives from the Pentagon on what to tell the natives
about Thanksgiving. The poor creature looked exhausted,
having no doubt spent the morning basting the turkey with
her bulb-baster. The rouge stood out on her inflamed cheeks.
The work she and daughter Jean, who seemed to have a good
relationship, had put into the food and the table setting, down
to the last nut-cup, was begging pathetically for notice. The
art that conceals art, Peter reflected glumly, was not an
American specialty. With his thumbnail, unobtrusively, he
peeled off the price-tag from his hand-crafted napkin.

As for 'Chuck', he was in a critical mood. He ordered the
carving knife back to the kitchen to be sharpened and dismissed the autumnal centrepiece, which was obstructing his
view, to the sideboard. Listening to the rasp of the combination can-opener and knife-sharpener in the pantry, Peter
surmised that they had had a family difference this morning.

Had the general been issuing the invitations, he suspected, there might have been fewer under-age deadheads on the list.

If you could ignore the commercials, the food was not too bad. Frankly Peter would not have guessed that the turkey was frozen, from the PX, if the hostess had not announced the fact with what he supposed was pride. In her place, he would have omitted the marshmallows from the candied sweet potatoes, but he approved of the hot Parker House rolls Jean had baked herself this morning, and the colonial stuffing spiked with brandy was O.K. The dinner plates, with the Air Force Academy coat-of-arms, were duly warmed in a sort of electric banket on a tea-wagon at the hostess's left. It was not her fault that, on this of all days, one of the waifs she had collected proved to be a vegetarian.

'Dark or light, Roberta?' queried the general, spearing a slice of breast on the point of his antlered knife. His daughter was holding out a plate destined for the tall girl on Peter's right. 'I won't take any, General Lammers.' It was as if an infernal machine, quietly ticking, had been planted in the room. The appalled general looked at his wife. He set down the carving-knife. *'No turkey?'* 'But honey, you didn't eat your shrimp cocktail either!' moaned Letitia. It was true, Peter realized: his neighbour had left a neat little pile of shrimps in her monogrammed glass goblet and eaten only the lettuce ribbons and the chili sauce. But the significance of it had escaped him. 'Is it Paris tummy, honey? We've got just what you need. Jeanie, dear, run and get the Vioform from my medicine cabinet.' 'She's a vegetarian, Mama,' said Jean. 'I forgot.' 'Oh, come *on*,' said the general. 'This is Thanksgiving!' His white hands, with black hairs on the knuckles, played impatiently with the carving implements. The girl held her ground. 'No, thank you. I won't. Really.' The rest of the company looked away. He essayed playfulness. 'I'm in command here. Mess Sergeant Jean, hold that plate where I can reach it.' 'She doesn't *want* any, Dad. Don't force her.' 'Pshaw!' He laid the slice of breast on the plate, which was already heaped with onions, mashed potatoes, sweet potatoes, and so on, placed there by his wife at the other end of the table. 'Take that to the young lady.'

Now everybody was watching her, some, like Peter, covertly. She had a long nose and short boyish-cut hair that rose in a crest over a 'noble' brow. Her eyes were grey, somewhat close together, and she had large appealing ears that reddened easily, as if people were talking about her, which might well be the case. She wore a grey dress made of wool, with a round white collar and a string of pearls, which had been appraised with care by the Frenchwoman, who had eyes like a customs inspector. Peter searched his memory for when or how he had met this dauntless girl before. Maybe in another incarnation. She looked like the title of a book the *babbo* was fond of recommending: *The Protestant Ethic*, but with pink cheeks and a shy grin. If he put a tricorn on her head, he could picture her as a revolutionary patriot dumping tea into Boston harbour. He felt sure he had seen her portrait, maybe in male attire, in the American Wing of the Metropolitan Museum or in some history text book.

'The stuffing, Chuck. Give Miss Scott some stuffing.' The girl opened her thin pink lips as if to protest, then bit the lower one and said nothing. Her plate was returned to the head of the table. The general spooned some stuffing onto it and, taking possession of the gravy boat, rapidly ladled giblet gravy onto her mashed potatoes. 'There!'

As her desecrated plate came back, she and Peter exchanged a dismal look. Catching the distress signal, he quickly passed her the cranberry jelly and looked around for olives and celery. 'Here, have some.' Angry with the general, he gulped down his Vouvray. Nobody would convince him that 'Chuck' was just insensitive, incapable of understanding that his own food habits might not be acceptable to the entire human race. Or that he was hurt by the girl's rejection of the sacred fowl, though that no doubt played a part. Unless Peter had gone stir-crazy in his solitary cell on the rue Monsieur-le-Prince, at the head of the table sat a vicious sadist wearing the jovial mask of hospitality. He had seized that gravy boat like a weapon in hand-to-hand combat. No wonder they had made him a brigadier general – at least that mystery was solved. Peter wished he had the strength to pass up the turkey himself, when his turn came, as an act of solidarity. But there were always others to consider; in this case, Letitia, who had been toiling harmlessly in the kitchen.

As an animal-lover, Peter, if he was consistent, should have been a vegetarian too. In Perugia he had been nauseated by those poor crumpled little birds the Italians loved to serve – the brain, believe it or not, was the choice morsel. On these occasions, Bob, ever the logician, had pointed out that those larks and thrushes, before being shot, had lived 'free as birds'; compare that to the existence of a battery chicken. This had not persuaded Peter to eat *uccelletti* but it had interfered with his enjoyment of broilers. Yet whenever he had feebly tried to interest himself in a naturist diet of fruit and raw vegetables, he had come up against his juvenile gluttony. He could live without steak and chicken, he had decided, but he doubted his present ability to forgo lobster and tuna fish. What he had not taken into account was the social pressures he would have to resist. He would need to be a hero, he now saw.

His other neighbour, a blue-eyed leathery lady with long ear-rings and grey hair cut in a fluffy bang, was waiting to engage him in conversation. During the first course she had been filling him in on the fact that her husband had left her for a German girl he had picked up hitchhiking on the *auto-route*. She now recaptured the thread. 'Letitia thinks I ought to go home to the States. But what the hell? I've gone to all the trouble to learn French, why *shouldn't* I stay here? He doesn't own Paris. He wants a divorce, but if I give him a divorce, they'll take away my PX card and my QC privileges. You can smile, Peter, but to me it's a tragedy. Twenty years as an Air Force dependent, and tomorrow, if I let him have his co-called freedom, the guards at the PX will tell me "Sorry ma'am, we can't let you by. That card has expired." Civilians don't dig what it means to us. Chuck and Letitia can entertain lavishly because, between you and me, they don't buy a thing on the French market. Not even a stick of celery.'

Ordinarily Peter would have felt sorry for this coarse-grained Donna Elvira. Maybe she loved the guy and was ashamed to mention that; it was odd what people were ashamed of, sometimes the best part of themselves, which they looked on as 'weakness', he guessed. But now though he kept an ear politely bent in her direction, his eyes slid to his right. Roberta Scott had not succumbed to the appetizing slice of breast in its casing of crisp brown skin. Instead, she was eating carefully around it: the onions, the rutabagas, the sweet potatoes, the Ocean Spray cranberry jelly. She avoided the mashed potatoes polluted with gravy and the stuffing contaminated by animal fat and juices during its stay in the oven. He followed the progress of her fork as it constructed fortifications against the giblet gravy, which ran between the banks of vegetables, lapped at the base of the tottering tower of jelly, divided into rivulets, and finally congealed. Peter was fascinated by these manoeuvres. It was like watching a game of jackstraws or a kid on the beach building a sand-castle as the tide was coming in. Others were stealing looks too. Only the general, content with his petty tactical victory, disregarded what was happening on her plate.

'Somebody ought to tell her parents!' interjected the grey-haired lady, tracing Peter's wandering interest to its source. 'Did you ever see anything *like* that? Look how thin she is.' Actually, in Peter's estimation, Miss Scott was in the pink of condition, compared to the fat sallow French girl in a two-tone taffeta blouse and to Jean, who today had a stye. She might be underweight, but her eyes were clear, and her breasts made two modest rounds under the thin wool of her dress. An image jumped into his mind of a healthy well-cared-for animal. Her long nose, made for sniffing and scenting, would be cool to the touch, and her hair invited stroking, like a shining pelt. She had gone to Bryn Mawr, he ascertained, and was working at the Institut Pasteur. She must be around twenty-three because after Bryn Mawr she had done a year of medical studies in Philadelphia, where her family lived. It was not hard to picture her as an interne, in a white coat, with a stethoscope.

Meanwhile the carnivores lifted forks that appeared to have grown heavy with their cargo of turkey and trimmings. They wiped grease from their mouths, quaffed wine, sought elusive food particles between their teeth with their tongues or a furtive fingernail; the older women's lipstick smeared. This Roberta did not seem to be wearing lipstick and she was not drinking her wine. That did not long escape detection. 'Don't you *drink* either, Miss Scott?' said the hostess, in a voice like the wringing of hands. 'I used to sometimes. But I don't really like it.' 'Not even *wine*? But you're in *France*.' 'I know.' 'A glass of milk then?' It turned out that she did not drink milk either. 'For Christ's sake, Leteetia,' said the general. 'Let's hear about something else.'

He got up and filled the glasses all around, but since Roberta Scott's was already full, indeed brimming, there was nothing he could do about it. He sat down heavily in his place and fixed his light-green eyes, like two probes, on the girl, searching out her secret. 'Roberta, Roberta,' he chided. It could not be denied that this fasting vestal was putting quite a crimp in the festivities. '*Vous êtes un trouble-fête, mademoiselle,*' the Frenchwoman said with a thin pretence of pleasantry. 'What is that in English?' 'A wet blanket. I know it,' Roberta said seriously. 'I'm really sorry, Mrs Lammers.' 'Don't give it a second thought, sugar. Just enjoy yourself in your own way. If *you're* happy, *we're* happy.' That of course was a lie. They would not be happy unless she conformed to their definition of enjoyment, which meant that she would have to be miserable to satisfy them.

Yet if she were old and decrepit or dying of stomach cancer or just unattractive, they would leave her in peace. The fact that she was cheerful and appealing, though not everybody's pin-up, was what threw them into disarray. Peter did not except himself. One part of him – he hoped a small fraction – had been backing the general in that contest of wills. He admired her force of character, but why *come* to Thanksgiving dinner if you were determined not to eat like the rest of the tribe? She could make an exception, just once, to be polite. On the other hand, if she started breaking her rule to please other people, she might as well give up being a vegetarian, he supposed. She had a right to eat and drink whatever she wanted. The trouble was, when she started exercising that right in public, she infringed on the right of the rest of the company to have a good time.

Take him. Like the other castaways, he assumed, he had been looking forward to the occasion, spot-cleaning his jacket, shining his shoes, drinking a litre of milk to line his stomach, hesitating over the choice of a tie. As the hostess had indicated, it was no fun to render thanks all by yourself in a crummy restaurant, which was the only kind a student could afford late in the month on his exhausted allowance. Now he felt like a dipsomaniac cannibal.

Her best solution, he meanly concluded, was to become a hermit. The Middle Ages had the right idea: anybody who wanted to mortify his flesh retired from the world to do it solo. She ought to live in a hut in the forest of Fontainebleau, eating wild berries and honey and wearing a shift made of bark. Even there, strangers would come to look at her, probably, and try to feed her, the way they did with animals in the zoo.

'How do you stand on honey?' he said abruptly. She turned her head, puzzled, chin drawn in, like a bird registering interrogation. 'I mean,' he said, goading, 'it's cruel, isn't it, to take honey from bees?' She pondered. 'I suppose it is,' she said, knitting her brows. 'I never thought about it. I'm not a strict vegetarian, though. With me, it's not a moral thing. When you study medicine, you learn not to worry too much about the sacredness of life. You have to experiment on animals in the laboratory. Anyway, golly, where do you draw the line? A tree is alive. How do we know it isn't conscious when we chop it down? It bleeds just like a human. I just know I feel better if I don't eat meat and some other animal foods.'

On hearing that it was not a 'moral thing', Peter felt immediately relieved, which was odd. He hoped she was telling the truth and not merely trying to make him feel comfortable in his carnivorous soul. The general's wife broke in. 'Is this a health fad or what, honey? What made you decide to take up vegetarianism? I don't mean to be intrusive, but tell us, do you really think it's cruel to kill animals?' So it was not only him. Even the general, who was carving seconds, paused with his knife in mid-air to await the verdict.

The girl repeated, in substance, what she had just been saying to Peter. He wondered how many times a week she had to respond to that query; in short, how often she was invited out to meals. In restaurants, did the waiters ask her? He ought to make her a present of his idea of a pocket tape-recorder that furnished standard answers to standard questions. But she did not seem to mind explaining herself at length. Unlike most people, she spoke, he noticed, in paragraphs – somewhat breathlessly.

'To answer your other question, Mrs Lammers, I really don't know what made me take up being a vegetarian. You could call it a health fad, I guess. But I've had a sort of "thing" about meat ever since I was little. They had to coax me to eat it. Then in boarding-school I overcame my prejudice. You know how hungry you get in school. The same in camp. And at home I have three younger brothers who aren't too fond of vegetables. My mother has to plan meals to suit the majority.

'But finally in college I started to think for myself. I got to understand body chemistry and I realized that I was being poisoned by what I was eating. Literally. I would keep falling asleep in my after-lunch class; they gave us our heavy meal at noon. Senior year I skipped lunch and ate carrots and peanut butter and dried figs in my room, and right away my marks in Latin – that was my two-thirty class then – went from C-minus to B-plus. But then I lost weight. I wasn't getting enough calories. So when I came to Paris this fall, I saw that here was my chance to experiment. They have these terrific vegetables in the markets, and I found an apartment with a kitchen, where I could cook all sorts of messes. For me, that was real independence. Freedom, golly me!'

'Liberty Hall,' said the general. 'It's small, but it's home. What I'd like to know, is there some theory behind this? Anything to do with cholesterol?' This year, Peter had observed, all the *croulants* were talking with bated breath about cholesterol, as if it were some new weapon in biological warfare aimed at shortening their lives. The exception was his mother, he was glad to say.

Cholesterol was not really the point, said Roberta. If you eliminated animal foods from your diet, naturally you eliminated animal fats also, thus reducing the cholesterol level in the blood. 'But the way vegetarians see it, a low-cholesterol diet based on lean meat, poultry, and fish may be almost as harmful to the body as a high-cholesterol diet. Man is descended from herbivores. His organs weren't designed for the absorption of animal flesh. We don't know when he became a hunter and an omnivore but we know that the habit isn't natural to the order of primates, with the exception of some of the baboons. Why, some people actually claim that it's a flesh diet that's turned man into a killer of his own kind! He has the tiger's instincts without the tiger's taboos. Of course that's only a hypothesis. One way of testing it would be for humanity to practise vegetarianism for several generations. Maybe we'd find that war and murder would disappear.'

'Do they have vegetarians in Russia?' the general demanded, emerging from a mental tunnel with a cunning look on his face. Nobody could enlighten him. Roberta guessed that most vegetarians in Russia had been Doukhobors and had emigrated to Canada a long time ago. Peter was interested in the Doukhobors. 'They were fantastic,' he said. 'Completely non-violent. They not only refused military service, they wouldn't even take up arms against wolves and bears. I read —' The general, with a chuckle, cut him off. 'Say, Roberta, why don't you go to Russia and make some converts? That's the place to test your theory. Organize a vegetarian movement.' 'Don't tease her, Dad.' 'I'm not teasing. I'm serious. If she has a plan for changing human nature, let her tell this Kosygin about it. He's her boy. "Everybody turn vegetarian or get sent to a slave-labour camp." ' 'Don't listen to him,' cried Letitia. 'Why, if you went there and tried to spread the message, they might arrest you as a spy.' ' "Anti-social element," ' muttered Peter. The general snorted. ' "*Might*"! You bet they would. They're not interested in eliminating Ivan's fighting instinct. But in the States we've got a vegetarian party on the ballot. That shows the difference, doesn't it? Did you vote Vegetarian, Roberta?'

'I think you mean the Prohibition Party, General Lammers,' she said mildly. 'Actually, if you want to know, I voted for Johnson. I'm not a crank; at least I hope not. I don't believe you can legislate reforms in people's habits. It has to be voluntary. Of course it's hard not to want to make converts when you see the change in yourself. I *feel* so much better physically and mentally since I gave up animal foods. It's amazing. My motor reactions are quicker. I need less sleep. There's a big improvement in my attention-span. It's not just a subjective thing. Even my French teacher notices a difference. I honestly think my IQ must have gone up by several points.'

'Well!' summed up the hostess. A pall settled again on the banquet, which was looking more and more like a replica of Belshazzar's Feast or the dream of the great king, his father, who was put out to eat grass. The *convives*, if Peter was a fair sample, had now started to worry about the damage they had been inflicting on their brains.

He stared at the huge drumstick bone, like a fossil remain, on his plate. A junior from Northwestern offered a ray of hope. 'You've got to remember evolution. If eating meat was bad for man, he wouldn't have survived. Or he would have kicked the habit back in the Stone Age. Man evolved as a flesh-eating higher animal. Maybe he's more intelligent than the apes *because* he became a meat-eater.'

'Hear, hear!' said the general. 'Well, Roberta, you've certainly given us food for thought, ha ha. What about booze? Are you going to tell us that monkeys don't use fermented beverages?' The girl calmly declared that she had given up drinking *for pleasure*. 'You'd be surprised. Truly. I have a much better time now than when I drank cocktails and wine. I like the taste of wine, but just one glass made me sluggish and torpid.' 'But you smoke,' loyally prompted Jean. 'Oh yes. And I drink coffee and tea. Lots.'

She had a high cheerful sturdy voice, somewhat childish for her age, as if she had been used to living with deaf people. It was true that her assertions were falling on deaf ears. In this group of sceptics, nobody would buy the idea that her abstemiousness was just an innocent form of hedonism, which was the conclusion you would be driven to if you accepted her explanations. In fact, Peter did not buy it himself. If she smoked and drank coffee, it was just protective colouration – the homage virtue paid to vice. He bet she did not inhale.

On the other hand, he recalled, there was the precedent of Epicurus. 'There was Epicurus,' he said, addressing the centre of the table. 'What about him?' 'Most people don't realize he was an ascetic. I did a paper on him for a course in ethics. He lived on barley bread and cheese and water because he thought the simple life was the way to achieve happiness, which he considered the *summum bonum*. Naturally nobody would believe that. Instead, they believed all the lies the Stoics spread about him being a gourmet and lecherous with women. So now Epicureanism means just the opposite of his teaching. But Roberta' – he stumbled – 'I mean Miss Scott, is a real Epicurean. She puts pleasure ahead of virtue, and nobody believes her because they identify pleasure with gross sensual satisfaction.' Everybody, including Miss Scott, was gazing at him in wonderment. 'Epicurus cultivated serenity of mind. He died with great fortitude of the stone,' he concluded.

'The stone!' shrieked the hostess. 'Do you mean gallstones? But that's cholesterol!' Peter was not attending. As when he had delivered a short harangue in class, his own distant words roared in his ears like the pounding of the sea in a conch shell. Then slowly he began to pick up fragments of the surrounding chatter. 'But what about your proteins?' 'Vitamin A?' 'Not even *cottage cheese*'? 'Green noodles.' 'But if you eat noodles, you're eating eggs, aren't you?' 'Don't you find it hard in the restaurants here? You never see a vegetable except in the markets. I always wonder what they do with them.' Peter recognized the languid voice of a Princetonian major in government studies. The clamour of agreement betrayed the anti-French sentiment ever ready to be mobilized when Americans in Paris got together. And as happened with anti-Semites merrily fraternizing, nobody at the table seemed to remember that there were French people present. 'I mostly eat in Italian restaurants,' the girl said, when the chortles had died down. 'They don't mind if you only take spaghetti with tomato sauce and salad and fruit. At home, when I cook for myself, I use the *Yoga Cookbook*.'

'I use that too!' cried Peter, who had bought his second-hand along the Seine. 'It has some great recipes.' 'Fantastic. Where in the world did you find yours?' Peter told her. 'The guy let me have it for a franc.' 'Me too!' she exclaimed, her eyes widening. 'Isn't that funny? Quai des Grands Augustins. I bargained.' 'Me quai Voltaire.' 'Do you have a Waring Blendor?' Peter did not have a Waring Blendor. 'Golly, you ought to get one. They're terrific for vegetable soups.'

Peter thought guiltily of his mother, who refused to touch a blender or a mixer; at that moment, in New York (9 AM Eastern Standard Time), she was doubtless pressing chestnuts or something through a sieve. 'Jean can get you one at the PX,' the girl went on kindly. 'You save a lot that way.' 'Thanks. Maybe I'll do that.' He must be out of his mind. His landlady would never let him have a blender, even if he were willing to scrap family principles and acquire one, and it would be a hard thing to hide in what passed for his closet. Yet could he ask this glorious crank to dinner and use a food mill? It came to him that he must be falling in love, but would she deign to notice a reedy college junior?

According to his mother, there was no such thing as un-reciprocated love. Love was something that happened between two people. It was not a solitary affair. But even if that dictum could be trusted, he was not sure that it applied to him. *After adolescence*, the fair Rosamund had stipulated. Maybe he had not finished adolescing. He still had that croak in his voice.

A piece of pumpkin pie had materialized before him. Assuming that egg and milk had gone into its composition, he hardly dared turn his eyes to his right. His own appetite had left him; he shook his head to a scoop of vanilla ice cream. But Roberta Scott was eating the pie. She must be hungry. Her nut-cup, he observed, was empty. Silently he exchanged it for his full one, which he had been saving for her – a present.

'Maybe you'd like to come to supper some night at my place. I could make some spaghetti and salad.' She considered this for nearly a minute, putting down her fork and chewing her lower lip; she had a way of looking you steadily in the eyes when you had made a remark, such as he had encountered among very poor people the summer before last in Umbria. 'Why, yes, sure, I'd like to. Thanks a lot.' A friendly eager smile replaced the clouds of perplexity on her features. 'Next week?' he said boldly. 'What about Tuesday?'

But even as he spoke he became aware of a pervasive silence. The general was on his feet and tapping on his glass for attention. He was going to offer a toast. To a character called Benjy, aged about eighteen, who had passed most of the meal in speechless obscurity. Peter had been introduced to him in the elevator. 'We're Leonard and Alice Burnside, from the Embassy, and this is our son, Benjy. Benjy, put that cigarette out and shake hands.' At table his wine intake had been monitored by his mother – a big crinkly-eyed woman with dimples in a magenta wool dress. Now, amid general astonishment, wriggling and pale, he was elevated to star billing. 'Is it his birthday?' someone wondered. But it was not Benjy's birthday. The kid was volunteering to take up arms for his country. That was what the clinking of glasses was about.

Glances of disbelief passed between the other young males at the table, numbering three: Peter, the boy from Northwestern, and |the ultra-WASP Princetonian, who bore the curious name of Silvanus Platt. They listened to Benjy's mother explaining to the French colonel that her son was so sold on the Vietnamese war that he could not wait to be

G

drafted. '*Il s'est rallié aux couleurs.*' '*Il a devancé l'appel,*' absently corrected the Frenchman. '*Je vous félicite, jeune homme. Et vous surtout, madame.*' He raised his glass.

The mother drank to her son. 'It was Benjy's own decision. "I've got to go, Mom," he said. Leonard wanted us to refuse our consent. Though he's only Benjy's stepfather. "Let him wait till he's drafted," Leonard said. But I couldn't say no to Benjy. I never have been able to. I guess I've spoiled him. But he's my only child.' Her face, which might have been pretty when she was young, crinkled and puckered like a wide seersucker bedspread.

During all this, her son had not opened his mouth except to engorge pie and ice cream. Benjy's worst fear, she went on, giggling, was that he might be sent to Germany, instead of out there, where the fighting was. At that point, the kid gave tongue. 'Yeah,' he said. 'That's right.'

Actually, Peter felt a revolted pity for Benjy. As transpired somewhat later, the kid was a 'problem' who had not been able to get into any college or find a job and had been hanging around Paris collecting traffic tickets while driving the family car – food for powder, in the words of Falstaff. Yet it would be surprising if he passed his physical, he was so awful and pathetic. His hobby was collecting matchbook folders. On the mental plane, the only message that had got through to him was anti-Communism. He wanted to be able to kill Viet Cong. And his parents, probably, were letting the poor creep volunteer in the hope that the Army would make a man of him – passing the buck to the Pentagon where they themselves had failed. That woman must know that she was in line to be a Gold Star mother unless the war stopped.

Slowly it came to Peter that, contrary to what you would expect in such a milieu, Benjy's parents were far from being proud of the patriot they had fledged. Even if he came back covered with medals, he would not get the fatted calf. To hear his mother tell it, she spent most of her time on her knees praying for peace. 'Though Benjy doesn't like me to. He hates it if I go into some little church and light a candle.'

'Yeah. I want to get some of those gorillas first.' '*Guerrillas*, please, Benjy.' She gave the *l*'s a Spanish pronunciation. 'He used to think they were real gorillas,' she explained, with a little gurgle of a laugh. 'He got that from listening to the radio.' 'I guess a lot of people make that mistake,' the general said easily. 'Well, here's luck to you, Ben.' He handed the boy a large non-Cuban cigar. 'Hope you see some action if that's what you want. In an "advisory" capacity, of course.' He chuckled. From Benjy, a strange ack-ack sound issued; like a kid playing machine-guns, he crouched in his chair, taking aim. 'Here they come,' he said, 'in a human-wave assault!'

Silence followed. Even Chuck appeared somewhat embarrassed by the potential hero in their midst. 'I guess Ben saw too many World War II movies when he was younger,' he suggested. 'The little yellow men in the jungle.' 'That's what I used to say to Leonard,' the boy's mother chimed in. ' "I don't see why the Embassy keeps showing those old war movies. They ought to think of the effect on the children." Didn't I say that, Leonard? And now look at the result. All he can think about is human waves and sharpshooters hiding in coconut palms and assassins in black pyjamas.'

'Holy cats, Mom,' said Benjy, puffing on the general's cigar. 'You sound as if I was a freak or something. Isn't a guy supposed to want to fight for his country?' That was the sixty-four-dollar question. 'Personally I want to stay alive,' said Silvanus Platt. 'How about you, Jay?' 'Me too,' said the boy from Northwestern. 'Me too,' said Peter, though in fact he was not sure that this ought to be his prime aim. 'Wouldn't you rather be dead than red?' said Benjy. 'No,' said Peter. 'Practically nobody would, when it comes down to it. They just think they would. All those Poles and Hungarians would be committing suicide if that idea was true. Anyway, this war isn't stopping Communism, so far as I can see. It may even be helping Communism by making people hate Americans.'

To his surprise, the general nodded. 'This is the wrong war in the wrong place, the way I look at it. Nothing will suit the

world Communist conspiracy better than to have us send a
land army to get bogged down in those mangrove swamps.
It's a diversionary tactic as old as war. The sooner the
US winds up its business out there, the happier all concerned
here at NATO will be. We know where the main enemy is
located – at the same old address, the Kremlin, Moscow. The
day the US lands ground forces on those Asian beaches, it
surrenders Western Europe to the Red Army.'

Peter had not thought of it this way. Still, he was interested
to hear a militarist espouse getting out of Vietnam. 'But
won't Johnson have to face some pretty rough domestic
criticism if we just pull out our advisers and leave the South
Vietnamese to cope?' wondered Jay Williams. 'For Christ's
sake, I said "wind it up." Hanoi has to come to its senses.
We could knock out that little country with one punch
tomorrow. You fellows know that as well as I do. *They*
know it.'

At these words, suddenly, the party got rough. Practically
everybody started shouting his opinion. The Frenchwoman
was shrilling about Foster Dulles and the chronic '*lâcheté*'
of the Americans. Always too little and too late. The betrayal at Dienbienphu. Suez. Her husband, more tactful,
sought to divide the blame. The French had betrayed too.
The Left. Mendès-France. Geneva. He barely stopped short
of attacking General De Gaulle, his own commander-in-
chief. A parliament of fools was in session. Roberta Scott put
her hands over her ears. 'But what would you have us do
now, sir?' said Silvanus Platt smoothly to the Frenchman.
'Granting that you're right in your analysis. That's all water
over the dam now. Where do we go from here? How do we
persuade Ho Chi Minh to call it quits?'

'*Mais la bombe, bien sûr,*' the colonel answered, throwing
out his hands. '*Une seule suffirait.*' 'Atomic or hydrogen?'
Peter inquired coldly, getting in return a pitying look.
'*Atomique, naturellement. N'exagérons pas.*' But General
Lammers was not convinced that an atomic bomb on Hanoi
would do the trick. You had to think of world opinion and
what the Russian response would be. If you decided to use

the bomb, it might make more sense to drop it on Peking, before the Chinese got theirs. That would give Ho something to think about, and the Russians would scarcely object. '*Ces Chinois s'en foutent,*' said the Frenchman. With the man-power they had, an atom bomb would be just a flea-bite.

'You have a point,' conceded Chuck. Still, on the whole, he did not favour dropping atomic hardware on Hanoi. 'We can do it with conventional stuff, if we have to.' 'But why should it be necessary, sir?' said Silvanus Platt. 'Wouldn't a clear warning suffice? As you say, they know we have the wherewithal to wipe them out tomorrow.' 'Yeah,' said Benjy. 'But they don't think we'll use it. We've got to *show* them.' 'Benjy!' '*Mais votre fils a raison, madame,*' said the French-man. *Le pauvre papa* Khruschchev had been willing to listen to reason; when Kennedy threatened, he understood. But these Orientals were fanatics. . . .

'We can't bomb Hanoi!' Peter burst out. 'I mean, it's im-possible for us to do a thing like that.' 'Why not?' said Benjy's stepfather, a bald man who had something to do with trade or economics. 'I don't say I favour it necessarily. I just want to know, why not? I was in the Air Force. We bombed Germany.' 'O.K., O.K.,' said Peter, feeling weary. 'I agree, we had to do that. Though maybe I would have been against some of those raids if I'd been alive then. I think you can draw a line between bombing military targets and bombing civilians.' 'The Nazis didn't.' 'But they were *Nazis*! For Christ's sake, that was the point, wasn't it?' 'What's so sacred about a civilian?' said the general. 'If he's working in a factory making war goods? Grow up, boy.' 'I think Peter's right, Dad,' said Jean. 'We have to be *better* than our enemy.' 'I agree,' said Benjy's mother. 'We *are* better than our enemy!' shouted the general. 'I haven't finished what I was saying,' objected Peter. 'Let him talk, honey.'

Peter started again. 'So we bombed Germany. And Hiro-shima and Nagasaki. My generation was born with that on its conscience. My mother says I started kicking inside her when Hiroshima happened.' 'If it shortened the war, it was worth it,' interrupted the general. 'Saved American lives *and*

Japanese lives. And if we hadn't bombed those dear German civilians, the Nazis would have had the bomb ahead of us. Put that in your pipe and smoke it.' 'Chuck!' 'Don't you think Truman could have dropped one teensy atom bomb on a deserted atoll?' said the woman on Peter's left in dreamy tones. 'That would have given the Japanese a chance to surrender when they knew what they were up against. If they didn't surrender then, it was their own responsibility.' ' "His blood be upon us and upon our children," ' muttered Peter. 'Maybe that might have been the best way, Helen,' said Mrs Lammers soothingly. 'But one man can't think of everything, you know, especially with a war on. We were certainly all grateful to President Truman when it was over. Now let's go into the other room and have some coffee and let Peter Levi have his say.'

'O.K., skip Hiroshima. We'll never agree about that. About Germany, I'll even concede that maybe our saturation-bombing helped shut down the gas ovens, though my father claims it was the opposite – it stiffened German morale. But anyway the Nazis were bombing England, which was our ally. The North Vietnamese aren't bombing anybody.' 'Just minding their own business, eh?' said the general. 'Are they helping the Viet Cong or aren't they?' put in Benjy's step-father, getting excited. 'Have you heard about infiltration? And atrocities? Civilians – women and children – ruthlessly murdered. Grenades tossed into theatres and other public places. Assassination of teachers and local officials.' 'Standing operating procedure,' said the general, nodding. 'Poisoned arrows,' said Benjy. 'And those punji stakes dipped in shit that they make traps out of. They don't abide by the rules of war.' 'Beheadings. Kidnappings. Standing operating procedure,' repeated the general. 'Do you approve of that kind of stuff, Levi?'

Peter groaned. 'No.' He was starting to feel sick. The general followed up. 'Maybe you think it's all us propaganda?' 'No, I guess not. I guess those things happen.' '*Happen!* Somebody does them. Somebody directed from Hanoi. Directed, supplied, and instigated. We have documentary proof and plenty of it. Now how are you going to put a stop to that?' 'I don't know,' said Peter.

He was getting the worst of the argument. Across the living room, Roberta Scott had her chin sunk in the palm of her hand, like a statue of Dejection; no help there. And the irony was that it was partly to curry favour that he had charged into the debate. You would think that a girl like that, from Philadelphia, would be a dyed-in-the-wool Quaker. 'Go ahead,' insisted the general. 'Give us your ideas. We're listening.' Peter's head was buzzing. It was like an exam nightmare. He tried to recall things Bob and his mother had said, things he himself had said, during the Goldwater campaign, which already seemed so long ago, like a Golden Age of clarity. And he remembered his father telling his mother that Peter might make a good judge but he could never be an advocate.

Put on the spot, he could not think of a single alternative to the unthinkable, which was bombing those frail little people in conical hats. The slogan 'land reform' floated into his ken, like a beat-up slug of printer's type. Give the South Vietnamese peasants something to fight for – a stake in their government? But even if land distribution was possible, it would take a long time and might not end the war but actually intensify it, assuming both sides became equally determined – had anybody ever considered that?

'We should negotiate,' he said at last. 'Great. Hear, hear,' said Mr Burnside. 'I couldn't agree more. But how are we going to get talks going? It takes two to negotiate. We're ready and willing to sit down and talk, but Hanoi claims there's nothing to talk about. We just withdraw our support and let the Viet Cong take over. Simple.' Peter licked his lips. 'But isn't that what we're saying ourselves? *They* should withdraw *their* support. Why should we have the right to demand that and not them? It's more their country than ours.' 'So you favour a Commie take-over,' said the general. 'No! But if I had to choose between that and bombing them, I guess I'd be for that.' 'So you favour it. You kids might have the guts to say what you think, instead of pussyfooting. Lay it on the line.' 'Maybe there wouldn't be a takeover,' said Peter, voicing his deepest wish. The general gave a bark of laughter. 'Oh, God, friend, where have you been all my life?'

The other youths, with the exception of Benjy, had been silent for a long time. It was impossible to tell on whose side they were now, apart from the question of their own personal survival. Roberta Scott was studying some little ivory chessmen on the table beside her; she looked as if every word spoken were making her unhappy. 'It's inconceivable!' Peter cried. 'Don't you see that? Doesn't *anybody* see that?' 'What's inconceivable, honey?' said Letitia. 'That we'll bomb North Vietnam. If we do that, I think I'll kill myself.' 'Is that a promise or a threat?' said Chuck, kidding. 'Hey, take it easy.' 'Why are you getting so worked up?' said Donna Elvira kindly. 'I don't like the idea myself, but it wouldn't be the end of the world, would it? What's so special about bombing Hanoi?' 'They can't retaliate,' said Peter, letting his breath out with a long sigh. 'And that's *why* we'd do it. To prove to them how powerful we are. If we thought they could retaliate, we wouldn't.'

Roberta raised her eyes and met his. She nodded. 'Yes. Golly, yes.' 'Since when is superior weaponry a reason for not using it?' inquired Chuck. 'This is war, not a horse-race, buddy.' Peter had had enough. Tears rushed to his eyes. 'You don't give a damn about your country, you stupid patriot. You don't care *what* it does. Or about its fair name. I *love* America or what I used to think was America. Listening to you, I don't recognize it any more.'

To his amazement, nobody moved to throw him out of the apartment. 'I think Peter needs a little fresh air,' Letitia said quickly. 'We all do. Let's get our things on and go out and play softball now. It gets dark so early these days. Though we ought to be grateful to French Daylight Saving . . .' Still chattering, she was guiding him to the bathroom. She turned on the cold-water tap. 'You just put this damp washcloth on your eyes and you'll feel better. We gave you too much bourbon. I always forget that it's a hundred-proof.' 'I'd better go home now,' said Peter, applying the cold cloth to his burning face. 'I'm sorry I was rude.' 'Just a good clean argument, honey. Good for the digestion. You'll forget all about it when you've had some exercise. I know Chuck will. Between you and me, it kind of got under his skin to see that girl refusing to touch her food. I saw that right away. He's such a wonderful host, loves to entertain.'

Peter nodded. 'Tell me the truth, Mrs Lammers. Are we going to bomb Hanoi?' 'I don't know, Peter. I wouldn't know a thing like that. Chuck wouldn't either. He was just talking off the top of his head. Got carried away. And that Benjy upset him too. We've known him since he was a toddler, when we served with the Burnsides in Madrid. They're *beside* themselves with worry. When you see a boy like that *wanting* to go out and get killed in that crazy war, it makes you wonder. Underneath, Chuck would a lot rather see him sign up for the Peace Corps. I want you to believe that.'

'O.K., I believe you, Mrs Lammers.' Peter rested his head against the cold tiles of the bathroom wall. 'Chuck agrees with you more than you realize. But we just can't walk away, can we? I mean, we have a commitment. If we walk out, our allies right here in NATO will start wondering whether they can trust us. There would be all these repercussions that the ordinary person doesn't think about. You *are* for the NATO shield, aren't you?' As she took the washcloth from his hands, she darted an anxious glance into his eyes.

'I guess so,' said Peter. He was not sure what he thought of NATO. His father said it was a necessary evil, which you could say about a lot of things without their becoming good. Still, as long as there was no fighting going on here in Europe, Peter found it hard to take an interest in NATO, one way or another. Which was possibly reasoning in a circle, since if there were no NATO, there might be fighting. Your opinion, he supposed, depended on your assessment of Russian intentions. But he did not want to use his brain any more this afternoon, if he could help it.

Out in the Bois, as Letitia had predicted, he felt somewhat better. He was on Chuck's team, and though he struck out his first time at bat, in the field he was fairly fast on his feet. The stars were the long-legged Roberta, in the pitcher's position, and the big Mrs Burnside at bat. The French colonel, surprisingly, was an agile shortstop and outfielder and fleet on the bases. Benjy was terrible. He would never survive basic training, even if he passed his physical; his nicotine-stained fingers were all thumbs, and he panted noisily trotting after an easy fly.

A small crowd of French children gathered to watch *les Américains* and to chase an occasional ball. Peter found he was enjoying himself and even enjoying the sense of being an American, as, waiting his turn at bat, he explained the game in French to the kids, who thanked him. Yet in the fourth inning, stationed in the outfield, he found he had the hiccups. Taking part in the national sport, on top of the national bird, had been too much. He tried holding his breath and swallowing accumulated saliva, hoping they would pass before anybody noticed. Instead, they got worse. When Chuck waved him in at the end of the inning, he was hiccupping so loudly, like a drunkard in a play, that the French *gosses* began to imitate him, whirling around, jerking, and making burpy noises. He could not even get his breath to tell them to scram.

Various remedies were suggested: drinking from the wrong side of a glass, hanging his head and counting to a hundred, getting a sudden shock. He went in search of a drinking-fountain. Needless to say, this being France, none materialized, though he walked for half a mile; the only water source visible was the distant lake, polluted, naturally, where he used to row. Chuck was at bat when he reappeared in their midst. 'Hic!' The general, making a foul tip, glanced at him with annoyance. Benjy offered to go with him and try to find a café.

When they had finally found one and Peter had drunk four glasses of Evian while holding his breath, the hiccups subsided. But then he had to wait for Benjy to finish a Pernod he had ordered. 'Would you like to smoke some grass?' said Benjy, feeling in his pockets. Peter shook his head. 'Let's get back to the ball game.' But it was a long way from the café. By the time they got to the Bois, dusk was falling; the little meadow where they had been playing was empty, and all the players had fled. Peter was bitter. 'Wouldn't you think they would have waited for us? Hiccups can be a serious thing. Christ, there've been cases of people who've had them for a year and finally kicked off!' 'Yeah. I read about one of those.' 'And that girl is supposed to be a *doctor*! Well, a medical student anyway. But all she was interested in was pitching. What about the Hippocratic oath?' 'But you're O.K. now, aren't you?' 'But they don't *know* that.' 'I see what you mean. You can't rely on most people, that's for sure. That's what appeals to me about the Army. The buddy-system. Like today. You had it bad in the windpipe, and I stuck by you. You'd do the same for me.'

Just then a voice called 'Hi!' Jean had waited for them. She emerged from a sort of copse. 'Mother was worried about you. She said to take you to the American Hospital if your hiccups hadn't stopped.' 'I'm O.K. now, thanks. It was nice of you to wait, though. What happened to the others?' 'Benjy's parents went home. And Roberta had to go to a concert.' 'Oh . . . She didn't leave any message?' 'Why, no. But she agreed with Mother that you ought to go to the American Hospital. They could give you an anti-spasmodic, she said.' 'She didn't say anything about dinner?' 'Dinner? Gosh, can you still eat?' 'I don't mean now. I asked her to dinner next week. A vegetarian repast.' 'Isn't that great of you, Peter! Do you know how to cook?' 'Yes.' 'I love cooking myself. What kind of dishes can you make?' 'Oh, *you* know, spaghetti . . . At home I used to bake cakes, but here I don't have an oven.' 'I'm crazy about baking.'

The three started walking through the landscaped wood. Peter could see that if he were not careful he would be entertaining Jean for dinner soon. And smoking grass with Benjy. Those two seemed to be his real friends. A final hiccup issued from his craw. 'Oops!' Jean giggled. 'Dad is a card. He thinks you can cure hiccups by will power. That's what he said, just now.' 'And Roberta, what does she think?' 'She claims they're a medical mystery. Doctors don't know what causes them or why they go away.' 'Like love,' said Benjy, astonishingly. 'Something in your chemistry that you can't control. Yeah.' They continued pensively walking in the direction, they hoped, of a Métro station. For a while they were lost in the wood.

Leviticus

IF it had not been for his draft status, Peter would have quit the Sorbonne. He was bored by his classes, which, being for foreigners, were on a childish level, like the course for *straneri* at Perugia. The lecture hall, thronged with humanity, was plunged in hyperborean darkness. True to form, the French were hoarding the electricity; the professor, doubtless under orders from the Ministry of Education, never turned on any lights, so that you could not take notes or draw pictures to alleviate the tedium. There was practically no ventilation, and when he could not get a place on the window-sills, Peter chose to sit on the floor, unable to stretch his legs without prodding somebody's bottom but hopeful that the air was purer down there.

It was not just *him*, as he tried to make clear to his family; the other 1,999 foreign kids segregated in French civilization felt bored and gypped too. In fact, the Left Bank was full of American drop-outs, not bothering to show up at classes any more, since nobody took attendance and their supervisor, if they had one, could not be more indifferent. At the end of the year, there was going to be an exam, which the majority infallibly failed, but even if you failed, you could get a 'certificate of attendance' from the professor – a meaningless document that only meant you were registered.

Most of the kids Peter knew were resigned to writing this year off as a total loss, academically, whether they did any work or not. Quite a few were switching to the Alliance Française, where at least they got practice in speaking; at the Sorbonne, all they gave you in 'intensive French' was grammar, and the professor did all the talking. But the kids who made that move could be ordered to report straight home for a physical, if their draft board wanted to get tough. You rated a student deferment by being enrolled in a recognized college or university, and going to the Alliance Française, though it actually taught you something, was like going to the Berlitz School at home or taking a correspondence course, as far as Selective Service was concerned. Up to now, as it chanced, General Hershey had not gone fishing in the draft pool of juniors abroad. But there could always be a first time.

Nobody's parents understood the score here. They could not use their imagination and realize that if a bunch of young aliens was isolated and ruthlessly exploited by a chauvinistic French university, naturally they lost all incentive to study; it was the same as in the schools in Harlem. The Sorbonne was only interested in collecting the tuition. As Dag had kept pointing out, it was no accident that the French civilization class was scheduled for 8 AM: they *wanted* the kids to cut it, for the simple reason that two thousand were registered for the course, while the hall seated five hundred. Dag was convinced that the curriculum had been devised by the French tourist industry to lure under-age foreign suckers to Paris. And he meant that literally. No wonder the poor methodical Marxist had got deported back to Norway; he had tried to expose the system to everybody he talked to, like the Enemy of the People.

But parents thought their kids were throwing away a wonderful opportunity. His stepfather wrote that he had counted thirty-seven negative words and expressions in Peter's last communication, which was only a page and a half long. In Bob's reckoning, 'finally' was a negative, as in 'My landlady has finally turned the heat on,' 'I have finally got a library card to work in the Bibliothèque Nationale,' 'The packages you sent finally came,' 'A French girl finally spoke to me in a café yesterday. She wanted to know the time.' Reading over his letter, which Bob had enclosed, marked with blue pencil, Peter had to agree that the omission of 'finally' would have given some of those sentences a more positive thrust. Evidently, he was bidding for sympathy, which his parents were unwilling to give. Self-pity in the eyes of Bob and his mother was a disgusting habit; if you were sorry for yourself, they would not be sorry for you – a duplication of labour, Bob claimed.

The *babbo* wrote that if Peter was unhappy in Paris, he might transfer next semester to a provincial university like Nancy or Montpellier. And he wondered why Peter had not investigated the special 'first year courses' the Sorbonne gave to qualified foreigners; he had heard them well spoken of by the French department at Wellesley. Though he did not thank his father for discussing his private affairs with the stupid Wellesley women, for a while Peter accepted the reproach. He too wished he had applied for one of those courses, instead of joining the mob in French civilization. Yet from what he gleaned, there was no cause for envy. What his father did not know was that those courses were mass-produced too and on a patronizing freshman level, as you could divine from the name if you thought about it; the lectures were just as moth-eaten, there was no class participation, no assignments were given, not even a reading-list, and the exam, when they finally sprang it, bore no relation to what the professor had been talking about. Every year most of the Americans flunked ignominiously, which was probably how the French had planned it – a national hecatomb.

In retrospect, he concluded that the real ploy would have been to get permission to audit lectures by one of the star professors at the regular Sorbonne or the *Hautes Etudes* and then take an exam or write a paper for his tutor back home; that way, he could have imbibed some genuine French culture and mingled with French students, at least in the sense of being in the same room with them. But you had to be pretty 'motivated' – his adviser's jargon – to attempt that and, not being enrolled, you risked being cracked down on by your draft board just as much as though you were hanging around playing the pinball machine in cafés or looking at old movies at the cinémathèques.

If he wanted to be sure of his student deferment, it was

better to stick it out in French civilization, going through the motions of studying for credit. That, at any rate, was the cynical advice they handed out at the Embassy; some guys in the class had asked. In short, stay in your slot. You might have to do your junior year over when you got home, but in the Affluent Society your parents would go on supporting you until you finally graduated and take you as a tax exemption. If they complained, you could point to the silver lining: you would be in the Class of '67 instead of '66, which would keep you out of the Army one more year. By that time, the war in Vietnam ought to be over.

Like most people his age, he guessed, Peter had a profound wish not to be killed. He was no different from those other guys at the general's Thanksgiving brawl. Though sorry for anybody who had to die in Vietnam, he faced with equanimity the idea that some unknown draftee – maybe even a Negro – should bite the dust instead of him.

He could see in principle that student deferment was a bad form of discrimination, that Selective Service – page Darwin – showed middle-class society red in tooth and claw, but just the same he had his education to finish. Would a nut like his mother want him to volunteer or go to jail as a co or what? She and Bob were opposed to the war, which was why they had finally voted for Johnson. Yet in their letters they had begun to say that he was reneging on his promises, not trying to achieve peace but plotting for a bigger war, now that the election was over. Give him time, Peter urged. At least wait for January, when he would deliver his message to Congress. He *must* have meant what he said about American boys not dying for Asian boys. Even the general, after all, was against landing troops, and as for bombing Hanoi, that was just the Air Force mentality.

For his own part, despite his bibulous statements that afternoon, Peter was not sure exactly how he stood on the war. In reality he worried what would happen to India which used to be one of his favourite countries, if the Americans let the Communists take over Indo-China. The best hope seemed to be some compromise, whereby the UN, maybe, could step in and supervise an armistice. That was what Roberta thought; when he had called her at the Institut Pasteur and asked her to dinner, she had invited him instead to a concert, and afterwards they had had a coffee. She had a lot of faith in U Thant.

He himself derived cheer from the reminder that if you stopped paying attention to these problems, they tended to get solved. Like Laos, which had had him sweating when he was sixteen, or the Berlin Wall. Even the Congo seemed to have simmered down, now that everybody was concentrating on Asia. It was the same as when you had a headache: you could make it go away by stimulating a pain in some other part of your body – your big toe or your crazy bone. He owed that prescription to his mother.

But since she and Bob were so excruciated by the Vietnamese war, shouldn't they be glad that Peter had his 2-S deferment? They were glad selfishly, he assumed, but the fair Rosamund would never like being glad just selfishly. He could count himself lucky that she was not on his draft board; if she were, it might be the sacrifice of Isaac all over again, minus the ram. It would have been interesting to have Isaac's point of view on that episode – something the Bible left out.

Recently he had decided that mercenary armies had made a lot of sense. He still believed in non-violence as a technique of persuasion, but there were some situations that persuasion did not cover. As the *babbo* said, what if Gandhi had been up against Hitler? Unless you were an all-out pacifist, you recognized that *somebody* had to bear arms, and why not somebody who had heard the call, like that poor nut Benjy? Instead of training every young kid to be a killer, it would be more moral, as well as more practical, to restrict the job to specialists. But ordinary twenty-year enlisted men, not just the officer caste, ought to be rewarded by society for the risks they ran, the way Iroquois Indians, who were sure-footed, got big money being high-construction workers – there were some of those *Peaux-Rouges* right here in France; he had read an article about them in *L'Express*. If he were in Johnson's place, he would abolish the draft and finance military training for qualified recruits by taxing people like his parents who could afford it and had children between eighteen and twenty-seven. Anybody over a certain income level who wanted to keep his offspring out of the Army – and ball-players and prize fighters and movie stars and Pop singers – would have to pay the price, so that the guys who volunteered to do the fighting would earn, say, what an automobile worker brought home on Friday night. What an instructor or a section-man got would not be enough to make getting killed attractive.

If he had the energy, he would send his plan to Johnson. He had another plan, along the same lines, to submit to socialist countries. That would be to give people who had degrading jobs like street-cleaners and sewer-workers or shoe-salesmen the highest rewards in the economy. In Paris, it was almost always Algerians, he noticed, that you saw sweeping the streets with those brooms made of twigs or laying sewer pipes. But there was no reason why the dirtiest jobs should be the worst paid. It ought to be the opposite. He was amazed that nobody but Peter Levi had thought of something so simple. And apart from the sheer equity of the arrangement, which was breath-taking in its neatness, like the Fool's Mate, it had another good feature: the materialists would rush down into the sewers, where they belonged, and artists and scientists and scholars would not be corrupted by money, as they were under the present system, even if, like his parents, they failed to recognize it.

He was hurt by the reception his idea got from his friend Bonfante, who as an old revolutionary ('*Papa, c'est un révolutionnaire; il a combattu dans le maquis,*' Irène explained proudly), ought to have been serious about it. Instead, Arturo, whom he found sweeping their apartment, was overcome with glee, laughing almost wolfishly as he wielded the dust-pan; his bald head was tied up in a red bandanna, and he wore a woman's ruffled apron over his trousers, which made Peter feel like Little Red Riding Hood visiting her grandmother. When Arturo had finally moderated his amusement and made a pot of *espresso*, he explained that Peter was too young to understand the relation between money and power. When a new class enriched itself, as had happened with the bourgeoisie before the French Revolution, it proceeded to seize power. What Peter was proposing, without knowing it, was a dictatorship of the proletariat. That was the big joke.

'Your ditch-diggers and sewer-cleaners would be the new rulers. The old Roman proletariat. Not even Marx's factory-workers.' 'But why should they want power?' Peter said sulkily. 'You mean they wouldn't be satisfied just to have the Cadillacs and the weekend *dachas* and sturgeon dinners at three-star restaurants?' 'If a Cadillac has no prestige, who wants it? When a worker is paid better than his boss, he will be the boss tomorrow. When the English king Charles lost his revenues, because of progressive inflation, he lost his head too.'

Peter did not see that a dictatorship of humble sewer-cleaners would be any worse than a dictatorship of fat Party bosses. 'They would not be the *same* sewer-cleaners,' Arturo pointed out. 'The profession would become overcrowded, and the weak would be pushed out. They would be forced to become actors or ballet-dancers – professions without prestige.' He gave his high Italian laugh. 'What is degrading is not the job, Peter, but the pay attached to it.' A surgeon's job was just as revolting as a plumber's. Maybe more so. In the Middle Ages, in fact, a surgeon and a barber were the same person and rewarded accordingly. 'But that proves my point!' cried Peter. 'It shows that society can change its mind about the value of a person's work. I guess sewer-cleaners are just as necessary as doctors.' 'Soon it will all be done by machines,' Arturo promised. 'When socialism achieves an advanced technology, no one will clean the sewers or sweep the streets.'

Arturo always invoked technology as the great solvent when they debated about the future. Europeans were idealistic about machines because they had not had to live with them. The Bonfantes were too impecunious to have a car or television or a washing-machine; they boiled their laundry on the stove. Arturo wrote a financial column for some provincial newspapers, which Peter guessed did not pay too well.

He knew all about the stock market and interest rates, but he did not even have a bank account. Elena kept what money they had in postal savings – the next thing to a stocking. Their apartment was in an old decrepit building, over a printing shop, and the presses often shook it, rattling the pictures on the walls. Everything in it was old-fashioned: their Model-T Frigidaire, which also rattled and made midget ice cubes, like a toy; their claw-footed bathtub, which they had bought at a *Démolitions*; their ancient modern art; Arturo's pre-war electric shaver; their gramophone and scratched monaural-78 records. Gas pipes for the old gas lighting fixtures had never been removed when electricity was installed and they crawled about the walls like lianas in a forest. Elena's mother, who had lived with them till she died, had covered every surface with Russian shawls, cushions, throws, and heavy draperies; they had pretty silver, some of it broken, that had come with her from Russia too, like the record of Chaliapin singing *Boris Godunov*, to which Peter was much attached. Her parents were Social Revolutionaries and had had to leave Russia with their few unworldly possessions when the Bolsheviks took over.

The most modern implement they possessed was an old vacuum cleaner, which Peter now noticed lying in a corner. He wondered why Arturo had been using the broom. There was a strange amount of dust in the room. Elena was at her job at the Mazarin Library, and the *femme de ménage* was sick. The vacuum was *en panne*, Arturo thought: every time he had used it lately, it had seemed to lack power. 'Maybe I can fix it,' said Peter, picking up the threadbare hose. He had often vacuumed for his mother in the dear dead days in Rocky Port, and Arturo, though fanatically tidy, was not much good with tools. Peter flipped the switch, and a cloud of dust and grit arose. In fact, the machine was blowing accumulated dust out of the bag into the apartment. 'Why, you've been working it backwards!' he exclaimed. '*O la la!*' said Arturo, crest-fallen. Elena and the children had been right when they claimed that whenever Papa cleaned the place, it seemed to get dirtier . . .

The manifest irony of this little *contretemps* put Peter in a better mood. Adjusting the suction, he ran the vacuum vigorously over the floors and rugs while Arturo meekly followed him with a feather duster, cupping his ear with his left hand to hear over the hum of the *aspirateur* as Peter held forth, from his wider experience, on the contemporary technological crisis. Maybe it would be a good thing, Peter shouted, if machines took over the more malodorous functions of society, such as getting rid of the garbage. That was already a *fait accompli* in large sections of America; he described the Disposall gadget his stepmother had on the Cape, which had practically eliminated those grisly trips to the dump. Of course you still had the cans and empty bottles to cope with, but eventually humanity might find some means of dealing with tin cans and old automobiles, besides making sculptures out of them. One solution might be to stop eating out of cans and driving automobiles, but that was too much to hope for in the present state of enlightenment. In any case, he was willing to admit that the Disposall made a real contribution to human happiness, although at the moment of installation in the Wellfleet kitchen he had argued with his stepmother that she would do better to keep a pig.

But each new invention, as far as he was concerned, ought to be viewed with suspicion until it could prove its innocence. In his ideal world-state, a patent office, staffed by moral philosophers, would replace the censors, scrutinizing applications for new processes and gadgets and deciding whether their ultimate effects would be good, bad, or neutral. Merely neutral would be kept pending for a period of years, on probation. Under a system like that, detergents, for instance, could never have reached the market.

Arturo rubbed his eyes, '*Détergents? Qu'est-ce que c'est que ça?*' Typically, he did not even know what they were. Peter flew out to the kitchen and returned with a bottle of washing solution. '*Ça!*' '*Mais c'est du savon!*' ' "Soap"!' exclaimed Peter with a pitying laugh. 'You're using detergents every day to wash the dishes without even realizing it. Probably your *femme de ménage* buys them. Over here, you're not aware that detergents are fouling up the rivers and poisoning the fish. In America at least we're aware of it. This horrible sludgy foam piles up in lakes and streams, killing all the wild life; it doesn't dissolve the way soap does. Pretty soon all the waterways and the ocean will be choked unless we can stop it.' Arturo raised a shoulder. '*Là, tu exagerès un peu, mon ami. Quand même!*' The ocean, he felt, would last out his time. ' "*Après moi le déluge,*" ' observed Peter. '*Qu'est-ce que j'y peux faire, moi?*' Arturo protested. The capitalists were to blame for manufacturing the stuff. 'But you don't have to buy it,' said Peter. 'You could tell your *femme de ménage*. All she has to do is read the fine print on the bottle. My mother and stepmother use only Ivory now or old-style soap powders. You can't wait for a revolution to stop the manufacturers. You have to educate the consumer. The trouble is, detergents are taking over. In a little while, it may be hard to find regular soap in a store. I heard the other day that the PX doesn't carry Ivory Flakes any more.'

Arturo appeared bewildered. The significance of Ivory was lost on him. 'You know about chemical fertilizers,' Peter firmly continued, 'and what they're doing to the soil.' '*J'en ai entendu parler,*' Arturo replied. '*Mais je ne suis pas exactement au courant.*' He laughed apologetically. There it was. Bonfante had no idea of what technology was actually doing, except in the field of weaponry, where, being anti-American, he was fairly well briefed. He knew about second-strike capability, but he and Elena had never tasted frozen food probably; he had never heard of a TV dinner, never seen a car graveyard, never walked on a tree-shaded street where he was the only pedestrian, not counting dogs . . .

You could not convey to him the tragedy of a nice little village like Rocky Port, where 'exploitation' was not the point at issue. If you mentioned that the laundress there had two TV sets, he thought you were trying to prove something favourable about the American way of life. Whenever Peter started describing the changes that had overtaken his old home in the space of only four years, he rapidly lost his audience. It happened again this afternoon. 'Listen, Arturo. It's important.' Arturo listened, blinking his eyes, which, strangely for an Italian, were a bright blue – the eyes of an old brigand. He was making an effort to comprehend, but gradually his eyes glazed over. He only brightened when Peter made reference to atom shelters. He nodded. '*Ils se préparent pour la troisième guerre mondiale.*'

All at once, Peter was overcome by a tremendous feeling of love. He was talking, he realized, to a totally innocent person, like some uncorrupted Papuan of the eighteenth century discovered by Captain Cook. A 'good European' so far removed in time from Disposalls, Mixmasters, thermostatically heated swimming pools, frozen-food lockers, motorways, U-Hauls, that even if you drew him diagrams he would never get the picture. And like some untutored savage presented with the white man's firewater, he responded with approval to the mention of instant tapioca ('*Très bonne idée*') and sliced bread. That there were no passenger trains any more in a large part of the US, that you could not buy a whole fresh fish on the seashore or a button in a *mercerie*, he simply did not believe: '*Tu plaisantes.*'

Arturo had his column to mail, and they walked together to the post office on the rue Danton. They discussed postal services. '*A New York, ça fonctionne très bien, à ce qu'on dit.*' Peter laughed; his friend's information was characteristically out-of-date. 'It *used* to be good, I guess. Now, there's only one delivery a day uptown, where my mother lives. '*Incroyable!*' muttered Arturo. '*Ici il y en a trois.*' He walked along in silence, shaking his head.

For the first time today, Peter had really made him wonder. It turned out that he knew a lot about the history of mail. For instance, in the War of 1870, the French had used pigeons to carry letters on microfilm, and, more fantastic, they organized a regular service of postal balloons, which the Germans tried to shoot down with telescopic-sighted Krupp guns. But the Boches only netted five balloons, while more than three million letters got through. 'So they invented air mail!' exclaimed Peter. 'As far back as that!' '*Bien sûr.*' Efficient and uniform free public mail delivery had been one of the great progressive achievements of bourgeois democracy; hence the stress in all the capitalist countries on the reliability and swiftness of the post. ' "Not rain nor snow nor sleet..." ' quoted Peter. 'It says that on the post office in New York.' The fact that there was only one mail a day now in the centre of world capitalism satisfied Arturo that the system was coming apart. 'Down in Wall Street, I think they have two,' put in Peter. 'And in the middle of town, where the big banks and offices are. But a lot of people, even my mother, use messenger service if it's something important.' Arturo nodded. '*C'est très significatif, ce que tu dis là.*' The US, like an old man in his dotage, was reverting to infancy, i.e., to private messengers to carry the post. The public sector was breaking down. According to Arturo, that would account too for the disappearance of trains – another productive achievement of bourgeois democracy in its phase of expansion. 'Trains aren't nationalized in the US,' objected Peter, who was nevertheless struck by his friend's reasoning. He would be glad to be convinced that capitalism was kicking the bucket in its headquarters, the United States, so long as it was a natural death.

They passed a big *marchand de charbon* coming out of his subterranean lair, all sooty, like Pluto, with a sack of coal on his back. '*Je viens chez vous ce soir,*' the black giant said to Arturo. He delivered wood for their fireplace. They were called *les bougnats* – why, Arturo did not know – and were said to come from the Auvergne, like wet nurses from the Morvan. '*Les enfants adorent ce bougnat.*' Peter could understand that. When he was young, he confessed, he had liked the idea of infant chimney-sweeps – small agile black demons clambering down flues. His mother had read him a book called *The Water Babies*, about a chimney-sweep named Tom who fell into a brook; he could not remember the rest. He had been sad when she told him that they did not exist any more, on account of child-labour laws. '*Les enfants-ramoneurs,*' agreed Arturo. In his childhood, he too had liked the idea. '*Oui, c'était pittoresque.*' He made a sudden grimace of disgust. He pointed to the *bougnat*. '*Un ivrogne.*' They were all drunkards, he said, because of the unhealthy conditions they worked in. Soon there would be no more *bougnats* – survivals of injustice and inefficient specialization. 'Won't the children miss them?' said Peter. Children could not miss what they had never known, replied Arturo shortly.

Peter disagreed, thinking of blacksmith shops and barber poles and those country fairs his mother talked about. He felt sorry in advance for his children, who would never see the *stoppeuse* darning in the window on the rue de Grenelle or the gilders with their golden signs or the lens-grinder with the big eye over his shop or the cobbler with his wooden shoe.

He pointed to a palette hanging over the emporium of a *marchand de couleurs*. 'Nice.' Bonfante gave a sombre laugh. He asked whether Peter could guess why the palette was there. 'For advertising, I suppose. I never thought about it. Does there have to be a reason?' '*Oui! Il y a toujours une raison.*' The explanation was that until the Third Republic the masses had been illiterate. You would not find such quaint signboards in *les beaux quartiers*, but here, where the poor lived, a few had survived. '*Saintes reliques de l'analphabètisme du peuple!*' He wrinkled his nose and stuck out his lower lip, the way all Italians did when they smelled something morally nauseating. '*Mon cher, il faut toujours se méfier du pittoresque. Ça pue.*'

Peter groaned. It was bad enough to know that everything he liked was doomed to disappearance without feeling obliged to be glad about it. And perforce that should include Bonfante, who was personally incapable of modernizing, whatever his grey matter said. If he were consistent, he would be living in some skyscraper in a housing development and driving a new *deux-chevaux*, instead of standing here on the corner tall and gaunt, with his bare bald head, like one of the nicer prophets in the Old Testament, his overcoat flapping in the wind, his chin sunk in his old plaid muffler. In fact, this fall when he had started driving-lessons, they had flunked him out of the auto-école.

When they parted, Peter felt another onrush of love. Maybe it was hopeless to try to shake Arturo's faith in technology. Yet he had to keep making the effort. A world in which nobody could work except a machine would be horribly boring, he thought. He could not understand why the only people, besides himself, to see this were a few artists, who were prejudiced by the fact that they worked with their hands and enjoyed it. If the right to work became the privilege of a few, which might happen with automation, that would be just as unjust as having leisure the privilege of a few. What was good about the Middle Ages was that everybody had worked: the knight fought, the peasant ploughed, and the lady cooked and made simples. Even a cat had a job – of catching mice. In a rational society of the future, the machine could have its allotted sphere, since it was here, as people said, to stay. Only it should be kept in its place. There would be no reason for everybody to write crummy poems or paint ghastly pictures, in order to feel creative, if they had the possibility, stolen from them by machines, of making something useful.

In an incautious moment, he had advanced this thought to his adviser, a sociologist hight Mr Small, who was probing him for his views on progressive education. Peter thought every child, starting in grade school, should be sent to learn a real trade, like shoemaking, under a master shoemaker, instead of fooling around with finger paints or making ceramics. The old guilds and corporations, with their distinctive dress and the system of masters and apprentices, had been an attractive feature of the Middle Ages, in his opinion; of course there was not much 'upward mobility' – only a cycle of replacement and renewal, as happened in the animal kingdom with individuals in a species.

'What interests me about birds and animals is that individuals don't count with them. That's one thing I've learned this year. It ought to be obvious, but I never thought about it before.' Mr Small industriously leafed through Peter's file. 'I don't find zoology among your subjects.' 'No. But you see I belong to this bird-watching group. We go out on Sundays. Birds don't have personalities, except tame ones. They only have collective personalities, like the hermit thrush or the cuckoo or the thieving jay. Or goldfinches, which are gregarious. Maybe you don't grasp the implications of that. But if I didn't have what's called a personality, I wouldn't mind death.'

'You think about death a great deal?' 'Well, yes. Everybody my age does, I guess, if you can judge by poetry. And of course there's the draft. Anyway, it seems to me that in the past people had less personality and were happier for it. They were more like animals, more natural. I mean, it's natural to die, after all. Rulers had personalities, like Charles le Téméraire or Saint Louis, but most people merged with their occupation and even took their names from it, like Miller or Baker or Skinner. My name, for instance, means priest. I would have been born a priest, literally – the way a bird is born to be a fisher or a fly-catcher.'

'You're anxious about the career choices open to you,' Mr Small noted, gazing out of the window. 'The junior year abroad is often elected as a decision-making device. A retreat and period of stock-taking. The individual is "closed for inventory", in business parlance. You're confronted with a bewilderment of choice, the concomitant of an open society. This naturally produces anxiety and evidently, in your case, a wish to regress to a closed, traditional pattern. Your rejection of individual freedom is so extreme that it leads to the fantasy of becoming an animal.'

Peter gulped. 'You can look at it that way, I guess. It's true, I have this thing about the past. But I always have had. It didn't come on just now. And it's partly because I care about the future. I don't mean mine. I mean humanity's. I keep thinking all the time about the direction we're going in and trying to figure out escape routes. Don't you get scared occasionally?' An eerie blaze lit up Mr Small's little green eyes; his pale-red lashes blinked angrily. 'Scared? I can't think of a more challenging time to be alive in for an American. All the options are open. No society in history before our own has given so-called mass-man such opportunities for self-realization.' 'To me, everything is closing in,' argued Peter. 'If I were a Russian or a Pole, at least I might have the illusion that things would be better if there was a revolution.

Or even gradual evolution. But here evolution just means giving everybody more of the same. Take a simple example: the Paris traffic.' 'Use the Métro.' 'I do. Or I walk. But I can't help worrying about those people stuck in cars.'

It was true. Some unkind fairy, finding his brain unemployed, must have set him the gruesome task of coming up with a solution for every current woe. And the Paris traffic problem was a much tougher nut to crack than the reorganization of society. So far, each of his *idées géniales*, such as the common ownership of all vehicles within the city circumference – you picked up a car, free, when you needed it and dropped it when you were through at one of a series of underground parking lots – ran up against some vested interest or was liable to abuse. 'Go on.' 'Well, every time I see a traffic jam, my mind automatically starts milling out plans to offer General De Gaulle or the mayor of Paris, if there is one. For instance, they could prohibit trucks from delivering except at night-time. That would help some. But then the trucks would keep people from sleeping . . .'

'Have you ever considered having psychiatric treatment?' 'No.' Not waiting for Mr Small's gaze to return from its bourne – the distant dome of the Panthéon – Peter donned his jacket. 'Excuse me. I just remembered. I have an appointment.' Small watched him fumble with the zipper-fastening. 'Very well. But keep in mind that the learning-process is not conducted exclusively or even mainly in the classroom. You come to me protesting that the instruction is boring. Well, widen your contacts with people. Talk to them in cafés, in museums, on the street. Don't brood in your room about the world's problems. Meet them, face to face. If you can come out of your protective shell, you'll look back on this year's experience as richly rewarding.'

'Ha ha,' Peter said to himself this afternoon, recalling that *dialogue de sourds*. In fact, a lot of the kids here used words like 'rewarding' and 'enriching', as though they were writing paid testimonials to 'My Junior Year Abroad'. Some, like the Smith girl, whom he still occasionally saw, figured that France was teaching them to appreciate America. 'It's been very educational,' she repeated in a cold smug little voice when complaining about French boys (they wanted her to pay her share if they asked her out), about the bad manners of postal employees (they made her lick her own stamps), about her landlady, whose only interest in her was collecting the rent ('She doesn't think of me as a *person*'). Many insisted that they were learning all by themselves to enjoy art: 'Paris has so many opportunities, Peter.' As though they had never heard that there were art galleries and museums at home, most of them free to the public, unlike the Louvre, which made the big concession of giving half-rates to students.

Others were bugged on the cinémathèques, like Makowski, who spent his days at the rue d'Ulm and the Palais de Chaillot discovering old American movies. 'You can do that in New York,' Peter remonstrated, 'at the Museum of Modern Art.' Peter was tired of Makowski, who had somehow obtained his address and kept dropping around to take a bath or go to the toilet, where he would camp for hours; he lived in a *chambre de bonne*. In principle, Peter did not mind being treated as a comfort station, except that Jan gave nothing in return. When Peter begged him to go to Autun with him one weekend to look at the sculptures of Gislebertus, Makowski could not miss a Buster Keaton movie that was playing on Saturday night. He had practically stopped going to his classes at the Institute of Oriental Languages, saying that he got more language-training eating at Chinese restaurants.

The principle seemed to be that the less you got out of your courses, the more you claimed to be soaking up on the side. It was pathetic, really; even the types who had given up totally on French and passed all their waking hours at the American Centre on boulevard Raspail and engaging in oyster-eating contests with each other on the day they got their allowance felt they were getting an education. At nineteen or twenty, Peter supposed, nobody, least of all an American, could face the idea of having made a bad investment of a whole year of their lives.

Yet they had a point; old Pangloss, his adviser, had a point about the so-called learning-process going on independently of any actual studying. Whatever his parents might think, he had made some progress here, for which he could thank Bonfante rather than his mouldy classes. The only 'intensive French' he got came from Arturo, who would not let him talk Italian with him. He was also picking up some basic Russian from Elena. And if, in the higher realms, he could observe a little growth in himself, he owed that to the Bonfantes, who were real intellectuals, he decided, unlike the academics he had been exposed to most of his life.

There were times when he could not help contrasting Arturo and Elena with his own parents, all four of them. Take that little thing called 'respect'. Up to now, the only respect he could remember getting had come from tiny children. His parents would be amazed if they saw the way he was deferred to in the Bonfante household. More than that. *'On t'aime, Peter, tu sais,'* Bonfante had told him today, with a quick soft smile, when they finally parted at the entrance to the Cour de Rohan; he evidently feared he had hurt Peter's feelings. Peter had to admit that he found a declaration like that 'supportive'. When the *babbo* hurt his feelings by not taking him seriously, he was never even aware of it: 'Why is the boy sulking?' he used to shout at his stepmother.

Yet a person had to be careful about letting anything positive that happened to him abroad influence him negatively about his own country and his home or homes. For one thing, the positive was so rare here for a foreigner that you felt like falling on your knees and kissing the hem of the garment of anybody who was kind to you, like the girl in the post office (he had been telling Arturo about her) who put new string for him on the messy Christmas package he brought to the window to mail to New York. Coming on an oasis in a desert made you tend to depreciate the well-watered pastures at home.

He entered his building. The curtain moved in the concierge's *loge*. A veinous hand extended. *'Votre courrier.'* There were four letters for him. One from his mother, one from his father, one from his former roommate, and one in a strange handwriting, with a Paris postmark on the envelope. He opened it. An invitation to sing Christmas carols next week at the house of some people whose name he did not recognize. On the bottom was written: 'At the kind suggestion of Miss Roberta Scott.'

His heart nearly stopped. He had made up his mind to go to Rome for Christmas, to get away from Paris and its clammy, unhealthy climate at least for a couple of weeks. The Bonfantes were taking their kids to ski in the Savoie during the *vacances scolaires*. That meant that if he stayed here he would be all alone over the holidays. He could make a call to his mother from the central post office on Christmas night, and that would be it.

If he went to the carol-singing, which was scheduled for the twenty-second, he would have to give up the project of riding his motorbike down through Provence and along the Riviera to Italy; he had studied the route on the map, to skirt snow-covered mountains, and allowing for sightseeing, it might take him practically a week to reach Rome at this time of year. Of course he could go by train, in a *couchette*, second class, again breaking a vow to the motorbike, but it might be too late now to get a reservation – the Bonfantes had had theirs for weeks. Every Christmas, they said, there was a mass exodus from Paris, starting the night the schools closed.

Even if he could get a place on the train, there was something else to consider. What if Roberta was staying here through the holidays instead of going off with the mob? He had not seen her now for nearly ten days. It would be madness to forgo the chance of having her all to himself in the empty city. The Institut Pasteur, where she worked, might not even *have* vacations. He halted on a landing and drew a deep breath. He felt the promise of Rome crumbling, like the plaster on the walls of the exiguous service staircase; and almost wished he had never got the invitation. At least he would have been spared what Mr Small, he supposed, would call the decision-making process.

If only he could be sure that Roberta would be staying here, he would gladly renounce Rome. Obviously, he could call her up and ask her, and, if she said no, he would shoot over to American Express and try to get a *couchette* on the train that left on the twenty-third. That would be the rational approach. He fingered a *jeton* in his pocket, started slowly back down the stairs, vacillated. His whole upbringing fought against a rational approach. To find out and coldly act on the finding would be cheap. As his mother always said, you had to be willing to sacrifice ... But *how much*? Furiously, he ground his teeth. Nobody ever told you the specifics; you were just urged not to play it safe, Peter. He continued the ascent to his apartment.

At this stage in his life-history, Roberta's company ought to be worth more than all the churches of Borromini and the Sistine Chapel. Except that he could count on the Sistine Chapel's being there, which was more than he could say for Roberta. He would be glad to play it safe if he knew what safe was. If some friendly jackdaw were to fly down his air-shaft with her pocket agenda in its bill! It was a case for a supernatural agency. Maybe he should consult his horoscope in the evening paper. Hating this bargaining his soul was doing with itself, he decided to toss a coin.

Joy to the World

IN his fifth-floor stronghold in the Albergo dei Re Magi, Peter put his eye to the keyhole and took a quick reconnaissance. The door of the wc, diagonally across from his room, was now ajar. He sped out of his room, shutting the door behind him without stopping to lock it, though he had left his wallet on the bed. There was not a second to lose. Even as he shot across the hall, other doors could be heard opening. If he had stopped to lock up, as the maid was always warning him to do, someone might have got there ahead of him, despite the favourable position his room occupied.

It was the same story as in those hotels in Paris. His day started with the race to the *gabinetto*; when he heard the ancient chain pull, he was on his mark. Followed the Herculean clean-up after its last tenant, only here he had to do it with sheets of thin slippery yellowish toilet paper, no brush being furnished. The big difference was that now he had a nice view through the open window of the red-tiled roofs of Rome and of plants growing in pots on neighbouring balconies. Across lines of bright laundry, he could even see the pale moth-brown angels with folded wings, like lifejackets, on the strange bell tower of Sant'Andrea delle Fratte. Afterwards he could saunter out and have a *cappuccino* at the coffee-store opposite the Propaganda Fide, buy an orange and a sugar bun, and go back for a second *cappuccino*.

So that he was glad he had not let himself be discouraged by American Express: no *couchettes* available, first *or* second class. Sitting up all night on the ordinary slow train, he had fortified himself with the maxim of William the Silent, which he recited to the clacketing of the wheels: '*Il n'est pas néces-saire d'espérer pour entreprendre, ni de réussir pour persévérer.*' He did not know how the person they called 'Guillaume le Taciturne' came to be part of French civilization, but he gave a good mark to the professor for introducing the class to that thought. Part of the night he stood in the corridor, having relinquished his seat to a Frenchman with a hideous baby. When he unclosed his gummy eyes for the *n*th time, it was the dawn of Christmas Eve; Italian officials were saying '*Buon giorno*' and asking for his passport and if he had any contraband. He was home.

Multas per gentes et multa per aequora vectus. Although it was a corny thing to do, after a late Roman supper of the traditional eels, he followed the crowd into midnight mass at Santa Maria Maggiore, by the station. They had a supposed relic of the Bambino's crib that the priests carried in proces-sion, and some wonderful mosaics around the high altar were all lit up and shining like a holy fire. Near where Peter stood was a confessional box in which you could tell your sins in Esperanto. Afterwards he lost his way and got swept along by another crowd, coming from the Aracoeli. Among these humbler worshippers were big dogs and a little goat, which he patted. He saw the statue, on horseback, of Marcus Aurelius and met the bagpipers from the Abruzzi, dressed like real shepherds, making their wailing music and passing a collection-plate. Returning to his hotel, he felt too excited to sleep.

The night porter, whom he woke up to get in, told him about a solemn mass at dawn in the church of Sant'Anastasia, at the foot of the Palatine; she had the same birthday as Jesus. He showed him how to find it on a map. It was another long walk. When Peter finally hit the sack after breakfast, he had not been to bed for two whole nights. That way, at least, he had circumnavigated Christmas. Waking up late that afternoon, he found it was already dark outside, since in Italy they did not have daylight saving in the winter. More-over, it seemed to have rained. He put in a call to his mother and mailed his letters of introduction in the post office at

San Silvestro, resigned to passing a solitary weekend on account of tomorrow being Saturday.

Incredibly, they all clicked. It was as if the lemons, cherries, oranges, and bells came up, one after the other, in some miraculous slot-machine attached to his telephone. Bonfante's sister invited him to lunch twice in her apartment; she was married to a professor at the University. A *contessa* who was an old friend of the *babbo*'s invited him to lunch too, with a pair of English pansies; she lived in a historic *palazzo*, and her menservants wore white gloves. Another friend of the *babbo*'s took him to a dinner *in piedi*, which meant a buffet supper, on the Via Appia Antica; that night he learned to do the twist. An art scholar Bob knew showed him through the *restauro*, where craftsmen dressed in white like surgeons operated on damaged frescoes, paintings, and sculptures. Everybody acted so sorry when they heard he had spent Christmas day alone, sleeping (*'Se avessimo saputo!'*), that he decided for the future to pretend he had not arrived till Christmas night.

It was an ill wind that blew nobody good. He now felt almost grateful for not having come on his motorbike. He would not have had room in his pack for the two changes of clothes with accompanying haberdashery that at the last minute he had stuffed into his suitcase. Even so, he had had to buy a new pair of too-wide black shoes on the Corso and he was thinking of taking the *babbo* up on the offer of a new suit. His father claimed to know a tailor here who could make him one in forty-eight hours for the price of a ready-made at home. He had instructed Peter not to let them put in any padding and to charge it, evidently suspecting that if he sent a cheque, Peter would just add the money to his savings and do without the suit. Or get a second-hand one at the old-clothes market near San Giovanni in Laterano, which in fact Peter had been eyeing – why squander a lot of *fric* on something that would hang uselessly in his closet once he got back to Paris? On the other hand, he had spilled *pasta* and Chianti several times on his grey flannel, and the talcum powder and salt they sprinkled on him did not wholly remove the spots.

His mother, too, on the telephone, had asked him about clothes. 'But I won't *need* any, Mother. You sound as if I was going to have a Papal audience. What am I going to do with a lot of white shirts? All I have on my programme is sight-seeing and taking in a few movies.' But it turned out that she was right. The Romans *were* hospitable, and Italian men, he had to admit, whatever their age and condition, wore dark suits, white shirts, and dark ties when invited out in the evening. He wondered what they put on, to mark the dif-ference, when somebody died.

His mother wanted to know what had made him change his mind about the motorbike. Of course she was happy that he had, on account of icy roads, but she said that it did not sound like him to listen to the voice of reason. 'It's too long a story, Mother. I'll tell you some other time.' 'And, dearest, I don't understand why you didn't leave Paris sooner, since the weather there is so grim.' 'Neither do I,' said Peter. 'Hey, Ma, this is long distance! Let me say hello to Bob.' Bob was inquisitive too. 'What kept you so long in Paris? Was it the Smith girl or the beautiful vegetarian?' 'Lay off,' said Peter. 'I had a lottery ticket, I had to study, I had a date with a Christmas carol. Pick the one that suits you.' He was not going to confess that he had been holed up in dreary Paris all those extra days, as it turned out, *for nothing*.

He still writhed when he thought of the fool's paradise he had carefully constructed that had fallen ignominiously to pieces at the first contact with reality. Taking '*Qui ne risque rien n'a rien*' for his motto when actually the gamble had been all inside his own mind. On the creeping train, he had plenty of time for mortification. The only comfort he could find in contemplating his downfall was that nobody but himself knew how high he had been flying. Yet that was clammy com-fort. If the sole spectator of your disappointment was your-self, it indicated you were a weakling or, at best, a nut. Nobody could split his sides laughing at you but nobody could feel sorry for you either.

He could laugh, but without pleasure, at the picture of himself buttoned into his flannel suit, engraved invitation in his pocket, hopefully ringing a doorbell on the rue de Lille and then walking through a garden with statuary to a house with all the windows lit up. His boats were burned, except for a little life-raft – the assurance that at least he would see her at this song-fest, and that he had decided was worth waiting for, whatever happened next. On purpose, he was late, so as not to be stuck with total strangers, and as his feet crunched on the gravel path he was chanting '*Auprès de ma Blonde*,' for which he had invented some new words: 'What would you give, my darling,/ to have your loved one home? I'd give the Sistine Chapel/and Buonarroti's dome./The coins in the Trevi Fountain, the Porta Pinciana walls./An ice cream at Rosati's, the Villa d'Este falls.' And all the while, the one eventuality that had not entered into his calculations was awaiting him, like death biding for Achilles at the Scaean Gate. She was not there.

Yet he had come to the right place. In a big high-ceilinged room with French windows and heavy white draperies, he found a number of compatriots whom he had already met at a rally of Americans-in-Paris-for-Johnson, an organization about which he was having second thoughts; he wished he had back the tithe of his October allowance he had donated to the cause. Trying to quell his apprehension (she might be late or have gone to the bathroom), he shook hands with a corporation lawyer, a trustee of the American Hospital, two bankers, a minister, a management consultant, an author of a famous book he had seen the movie of, a Negro actor, a travel agent, a guy from the American Centre, a professor who was writing a book on De Gaulle, and some miscellaneous women in glittering dresses; this, he guessed, was the infrastructure of what they called the American liberal community – plus the hostess's French teacher.

The hostess, a tall thin nervous blonde in a long grey velvet dress that matched the walls, was passing out mimeographed programmes with the words and music and urging the guests into a small white music room that contained nothing but an expensive-looking clavichord, a music stand, and two gilt chairs. 'Is everybody here?' she kept asking, tapping on a list. 'Harry, is everybody here?' Her husband consulted *his* list, on which with a small gold pencil he had been putting little checks. He was tall too and wore a dark grey velvet smoking jacket, gold-rimmed glasses, and a tie that looked like a stock. It came back to Peter that this guy had passed the hat for the Johnson outfit; he was a fund-raiser for an international church group. 'I count one to come still. Shall we begin?'

In the general move forward, Peter found he was stepping on the hostess's skirt. While he was apologizing, the doorbell chimed three times. He gave a cry of relief. 'Hey, that's her – Roberta!' 'Roberta?' the woman said, still inspecting the damage to her train, on which Peter's foot had left a large damp print. 'You mean Bobbie? But she's gone away. Didn't she tell you?' 'Gone away? For *good*?' 'No, no. Just for the holidays. She and her friend have a fascinating itinerary worked out. They're going to do Romanesque abbeys in Burgundy. Not just the obvious ones like Vézelay and Cluny but the little *recherché* ones.' 'I guess she'll go to Autun,' Peter said glumly. 'Oh, surely. Do you know Gislebertus?' 'Only from a book I had.' For Christmas, he had sent his mother his copy of *Gislebertus, Sculpteur d'Autun* and some pans and a conical sieve called *le chinois* from the Samaritaine. Envy added to his sense of betrayal. He loved the little raisin-eyed people in that book, especially one of the Magi who looked like Harold Macmillan and a tiny brave naked warrior with a big dagger riding into combat on a gigantic bird.

The hostess was giving her cheek to the new arrival to be kissed and making purring noises. 'So naughty of you to be late. Mr Levi, here's another friend of Roberta's. Silly, do you know Peter Levi?' Peter recognized the heavy eyebrows and thick silken eyelashes of Silvanus Platt. 'Hi.'

'Will everybody put out their cigarettes, please?' With an ill grace, Peter let himself be lined up among the basses. He considered that he had been tricked into coming here. The invitation had not specifically said that Roberta would be present but it had certainly left itself open to that construction. Nor did he like the idea that the Princetonian, who sang tenor, had been seeing her unbeknownst to him.

His old antipathy to music-lovers refuelled. There was no Yule log burning merrily in the living room, and he saw no sign of refreshments. Instead of pictures on the walls, they had grey blown-up photographs of prints of antique instruments. Less-is-More appeared to be the house rule. Everything was grey, black, or white. The hostess blew into a recorder, and the host tinkled away inaudibly on the clavichord – his wife's Christmas present to him. On the programme, the words of the carols had been written out in olde Elizabethan spellyng with ampersands, which reminded Peter sourly of Rocky Port. He did not know any of the carols they had exhumed from library stacks and he could not read music, not that it mattered, since he was unable to stay on key. Most of the other carollers seemed to be in his situation. It made him think of those awful mornings in chapel when the headmaster decided to stir things up by posting a new hymn.

He would almost rather be lending volume to 'O, Come, All Ye Faithful' or 'Silent Night'. It struck him that these rich amateurs needed somebody like his mother or Richard Dyer-Bennet to instruct them in the art of the possible. When they had carols at home or at his aunt Millie's, the sisters always included a few that everybody knew, like 'What Child Is This?' which had the same tune as 'Greensleeves', and 'I Saw Three Ships Come Sailing In' and 'Once in David's Royal City' – Peter was partial to hymns and carols that had Jews in them.

The purpose of tonight's exercise was obscure to him. If the hosts wanted to play a duet, why couldn't they do it by themselves, instead of recruiting a lot of supernumeraries and giving them sheets of music to hold in their hands as stage-props? The whole occasion was like a long-drawn-out punishment of Tantalus. He guessed there had been a fatal decision to do something 'different' this year, which any child could have told them was playing with fire when it came to something like Christmas. Peter felt defrauded not only by the unfamiliar carols but by the tree this couple had, which was trimmed with glass icicles, transparent glass balls, and white roses and carnations that were distributed, when the programme finally ended, to the guests according to sex.

At that point, the host ladled out some mulled wine which, the hostess explained, ought really to have been warmed with a hot poker instead of being heated up on the stove. People like that, Peter had noticed, seemed to think that knowing the right way of doing something excused you for doing it the wrong way, as though knowledge was all that mattered. Installing the carnation in his buttonhole, he decided that this could not be more different from the general's home atmosphere, and yet it seemed just as American, in a sinister way he could not define.

He was surprised that this pseudo-worldly pair knew Roberta well enough to refer to her as 'Bobbie' and not so surprised that they knew Silvanus Platt, whom the hostess addressed as 'Silly' and sometimes 'Silly Boy'. Peter hated to think what it must have been like for the poor guy in school. Tonight he was wearing a paisley waistcoat and a pocket watch with a gold chain on which hung a Phi Beta Kappa key. Maybe it was his father's, or he had bought it at a pawnshop. Even at Princeton, nobody could earn one before the spring of his junior year, and for that you had to burn the midnight oil, whereas Silvanus's specialty, it appeared, was burning the candle at both ends.

He was prattling to the hostess about girls, ski resorts, night clubs, poker, somebody's wine cellar. Peter was getting ready to make his escape when he heard the name Bobbie. Silvanus could not understand why a vegetarian teetotaller would want to do a tour of Burgundy, of all places, where the whole point was eating and drinking. To be fair, the same thought had crossed Peter's mind. 'Food for the soul,' the hostess said, puffing on a cigarillo. 'You wouldn't dig it, Silly. Darling Bobbie has this *béguin* for the Romanesque. So pure and grand and austere.' 'But why does she have to go to Burgundy? Isn't there Romanesque around here?' 'Nothing to write home about. Use your eyes, darling. Of course there's Normandy. Jumièges, which has some delicious Carolingian bits. And that one where they have the plainsong.' 'St-Wandrille,' supplied Peter. 'But what's great here in the Ile-de-France is the Gothic. Have you been out to St-Denis? You can see right there where it originated. And you don't have to have a car or anything.' 'Bobbie wouldn't *look* at a Gothic cathedral,' said the hostess with a little laugh. 'All those fussy crockets and overloaded gables.'

'I *like* Gothic,' protested Peter. In fact, one of his plans, if Roberta had stayed here for the holidays, had been to take her to look at Amiens, which, according to a book she was reading, was the Gothic Parthenon. To learn that she was a zealot of the Romanesque was another bad surprise. He felt a loyalty to the Gothic, which he regarded as his personal discovery, and the fact that there was a lot of it around, readily accessible to the modest Paris-based day tripper, was an additional merit in his eyes. He had nothing against the Romanesque, as his love of Gislebertus proved, but a girl who could be unfair to Gothic cathedrals was not likely to care for Peter Levi, with his tall attenuated form and crazy soaring pinnacles. 'You do?' said the hostess with a thoughtful air. 'One has to see Chartres, of course. Marvellous. But Harry and I aren't so *emaballés* by church architecture. We're mad on *châteaux*.'

Peter remembered his mother saying that you could divide people into those who liked churches and those who liked *châteaux*. She meant the guided-tour kind where you admired the furniture, not ruined castles with dungeons, which you could visit by yourself. According to her, social climbers, even those claiming to be interested in art, got rapidly bored by churches unless they had lots of loot in them in the form of gold, marbles, and precious stones. She had a point, Peter decided, listening to this woman briefing Silly on the *hôtels particuliers* of the Marais. In his mind, he sketched a Last Judgment, with a Weighing of Souls: two little *château* people, resembling the hostess and her husband, were sitting in a balance pulled down by a horrible demon, while in the other basket he and his mother, light as eggs, were mounting upward, tenderly claimed by an angel holding the scales.

The party was breaking up. A servant opened the door to the dining room and then hastily closed it. No boar's head was forthcoming. A long table with twin candelabra was set for two. An insane thought struck Peter. All was not lost. What if he were to go to Autun tomorrow, on his own? It was as good a place as any to spend Christmas, and he had a fair chance of running into Roberta, provided he stayed put. She was bound to visit the cathedral, and he could entrench himself there with his binoculars. A guy could spend a week studying the tympanum and the capitals without getting too bored or (he hoped) catching pneumonia.

Silvanus, who had his coat on, was proposing they go eat some oysters. 'O.K., but wait a minute.' Peter turned to the hostess. 'Thank you for a nice time,' he lied. Then he took the icy plunge. 'I wanted to ask you something. About that tour Roberta and this girl are doing . . . I might be in Autun myself next week some time . . . On my motorbike. It would be fun if we could make connections. I thought maybe you'd know what her plans were, more or less. I mean, is she going to Dijon first or . . . ?'

Something was wrong. The woman was looking at her husband and lifting a pencilled eyebrow. 'I haven't made up my mind yet,' Peter continued, hedging. 'There's this Pole who thinks he might come with me. But I might go to Rome instead. Though they say the trains are pretty full.' The woman eyed her husband again. She made that purring noise. 'Go to Rome, darling.' Other guests were waiting to say good-bye. 'Have a scrumptious Christmas.' 'See you at Klosters.' Peter tried again. 'About Autun —' The host put his oar in. 'My wife says go to Rome. And my wife is a wise woman.' He held out Peter's coat. Peter took umbrage. 'I don't get it. What's the mystery? Why shouldn't I see Autun if I want to?' The woman gave her husband one of those shall-we-tell-him glances. 'Of course you can see Autun. But you might be *de trop* right now. Don't look at me that way, Harry! After all, it's not a secret.' She spoke loudly and defiantly, thrusting her pale head forward almost into Peter's face. 'Bobbie isn't with a girl. She's with her *petit ami*.'

'Cynthia,' her husband sighed. She whirled. 'I have a perfect right to tell him. Bobbie's my goddaughter. I'm her mother's oldest friend.' 'That's a funny reason, darling.' 'It's not!' 'Well, thanks,' put in Peter hastily. 'Thanks a lot really. I wouldn't want to butt in. It was just an idea anyway. I can go to Autun some other time.' '*Of course,*' soothed the woman, resuming her social mask and turning to look at herself in a long mirror as though to make sure she had it on straight. 'Probably I'm over-protective about Bobbie. But her friend is French and a little bit stuffy. He might not be pleased to have an American boy on his trail. Like one of her younger brothers.' ' "Sister, sister," ' said Silly Boy, ' "what's that naughty man doing in your bed?" '

'Come on,' urged Peter. 'Let's go.' He had no desire, not even a morbid one, to hear any more. But Silly was curious, so they had to stand there, with their coats on, listening to the gory details. The *petit ami* was a research doctor, separated from his wife. And Roberta's parents knew. 'I imagine they expected something of the sort when they sent her over here. At home, she'd had an unhappy love affair with some man who lived on peanut butter and stood on his head.' 'Apple butter, darling.' 'Are you *sure?*' 'Oh, absolutely.' 'Well, anyway, this young doctor couldn't be more normal and *comme il faut.* Does the *chasse à courre* on weekends. Bobbie's always been a passionate athlete. His not being divorced is a convenience, really. If she wants to go ahead with her career, she'll have another two years of medical school and then interneship. And then the residency. It's a terribly sensible arrangement. If it lasts, she can do her interneship at the American Hospital. None of the complications of marriage and the inevitable children.'

'Yeah, it makes sense,' said Peter. Actually, to his stupefied brain, it made no sense at all. In his private order of credibility, a Roberta *dépucelée* ranked far below the Virgin Birth and the Immaculate Conception. If she had not been a virgin unspotted when he had met her at the general's on Thanksgiving, then he would swear no more oaths. But maybe even then she had been bedding down with this doctor. Maybe it had already happened with the headstander. His imagination balked at the thought, just as it had declined when he was little to picture his parents doing it; he preferred to think that he had originated in a cabbage leaf.

Yet had he not hoped to deflower Roberta himself? He was no longer sure. If he had, the hope had been founded on the sheer unlikelihood of the proposition. Hoping against hope seemed to be the only course open to him where sex was concerned. Imagining his own initiation by some practised hand was repugnant. He did not want to be a hapless Adonis pursued by a hot-breathing Venus; rather, a pure mortal youth loved, while he slept, by a chaste Immortal, like the moon stealing down on Endymion. While feverishly dreaming of trapping the maiden in his snare, he had not once thought ahead to the act that presumably – what else? – would reward his devotion. His mind had drawn a veil. It was true that he had had a mild curiosity about her breasts, but really he had been enamoured of her as a radiant totality that included her Waring Blendor and her nutty food ideas; if he had to pick some part of Roberta that summed up the whole, it might have been those flags of colour in her cheeks.

He did not know whether this was natural or whether it was not just another illustration of his being a grotesque anachronism. In movie houses he was always embarrassed to see couples pawing and nuzzling each other, on or off the screen. All he knew of love's raptures came from reading poetry, and the poets, like him, usually did not let their imagination stray much below the waist unless they were rejected and angry. Yet it looked as if the world had changed. To listen to most guys talk today, all they were interested in was some girl being 'stacked' and whether or not they could 'get laid' by her.

Peter had only fitfully had such coarse thoughts himself and then about streetwalkers or unattractive girls reputed to be pushovers. And when he had them, he was ashamed, since they violated the great commandment he still carried in his wallet: 'The Other is always an End: thy Maxim.' If a woman was a tool for obtaining gratification for your tool, she could not be an end. Of course that was the whole logic of prostitution: you used them as a means of getting laid, and they used you as a means of getting dough. So that you could say that it all squared off there, in a sordid realistic way. And if a girl wanted sex and you wanted it too, that could be a deal, he supposed. But in those arrangements, he suspected, one party was usually cheating.

If memory was not lying to him, the *most* he had imagined with Roberta was taking her to Amiens on the train, taking her out to Trappes and showing her the moorhens and the fieldfare in the winter ponds and hedges, maybe taking her skating on one of the big rinks, feeding her jasmine tea in his apartment and toast with rose-hip jam – little extensions of his confidence that implied no fell design. Yet as he walked with Silvanus towards St Germain des Prés, he discovered a strange thing. His love had died on the spot. One swift blow had done it. And he did not feel half as much anguish as when his plant had bit the dust. Only anger with himself and a sense of wasted time. Now he would have to begin all over, trying to find an interest in life beyond the daily grind. It was depressing not to have anything to look forward to any more. True, that had been his state when he had met her, so that he was only back where he had started. Yet there was a limit to a person's resilience. To be repeatedly sent back 'home', like a man in parcheesi, by a single throw of the dice, could finally make you resign. Let the others play. Instead of going through the weary ordeal of trying to get to Rome, which would probably disappoint him, he could cable his family to send him an airplane ticket to New York. One-way.

In the café, over their second dozen oysters, annoyance with the virtuous Roberta began to surface. 'Frankly, can you swallow that story? Do you see her checking into a hotel room with a man? After all, they ask you for your passport. Don't forget that.' Silvanus nodded. 'I would have bet anything she was a virgin,' continued Peter. 'Me too.' 'The fact that they travel together doesn't necessarily prove anything. Maybe they sleep with a sword between them.' 'The guy is French, remember?' 'But I *saw* her about ten days ago.

We went to a concert. She seemed just the same. You know, sort of fresh and wholesome, like an American apple.' 'The one the doctor ordered, ha ha. But she really was a nice dish.' Silvanus fetched a sigh. 'I took her out once myself. Skating.' 'Oh?' 'That's all. We had fun. And she paid her own admission. There aren't too many attractions in Paris-after-dark for a vegetarian health fiend.' 'But that was what was so *misleading*,' said Peter. 'You assume that if somebody's a puritan, they're a puritan all the way down the line. You'd think you had the right to assume that.' 'Girls are funny.' 'Maybe being a vegetarian is the explanation. A person's physical nature has to find *some* outlet. A girl that doesn't drink or eat meat and butter and stuff is available for sex, no?' Silvanus shook his head. 'In my experience, you have to get them a little high the first time. Not loaded, because they might be sick, but high.'

Peter remained silent. He was thinking that if he went on a strict vegetarian diet, he might be able to lose his own virginity. 'You can usually tell,' Silvanus went on, 'when a girl will. I mean, when a nice girl will. I can't stand tramps.' 'How do you tell?' 'Oh, there are lots of little ways. Sometimes I study them when they come out of the Alliance Française ... Some of those Swedish chicks are virgins. Contrary to what you hear.'

They ordered a third dozen oysters. Silvanus was having Belons, and Peter was sticking with Claires. 'Silvanus —' 'Call me Silly, if you want. I don't mind. In fact I'm learning to love it. It disarms the opposition. If you can get a woman to call you Silly, you're in. Especially an older woman. "Oh, Silly, don't do that!" ' He mimicked a female voice. Peter sought another topic. There was a question he had been wanting to ask. 'What kind of a name is Silvanus?' 'It comes out of the Bible – the Epistles. He was one of Saint Paul's disciples. It's another name, most likely, for Silas, in Acts. There were a lot of Congregational ministers in my father's family, way back, and in each generation we have a Silvanus. People think a name like that is a handicap. They're so wrong. In the first place, it helps you develop an armour early. Second, it makes the general public remember you: girls, headmasters, professors, party-throwers. Third, it makes the whole world feel sorry for you. "How could your parents have been so cruel as to give a tiny child a burden like that to carry through life?" ' Peter gave a weak assenting grin. 'Fourth, it's a conversation-starter. If somebody you meet asks you your first name and you say "Peter", that's the end of it. No mileage. But if they ask *me* my name, it's an opening for me. Right away, like you, they want to know what kind of a name is that, and we're off.'

'Don't you ever get fed up with explaining it?' 'No. Why should I? It's less of a drag to repeat something you already know than to try to think up some boring fresh gambit. Anyway, I vary it a little. I haven't given you the bit about Silvanus, Roman god of woodlands, hence "sylvan". My uncle Sylvy goes to town on that, reciting Vergil and Horace. *"Horridi dumeta Silvani . . ."* It's a ball. Then there's the bit about Silas being maybe one of the authors of the Gospels.' 'I never heard of that.' 'Neither have most people. But you're interested, aren't you?' 'Well, mildly. Go on.' 'No, I just wanted to show you the possibilities. At some point, the other person, if it's a girl, chimes in with "Don't you think children should be allowed to choose their own names?" Or "I love the name 'Ermentrude', but I wonder if I'd have the courage . . ." Did you notice the time when we ordered these last oysters? "Silvanus", if you include "Silly", is usually good for a fifteen-minute chat.'

Peter burst out laughing. He was warming to this boy, who reminded him of someone, though not physically. He searched his memory. Someone he knew quite well, he thought . . . Then he got it. It was himself. As he might be in the fourth dimension, turned inside out. Or reincarnated. 'I think a lot,' explained Silvanus. 'Though I'm not meant to be very brainy. My brother Barnabas got all the grey matter in the family. But I analyse situations and work out strategies. And I study people. While I'm talking to them, I'm watching their reactions to me. I couldn't do that if I was self-conscious, like you. You have to practise to develop your armour.'

'You're a funny guy,' said Peter. 'Let's see each other when I get back.' 'Where are you going?' 'To Rome, I guess. Would you like to come along?' 'I've got to go to Klosters. With Cynthia.' He raised his eyebrows suggestively. 'You mean that woman tonight? But she's old enough to be your mother!' 'Hardly. She may be old enough to be somebody's mother, but *my* mother is *old*.' 'Doesn't her husband suspect?' 'So what? He's probably used to it. She says he's impotent. They're "like brother and sister". Though they all say that.' 'But weren't you talking to her about girls tonight?' 'I make a point of that. It lets her know I'm a free agent. You know, just a butterfly flitting from flower to flower. And it makes her feel brave and generous. Actually, she's rather a tightwad. Or maybe it's him. She comes from one of those breakfast-food families – Grape-Nuts or Ralston's, I forget. But they play poor little church mice, squeak, squeak. In Klosters they have a rather grand chalet. Bobbie stayed there. But I don't expect Santa Claus will put much in poor Silly Boy's stocking. No Cartier watches or diamond cuff links. Something thoughtful, for his soul. *Timeo Danaos et dona ferentes*, as my uncle Sylvy says when he goes to stay with our rich cousin. They're paying my air fare and sending a car to meet me, which is a help, but then there are the tips to the servants and my own wee thoughtful presents . . .'

'You shouldn't go,' said Peter, 'if you dislike that Cynthia as much as you give the impression.' 'Do I sound as if I disliked her?' 'Yes.' 'It's so hard to know what one feels, really. But in cold, cruel fact, I confess I'm going for the skiing. It's my first crack at the Swiss Alps. I couldn't pass that up, don't you see? Then I have this dream . . .' 'What's your dream?' prompted Peter, looking at him with curiosity. Silly crossed his fingers; he knocked on wood. 'To get taken on as a ski instructor,' he confided. 'You're kidding.' But Silly was serious. 'A guy I know put me on to it. The thing is, you have to connect with some English-speaking group that wants lessons. The instructors up there only know how to talk German, so it's an opportunity for an American to cash in. Unbelievable!' He sighed. 'With my room and meals free,

I could clear maybe a hundred and fifty dollars. This guy knew another kid who did it last year.' And unlike this other kid, Silly had experience. He had been a ski instructor before once in Vermont; a family had hired him to teach their children. But it was easy; anybody could do it that understood the fundamentals. The problem was really contacts. Harry and Cynthia would have to fix it so that he could meet the English and American crowd. 'I haven't told her yet. She says she wants to be "quiet". I've got to make her give a party for me, right away, when I get there. She has to see how important that is for me.' He wiped some little beads of sweat from his forehead. 'But don't the people who go to a fancy place like that already know how to ski?' 'Yes, but there always have to be first-timers, who want to make it socially. They feel out of it, not knowing how to ski and not knowing the language. That's where my English comes in. I can organize them in a class. It's a question of finding them before they sign up with another group. You can give private lessons too, if you get known. Rich guys and women who need some special attention.'

Peter listened dubiously. It seemed clear that this far-fetched project was close to Silly's heart. Maybe kids on their own over here got that way when they overspent their allowance. To deter him was probably impossible, yet Peter felt he should try. Perhaps it was his own pessimistic nature, but he was convinced that nothing would materialize for poor Silly up in those Alps but sorrow and disappointment. Even if he could connect with a job, the woman would find means of keeping him away from it. She had looked tough and selfish, Peter thought, and she was not paying Silly's expenses to have him gambolling on the slopes with other women and girls. In Paris, he might be a free agent, but in a chalet he would be her plaything, like a talking doll.

He pointed that out. 'Yes, I know. It could turn out like that. I told you it was my *dream*. The old fairy gold. And if the weather should suddenly get bad, it could be a grim little house party. They play cribbage, and Harry does *petit point*. And they believe in keeping the heat way down and wrapping themselves in shawls. If they turned up the thermostat, somebody might think they were Americans.' He became extremely dejected, which awakened compunction in Peter. In his private book of Leviticus, there was a precept for parents and pedagogues: never throw cold water on an enterprise unless you can offer an alternative. 'Listen, Silly,' he suggested, 'why don't you go to Switzerland on your own? You could get taken on as a ski instructor just as well in some other centre. Then you'd be independent, don't you see? The fact that you haven't told her shows you're worried yourself about how she might react. You could go to St Moritz or . . . What are those other ones?' 'Gstaad, Davos, Zermatt.' 'Yes, why not one of those? You could post notices in the hotels. "Experienced American gives skiing lessons." ' He hoped he was sounding persuasive. His ignorance of winter sports, skating aside, was deep and principled, and, for his own part, he would much rather be drafted into the Army than arrive seeking employment in a mountain village packed with sunburned skiers who knew not Peter Levi. But Silly was manifestly different. He knew his way around.

'It's too late. I promised. Besides, I'm stony. Really stony.' Peter reflected. A man of words and not of deeds was like a garden full of weeds. 'I can lend you some dough, if you like. I have plenty. You can pay me back out of your profits. And, listen, you don't need to take a plane. There are trains. And if you don't land a ski-instructor job right away, you might be able to wait on table. Or baby-sit. A lot of families take their kids with them to the *sports d'hiver*.' 'Thanks, I can baby-sit in Paris if I want to.' His voice was dry, and he was regarding Peter with something like pity – or was it simple amusement? – from behind that fringe of eyelashes. Peter saw that he had made an error in strategy: the battle for Silly Boy's soul was over. He did not know why he had wanted to reclaim the foolish youth, unless he felt he had 'good stuff' in him, as the headmaster used to say about some hopeless delinquent. Without further discussion, they rose. Silly covered a yawn and wound a long white cashmere scarf around his neck. They had paid the bill. 'Thanks, honestly, for the offer of the loan. It was a nice thought. My ransom.' 'Well, have a good vacation anyway.' 'You too. I can't wait to get on those slopes and pick up a tan. Fresh air and exercise!'

In Rome there were fresh air and exercise, as well as churches, fountains, hills, domes, sword-brandishing angels, *palazzi*, clocks, bells, and friendly inhabitants. Investigating Rome, Peter was happy. It was a nice town to walk in, despite hazardous traffic, and, on his father's recommendation, he had bought himself the TCI guidebook, in Italian, from a pushcart near the Porta Pia that specialized in second-hand guides. He was philosophical about overcast skies and the few drops of rain; they made him appreciate the brilliant days in between, when the sky looked like a tent of pale blue silk stretched over a circus of gravity-defying shafts, towers, lanterns, flying statuary.

Imperial Rome did not interest him greatly, but he liked the early Christian churches, especially Santa Maria in Cosmedin. In the Piazza Navona, he loved the stalls set up for the Befana with candies and toys and crib figures of the animals and the shepherds and the Magi; there were dolls of knights in armour and beautiful ladies like the Queen of Night and Harlequins and Franciscan friars and, naturally, tanks and spacemen and bombers in plastic, which would eventually no doubt take over, but it had not happened yet.

He made a pious pilgrimage to San Giovanni dei Fiorentini and he looked in on San Luigi dei Francesi, where the priests were French. He visited the ghetto, entering by a street with a name like the Wailing Wall – Via del Pianto. It was not the Jews, though, that were meant to be weeping but the Virgin Mary, in a little hidden church around the corner. The guidebook said she was crying on account of the stubborn *Ebrei*, who would not recognize her son as their saviour – he was glad to see from the kosher signs that they were still holding out, because when they were converted, it would be the millennium, and the world would come to an end. Nearly everywhere he went, he met the bagpipers from the Abruzzi, and everywhere, like an aura, there was the inviting smell of roasting coffee.

In Rome, he never got lonely, he found; there was always somebody eager to start a conversation and to compliment him on his Italian: '*Come parla bene!*' And waiters and countermen and sacristans, like the old woman who sold him his breakfast orange, all wanted to hear him say that their country was beautiful. '*E bella l'Italia, signorino?*' '*Si, si!*' At night in his room, he studied the guidebook, preparing the next day's expedition. This gave him a purpose in life; he could hardly wait for the morning to get up, run the gauntlet to the toilet, shave, and foray out. His hotel, it turned out, was in Borromini territory, which he took as a sign; he was resolved to see all the master's works and he was succeeding, though some were hard to get in to, with peculiar visiting hours or keys to be hunted down. '*E chiuso! E chiuso!*' a voice would bawl from a neighbouring top-storey window. But in Rome, unlike Paris, they eventually relented, just as in Rome they would let you stay in a museum till closing-time.

The only drawback about dear cracked Borromini was that so often you had to see Bernini, his cruel worldly rival, beside him or combined with him or sneering at him, as in the fountain in Piazza Navona, where the Nile was supposed to be covering its face so as not to have to look up at the 'top-heavy' façade of Sant'Agnese and the Plate shuddering and raising its hand to keep it from falling down, like those joke photos of tourists holding up the Tower of Pisa. Peter hated Bernini and made the sign of the figs at him whenever he could, unobserved. He personally could not find anything to object to in the proportions of Sant'Agnese, except that the saint's statue with her finger pointing to her breast was perched on one end of the front balustrade rather than in the middle: where were the other 'errors' that Bernini found so laughable? He bought a jumbo postcard of the piazza and sent it to Bob, with an arrow pointing to the church and the message 'What's wrong with this picture? Please inform. Peter.'

He was starting to acquire catalogues, postcards, large glossy reproductions; he invested in a pocket history of architecture, a pocket-mirror to look at the ceiling of the Sistine Chapel, a pocket engagement book, a notebook in which to scribble his reflections. He even wished he had a camera with him. Or that he had been taught how to draw. Though he used to chide his mother for extravagant purchases of postcards, telling her she should rely on her memory, he now felt heartsick when at Anderson's they could produce only one measly reproduction of the marvellous bird angels nesting in the vaults of San Giovanni in Laterano. He had hoped to find a whole flock of *particolari* to choose from, to remind him, back in Paris, of the morning he discovered that fantastic aviary of cherubs and nearly fainted with pleasure.

If it had not been for Borromini, Peter was not sure that he would have liked the baroque and he wondered whether he did not like *him* for what somebody like Bob might consider the wrong reasons – because of the downy pennate creatures he put everywhere, standing in belfries and nesting in vaulted ceilings, hiding in egg-and-dart mouldings, pretending to be columns, peeking down from pediments. Borromini must have loved wings, since he usually gave his angels two pairs, like little garments, one folded and one open. And he loved stars, vegetables, leaves, acorns, flowers. Peter got attached to the little rhymes of concave and convex that seemed to be the master's 'language' and to the ribbony movement of plaster around windows that reminded him of his mother's boiled frostings as it swirled from her knife onto a birthday cake. He sensed coded messages coming from Mother Nature in the giant heads of the stern-eyed falcons (they had breasts like women) surmounting pillars on Palazzo Falconieri and in the acorns that hung like ear-rings on the Sapienza and on the Propaganda Fide, piercing small holes in its stone flesh. The guy had a strange sense of humour. Yet Bob said he had committed suicide.

When he looked at Borromini, instead of thinking about space and 'volumes', Peter had the feeling he used to get from

fairy-tales: that the world was in constant metamorphosis.
Capitals and columns were turning into vegetable and bird
forms; doors and windows were faces with ears. Invariably,
he was the only visitor to those hidden chapels and oratories
– as if he was the sole member of the human species who, led
by some croaking frog or talking raven in the shape of an
ancient custodian, had ever been introduced into those
zoomorphic interiors, which were buried, like the kernel of a
walnut or the secret of life, inside a neutral brown, hard-to-
crack shell. Nobody would guess, for instance, that the vast
Propaganda Fide, bustling with missionaries, across from
where Peter had his morning *cappuccino*, concealed the little
cenacle of the Re Magi, though the name of Peter's hotel was
a sort of password, if anybody stopped to think. Even the
light that streamed in there seemed to be a visitor guided by
a special angel.

When Bob's friend Sergio was taking him to lunch, at a
place called Il Buco, Peter broached the subject: where could
he find a good book on Borromini? He had been reconnoitring the bookshops to no avail. Naturally there wasn't one,
at least that Sergio knew of, unless Peter read German. He
seemed surprised by Peter's interest. Like most older people
(he was thin, elegant, and fortyish, with wrinkled laughing
eyes), he began digging for a motive. Was Peter planning to
study architecture? Was he taking a course in the baroque?
That a layman could 'just like' Borromini sounded pretty
evasive; it was the same as with watching birds or keeping a
plant in your room. A full explanation was called for, though
if a kid was interested in cars, nobody asked him if he was
planning to be a garage mechanic. When Peter ticked off the
churches and chapels he had been visiting, Sergio threw up
his hands. '*Come mai? Un ragazzo di dicianove anni!*' He
could hardly believe that a nineteen-year-old with no training
in art would simply look under 'Borromini' in the guidebook
and follow up the page references – seventeen, to be exact.
'*In Francia ti piaceva il barocco?*' Peter had been unaware that
there was such a thing in Paris as the 'Jesuit style' – the French
name, it appeared, for the baroque – and did not think he

had seen any examples of it. '*Ma certo. Les Invalides!*' And the church of the Sorbonne, for that matter, which was practically in Peter's back-yard. '*E un capriccio,*' summed up Sergio, who in reality liked Borromini himself. A restless genius who came from the north and had not fitted into the Roman Counter-Reformation picture. His filiation was Gothic, and if Peter wanted to trace his influence, he should go to Turin . . .

Hearing the word *Gothic*, Peter experienced a funny thrill. The short hair, newly clipped by a barber, rose lightly on the back of his neck, and he shivered. It was a moment of confirmation. The *principium individuationis* had affirmed itself in the seemingly chaotic perceptions of that *flatus voci*, Peter Levi. There was a *reason* underlying his old predilection for Borromini which, independently of any instruction, had brought about an act of recognition, just as had happened to him with St-Denis and the Abbé Suger. His choices were stemming from an inner unity, a Tree of Knowledge branching in him. Contrary to what he always feared, the objective world and Peter Levi were in touch with each other. He existed, he was real. If asked to write a paper on 'Gothic Elements in the Borrominian Structure', he could not point to any. But they were there, art historians knew about them, and his soul had felt their presence. The hair on the back of his neck subsided; he supposed this was the closest he would come to having a mystical experience. Seeing him shiver, Sergio was afraid that he might be catching a cold. The Roman winter was treacherous; you had to be careful about sitting on the Spanish Steps in the sun.

Peter laughed. He knew he was not going to get sick in Rome; he had too much to see and in such a short time. Feelings of power and mastery coursed through him. He accepted a *grappa* on the house. Leaving the restaurant, he realized that the thing tourists always talked about had happened. He had fallen in love with Rome. When and if he loved a girl really, it would be something joyful like this. And Rome was reciprocating. As his mother said, it took two.

That afternoon, when the stores opened, he went shopping.

He picked out an umbrella for Elena Bonfante and a bold striped tie for Arturo, pink gloves for his mother's birthday, and a handkerchief for his landlady. He stopped in at the *babbo*'s tailor and had his measurements taken. In the Piazza Navona he had a stand-up coffee and a chocolate *tartufo* and chose some crib figures of shepherds and the Three Kings to be distributed to his half-brother and -sister and the Bonfante children.

Everything seemed cheap here, in comparison to Paris. In restaurants you could eat just one course if you wanted or take half an order of *pasta*. Moreover, they were nice about cashing cheques at American Express. In the post office at San Silvestro, they had typewriters, free, for sending cables on which, with two fingers, Peter tapped out letters home. At San Silvestro, they also wrapped up his packages, at practically no cost, for mailing to America, and the public scribe sewed a dangling button on his raincoat. He left his watch to be cleaned because in Rome he did not need it; every quarter of an hour, wherever you were, a half-dozen church bells sang out the time. In the market, he bought *tuberose* for the kind plump signoras who invited him to meals, and when he climbed on a trolley bus with them, during the noon rush, the other passengers would smile and make room for him, so the flowers would not get crushed; everybody commented on the fragrant smell (*'Che profumo!'*), as though he were making a donation to the general happiness.

In the narrow streets of Vecchia Roma and in Trastevere, he saw scabby palaces and tenements and plenty of poor people, but this did not upset him the way it would have in Paris. On sunny days, caged birds swung from windows, women sat mending in their doorways, workmen making deliveries sang. If he watched a handsome woman drawing water from a fountain, he did not stop to think that this meant she had no *acqua corrente* where she lived. He guessed it was true that poverty seemed more acceptable in warm countries.

The world's problems did not clamour at him for solutions here. When he passed the Senate in Palazzo Madama (*note-*

vole facciata barocca) or the Chamber of Deputies in Palazzo Montecitorio (*iniziato nel* 1650 *dal Bernini*), it was hard to remember that there were legislators inside fighting. *Ars longa vita brevis est* was a truth that could not be argued with in the Eternal City, where the monuments were big and the inhabitants rather small and grasshopper-like. He endorsed the *apertura alla sinistra* without feeling too hopeful about what it could accomplish. The very fact that the Roman poor seemed so exceedingly numerous compared to the Roman rich made you doubt that land reform or redistribution of wealth could do much to change what looked like a natural state of affairs.

The *Messaggero*, which he read in preference to the *Corriere* and *La Stampa*, was short on what were known as current events and long on the *cronaca* of local stabbings, shootings, poisonings, suicides, frauds, burglaries, arson, as well as national scandals involving adulterate wine, milk, olive oil, building cement; it also featured avalanches, train wrecks, floods, explosions, and ordinary traffic deaths. Each day on finishing the paper, Peter marvelled that there was anybody left around to read it, except the police and the fire brigade. He was amused by the thrifty Roman house-painters, who at work wore hats made of folded newspapers, shaped like children's paper boats, from which stared gruesome headlines: BRUCIATO VIVO, STRANGOLATA, IL MOSTRO DELL'AVENTINO. He would be sorry to get back to a town where nothing much seemed to happen but world news and addresses by General De Gaulle.

That was not how the Romans felt. They envied him for living in Paris. To them, it was the main stream. It startled him to find that an American kid domiciled on the Rive Gauche was welcomed here as an authority on what was taking place in the headquarters of fashion, art, music, theatre, NATO, avant-garde politics, and *le nouveau roman*. He was expected to bring the word on hair styles, the Salon de l'Automobile, Althusser, who Sartre was dating, Britain and the Common Market, poor old Khrushchev's fall. Examined by the *contessa* on structuralism and Malraux's cultural offensive, he began to wonder whether he had actually been living in Paris, so much seemed to have been going on there that he knew nothing about. At the same time, being an American, he was supposed to be up on the Berkeley Free Speech movement, President Johnson's cardiograms, the Alliance for Progress, did-the-CIA-kill-Kennedy? Above all, Vietnam. What was the public sentiment on peace negotiations? Troop commitment? Bombing Hanoi?

'But I haven't been home since early October,' he repeated. 'All I know about America is what I read in the paper.' They read the papers too and more attentively than Peter did – that was obvious. '*Questo Mario Savio, com'è?*' To the disappointment of the Roman academics, Peter did not know the student leader and had no firm position on the free-speech controversy. 'Berkeley is horrible,' he explained. 'One of my stepfathers used to teach there. You have to swear a loyalty oath. It's like a great big factory. I guess it's natural that the students would finally rebel.' But Bonfante's brother-in-law, who had met a professor from Berkeley last year at the American Academy, was receiving weekly bulletins that he wanted confirmation for: would Peter agree that the student organizers were using neo-fascist methods? Peter could not help him. He felt he should apologize for his father, who in his letters had never mentioned the topic. 'Wellesley's a long way from Berkeley, you have to realize.'

When pressed about civil rights, he was more in touch. But not enough. His questioners were sure that, living in Paris, he must have met James Baldwin. 'No. Our paths never crossed.' '*Strano. A Lei non interessa il problema dei neri?*' '*Si!*' What was strange to Peter was the assumption they made that, in his place, they *would* know James Baldwin and Samuel Beckett and Graham Greene and the widow of Richard Wright, not to mention Professor Lévi-Strauss and Professor André Chastel and a cross-section of French students. For them, Paris was a city of opportunities, of lost opportunities as far as Peter was concerned. His only score, in their eyes, was meeting an American general, which was the part of his Parisian experience he would soonest have done without.

'*E cosa diceva del Vietnam, questo generale?*' '*Stupidaggini.*' He refused to enlarge. Among these curious, albeit 'concerned' Italians, he felt a certain protective loyalty to his country, and to quote some of the general's utterances might help make them come true, like a bad dream told before breakfast.

That insane news-hunger was the only side of the Romans with which he could find fault. It continually amazed him that people privileged to live in this wonderful ochre- and tangerine-coloured city of cypresses, fairly frequent blue skies, art, and parasol pines should be so concerned with information feed-in, storage, and retrieval *re* the darkling plain he had been inhabiting and was fated soon to return to. He supposed it was in their tradition – '*nihil humanum mihi alienum puto*' – but to him they were most human when, like the *Messagero*, they concentrated on the *cronaca*. As his time grew shorter, he sought asylum in the Vatican, having finished his Borromini itinerary. In the Sistine Chapel, he could be safe from nine until closing-time.

A Sibylline Interlude

ON the day after New Year's, Peter sat down on his accustomed bench, just outside the marble screen, facing the Delphic Sibyl. This would be his last crack at the Michelangelos, since he planned to leave on Tuesday. Sunday the museum would be closed, and Monday Sergio was taking him in a car to Frascati to see a villa with the ultimate Borromini. The place was already packing up with guided tours. He recognized the busload of Germans who had invaded his hotel the night before and monopolized the toilet since shortly after dawn. But he had learned not to be bothered by the crush of humanity and the horrible Babel of tongues; his most recent acquisition was a pair of ear-stoppers. In the summertime, he understood, the crowds were a lot worse; the room actually stank. The thing to do then, he guessed, was to carry your private Airwick. Modern society provided its own antidotes, if you were resourceful enough to use them in emergencies not dreamed of by the manufacturer.

At this season, though, for ten minutes at a time the chapel would be almost empty, as though a tide had receded; the throng would rush off into the Stanze di Raffaello. When the Sistine Chapel was full, the 'School of Athens' was practically deserted, and vice versa. An oceanographer might be able to chart these human tides and currents, which had a strange regularity of ebb and flow. During one of the longer ebbs this morning, as Peter trained his pocket mirror on the vault above, stopping now and then to consult his books of reference, he became aware of a short, vaguely familiar figure sitting on a bench against the entrance wall, beneath the

Prophet Zechariah: Mr Small, his adviser, but wearing the beginnings of a reddish beard, a turtle-necked jersey, baggy pants, boots, and a duffle coat. He looked like one of the older Beats on the Spanish Stairs.

Peter for a minute was not sure it was him, and the professor gave no sign of recognition. Maybe that was understandable. From the point of view of the other, each of them was in disguise. In their previous encounters, *he* had been unshaven, tieless, in his sheepskin coat, whereas Small had been wearing a tweed jacket, a woollen necktie, and loafers. Now Peter was attired in the *babbo*'s new suit and had recently had a haircut and a shoeshine. It was as if they had exchanged clothes, like Leporello and Don Giovanni.

Peter wondered whether he ought to speak. His adviser might be ignoring him on purpose. He might be here in Rome on some squalid adventure. Mysteriously, he was not looking at the frescoes; he was making notes on a pad. Every time a new tourist or group entered, he scribbled rapidly. You would have thought he was taking attendance. Now his eye was roving over some Italian schoolgirls led by their priest in a cassock. Humbert Humbert had been a professor too. But the little girls moved on, into the inner chapel, and Mr Small's scrutiny turned to some elderly American women with glasses around their necks. Maybe he had a rendezvous here, and the other person was late. Golly, what if he was working for the CIA? They met their contacts in funny places.

Eclipsed behind a mass of turbaned Indians surrounding a lady guide, Peter considered this hypothesis. If you could believe Makowski, at least half the American professors doing 'research' abroad were on the CIA payroll. He said one of them had tried to recruit him to write weekly reports on pro-Peking activities in the Institute of Oriental Languages. When Makowski ('for kicks') made up his mind to play along, two agents took him, blindfolded, in a car to an apartment in the suburbs with the shades drawn, where they gave him a lie-detector test, which he flunked. That was the most believable part of the story, Peter had promptly decided, but now he began to wonder ... Makowski's assignation with the

Spooks had been guess where? At the Cluny Museum, in front of the 'Lady and the Unicorn'.

In the doorway, two young US Air Force men, with crew cuts, seemed to be asking directions. Then they shouldered their way forward to the 'Last Judgment', which they stood contemplating, their hands on their hips. The professor followed in their wake and edged himself onto a bench at the far end, beneath the Prophet Jeremiah. Peter rose to get a better view. For all he knew, the Sistine Chapel, on account of Michelangelo, might be a well-known pick-up point for foreign queers. If he spoke, it might embarrass his adviser. On the other hand, it might be a kindness to let him know he was observed. Collecting his gear, Peter quickly installed himself opposite, below the Libyan Sibyl. 'Hi, Mr Small.'

The professor raised his small pale eyes. 'Why, it's Levy!' he cried. 'For the Lord's sake, what are you doing here?' He appeared pleased and surprised to meet Peter, who politely took out his ear-plugs and joined him on the other bench. 'Come out and have a smoke.' Peter shook his head. 'This is my last day here, and I don't want to lose too much time. You see, it was closed yesterday, on account of the holiday. And this morning I was late because of some Germans in my hotel.' 'Germans?' 'They moved in on the toilet so that nobody else had a chance. There's only one toilet to the floor, and they had this big guy standing guard outside it. So I had to wait for American Express to open. It's around the corner from where I'm staying. But I found out they keep the cans there locked. Some stupid new rule. You have to ask a clerk for the key.' Mr Small evinced sympathy. He asked some questions about Peter's hotel. Then he started taking an interest in the TCI guidebook and the *Itinerario Pittorico dei Musei Vaticani*, which had slid from Peter's lap to the floor. The professor picked them up and examined them. 'Where did you find these?' he asked sharply.

Peter began to tell about the second-hand book cart, but Mr Small, as though dissatisfied with this explanation, leafed through them frowning and pulling curiously at the red and green ribbons that were marking Peter's place. You would think he had come upon some undecipherable Roman papyrus or scrolls from the Dead Sea. The TCI volume with its folding maps and plans seemed to fascinate him. 'It's just the ordinary Touring Club guide,' Peter felt obliged to point out. 'They have them for all the big cities and the different provinces. Like the *Guides Bleues* in France, only these give you better information.' The professor read aloud the date on the copyright page. '1940! Lordy me, could you find something more contemporary?' Peter had not noticed how old his treasured guide was. ' "*Ristampato giugno* 1957," ' he said, reclaiming it. 'My mother used to go around with a pre-war Baedeker and a guy called Augustus Hare.'

Mr Small leaned his head back and let his eyes rest on the ceiling. 'I never carry a guide or a map. Of course I'm a very visual person. If art doesn't say something to me directly, without mediation, I'm not interested. When I visit the Sistine Chapel I don't need all that fine print to tell me what I've been experiencing. Wonderful colours, beautiful forms, marvellous light. You ought to get rid of that portable reference shelf. And these crowds here, contemporary, constantly changing, are just as exciting as any fresco.'

The word *contemporary* was high on Peter's aversion list and it seemed to be a favourite with people who weren't. The fact that his adviser thought he was being helpful did not lessen Peter's irritation. He hated being told how he could save his labour, which nine times out of ten only showed the other person's ignorance. 'You haven't really seen the Sistine Chapel unless you've studied it,' he objected. 'You just think you have. I made that mistake myself when I came here with my mother a few years ago. But there's an awful lot going on in that ceiling. Like those *putti* holding up the pillars. You don't see them at first. They sort of emerge if you sit here long enough, like animals that will come out if you wait in the woods without making any noise. And those other *putti* on the tablets beneath the Prophets and the Sibyls. Look at that scowling one, under Daniel. He's having a tantrum. That's what's so great about books. They make you see things you might have missed on your own. There are two kinds of *putti*, one flesh-coloured and one marble-coloured. And they have different personalities.'

Needless to say, Mr Small had been unaware of any *putti*. He had not even observed the *ignudi*, those heroic pagan youths with laurel wreaths and prominent penises of whom Peter was particularly fond and who, to his eyes, practically whirled off the ceiling at you, like naked athletes playing a game of Statues. To cover up this oversight on the part of his adviser ('*Where?* . . . Oh yes, of course'), Peter started discoursing about the spandrels. 'See those triangles over the windows. They're supposed to show the ancestors of Christ. But there must be more to it than that. To me there's something sad and almost sinister about them, sort of crouching in the shadows or just staring ahead into space. As though the light of Genesis had gone out or dimmed, like a bulb fading. Look at that young mother there, just above us, next to Jeremiah. Between him and the Persian Sibyl. She's got on a pale green blouse and a yellow skirt. Well, she's cutting her skirt with a big shears. Why? For that, you'd have to know the story, and these books I've got don't tell it. So if I want to understand, I need *more* books, don't you see? Like the Bible.' He offered his adviser the mirror. 'Can you make out the scissors? The other day a lady let me use her opera glasses. I forgot my binoculars in Paris.'

Mr Small handed back the mirror. 'Primitive people often cut up their clothes as part of the mourning ritual. I believe it's still customary among orthodox Jews.' 'I bet you're right! Hey, you've got it, Mr Small! What do you suppose she's mourning?' 'Perhaps the Babylonian Captivity. "By the water of Babylon." But there's no need to look for literal meanings in these accessories. We're not interested in those old Bible tales; probably Michelangelo wasn't either. He had to put them in to satisfy the Pope and his court. What he really cared about, being an artist, was form, line, colour. For him, the whole cycle might as well have been an abstract design. Why make a puzzle out of it?' 'You're so wrong, Mr Small,' said Peter, his voice rising. 'Michelangelo wanted to *say* something. I haven't got the whole message yet, but it's there. If my stepfather was here, he'd agree with me. He teaches history of art. Maybe it was different in your day, but now they put a lot of stress on the iconography.' He felt slightly ashamed of invoking authority in a discussion, but Mr Small seemed to be tickled by that feeble blow below the belt. He gave an indulgent laugh and stretching his arms wide embraced Peter in a sort of half bear hug, as if to say they were buddies despite their difference of opinion.

'I'm aware of the new academicism. Entrenched interest groups resent the boom in museum attendance, the avail-ability of cheap reproductions and colour slides. They can't accept the fact that art is now within the reach of the masses. In consequence, as one might expect, there's a drive on to restrict the understanding of art, if not the actual experience, to a tiny coterie of privileged specialists and cultured dilet-tantes. They'd like to turn this wonderful spectacle over our heads into a private field of research, their own little hunting preserve – "Trespassers Keep Out." Why, if they had their way, they'd institute screening procedures at all the great museums, to bar the vulgar public!'

The idea in fact had crossed Peter's mind. Looking down the chapel, he saw the usual maelstrom. Every corner was occupied by dark serried groups, reminding him of flocks of starlings, drawn up in formation around their leader. When they moved, a new flock descended. In the middle of the room, well-to-do Americans stood with their individual cicerones. On the bench Peter had left one old man remained stationary, having fallen asleep; his white head nodded and jerked. A mother carried a tiny baby wrapped in a yellow shawl and sucking on a pacifier. In its father's arms, another baby cried. On the far side of the *cancellata*, a German in *lederhosen* opened a tripod stool and sat down where he could watch the lady copyist copying a Botticelli. There were nuns, priests in skirts, priests in trousers – cassocked priests, for some reason, favoured a folded-arm pose when studying the frescoes. On the raised platform, for the pope's chair, some student types were lying, using their coats for pillows. Every now and then a custodian in a grey uniform with gold buttons would clap his hands loudly to make them sit up. A girl in a tight sweater who looked as if she had gone to Bennington paced around with long gliding steps, her hands clasped behind her back and her long straight hair tossing, like the 'lost' heroine of some neurotic ballet. A sort of permanent hum rose from the chapel – from so many people reading aloud from guidebooks and brochures – and competing with this natural human-hive sound were bossy guides rapping for attention: '*Links, Gemälde Paradiso, recht, Inferno mit Teufels.*' Along the wall, open compacts and hand mirrors flashed. People squinted, shaded their eyes, massaged cricks in their necks, bumped into each other. Two vague soft old ladies attached themselves to an English-speaking tour. 'Do you folks mind if we listen in? We've wasted a whole half-hour here looking for the Michelangelos and we can't seem to find them.' A student sat up and laughed coarsely. 'Christ!' 'Christ, yourself!' said Peter. 'They probably expected to see statues. Why is that so stupid? In case you don't know, he was a sculptor, primarily.' He turned to his adviser. 'If I don't wear my ear-plugs, I keep getting into arguments. That's the effect this mob has on you.' The confused incessant movement and medley of tongues made him think of an air terminal where half the flights had been cancelled. The Seers above looked down on a sort of Exodus or final Judgment of the tribes and peoples. Whatever Mr Small thought, some authority, in Peter's opinion, was going to have to separate the sheep from the goats.

'I know screening sounds repulsive, but we do it in colleges, don't we? You must do it in your own seminar when you limit the class to fifteen or whatever.' Mr Small retorted that soon all education would be conducted by TV; the small hand-picked class, a vestige of the age of privilege, would be swept away. Peter groaned. 'All right, then put all the art on TV too. Maybe eventually that will cut down on attendance, like with night baseball. But I can't wait for that. I want to be able to look at art, live, now, while I'm young, before the Army gets me. Won't you even admit there's a problem? And actually it's not so bad here as in some other museums, though the noise is worse. At least most of the stuff is on the ceiling. Think of the "Mona Lisa" in the Louvre. It would take a giraffe to see it. Hey, maybe you could invent a periscope!'

At that point, the custodian at his little desk shushed them. *'Per piacere, signori!'* 'O.K., see you later, Mr Small,' Peter said hastily. He supposed the guides had the right to lecture at the top of their voices to the droves who were paying to be herded by them, whereas he and his adviser, being unpaid, had a duty to be quiet. Mr Small, however, was anxious to pursue the conversation. Peter yielded. 'I guess we'd better get out of here, though,' he suggested. 'By all means do,' a woman's voice interposed. 'Why are such ruffians admitted?' she went on in a loud whisper, evidently misled by Mr Small's slummy appearance and bearing out his description of the attitudes of the once-happy few. Peter led his adviser into the Borgia Apartments, which were usually empty. It puzzled him that this rather disagreeable teacher should be so eager to talk to him, unless he was just lonely, not knowing any Italian and without even a guidebook for company.

But Mr Small, it turned out, had method in his madness. He wanted to poll Peter for a study of tourism he was doing. 'Tourism? You mean like here?' 'The idea surprises you, does it? And yet tourism is all around us, a central fact of our mobile civilization, so much taken for granted that nobody has stopped to ponder on it.' That was so, Peter reflected. He supposed statistics got collected somewhere on how much of their income tourists spent abroad, what carriers they used, and so on. There were stories with tourists in them, poems with tourists in them, Steinberg cartoons with tourists in them. But if he were asked, now, to draw up a reading-list on the subject, not a single 'general' title, he realized, would come to mind. Not even a magazine article in some place like *Harper's*. If he had seen one, he would have read it. Maybe Mr Small was right that most people carried in their heads a 'stereotype' of the tourist that it might be a good idea for research to dispel.

What was really peculiar, though, and worth a study in itself, was that this rich research territory had not already been prospected. Even if the stereotype summed up all there was to say – that the average tourist was an omnipresent insecure guy slung with cameras and carrying drip-dry suits on a hanger in a plastic bag – that did not normally deter sociologists, who, as the *babbo* said, could only 'discover' things that everybody knew anyway. Peter would like to hear a Marxist explanation of the fact that a world-wide industry feeding millions of mouths – billions probably if you counted automobile workers, workers in aircraft plants, luggage-manufacturers, Eastman Kodak, Agfa, Zeiss, all the makers of film and cameras, doctors giving shots, manufacturers of life-jackets and throw-up bags, authors and publishers of travel books, whoever it was that made passports – had been overlooked by the so-called social disciplines until Professor Beverly F. Small came along and 'happened' to have this brainstorm while sitting at the Deux Magots one Sunday morning idly watching the crowds and eating a *croissant*.

Like Newton under the apple tree. No wonder he was pale and excited. A foundation, naturally, was interested in the project and paying his expenses for a 'dry run' in Rome. On the basis of that, he expected to get funding for three years' research. At Easter, he would fly to Athens and cruise around the Greek islands. In the summer, Spain or Mexico. 'Hey, that's great, Mr Small! You don't need a helper, do you?' But his adviser had to be alone during the early stages of a project; he would be using his vacations to lay down guidelines for his students, who would take up the work next fall. In the fall, he hoped to fix it with his university so that he could travel with his advanced class on an extended field period. Or he might have to arrange a leave of absence.

The financing sounded like the easiest part. If his grant ran out before the study was finished, he was pretty sure he could get additional subsidies from countries like Spain and Portugal, which needed more background on tourist-expectations in developing their reception facilities. Other backing should rapidly become available for a study of this magnitude. In Paris, he had been talking with some of the lesser airlines – Air India, Air Afrique, Aer Lingus, and the like: whatever he and his students discovered about the travel pattern would rebound to their advantage in planning and promotion.

'India! Africa! Do you think you'll visit the game reserves, Mr Small?' His adviser, who now resembled a mushroom, would certainly get a good tan. A doubt crept into Peter's mind. 'You don't think you're trying to cover too much territory? Maybe you should concentrate on something small. Like a Turkish fishing village that's been written up in *Holiday*. Find out what happens.' Mr Small snorted. Villages were crawling with *au pair* sociologists doing interminable 'careful' investigations of the type Peter mentioned. 'The impact of modernity on the folkways! All trivia! Who cares what happens in a village? Now that we have the computer, research must take broad new free forms. CinemaScope. The wide screen.' As he had emphasized in a memo to the foundation, the structuring of the study should emerge from the data itself; it was important to avoid methodological traps that determined the findings in advance. 'For the present, I'm feeling my way, using aleatory techniques.' I.e., so far, he had just been going around Rome with a tape-recorder, interviewing people at the Trevi Fountain, on the Spanish Stairs, at American Express and Alitalia.

This morning he had had his first setback. The Vatican guards had made him check the tape-recorder at the entrance, together with his Rollei and briefcase. 'Isn't that the limit? I couldn't convince them that a tape-recorder is an essential piece of modern scholarly apparatus. They simply kept pointing to the checkroom and repeating *"Guardaroba,"* as if they knew no English – a familiar dodge, of course.' He had then sought to telephone to the cultural attaché at the Embassy, to get him to use pull, but first he could not find a telephone and next he could not find a *gettone*, and finally the cultural attaché was giving a lecture to the Rotary in Siracusa.

'You wouldn't come and talk to the guards for me, would you, Levy? You seem to have learned some Italian.' He gave Peter's arm a pleading little squeeze, as though he was a blind man deprived of his Seeing Eye dog. 'It wouldn't do any good,' said Peter, resolved not to go on this stupid errand. 'If this was a state museum, they just *might* let you by with it. But the Church is tough. You have to have all sorts of permissions to take photographs or do anything that's not in the rules. I know, on account of my stepfather. They don't like art historians or tourists, really. To them, they're sort of sacrilegious. That's why they give them a hard time. Haven't you noticed all those signs – "*Questo è un luogo sacro*" – outside churches, about being properly dressed? And honestly I don't think they'd care for the idea of interviews in the Sistine Chapel, Mr Small. Why don't you do it outdoors, on the street? Catch people when they're leaving?'

Mr Small supposed he could. But tourists leaving a museum were likely to be in a hurry. He needed a relaxed, informal atmosphere. It worked out best when an interview 'grew' out of a seemingly casual conversation. 'What are you doing in Rome?' 'Where are you from?' 'Do you have family here?' and so on. This was going to be a depth study, he emphasized, not the usual superficial survey made in airports. To Peter, Mr Small's scientifically framed questions sounded suspiciously like the ones he had been answering ever since he left his native shores – with those old schoolteachers, for instance, on that gruesome train ride from Le Havre. And in his eyes Mr Small's costume and sprouting beard, which he wore, he explained, so as not to look like a professor, far from putting a passing tourist at his ease, might suggest he was sidling up for a hand-out or selling contraband.

In fact, right here, the guard had his eye on them. The gloomy Borgian Sibyls' Chamber (*affreschi di scolari del Pintoricchio molto ritoccati; fu in questa sale forse che Cesare Borgia fece uccidere il cognato*), hung with Flemish arrases like the closet where Polonius evesdropped, seemed to oppress Mr Small with its musty reminiscences of conspiracy.

Whenever the guard glanced in the doorway, the professor lowered his voice and bent close to Peter, as though the walls had ears. He talked feverishly of the shattering of precedents his undertaking involved. 'I'm prepared for attacks, naturally, from the academic Mafia. Some of the small minds in human-istic studies will have their knives out. That's the price one pays for having a certain charisma. Even at the Foundation questions have been asked about the utility of this kind of research and the deployment of tax-free resources for fresh ends and novel approaches. In my university, I can expect talk of sinecurism, based, as usual, on envy.' 'Yeah, I can imagine.'

Peter chortled. He had to hand it to Small. When he thought of poor Bob, who was forced to spend a certain number of summer hours in hot libraries and dusty archives when drawing an allocation for studying some obscure Mannerist painter, he felt a certain delight in the picture of his adviser, free to lie on a beach all day long or submerge in a snorkel – *anything* he did could not help contributing to his knowledge of tourism, and the less he exerted himself, the more his knowledge would broaden. Eventually he would have to write up his findings or get his student myrmidons to write them up for him, but that was a long way off, and before he was through he might be looking into moon travel.

'Have you thought of getting a shopping and souvenir subsidy?' 'What do you mean?' 'Well, you know, to buy Swiss watches and Japanese cameras and Florentine leather. All that junk that tourists bring home with them and try to smuggle through customs. The idea of loot is pretty funda-mental to the tourist experience. So you should have an expense account to go shopping and learn how it feels.' Mr Small took offence. 'Do you find something amusing about tourists or about making a serious study of them?' 'Both, I guess, a little.' 'But you're aware of the importance of the phenomenon?' 'Oh yes.' Peter sighed. 'And I know I'm part of it.' 'Such humility is becoming. I feared you might be one of those snobs who distinguish between class tourism and mass tourism.'

Peter flushed. 'Well, I have to admit I like tourists a lot
better in units of one or two than in units of thirty or fifty.
But the difference doesn't have to be based on dough. I
mean, you see young couples or boys and girls roaming
around by themselves who don't look all that prosperous.' A
sturdy young girl with blond pigtails and bare chapped legs
raced through the room and up the stairs. 'Take her. She
comes every day. She's Dutch or German and spends most
of her time with the Blessed Angelicos, I think. I saw her
once in Piazza Navona with a knapsack. To me, she's a
"class" tourist.' Mr Small dismissed the northern maiden
with an impatient gesture. 'Tourism today is a mass industry serving a mass market. The fact is finally being recognized, and adjustments are being made: improvement of
mass carriers – planes, ships, and buses – expansion of hotel
and camping facilities, introduction at key points of super-
restaurants with self-service. The single tourist unit, as you
call it, will soon be as outmoded as the coach-and-four. Even
the upper crust will travel in groups on yachts, private planes,
and the like. No one will be able to reserve individual space.
All block booking.'

'I can imagine,' said Peter, who had his private crystal
ball. 'But this process you're describing, won't it be self-
defeating in the end? Isn't the point of travel to have a
change of scene? With those giant hotels and cafeterias,
every country will look the same. I've been thinking about
those Germans in my hotel. They haven't heard anything
since they got there but German and broken German.
They'll have lunch in some place where "*Man spricht
deutsch*" is advertised, and their guide will tell them in
German about the catacombs. They probably won't even
have to change into Italian money. Their beds and meals will
be paid for in advance, and they won't tip the waiters or the
chambermaid. They might as well stay home and have a
plate of deep-freeze spaghetti and see the Sistine Chapel on
television.'

'We don't know yet why people travel, Levy. Nobody so
far has examined the question culturally and sociologically.

Economically we do know something. Package tours for lower-income groups, on the balance sheet, are proving to be more profitable for the host nation than the old de luxe tourism engaged in by the higher brackets. Even the fancy hotels aren't turning away package tours these days. It's the same with any commodity handled in bulk. They're easier to process in and out.'

'I don't see that. Most tours don't stay more than a couple of nights, maximum, in a town. Tomorrow morning, when those Germans leave, my hotel will have to change all their sheets. With the single tourist unit, like me, who's a slow mover, the hotel only has to change the sheets once a week.'

This argument caused Mr Small to give one of his sudden effusive little hugs. He went back to the question of tourist motivation. What caused several million Americans to seek out other scenes? 'In what way is this culturally determined? What part is played by economic factors, education, social background, geographical distribution, ethnic origin? And how are these, in turn, related to the length of stay abroad? What about "repeaters"? Statistics, of course, can help us. For instance, it now seems to be established that a far higher percentage of US tourists in Asia comes from the Pacific Coast than from the Eastern seaboard. Isn't that intriguing?'

'I think I could have guessed it.' 'Guessed it, yes. But to *know* it! For example, I can form a hypothesis as to what brought you to Rome at Christmas-time, which might have served well enough for an old-time writer of fictions. Say a disappointment in love. But as a sociologist, I must make no facile assumptions.' He took out his ballpoint. 'Of course the reasons immediately apparent to you may not be the real reasons or only the tip of the iceberg. Undoubtedly, there's a certain amount of atavism in the travel pattern. Rome, as the centre of the Christian world, evidently acts as a magnet during the Christmas and Easter festivals for people of long-standing Christian orientation, even though they may be unaware of the papal city as the New Bethlehem. Tourism tends to confuse itself with the traditional pilgrimage to the holy places. But we can exclude that in your case since you're Jewish, I assume.'

'Half. But the other half went to midnight mass on Christmas Eve. You may have something there about the atavism. I'm not religious or anything. My feet just took me. But let me tell you something else strange. Really strange. I don't know whether you noticed, but in the Sistine Chapel, on the left-hand wall, there's a fresco by Signorelli and Bartolommeo della Gatta. To the left of where you were sitting. Right above and behind where I was, though I guess you didn't see me. Well, every day I've been sitting on that same bench, trying not to look at anything but the Michelangelos, so as not to get distracted. Of course I move around some but I always come back to that bench. Then the last time I was there, I had this weird feeling, as though I ought to turn around. Like a tap on the shoulder. And what do you think? Behind me, over my right shoulder, in that Signorelli fresco, I saw a nude youth with golden hair, wearing a sort of locket and a red scarf around his loins. Do you remember him? He looks like a tender captive. All the other figures have clothes on.' Mr Small did not remember the ephebe. 'O.K., if you go again, look at him. Do you know who he is, according to the guidebook? The personification of the tribe of Levi. That's how we pronounce the name in our family, actually – the same as in "Levite". Not "Levy". So he's my Renaissance cousin. You know, idealized and pagan, like a young god or martyr ready for the sacrifice. The title of the fresco is "The Testament and Death of Moses". Do you think it could be racial memory that made me sit down on that particular bench, in front of my archetype and finally made me turn around and meet his eyes? He has a tear, like a cast, in one eye, as though he was crying, but maybe the picture is damaged. Or maybe he's naked and crying because he has no property. The Levis weren't allowed to own land.'

'Curious,' said Mr Small, taking an extensive note. 'You should read your Jung.' Then he brought Peter back to the weary subject in hand: why he had chosen Rome for his winter holiday. Of course Peter could not answer. If he knew why he had come to Rome, his inner self and mainspring would have no more secrets from him. All he could think of was Borromini and the Sistine Chapel. 'Nonsense,' said his adviser. 'Those are your ostensible reasons, pretexts you gave your family to justify your trip. There are plenty of fine museums in Paris, for anyone who takes the trouble to stroll through them. Let's dig a little deeper. I think you said you'd been here before, with your mother. Did something significant happen to you on your earlier visit?' 'Borromini and Michelangelo.' 'Bob' had happened to him on his earlier visit, but he had not come back to see Bob, so why bring him up? 'Yes, yes! You convince me that they are meaningful to you emotionally. But why?' 'I don't know.' 'Let's take the Sistine Chapel. Was there some particular feature that stood out in your memory?' Peter sighed. 'O.K., the Delphic Sibyl.'

Mr Small's ballpoint flew. 'Does the figure remind you of anyone? A girl? Or a boy perhaps? You know Michelangelo's proclivities?' 'A girl.' In fact his favourite Sibyl did remind Peter slightly of Roberta but also of his pensive mother, whose arms were muscular from playing the harpsichord. 'Unusual that a clothed, asexual figure should excite erotic fantasies in someone your age.' 'I didn't say erotic,' Peter replied stiffly. 'And to me she's the height of girlishness. Miss Nature before she got to be Mrs. I love the Prophet Isaiah too. I suppose you think he's effeminate, with that raised eyebrow and drooping hand. To me, he's young Jewishness in a pure, refined state, the way we were before the Diaspora. Intellectual beauty, like in that poem by Shelley.'

' "Before", "before",' Mr Small chided. 'It's curious that you show so little interest in the "Last Judgment" – a much more powerful and gripping design to my mind.' 'The "after," ' said Peter, with a wan grin. 'I agree, it doesn't appeal to me much. I like Genesis and the Prophecies.' He thought he had made a nice discovery: it was the Prophets and the Sibyls who upheld the whole structure by their mass, weight, and volume, e.g., the old gaunt Cumean Sibyl, in her white cap, bent over her green tome, with an arm like a blacksmith's and gnarled fingers gripping the pages. They were bigger than the other figures, as if to show that their vision of the Redemption surpassed any temporal event. Maybe that was Michelangelo's Platonism, the Ideas being greater than their puny reflections on the wall of the cave. By contrast, the newly emerged Eve, praying, was just a stumpy little fetish. Peter had not decided how the *ignudi* on their pillars fitted in, but they must be another *redeeming* feature, contributing to the uplift, a triumph of something natural over something else. What was clear, though, was the pitiful shambles that followed the magic bright moment of the Creation of Man, with God's forefinger passing the spark to Adam's, to call him forth from the deep of His intention. A plan that started with the separation of light from darkness and ended with the drunkenness of Noah left you feeling that the Almighty might have been wiser to stop with the Creation of the Fish. And the four big vengeful spandrels in the corners carried mysterious and sinister messages: David finishing off the fallen Goliath, Judith and a maid tiptoeing out with Holofernes' head on a platter, Haman being nailed naked to a tree, the Children of Israel in the coils of fiery serpents. Every one of those barbarous episodes, when you thought about it, was an execution. Yet the Prophets and Sibyls, intent on their books and scrolls, were apart from all that, and the sun, when there was any, lit up their garments, which made you know there was hope. Michelangelo must have known that a finger of winter sunlight would touch the yellow mantle on Daniel's right knee, weather permitting, at a certain hour of the morning as long as the frescoes lasted, and every time Peter considered that, he felt joyful, as when somebody kept a promise.

'Well, let's go on. Based in Paris, as we've established, you had a variety of travel options. Was Rome your first choice?' 'Yes. No, I take that back. A while ago, I had the idea of going to Warsaw with this Norwegian I knew. I'd like to see a Slavic country in the snow. Then that fell through. He got deported. Later, I was toying, for about a half an hour, with going to Autun.' '*Autun*? Why in the world?' Peter told him about Gislebertus. He was not going to mention the faithless

Roberta, even if it was omitting something important. 'You seem unfocused,' Mr Small commented. 'All over the place. No clear line of direction. Why are you so art-oriented, all of a sudden? The last time I saw you, you told me you were interested in entomology. Something about becoming a bug.'

It was typical of adults that they seldom remembered anything straight about a younger person, which showed their real lack of concern. 'It was birds,' said Peter. 'Oh, sorry, what was I thinking of?' ' "The Metamorphosis", by Kafka.' 'Jove, you're right. Have you read it?' 'No. But I know the plot.' Mr Small kept straying from the subject, but possibly that was part of the strategy of a depth interview. Peter grew impatient, thinking of the little spandrels above the lunettes. He had resolved to go without lunch to study them, but already he was way behind schedule and it was a grey morning. On a day like this the light faded fast in the chapel; after one o'clock it would be too late to make out those dim shadowy figures waiting, if that was what they were doing, for the Advent.

'Would you mind if I went back now to the Sistine Chapel?' 'Sure, go ahead. Just let me ask you a couple more questions. Have you had any contact with other Americans here? The Beats, for instance?' There was a sudden, bated eagerness in that last 'offhand' query, which made Peter wonder if the whole interview had not been leading up to it. It was funny how older people got excited by thinking about the Beats, as if they were some new form of pornography. 'No,' said Peter. Mr Small was disappointed. He had hoped Peter might help him; it turned out that one of his main purposes in Rome was getting to know them better. Amazingly, in Paris he had already picked up quite a few in the Place de la Contrescarpe, near where they had their pads. 'They gave me a lot of data. Fascinating stuff. I have it all on tape. Some of course were unwilling to be drawn out, taking me for a spy from the Establishment. In Paris, with my Embassy and academic connection, I had to be somewhat circumspect. The place to find their counterparts, they told me, was on the Spanish Steps. Anywhere else that you know of?'

'American Express. Maybe Cook's. You could put an ad in the *Rome American*.'

Mr Small gave a brisk shake of his head. Advertising his purpose would defeat it. Unobtrusive, in his drop-out disguise, he hoped to be accepted by the tribe in Piazza di Spagna and gain their total confidence. 'It's like any anthropological field trip. You have to talk to them in their own language and respect their value system. Some of them are extraordinarily attractive, as human beings. Last night, I smoked grass with a diversified group and collected their stories.' Peter grinned, thinking of Sherlock Holmes in the opium den. 'Weren't you afraid of getting stoned, Mr Small?' 'It's fairly simple to simulate inhalation. What's meaningful for them is the communion-rite. Sharing the "joint". The feeling of brotherhood. "Man." Isn't that beautiful? Not "Mister". "Man." ' 'Did you tape them?' 'Not yet. We just sat around and got acquainted. Later they'll feel more comfortable, and I can use my machine. I want to be introduced to the pads where they live. They have this idea of community, both sexes intermingled, few or no possessions. I'd like to get that on film. In Paris, I found them camera-shy, like many primitive people. My little Minox created the suspicion that I might be the "fuzz".'

Actually Mr Small's findings were not devoid of interest. Peter saw that he was going to have to give up on the spandrels. He looked at his watch. It was too late even to catch a sustaining bite in the priests' bar in St Peter's, which was one of his favourite refuges. Sergio had steered him to it. You went through a corridor to the left of the transept, as if you were going to the Treasury; then you came to a room all panelled in intarsia, with stars and flowers, and you opened a small door on the right, just like in *Alice in Wonderland* – if nobody had told you, you would never suspect there was a door in that wall. Inside, there were always a lot of priests, the trousered type, drinking beer, but they also served sandwiches and Campari-sodas. Around noon, though, they closed. He knew another secret passage, which he had found on his own, in the Stanze di Raffaello. You walked through a door marked 'Leo x' in the wall beneath the 'Incendio del Borgo' and discovered nice clean toilets. On Mr Small's expressing a desire for the men's room, Peter was now able to conduct him there. For once, he had impressed his adviser. 'Why, it's a regular labyrinth,' he commented. 'Goodness me, how do you get your bearings?' Then he wanted to eat, and Peter, feeling hungry, consented. He had blown the day anyhow. They ransomed the tape-recorder and camera and took a taxi to a *trattoria* in Trastevere Mr Small had been told about. As might have been predicted, it was full of American tourists, which did not bother Peter but put Mr Small slightly out of countenance. 'I don't see anything "typical" about this,' he said fretfully, as they waited in line. 'I suppose it's been discovered.' 'Who told you about it?' 'The cultural attaché.' Peter shrugged. 'Well! Anyway, you can tape them.' 'Too noisy.' 'Go on about the Beats,' Peter urged when they were finally shown to a table. It amused him that his adviser had been studying the migrations of the Beats as though they were salmon or birds. He had even picked up some of the lingo you came across in bird books and Nature-study columns.

The way he put it, few of the Beats were sedentary; they moved on, usually with the onset of winter to warmer climes, and always driven by the need of drugs, which were the same to them as the food supply. There was a whole colony of them, for instance, now established in Nepal, and yet nobody could explain how word passed between them as to where they should foregather next. They appeared to respond to a common 'urge' which had a destination coded into it, like an airplane ticket.

Peter laughed. 'You mean they have flyways.' Mr Small nodded. What he expected to learn from his research was that tourists in general had flyways. If these could be charted and shifts in schedule and direction predicted, it would be extremely interesting. Already data was being collected at unexpected posts of observation; Breton peasants made an annual note of the first spring tourists as they did of the return of the swallows, and in time such 'sightings' would be stored in computers for analysis. The Beatniks were the clearest example of the post-industrial wanderlust and the easiest to investigate, because of their manner of dress, which made them conspicuous, their herding habits, and their dependence on narcotics. Any change in the narcotics laws, any slight relaxation or stiffening in enforcement produced immediate population shifts among them: an exodus or an invasion.

Something similar could be observed with homosexuals, who were also readily identifiable by their dress, voice, and so on. They too had a herding habit and could be found at certain familiar stations at certain times of the year. They were sedentary, Mr Small understood, in Capri, Venice, Tangiers, Athens, Taormina. 'Amsterdam,' supplied Peter. 'Oh?' 'From what I've heard, anyway.' Mr Small made a note. 'I wasn't aware that they congregated so far north. One might be able to look into that during tulip-time.' Many of them were nest-builders and, unlike the Beats, they generally travelled in pairs. They were gregarious at their meeting-places, but while in transit each individual pair tended to eschew the company of other pairs. You would not find them banding together, like heterosexual similars, to charter an airplane or a bus. Their migrations too could be understood in terms of the food supply, if that was interpreted in a broad sense to mean readily available adolescent boys. And again, as with the Beats, the food supply was dependent on police attitudes, reflecting of course the attitudes of the community.

The behaviour of these deviant minorities, scientifically probed, ought to throw considerable light on the whole tourist phenomenon. A striking parallel could be detected between hostile community reactions to Beatnik or homosexual colonies and hostile community reactions to campers, trailer aggregates, and the like. Commonly one fraction of local opinion encouraged the influx of the outsiders, for evident commercial motives, while another fraction sought to expel them, often on the pretext of sanitation. Moreover, among the so-called invaders themselves, you found a most interesting tendency to identify with the host community and its xenophobic prejudices, to the extent that individuals and even whole groups in the tourist population manifested anger at the presence of other tourists.

'That's it!' cried Peter, looking up from some noodles *al burro* he was winding around his fork. 'You've got it in a nutshell, Mr Small. There's a logical contradiction in the whole tourist routine. The dragon swallowing its own tail. Or maybe I mean a paradox. "Oh God, tourists!" you hear them moan when they look around some restaurant and see a bunch of compatriots with Diners Club cards who might as well be their duplicates. Sort of a blanket rejection that, if they sat down and analysed it, would have to include themselves. Only nobody does. They can't. Instead, in the Sistine Chapel, you start thinking of reasons why *you* have the right to be there and all the rest don't. The only tourists you don't look on as gate-crashers are solitary art-lovers you can put in the same class as yourself. Like that Dutch or German girl we saw. But if she was multiplied, I'd start to hate her, I guess.'

Halfway through this speech, it came back to Peter that Mr Small himself had not been too pleased just now to find other Americans here. Nor was it unlikely that he had a Diners Club card. But when he dared glance across the table, the professor was fiddling with the tape-recorder, which he had quietly moved into position. His head was cocked over it, and he was listening to Peter with an encouraging smile. 'Beautiful!' he said, patting Peter's arm. 'Just give me that bit about the Diners Club again.' The crowd in the restaurant had thinned out. 'Oh, I forget,' said Peter. 'You hear the same stuff all over the place. Like this morning in American Express, there were these women talking to the clerk. "Pompeii, isn't that awfully *touristy*?" We saw them again in the Sistine Chapel, with a guide. You know what they decided about the ceiling? Too "busy".'

Mr Small put his ear to the machine again. 'Lovely! Just go right ahead. Don't be diffident. Forget about the machine. Pretend you're talking to me directly.' 'O.K. Can't you see that it's to the interest of everybody, including tourists, to discourage tourism? Not counting travel agents, naturally, and other parasites. But to the interest of tourists most of all. The inhabitants, so far as I can see, mind tourists less than other tourists do. I don't mean because they make a profit on them. The inhabitants sort of enjoy tourists, up to a point. They lend a little variety.'

'Go on.' 'Well, the nice thing about travel is the chance to be by yourself in an unspoiled pristine setting. Or with one person you like a lot. Isn't that the principle behind honeymoons? In English freshman year we read some of Dr Johnson's *Lives of the Poets*, and it told about how Milton travelled through Italy in the company of a hermit. That must have been just about ideal.' Mr Small smiled. 'Have you considered the drawbacks?' 'You mean lousy inns and bedbugs? Would I really want to go back to that? I guess maybe I couldn't, on account of my conditioning. But people can take more than they think. Look at the Army. If a guy can accept hardship because he's drafted, he ought to be able to stand a little inconvenience when he's going somewhere for fun. I mean, I sat up all night on the train to here, and it was a lot more rewarding than being strapped in on a plane. In comparison, you could say it was an adventure.'

'Air travel was once an adventure.' 'Maybe I would have liked it in those days. Now the only adventure you can have in a plane is when it crashes into a mountain. Everything's upside down. If you wanted a novel experience today, you wouldn't hop on some jet just off the drawing-board, would you? No, you'd get on a mule or go up in a balloon. Being in one of these old crumbling cities on your own is like being the first white man or whatever to walk in a virgin forest. Or like coming out of your house in the morning after a big snowfall and almost hating to make the first human footprint. My generation doesn't have experiences like that very often, which is why we come abroad, I guess. There isn't much unspoiled Nature around any more, and the places where people like poets used to look for it – the mountains and the seashore – are all jammed up with humanity and bottle-caps. So arriving in a strange town by yourself, with just your guide-

book for a compass, is the nearest equivalent we can find to
being alone with Nature, the way travellers used to be in the
Age of Discovery.'

Peter paused and chewed a mouthful of salad. He did not
want to sound like a misanthrope in front of the tape-recorder.
'You can't blame the multitudes for wanting sun and swimming and fresh air. Nobody should have a monopoly of that.
If factory- and office-workers get vacations, they have to have
some place to go. Beaches should belong to the public, even
if it mucks them up. But there has to be *something* left to
explore. To give you the illusion that you're blazing a trail,
although you know that thousands of others have been there
before you.'

'Have you ever thought of camping in the north woods? If
you want real Nature, that's it. Absolutely untouched. The
rangers in the parks see to that. No hunting or fishing, no
swimming, no dumping, put out your campfires, bring your
own firewood and your grub. My wife and I used to do it
every summer with the kids. Our only contact with civilization was the chief ranger's radio.' Peter made a noncommittal
noise. To him, this sounded more like an al fresco meeting
with Big Brother than like communing with the infinite. He
wondered where Mr Small's wife was. 'We're divorced. One
of those things. She was envious of my relationship with my
students. She's basically a cold person, and I'm a warm
person.' 'Oh. Well, I guess those pack trips can be fun. I've
never tried. But I went bird-watching once on the Appala-
chian Trail. I remember the scary feeling when night started
coming on fast. I thought I could hear it stalking me in the
woods. To me, Nature has a scary side even in the daytime,
with twigs and branches snapping at you. Sort of an underlying menace. I suppose, out camping, you can sense that
pretty often.' Mr Small misunderstood. 'Nothing to be afraid
of. The trails are well marked; no fear of getting lost. And if
you come down with an appendicitis, a plane will take you
out. Sometimes at night you hear bear, but there are always
other campers in the next cabins. All you have to do is holler.'

Peter returned to his theme. 'If you love someone, you

want to be alone with them. The same with art. There ought to be churches and museums where you don't have to meet gangs of tourists, where you can just sit and contemplate. You can't do that any more unless you're on the track of some nut like Borromini that the average person hasn't heard of. If I follow up on the logic of that, I'd decide never to see any of the famous masterpieces because it's so horribly frustrating to get there and *not* to see them.'

'Still, you seem to have managed.' Peter shook his head, thinking with bitterness of the spandrels, not to mention the lunettes. 'Only a little, really. And only by being tricky. Listen, I heard about this rich *studioso* who gets driven by his chauffeur every morning to the Sistine Chapel at nine o'clock and leaves at nine-fifteen. That way he outwits the crowds. I wouldn't want to be him. Yet maybe in time I'll be like that, studying all the angles, to get my cut of the available art. That's what the modern world leads you to.' He sighed. 'Mr Small, how can a person be for peace if he's never experienced a feeling of peacefulness? For that you need to be alone and enclosed in something vast like the ocean. An element bigger than you are that will still be there when you're gone.'

'The stars in those north woods. Remote universes, yet you feel you can reach out and touch them.' Peter could not deny that the stars communicated the feeling he had described. Or had at any rate before *il pallone americano* had muscled in on the firmament. 'I was thinking of Rome. In Rome, the inhabitants don't intrude on your thoughts, any more than the fish in the ocean. They're part of the element. But mobs of tourists are just garbage dumped here by planes and sight-seeing buses, with the guides and storekeepers diving for them like scavenger gulls!'

The Recording Angel in the black box was taking note of his words, he recalled. 'If you want me to say I'm part of the garbage, O.K., I agree. I'm fouling up the element. When I'm in the Sistine Chapel, I hate my fellow-man. There's something basically wrong with a situation like that. If a guy is in the presence of beauty, he should be having noble thoughts. That's what finally made me get the ear-plugs. Not just to tune out those ghoulish guided tours but to keep from having evil thoughts about them. "Avoid the occasions of sin", is one of my father's recipes. He got it from the Jesuits.'

'Do you accept democracy, Levy?' Mr Small shot out the question like a district attorney moving in for the kill. One minute he was giving those encouraging little pats and ingratiating hugs, and the next he had you in the box, as though he was his own stool pigeon. Peter essayed a soft answer. 'I always thought I did. But there are some things you can't slice up evenly, like that baby in the Judgment of Solomon. I'm coming to the conclusion that the principles of democracy work better when there isn't too much cash around. The way it used to be in Athens. If we could only get back to that . . .' ' "Barefoot in Athens".' His adviser's pale foxy eyes looked at him pityingly. Peter read his thought. He began to be angry. 'All right, so they had slavery. Jefferson had slaves. Don't you think I know that? But just the same, democracy, the way I see it, is something civic, involving a little free space. There's nothing democratic about huge herds of travellers stampeding for the same point. If it's a herd instinct that tells them to converge on the Sistine Chapel, that instinct ought to be redirected to something more appropriate, like a football stadium!'

'Appropriate to whom? What makes you so sure that the Sistine Chapel is appropriate as an end for you and not for the masses?' 'It's obvious,' said Peter, no longer caring that he had shifted his ground. 'You saw that mob scene this morning. They don't even listen to their stupid guides, who half the time tell them everything wrong anyway. Mostly they're bored stiff and yawning, because they had to get up early and join their tour. Instead of looking at the frescoes, they're peeking at their watches. This professor I know says it's the same at the Uffizi in Florence in the summertime. You know what I think? A tourist ought to have to pass an entrance exam to get to see the "Mona Lisa" or the "Last Supper" or the Sistine Chapel. It's the only way.'

'The "*only*" way?' Mr Small appeared amused. 'Honestly,' said Peter. 'I've given a lot of thought to it. Prohibiting tours would help, at least in the winter, which is when most of the old folks come, because they get the off-season rate. Or you could restrict tours to certain hours of the day, but the trouble is there aren't so many hours when the light is good. Or you could have one day a week when only tours would be admitted. That might be more fair. But I realize that even a measly half-measure like that wouldn't have a chance under the present set-up. Under capitalism, you can't have the mildest reforms because art gets milked for profit like everything else.'

'Would it be better under Communism?' 'Well, at least there wouldn't be any American Express.' 'What about Intourist?' 'Actually I was thinking more of socialism. You'd make more museums for the people and distribute the art around more in the provinces. But still you'd have a problem. So you'd educate the public to see the rationality of an entrance exam. If a person passed, he'd get a card that would admit him to all the three-star attractions, like the "Birth of Venus" and so on. And if he didn't, there'd still be a lot of art to look at. Then, so as not to weight the scales in favour of intellectual people who were good at passing tests, you could have a lottery too. Prizes would be books of tickets entitling the winners to see twelve masterpieces of their choice. Like rationing during the war: a guy might want to use up most of his tickets on the Sistine Chapel and skip the "School of Athens" or whatever interested him less. I forgot to say that under my system schoolchildren could get in without taking any test. The little kids that come to the Sistine Chapel with their priest or teacher always have a ball. I love to watch them looking up at the ceiling with big round black eyes and twirling around like tops till they're dizzy. They point and ask questions. *"Una sibilla, cos'è?"* If the priest is any good, he shows them the *putti* playing, and they wonder if they're angels. *"No. Sono fanciulli come voi. Giocano."* '

Peter spoke rapidly, ending with a nervous laugh. A sarcastic smile glimmered on his adviser's features, and Peter feared it might refer to a fact he had just noticed himself: his plan had an Achilles heel. Under socialism, i.e., in an ideal republic, just about everybody would be able to appreciate art, so that there would be no reasonable basis for exclusion, and the museums would be even more packed than they were now.

But Mr Small had failed to observe the hole in his reasoning. The sneer on his face had another referent. Abruptly he turned off the tape-recorder. 'Enough of this modish drivel,' he said. To Peter's disbelieving ears, he launched into a defence of capitalism, which was the best system yet invented – or likely to be invented – for technological progress and an equal distribution of goods. 'Of course it's flawed, but what human system isn't? Don't tell me socialism hasn't been tried yet! We've had it in all its varieties, mixed and straight, and look at the record. Take a good hard look.' And he began to hold forth about something he called the market mechanism, which worked (with some correction) like the mills of the gods, to spread the wealth, remedy social injustice, multiply choices, advance basic research, apply technology to formerly insoluble human equations. The way he described it made Peter think of one of those mixers the fair Rosamund hated that did everything but chew your food for you.

'Wow!' said Peter. 'You surprise me, Mr Small. I thought you were some sort of far-out radical. Like a tribune of the people. I couldn't understand how you could reconcile the ideas you seemed to be for with wanting to work hand and glove with air lines and reactionary governments.' 'Those terms have no meaning for a contemporary mind. In my youth I was fond of them too, during a brief romance with that mythic animal, democratic socialism. Today there's no excuse for that kind of ignorance, when any reader of the newspapers can see that Right and Left, if we must use the old vocabulary, have so clearly changed places. Yet the glib slurs on capitalism remain fashionable.

'Capitalism, if you were only aware of it, has shown itself to be the most subtle force for progress the world has ever known. In its post-industrial phase, an insidious, awesome force. Boring from within the old structures, levelling, creating new dreams, new desires, and having the technical knowhow and the dynamism to satisfy them. You're living in the midst of a vast global revolution originating in the United States and you seem not to take the slightest interest in it, except to go through some feeble motions of dissent. From your ivory tower, you look down disdainfully on that revolution and pretend to yourself that you'd welcome it if it bore the name of socialism. I can assure you that you wouldn't, my friend. "Socialism" is your alibi for rejecting the real progress capitalism has made, the levelling you abhor, if the truth were told. "Garbage", you said just now, in a moment of outspokenness which no doubt you regret. That was your epithet for the common man.'

'Hey, you misunderstood me! I don't think those crowds are garbage in their natural setting. It's the processing that does it to them. That's the word *you* used. The same with real garbage. Before it's processed into that state, it's just food – plain healthy food. And if you take out the tin cans and compost it back into the soil, it will be food again.' 'Why don't you meet the argument instead of taking refuge in childish verbal fencing?'

'I'm not going to argue with you, Mr Small. I feel too tired. Just listening to you makes me exhausted, and I'm not saying that to be rude. To have any real discussion, we'd both have to go back to the letter *a*. And honestly you're too old for that. Maybe you're right about capitalism being a revolutionary force. Sure, it can produce abundance, but abundance of what? I admit it's bringing about changes. But those aren't the changes my generation wants. If capitalism is so great, what has it done for civil rights?'

'Christ! You privileged kids are all alike. You despise the common man, as long as he's white. But you suddenly love the Negro. If CORE had been holding a caucus this morning in the Sistine Chapel, you would have slavered with joy. All right, I'll tell you what capitalism has done for civil rights. The market mechanism plus technology has brought the black man off the fields and into the cities. North and South. In the cities you got overcrowding, slums, unemployment, welfare, rioting – an explosive situation produced by the restructuring of agriculture. But out of that miserable crowding, those festering slums, the civil rights movement was born. Your field nigger, as they called him, never knew he had any rights. The whole thing is an urban movement generated by the dynamics of post-industrial society. If it had been left to you, the black man would have stayed on the land forever, close to Nature, peacefully farming or share-cropping. Which means he would have remained an Uncle Tom!' He struck his fist into his palm with a smack that made Peter jump.

'That's a good point,' he acknowledged, swallowing several times. 'I never thought of it that way. I guess I only looked at one side of the picture. To me, the slums were bad.' Mr Small grew more affable. 'You might say the ghettoes with their high crime rate and juvenile delinquency were a high price to pay for the returns, so far, in actual civil rights gained. But change is often seen as costly in the immediate perspective. Capitalism in time will eradicate the slums because it can't afford them. Slums mean under-consumption; it's as simple as that. I can promise you that in the forseeable future, with automation and full productivity, the remaining pockets of poverty will be wiped out in the us. We will look back on the ghettoes as the inevitable way-stations on the highway of development.'

'Yes. Maybe.' Now that the meal was over, Peter was disinclined to prolong the debate. He was glad to see that his adviser was feeling mellow again. It was strange that, unlike the original Dr Pangloss, who had a sunny outlook, his descendant was of a variable temper, hard to forecast and seldom *sereno*. Dr Pangloss's insulation from reality had made him a good travelling companion, but Mr Small's personal plexiglass bell evidently caused a kind of itchiness or inflammation that kept him irritable and peevish – Peter would not have cared to go through the Lisbon earthquake with him even to be in on the happy ending of seeing him hanged by the Inquisition. Maybe the idea that all was for the best was harder to hold onto nowadays, and a guy like Small had to be satisfied with thinking that *he* was for the best, brimming

with good will and faith in the market mechanism all the time
that really, if he only knew it, he was stewing in doubt and
rancour. He had a higher ɪꞯ, Peter estimated, than Candide's
companion, and perhaps that was part of the problem.

Now he played a few sentences back on the tape-recorder,
listened as if to music, and lovingly replaced the cover. He
seemed so tender with that instrument that Peter wondered if
it was new. 'Don't mistake me, Peter. I'm not insensitive to
your *Angst*. I have my own ambivalences toward this abrasive
new society we're making. "The world is too much with us;
late and soon, getting and spending, we lay waste our powers."
Yes. Nor do I see remedies in the foreseeable future for
the sheer increase in man's numbers, though I'm confident
they will be found. I believe in man.' It occurred to Peter
that Mr Small had been successfully analysed; that might
be what was the matter with him. He was lighting his pipe.
'I know you reject the techniques of psycho-therapy. But if
this solitude you speak of is so important to you, perhaps you
ought to try some of the mind-expanding drugs. My "Beat"
friends may have something to teach us. With drugs, they
don't need the vicarious experience of art. Every "trip" is a
tour of the unexplored resources of consciousness. We
should ponder the semantics of that word. What if they've
found the answer to the very real dilemma of tourism you've
noted? A partial answer, anyway. They perhaps show a
greater adaptiveness to the changing environment we live in
than those of us, like you, who persist in the traditional
patterns. And their solution, in due time, will be within the
reach of every housewife, every old person. There's no doubt
in my mind that pot will soon be legalized and marketed
through the normal channels at an acceptable price. The
cigarette industry, in trouble over cancer, will see the
opportunity. There's your market mechanism, don't you see,
with its inherent thrust forward, to open new vistas, resolve
old problems!'

' "Don't take that trip up the Nile. Turn on with a Camel."
Yeah.' Feeling no eagerness for this alternate future either,
Peter added up his share of the bill and put down a thousand-

lire note. 'Oh, the bad news! Shall we split it?' Peter had had
no notion of splitting, since his adviser had consumed a
bistecca fiorentina, a half-litre of wine, and a *cassata siciliana*,
while he had had noodles, a salad, and a small San Pellegrino.
But some affluent people were like that; they never noticed,
when they offered to divide the bill, that they had had the
more costly items.

'Let's see,' said Mr Small. 'It comes to about 3,000 lire.
You put down another five hundred, and I'll leave the tip.'
Peter, who had hoped for some change from his original
contribution, felt himself turn red. 'The service is included.
See, there it is.' He indicated the item on the bill, trusting
that this manoeuvre would inspire his adviser to make a
detailed cost breakdown. 'Oh, fine,' said Mr Small, ignoring
the bill and waving to the waiter. 'What do I give him extra?'
'Oh, a couple of hundred.'

The waiter was waiting. Peter found himself in a familiar
sort of quandary. Leaving aside the selfish motive of his
depleted funds (with the five hundred lire and his rightful
change he could buy his supper at a counter and part of his
breakfast too), he asked himself whether he did not have a
friendly obligation to set his adviser straight. If Small, afterwards, were to realize his mistake, he would wish Peter had
spoken up. An honest person must always be glad to be saved
from cheating another person, especially a younger one. If it
was Peter, he would want to be told. But Mr Small was not
Peter – that seemed to be clear – and there were people who
would rather walk around with their fly open than have
someone tell them about it. His mother, for instance, always
got mad if he said her slip was showing. 'Don't you want to
know, Mother?' 'No.' Money, he guessed, could be an even
more sensitive area in the adult soul. And Mr Small might
have alimony to pay and maintenance for his kids – he had
not revealed how many. Would it be cowardly to take the
easy course and fork over the five hundred lire? Or Christian?
Was deciding to be 'Christian' just an excuse for being a
coward? Peter wondered what that contemporary sibyl,
'Dear Abby', would advise. 'Gently draw the error to your

companion's attention?' But that 'gently' was a typical sibyl-
line evasion. There was no gentle way of telling somebody
he was rooking you.

Peter's hand went slowly to his wallet. Then he remembered
the foundation. And Mr Small, evidently, remembered too.
'By the bye, would you mind telling the waiter to bring the
check back? And have him mark it "Paid". I'd like to have
it for my records.' Peter got it. The guy was planning to
collect from the foundation on Peter's lunch as well as his
own, which would put him not just even but ahead of the
game. The fact that he avoided the term 'expense account'
showed he had some shame left. But not enough. He had dug
his own grave. In it the worm turned. 'In that case,' said
Peter, 'you'll want separate checks, won't you?' He spoke to
the waiter. '*Faccia due conti, per favore, Scusi*'. The man
somewhat grumpily redid the addition. As Peter pocketed
his change, his eyes avoided Mr Small's. It was better not to
gloat over a fallen adversary. Victory was sweet, but the wise
man did not seek to savour it.

Outside the restaurant, undeterred by the heavy equipment hanging on straps from his shoulders, Mr Small managed a final effusive embrace. Then he held Peter at arm's
length. 'What a wonderful day we've had together.' It was
hard for Peter to imagine that this affectionate burbling
person had tried to gyp him on the check. 'Wait just a
minute, Peter. Stay there!' He darted across the piazza, the
tape-recorder bouncing against one hip and the camera
against the other. He had left his briefcase on the pavement.
In a minute he came running back, having found a local
passerby who was willing to take their picture. Extracting
the Rollei from its case, he hung it around the man's neck,
showed him how to use the viewer and press the button.
After peeking into the viewer he set the speed and posed
himself and Peter, arms linked, against the background of a
fountain. Peter faced the camera, feeling the snug pressure
of the professor's arm, undeniably 'warm', upon his and
trying to fight off a sense of total unreality. If today was to
figure as a sentimental *ricordo* in Mr Small's memory book,

then one of them had to be nuts. '*Un sorriso, per piacere.*
Smile, please, misters.' Mr Small had already obliged. Peter
forced a peaked grin to his own lips. He nodded. He was a
snob. He preferred most art to most people. He was guilty of
juvenile coldness and non-participation. When he had not
shared whatever it was the sociologist thought they had
experienced, the least he could have done was consent to an
equal division of the check.

Two-thirds of a Ghost

Coming back to Paris, with his soul refreshed, Peter encountered a 'disagreeable' he had managed to erase from his memory – the *clochards*. In Rome, there were no *clochards* because the Italians were not vinous. One of the world's problems you could ignore there was acoholism. In the street you seldom saw a drunk person, not counting foreigners. In Rome, there were only ordinary beggars, mostly cripples on church steps and ragged gypsy women with babies in their arms that his ex-roommate claimed were rented. You forked over some *spiccioli* as a matter of course, and the strays, if any, that preyed on your conscience were the homeless, hungry cats.

In Paris, regular beggars were rare and hung out mainly in the subway. He met one – a blind man with an accordion – on his way home, when he had to change at the Gare d' Austerlitz stop, and, keeping to Roman habits, he searched for a donation among the small coins in his pocket, though it meant putting down his heavy suitcase, which at once became a traffic obstruction. To the sundry '*Merde, alors!*' hurled at him by the jostling throng, he replied mechanically, '*Ta gueule.*' In Paris, beggars almost never thanked you, and he was startled to hear the blind man call out after him something that sounded strangely like '*Merci!*' '*De rien,*' Peter mumbled. '*Monsieur!*' the man reiterated, rapping on his begging-cup. Eventually Peter dug. In his confusion, he had dropped some small lire along with the one-centime pieces into the plastic cup, and the blind man, by touch evidently, had detected the fraud. He was angry. Peter put down his suitcase again and fumbled in his pocket; he had no more French coins. He drew a crumpled five-franc note from his wallet – a dollar. The man smoothed it out and felt it carefully, as though it might be counterfeit. '*Ça va*,' he said finally.

This little incident assured Peter he was home. Only in France, he guessed, would a subway beggar, on getting a handout, act like an incensed storekeeper presented with a wooden nickel; he was probably lucky the guy had not called the police. Yet when he thought it over, he found less cause for mirth. The blind man had made sense. If a person gave charity, it was because he decided he owed it, maybe not to a particular individual but to the other half of humanity, and the creditor had the right to expect the account to be settled in the coin of the realm. Just the same as a storekeeper – why not? French logic had punched holes in Peter's philanthropy, which seemed to have been based on the rotten assumption, Beggars can't be choosers. Of course it had been an 'innocent' mistake, yet not all that innocent underneath. Peter knew he would not have been so careless with the merchants in the Marché Buci. He ought to be glad to be back in this unsentimental country, where icy reason had its temples and everything taught him a lesson.

But the *clochards* were something else. Making his way home that night, along the Boulevard St-Germain, from the Bonfantes', where he had delivered his offerings and been persuaded to stay for supper, he stumbled over one sleeping on the Métro grating. They did that in the winter to keep warm; often, near the Odéon stop, between the rue St-Grégoire-de-Tours and the rue de l'Ancienne-Comédie, there would be two or three dark shapes stretched out or huddled on the big iron ventilator grill, which they treated as a hot-air radiator. Normally he picked his way with care to avoid them or even, like the bad Levite in the story of the Good Samaritan, walked on the other side of the street. But tonight he forgot.

His foot trod on something soft and yielding, which stirred under him. He let out a yell of horror. He was walking on what seemed to be a human stomach, but it could be a pair of breasts. The creature was all wrapped up, like a bundle, in a sodden piece of cloth that might once have been an overcoat, and he could not tell its sex or find its face. At least it was still animate. He heard its voice mutter. Then it turned, stretched, settled itself in a more comfortable position; a head had thrust out, and under the street light he had a glimpse of a grey unshaven jaw. Apparently no vital organ had been crushed by being stepped on, but how could he be sure? Alcohol was an anaesthetic; in the old days they used it when performing operations – Lord Nelson was crocked when they amputated his arm after Tenerife, or was it while he was dying, at Trafalgar? An awful sour smell came from the recumbent form; on the grill, a few feet away, lay an empty wine bottle.

Peter picked it up and took it to the trash-basket on the corner. If it was left there, somebody could trip on it and hurt themselves. On second thoughts, he went back and retrieved it. The guy must have paid a deposit on it, and in the morning he could get a few centimes back for the empty – enough for a cheap cup of coffee maybe. Overcoming his repulsion to touching the inert, stinking heap, he thrust the bottle firmly beneath its arm. The *clochard* responded with a hugging, cradling motion, as though the *gros rouge* was a baby. Disgusted, Peter turned away.

It was no use calling the cops to take the bum to a hospital, in case there might be internal bleeding. The gendarmes just laughed if a foreigner tried to get them to do something merciful about a *clochard*. That had happened to Dag, who found one slumped over the wheel of a car in the entrance to his building and thought it was somebody who had had a heart attack. And even if Peter were able, which he doubted, to haul the body home for first-aid, his concierge would probably hear him and bar the way; she had a complex about *clochards*. He started walking towards the *carrefour*, endeavouring not to quicken his steps. He felt furtive, like a motorist leaving the scene of an accident. Every few paces, he turned to look behind him. When he reached the intersection, the *clochard*, to his relief, was stirring. The shapeless hump rose with slow laborious movements like a dinosaur emerging from primeval slime and wove off in the other direction down the boulevard, holding the bottle and, for good measure, Peter's new carryall, which he had used to transport the Bonfante presents and which he could not remember having dropped.

What a reception committee! He felt so weak and sweaty that he could hardly make the stairs leading up to his street. Between the beggar and the drunk, he seemed to have run the gauntlet in some fiendish initiation rite. His heavy boots were slippery from the bum's vomit, and he sat down, holding his breath, and cleaned them with his handkerchief, which he then threw away.

After this, for a while, he encountered *clochards* everywhere, looming in his path, clutching at his sleeve, shuffling past him to a *zinc* or a *pissoir*. He wondered if they could be a form of DT's and instead of snakes or pink 'elephants he was seeing bottle noses, red rheumy eyes, purple veins, laceless shoes stuffed with newspapers, torn flapping overcoats, and layers on layers of indeterminate clothing stained with wine, spew, mud, and snot. He saw these apparitions zigzagging out of bars, sitting and lying on public benches, fumbling in the morning garbage, staggering along sidewalks, leaning against lamp-posts, propped in doorways, collapsed on the Métro steps, occasionally panhandling, and always at night extended on the various grills, grids, and gratings through which the hot stale breath of the Paris underground lung system was exhaled into the atmosphere, as though Paris itself was a vast unhygienic Russian stove on top of which snored these muzhiks in their bast and rags.

On his walks, he took to counting the grids in his neighbourhood that might serve as their night-time couches; he would not have imagined there could be so many, square and rectangular, of diverse sizes and patterns – not just Métro ventilators, he came to realize, but ducts from bakery ovens, conduits from every kind of infernal furnace and combustion-unit sending up blasts of contaminated air. Unless you had

K

a special interest like his or were walking with a girl wearing high heels, which were likely to get caught in the grillwork, you would never notice they were there.

He became conscious, too, of the number of empty bottles lying around in the *quartier*, on sidewalks and in gutters – flotsam warning him of the vicinity of some human wreck. He could not rid his mind of the subject. In the Métro, he watched to see whether anybody but him was reading the anti-alcoholism propaganda and taking it to heart. Where he used to ask himself whether women he saw on street-corners might be prostitutes, his speculations now anxiously turned on whether young workmen tossing it back at a *zinc* might not metamorphose tomorrow into *clochards*. What made a heavy drinker turn into a derelict was a mystery, he guessed, and for a born hypochondriac like himself this rendered the sickness more scary, like multiple sclerosis; you never knew where it might strike. He did not quake on his own behalf (when he drank too much, he got sick, which his aunt said showed he could never become a drunkard) but altruistically, which was worse. He began to look with pro-phetic dread on crones in the *épicerie* with a pair of Postillon bottles tucked into the bottom of their shopping baskets, husbands of concierges, waiters with trembling hands, the oyster-opener across from the Deux Magots, the customers in Nicolas, even priests.

At least he did not have to worry about his concierge. Though she occasionally lifted a medicinal glass with her aged *copines*, the bottle of nice wine he had given her for Christmas (acting on a bum steer from his father) was still standing on her buffet, like an altar ornament, next to a vase of yellowed 'palms' from Palm Sunday and some framed tinted photographs of her relatives and Queen Fabiola. In fact, she had a horror of *clochards*, and if anything could cure him of his own obsession, it was listening to Madame Puel on the topic.

She read about their misdeeds in a concierges' newspaper and exchanged atrocity stories with her pals along the street. To judge by her accounts, her broom and mop got more exercise driving out the poor wretches she found asleep in her hallway than in their normal functions. As the nights got colder, she tightened the rules of the building. The big front door was locked at six o'clock, and when Peter came home after ten, it was not enough now to ring six times; he had to announce himself, which he hated, as he passed the *loge*. '*Levi.*' If the tenants expected a guest after that hour, they had to come down themselves and open, by pre-arrangement. Yet despite these new security measures, the *clochards* somehow slipped in, almost, Peter felt, to Madame Puel's satisfaction, as though their breaching her defences sharpened her relish for battle. Just as she seemed to enjoy telling him, by way of a morning greeting, '*Votre camarade a laissé la porte ouverte,*' meaning, usually, Makowski, who often failed to close the front door when he left, though not as often as she pretended.

Sometimes when Peter got home she was lying in wait for him in her bathrobe and *bigoudis*. '*Levi.*' To break the monotony of hearing his name issue from his own lips, he now and then used a falsetto or a sepulchral bass. He loathed it when her door unlocked before he could get past. '*Ah, bon soir, Monsieur Levi. J'en ai chassé un déjà, vous savez. Une femme.*' Like his mother with a mouse-trap, she kept score. One triumphal night, when the people on the fourth floor left were having a party, she caught three in a row.

He wondered if Madame Puel guessed how miserable it made him to hear about these things and often he suspected she did. She thought he was 'soft' on *clochards* because he had dared ask her one icy day what harm it would do to let them sleep in the hall or in the service stairway. '*Ah, monsieur, vous parlez. C'est pas un asile, notre immeuble.*' Who was to clean up their filth after them? '*Vous, Monsieur l'Américain, ou moi, l'employée?*' Peter allowed that he could do it. The beldame laughed. He would not get the opportunity. It was easy for him to talk. Up there in the mansard, what did a strong young man have to fear from those *salauds*, while she, an old woman, on the ground floor in her *loge*, a widow, could be murdered in her bed?

Peter begged her to try to make distinctions. A *voyou* was one thing, but had a *clochard* ever knocked off anybody that she knew of? In his observation, they were too far gone to hold a bottle, let alone a weapon. '*Vous dites*,' she replied. About a week after this chat, he was surprised, at breakfast, by her rapping at his door. He could tell something important had happened; it was the first time she had been to his room – she used the elevator to reach the other tenants and left the back stairs to be swept by a slave on Saturdays. She was breathless, having made the rounds of the house. But she would not take a cup of coffee or even, at first, sit down. He had asked her, had he not, what harm a *clochard* could do? Could he guess what she had found last night on her third-floor landing when she had chased one of *them* out of the elevator? Peter could not guess. '*Deux mégots, Monsieur Levi! Vous vous rendez compte?*' In her withered palm, she held out two cigarette butts. '*Voilà!*'

Peter nodded. He could see her point. The whole old fire-trap building could have gone up in smoke. But how could she be sure that the butts had been left there by the man she chased? '*C'était une femme*,' she corrected. '*Toujours la même.*' Earlier, Madame Puel had smelled cigarette smoke and crept up the front stairs to investigate. But seemingly there had been nobody, and she had gone back to bed. The way she reconstructed it, the woman, hearing a noise, had hidden in the elevator. Then she had fallen asleep, and her body had slumped against the elevator door. That was how Madame Puel had found her, at 2 AM, when a nurse on the fourth who worked nights had walked up, because the elevator was stuck, and seen what she thought was a cadaver inside.

It was lucky, said Peter, with a compassionate shudder, that the *clocharde* had not set fire to her clothes and burned up, trapped, in the elevator. Unlucky for *her*, thought the concierge; a creature like that was better off dead. Then at least she could not be a threat to others. For herself, Madame Puel did not care. '*Mais vous, qui êtes jeune, qui avez la vie devant vous ... Et tous les autres, avec leurs familles, leurs*

distractions. Griller dans un incendie, c'est pas gai.' She stared
at the cigarette butts in her hand and let them drop on
Peter's table. *'Eh bien, voilà. Je suis venue vous le dire. C'est
tout.'* QED.

Looking into her parched ancient face, Peter had no recommendations to offer. It was pointless to argue that the old
run-down building ought to install individual buzzer systems,
like in the United States (the skinflint owner would rather
collect the fire insurance and retire to the Côte d'Azur), and
the joke he considered making ('I suppose you could put up
"No Smoking" signs') seemed inopportune. To his surprise,
poor old Madame Puel, now that her point was proved, had
become nicer.

*'Je suis bonne catholique, Monsieur Levi. Je sais bien que ces
salauds sont des êtres humains en quelque sorte. Mais j'suis pas le
Christ.'* It was no pleasure, she assured him, to have to drive
them out night after night, but that was her job. *'J' suis
payée pour ça.'* When her little dog had been alive, it had
been a different story. He barked fearlessly at all intruders. In
his day, the building was a fortress; no *clochards*, pedlars, or
other unauthorized persons dared set foot in it. But then he
nipped at the mailman, and they made her put *'Chien méchant'*
on a placard hanging on the *loge* door. *'Chien méchant!
Figurez-vous. Quelle honte.'* For *her*, Peter assented sympathetically. But the dog, after all, could not read. Madame
Puel tossed her head; her nostrils flared. Boy had *sensed* the
shame of it, and, shortly after, he had died. Of mortification.
'Mon vieux compagnon.' Her eyes filled with tears. Boy had
been the building's protector for nearly fifteen years, poor
fellow, and all the thanks he got were objections to his barking – not even a marker in the dog cemetery. And now she
had taken his place. *'Un chien de garde!'*

She was nothing but a watchdog. And everyone held it
against her. *'Vous aussi, Monsieur Levi.' 'Mais non!'* protested
Peter, though of course she was right. He *had* held it against
her, but he would not any more. *'Je comprends,'* he added.
'C'est une grande responsabilité.' He went to the stove and put
on water to make her a fresh cup of coffee. *'Ah, comme vous*

êtes bon! Toujours si gentil avec moi et courtois. Vous, un étranger!' She wiped her eyes. He tried to think how to say in correct French that he would like to have known her dog.

It was human nature, he supposed, that as soon as she recovered she would start attacking *clochards* again. They threw up; they were incontinent; they had vermin; they stole. And if you let one stay, the next night there would be four. They were clever and tightly organized. *'Comme les juifs,'* murmured Peter. And yet maybe it was true. It might even be true what anti-Semites said about Jews sticking together and if-you-knew-one-you-had-to-know-their-friends. Making exceptions was usually a poor idea, he found; it was the same principle as 'Just one won't hurt you.'

You had to be willing to let the exception *be* the rule. And for that you would need to be Jesus Christ, as Madame Puel said, or a *'Parfait'*, like the Cathars in Languedoc he had been reading about, who thought the whole temporal world was a creation of Satan.

The worst, Peter decided, was the casuistry people practised in going along with the temporal *status quo*. Even if, like the concierge, they had no choice – the way the world operated – but to give some unfortunate the bum's rush, they could not leave it at that. They had to *talk*. She had convinced herself, for instance, that drink made *clochards* insensible to the cold. *'Ils ne sentent rien, Monsieur Levi. Ils ne sont pas comme vous et moi.'* She really seemed to think that was a proved scientific fact. But if they did not feel the cold, why did they hole up in her elevator and in her entry hall? It never occurred to her to put the two things together.

Most of the American kids here had the same attitude. Some were actually obscene enough to give them the hotfoot, in a spirit of scientific experiment, to see if they would react. Among the guys and girls who sat around at the American Centre, there was a lot of shocked discussion and comparison of notes. The *clochards*, they decided, were a wholly different species from Bowery bums, tramps, hobos, or any other kind of floater or hopeless drunkard they knew. Like Peter, they could not get over finding them underfoot at night. 'Aren't there shelters or anything, for Christ's sake?' It bothered them that the *clochards* would not behave normally, like American bums, who sidled up with a hard-luck story and asked for a handout. Instead of begging for dough to make a phone call to their sick old mother in Metz, the *clochards* just glared at them from wild inflamed eyes, like filthy prophets. And when, infrequently, they asked for money, it was more of a brusque demand than an appeal.

Some of those American nuts were avid to draw them out, get their life stories – no doubt to pad out their boring letters home. 'They won't talk to me,' a girl mourned. 'I've tried and *tried*.' 'They're French,' said Peter. He would never have dared venture more than a *'Bonjour'* to a *clochard* himself. To him it was unthinkable to want to ferret out the history of a down-and-outer: 'What brought you to this, my good man?' He occasionally dropped a franc on some comatose form and then fled, as if he had committed a trespass. Like most of the other kids, he guessed, and like Madame Puel, he was afraid of *clochards*, the way people were afraid of snakes, even though they knew they were harmless. The pain these bums gave him was moral.

He was ashamed of being so ignorant of a subject that was so much on his mind. But the data gathered by his peer group came chiefly from café waiters and added up to the fact, if it was one, that the *clochard* community was a microcosm of France: you could meet all kinds among them, *agrégés*, doctors, actresses from the Comédie Française; the distinguished toper with the baby carriage who went around the *quartier* collecting rubbish was a former banker . . . But that was what the census-taker would note in any hell, e.g., Dante's. That they lived by selling the rubbish they collected and on sponging – mainly off each other – was somewhat more informative, though it left you wondering why, if they were capable of organizing, they did not go a step farther and arrange some minimal housing – even discarded pup tents or sleeping-bags.

According to Silly Platt, who was an authority on *clochards*, Peter's question showed he had not grasped their psychology.

'They don't feel the cold the way we do.' 'That's what my concierge says.' 'She's so right. They feel it up to a point but not enough to do anything constructive about it. In fact they'd *rather* mess up the hall of a building that somebody has just swept or wallow in their puke on the sidewalk. Have you ever seen a bear's wallow? Muck they like to roll in. That's what these bums go for. They're animals. I gave one half a franc the other day (*"Donnez-moi; j'ai faim"*), and when he leaned over to thank me, sort of bowing, he threw up on my shoes. It's really crazy. He must have thought he was showering me with gratitude. And I watched another one on the Boul' Mich'. He was shitting down his pants leg. Right in broad daylight. And he just staggered on with this smile on his face, as if the oily stuff slithering down his leg and leaking on the sidewalk was perfume. Guerlain Number Two.' '*Basta*,' said Peter, gagging.

He was only half persuaded that Silly knew whereof he spoke. 'You don't think they do it more as a revenge on society?' 'You make it too complicated. If you just look on them as animals, they won't bother you any more. Actually I get sort of a kick out of them.' Silly was an authority on several aspects of French life, high and low. He had figured all the angles and liked to live dangerously. A few days after classes started, Peter had run into him on the Métro platform, preparing to ride first class on a second-class ticket. He had some old punched first-class tickets in his pocket, in case the *côntroleur* passed through the car, checking up. 'Come on!' Reluctantly, Peter boarded. He had never been in first class before.

'Watch this!' said Silly. 'I'm going to have some fun.' Obediently, Peter watched a middle-aged Frenchman in a beret who was sitting on a *strapontin* opposite them. Silly's penetrating grey eyes were drilling holes in him, compelling him to look up from his newspaper and meet that transfixing gaze. The man gave a wondering glance sideways at Peter, turned back to his paper, then peered out again. Meanwhile Silly's orbs did not waver. To Peter's astonishment, the man accepted the challenge. Their eyes crossed swords. It was a staring match. Finally the Frenchman's eyes dropped. At the next station, muttering, he got off. 'I make them get them down,' announced Silly. 'Get what down?' 'Their eyes, don't you see?'

He selected another victim and went through the same performance. 'I always win. The guy that starts has the advantage.' 'But why do you do it?' 'To test my will power. Watch!' This time it was a youth about their own age, sitting with his mother. He was harder. Silly leaned slightly forward. 'Get them down, get them down,' he was murmuring, like an incantation. Then the mother caught on. She nudged her son. '*Jean! Qu'est-ce que tu fais là?*' That did it. 'Watch now. They'll move.' Sure enough, the woman, with an angry look backward, led the boy to another part of the car. 'It's more amusing when they retreat right off the train. Like that first guy in the beret. You could tell it wasn't his stop.'

On the Champs-Elysées, after Silly had turned in an airplane ticket, they went to a café. Peter was curious about the expression 'Get them down.' It was a sort of code, Silly guessed, for getting the French down. 'If you don't practise all the time, they have the upper hand, don't you see? They're one up on us, knowing French. You have to stay in training.' This eyeball-to-eyeball exercise, he explained, was just one of the power games he made a point of playing with the French, especially shopkeepers. 'They always expect the foreigner to yield first. When you don't, they're at a total loss. Completely off base. It's crazy.' The thing was never to accept their rules; invent your own.

For instance, the markets. 'You know that old gag about making you buy a kilo?' Peter groaned. 'God, yes.' 'You don't mean you still go along with it?' 'All the French do,' argued Peter. 'We're not French! We're Americans!' 'O.K., but I don't see how you get around it.' 'I have a system. Listen.' When he went marketing, Silly never took more than a few francs along. He looked over the vendors' merchandise and decided what he wanted to buy. 'Say it's cabbage. I take two francs out of my pocket and tell the guy,

"Give me two francs' worth. That's all the money I have." '
'And it works?' Not only did it work; he got more for his
money that way. 'Look. If four oranges weigh out at two
francs and twenty-five centimes, they let me have them for
two. They're not going to take a slice off the fourth one. It
never fails.' Peter felt torn between admiration and envious
scepticism. He relaxed a bit when he heard that Silly did his
shopping on the rue Mouffetard. He doubted very much that
the system would function at the Marchè Buci.

Instead of debating that, he asked what had happened in
Switzerland. 'You were right,' Silly admitted. The ski-
instructor job had not materialized. But he had got a good tan
and really scored playing poker. Moreover he had met a
fantastic French girl who had invited him to her home in
Versailles. 'I'm getting around quite a lot now, as a matter of
fact.' He had been given hospitality in a number of 'homes',
which Peter translated to mean rich French people's houses.
'How do you do it?' said Peter. 'I mean, get to know them –
any kind of French?'

Naturally Silly had a system. 'Have you noticed that I
never wear a watch?' He did that on purpose so as to be able
to ask for the time. Also, he did not carry a lighter or matches.
'But what use is it if they give you a light or tell you what
time it is? In my experience, a hand just delivers a box of
matches, and that's it. No words wasted. Honestly, I've been
going to the same café near where I live since I got here, and
not even the waiter speaks to me.'

'You should circulate more. And when somebody French
gives you a light, don't just say "*Merci*." Start talking. Don't
wait for them to make the move. And once you have your
opening set, you have to be ready with the follow-up. Plan
ahead, like in chess. All the time be thinking about how
you're going to shift your chair around to pull it up and sit
down at their table. In fact when you come into a café look
the terrain over and pick the table you want to be next to.
Not a group that's practically finished and getting ready to
pay the check. Not lovey-dovey couples. Never Americans,
because they'll try to pick *you* up, and that's fatal.'

'Fatal?' 'For both sides. If an American girl picks me up, it's because she's decided I'm French. They want to meet French boys, to practise French on them; American boys vice versa. And older American tourists just want to pick your brains for restaurants and night clubs. Or they have a daughter who's a student who'll be joining them. American girls bore me over here. I make a point of not knowing any, if I can help it. I mean the student crowd. They're a drag. You should do the same. The idea is to be stripped for action.'

The advice was wasted on Peter, but it was nice of Silly to give it. Peter could not help liking him for the candid way he shared his know-how and elucidated his ploys. Like the Phi Beta Kappa key he wore, which he had rented from his brother, Barnabas. 'But isn't that sort of dangerous? If you run into a real Phi Beta Kappa, won't they start asking embarrassing questions?' 'And do what? Call the police? It's just another ice-breaker, don't you see? Everybody that's been to college knows right away that I'm too young and giddy to be a real Phi Beta. So they get interested in how I came by it, and I tell them. I'm not really fooling anybody. And the French, who don't know what it stands for, can't wait to have their curiosity satisfied.'

He evidently thought that Peter was an unsuccessful operator in need of a helping hand. As a former fellow-sufferer, he sympathized with Peter's shyness, as though this condition made them a single person, like the same thing, before and after treatment, that you saw in ads for curing baldness. This was a mistake that Peter could not bother to clear up. But though he did not feel much like Silly and would rather remain in his shell than grow what the guy called 'armour', it was surprising how much they had in common. Even in politics they were not so far apart. Over here, Silly felt more liberal, he revealed, though he expected he would revert when he got back to Princeton and the government-studies routine. He was more conscious of poor people here. His father, who was a town planner, kept him on a tight budget, and it interested Peter to learn that Silly, except in his dress (he was wearing a golden corduroy suit and another flowing cashmere scarf), was even more economical than himself. He lived with five other kids in an apartment near the rue Mouffetard, surrounded by Algerian cafés where knife fights went on. There was a kerosene stove for heating, but it was so cold you could see your breath. The toilet out in the hall they shared with three other people, and girls were afraid to go to it, on account of vd. They had rigged up a portable shower in the living room, where Silly slept on a cot between blankets, without sheets, to save on laundry. By cooking his own meals, he could get along, he figured, on $1.75 a day, if he had to.

Amazingly, he liked animals, and they discussed going to the zoo at Vincennes together, when it got slightly warmer. Silly had studied zoology and he had a bear he called 'his' in the menagerie at the Jardin des Plantes. Whenever he was depressed, he went and visited the bear. He also liked motorbikes, but his father had made him sell his before coming over. If his aunt would send him the money, he might buy Peter's.

Peter's heart leapt. 'Would you like to come and see it?' Together they went to Makowski's place, where they inspected the motorbike and powwowed about the draft and Vietnam. The stolid, sombre Pole did not take to Silly Boy, who had a lighthearted theory that the us and Hanoi were merely playing poker: Hanoi had all its cards face up on the table, which gave it an advantage, because the us did not want to uncover its hole cards but was gambling that Hanoi would cave in without 'seeing' the us royal flush of bombers and Marines. 'And what will happen when the crunch comes?' 'There won't *be* any crunch. It's a game, see.' He knew a girl's father who worked in the quai d'Orsay. The Russians were in a deal with the us to fold up the game and deliver Hanoi to the peace table. At a new Geneva Conference. It was shaping up right now. Makowski did not believe it, and if there was such a deal it would be a sellout to Communism, just like in Eastern Europe. Silly said no, Vietnam would be neutralized, like Austria. Both players would get their ante back.

When they left Makowski's room, Silly said he was sorry
that he could not bring Peter to his apartment. They were
having problems. The other tenants were circulating a petition to have them bounced out on account of the noise they
made and the parties they threw. His roommates took it
seriously, though to him it was a laugh. He thought it was a
sort of feather in his cap to have brought the neighbours to
the point of petition and assembly. 'But pro tem we can't
invite anybody. Anyway, the place is a mess.'

Peter found Silly, as a companion, a welcome relief from
himself. His hyperactive brain, unlike Peter's, seemed to
work full time for his airy will. It did not go looking for
trouble. Silly's will, Peter estimated, could not be farther
from the moral will of Kant, yet there was something innocent and childlike in its operations. If other people were
means to him, they were also in a strange way ends. He did
not even seem particularly ambitious underneath his patter.
'My father really worries that I might become an opportunist,'
he confided, which made Peter laugh. 'You mean you think I
am one already?' Peter was not sure. 'Paris is my chance to
test myself, don't you understand? Have you noticed how
many mirrors there are here? Oh yes. It's fantastic. You
should try counting. Frenchmen look at themselves all the
time. I feel I was predestined to come to Paris. I have to find
myself. Put myself together out of all those bitty reflections I
see in their eyes.' Peter laughed again. 'That would make you
a mosaic, Silly.'

Following this he heard no more from Silly. It was typical
of that butterfly to vanish after a seemingly serious heart-to-
heart and a pending deal on the motorbike. But Peter had
other things on his agenda: the Wellesley girl had written
that she was coming to Paris; Roberta had written and asked
him to tea; his mother wrote that she might be passing
through Paris around Valentine's Day on her way to play in
Poland and wanted him to find her a hotel ... The ground-
hog had failed to see his shadow, so spring might be on winter's traces. When his allowance came, he thought of inviting
Silly to join him in another oyster-eating orgy – this time *chez*

him. He had acquired an oyster-opener. But since they both
had no telephone, he procrastinated.

He met him next at the dentist's, when he kept an appointment to have his teeth cleaned, for which a reminder card had
been sent: Monday, 8 February; 10 AM; 33 boulevard
Malesherbes. Peter had almost not showed up, after the night
he had spent, the grimmest of his life. But because his mother
was coming, he made himself obey the summons. When he
came into the dentist's waiting room, with the morning
papers under his arm, he was crying, and the last person he
would have wanted to find, reading *Anaesthesia Progress*, was
Silly Boy Platt.

The night before, on a premature busman's holiday, he had
taken in a horror movie – the ten o'clock show. Coming
home, he had noted the usual *clochards* on the Métro grating.
All was quiet at the concierge's when he passed. Then, on the
second landing, he found it – what looked like a human
puddle in the weak light of the *minuterie*. Mechanically, he
circumvented it and continued his climb. He had seen that it
was a woman, rolled up in a brown coat resembling a horse's
blanket. That checked out. He felt no surprise, only a horrible
weariness. His head was nodding up and down in recognition
of the event. This had been waiting for him, he should have
known, like a big package with his name on it: Peter Levi,
Esq., Noted Humanitarian. In fact, it was overdue. A man's
character was his fate – Heraclitus. Old Atropos had taken
his measurements as if for a suit of clothes. All afternoon,
while he peacefully watched birds in the Yvelines, the plot
against him had been thickening.

Nevertheless, he went steadily on, up another flight. Then
his steps lagged. He halted and considered. So far as he could
tell, the rest of the building was asleep. Waking Madame
Puel, to get her to cope, was not a possibility, despite the
pleasure it might give her. Also eliminated was kicking the
bum out himself. He could not. The alternative was what he
was already doing: leave her down there on the landing and
pursue his course to bed. To him, it was cold and draughty,

but to her, it was doubtless cosy, compared with the street. She had the coat over her and probably a lot of filthy sweaters underneath. In the morning, she would be stiff, but it would not take her long to get oiled again.

Till morning, nobody could find her. Madame Puel would not be prowling up the service stairs, and even if that happened, she could not know that *Peter* had seen the bum and failed to react. The woman could have crept in after he had gone to bed. Maybe when that night nurse came home, tired, she could have left the front door ajar. There could be lots of explanations.

The *minuterie* went off. In the dark, its natural element, the voice of conscience bayed. A Peter Levi law said: Do not do what thou wouldst not be known to have done. If an action tempted you to disclaim it, you had better think twice. He thought, groping along the wall for the light button. The pale light came on again, showing him the worn splintery stair treads. Highly inflammable. And of course it was the same *clocharde*, the heavy smoker. It had to be. He acknowledged the other alternative that had been picking at his sleeve, like a person waiting to be recognized.

Even when she opened her bleary eyes, the drunk woman did not understand what Peter wanted. His French did not get through the fumes of alcohol to her. He tried pointing upward and making encouraging signs, but her brain could not grasp that they were going to his apartment. At last he had her upright, and they started climbing, he leading the way and beckoning to her to follow, like Eurydice. She was younger than he thought at first – maybe only in her late thirties – and her features, though blurry, were soft and still feminine. She smelled of tobacco and sour stale booze, but at least she had not vomited recently. On the fourth-floor landing, she fell down, and he had trouble getting her to her feet again. She broke away from his grasp and began rolling heavily down the circular stairs. The last flight was an uphill battle all the way, with the *minuterie* constantly going off and plunging them into darkness. She took advantage of the dark to crawl away. Also she made quite a lot of noise. He was afraid his landlady would wake up. This showed him that his law needed some revision. There were times when you would not want to be caught performing a *good* action. While embarrassment played a part in his desire not to be discovered in the act of dragging a *clocharde* up to his apartment, his main motive was the fear that somebody would prevent him from carrying out the project. It was strange. Even now, the wish closest to his heart was that this female shambles would melt away, like a bad dream he might still wake from, yet at the same time, contradictorily, she had become an assignment he was determined to complete. And a big element in his determination was the resistance he could count on meeting in others, which in fact he was already meeting in the inert object herself.

Unlocking his door and switching on the light, he saw that she was cowering, afraid to come in and afraid, he guessed, to run away. The glazed terror in her eyes told him clearly that she expected *him* to murder *her* – a realization that made him laugh dourly. Maybe a female *clocharde* had reason to shrink from "normals", and his reassuring smiles, far from accomplishing their purpose, might be scaring her stiff. He could be a grinning sex maniac. Nevertheless, having looked around the room, she consented to come in.

He fixed her a place to sleep on the floor, next to the radiator, using his sheepskin-lined jacket and a chair cushion and praying that she would not be sick. He rolled up some sweaters for a pillow. Then he led her into his toilet and shut the door. When she failed to come out, he knocked. No reply. Eventually he went in and got her and propelled her to the bathroom with a clean towel. Again she did not emerge. For her, these were hiding-places. He found her huddled in the little bathtub. She had not washed. He guided her back into the living room. '*Voici votre lit, mademoiselle.*' For some reason, he could not call her '*madame*'. Then he showed her his own bed, to make it clear that she was safe. She responded only to signs, and the few thick unintelligible words she mumbled from time to time seemed to be addressed to somebody who was not him. After that, he got out a partly full

bottle of wine and poured her some in a glass. He gave her a
piece of stale bread, which was all he had, and some cheese.
She drank the wine and stretched out her glass for more.
'*Après*'. He pointed to the bread and cheese. '*Pain*'. Then
to the wine bottle. '*Puis vin*'.

So long as this dumb show went on, it was not so bad. But
finally the time came when he had to turn out the light. In the
dark, he slipped into the bathroom with his pyjamas, to get
undressed and washed. On reflection, he decided to sleep in
his pants and jersey, taking only his jacket and shoes off. He
could not tuck himself in, like a good little boy, in his nice
clean pyjamas, while the woman lay on the floor in her dirty
ragged coat. It did not seem right, even, to brush his teeth.

From his bed, he was unable to tell whether she was awake
or not. She hacked and hawked repeatedly, with a smoker's
cough, but perhaps she did that in her sleep. The hawking
made him feel sick, especially when it turned into choking and
a long-drawn-out noise like retching. He put his head under
the blanket and covered it with a pillow. He could not smell
any vomit, but the window was open. He wished he had a
flashlight so that he could creep across and make sure that
she had not puked over the landlady's cushion. But if she
had, what could he do? The only thing was to go to sleep and
forget about it till morning. But he could not fall asleep,
though after about an hour the *clocharde* was finally quiet.

He recited all the poems he knew and reviewed the Sistine
ceiling. Then as he started to drift off, a terrible thought hit
him. She might wake up and start smoking. After all the
fresh air he had had today, if he dropped into the arms of
Morpheus, he might never know the difference. In bringing
her up here, he had never thought of that. It meant that he
had only transferred the problem several stories higher. She
might still set her clothes on fire and burn up the building. It
was no great consolation that he would be among the first to
be incinerated. He thought sadly of Madame Puel. She would
never forgive him if she died on a widow's pyre.

He tried to remember what you did to put a fire out. You

were not supposed to use water but smother it with blankets. But he had only one blanket. He should have taken the woman's matches before he turned out the light. Now it was too late. If he woke her now, it might frighten her. He tiptoed across the room and put an ashtray beside her. Yet that was inadequate precaution. He saw what he had to do: stay awake and keep vigil, like the Dutch boy with his finger in the dyke. He did not believe that you had a duty to yourself nor maybe even to your family, but you owed something to a unit as large as a building.

These anxieties were giving him a perverse craving to smoke himself. In the toilet, he lit up. It had a tiny skylight, which he opened, so that the cigarette smoke would not filter under the door into the living room and put ideas in her head. But this stratagem destroyed his pleasure. He threw the cigarette into the toilet and flushed it away. There was an awful groaning and clanking of water pipes, which he feared might alert his landlady; he had strict orders never to pull the chain after 1 AM. When he came back to bed, the *clocharde* was snoring and making a gurgling noise herself.

Now that sleep was forbidden him, of course he got sleepy. But just as he was slipping into oblivion, a massive depression laid him low. It was the *clocharde*. A sort of swampy miasma was coming from her that he could sense, like something physical. She was poisoning his good deed.

He sought to analyse the bitter melancholy rising in his soul like heartburn. O.K., you were not meant to do good actions for *enjoyment* exactly, but they ought not to be so positively repugnant that you had to hold your nose morally while performing them. And that was just how he felt. Instead of being glad that he had helped somebody out, inexplicably he stank to himself. The only moment, he could honestly say, that had given him any pleasure was when he got her to eat the bread and cheese. Yet that was when he was teaching her, with a primitive little reward system, not to be a *clocharde* at least while she was in his apartment but to obey his house rules and drink her wine with food. Act like a fellow-creature. In short, she was only bearable for the few false minutes when he kidded himself that he was reforming her. But he had failed with the clean towel.

It had been a hideous mistake to share his four walls with misery and indigence even for one night. In fact he had no business bringing her here, unless he meant to keep her, which of course he did not. The sole ray of hope was that this cruel and unusual punishment could not last long. In the morning she would scram. She had stopped snoring. Maybe she too was counting the minutes till dawn. She would be no more eager than he was to repeat this experience. On that he would take a bet.

Yet the worst was that, even furnished with hindsight, he did not see what else one Peter Levi could have done than exactly what he did, which made the mistake in some crazy way irreparable. He could walk away from the problem in the street but not in his own building. The problem, as they said, had come home to him. He supposed he might have given her some money for a hotel – bribery.

Madame Puel had hit the nail on the head. '*C'est pas un asile, notre immeuble*'. In the Great Scheme of Things, the building had not been intended to be a *clochards'* dormitory. But what could you do when some *clochards* were insensible to the Great Scheme of Things and refused to *know their place*?

There was no solution. Silly's advice, to look on them as animals, did not meet the problem at all. Tossing in his sheets, Peter was feeling a nauseous repulsion which he would certainly not feel toward an animal. Between himself and this woman was an immeasurable distance that proximity of breathing accentuated. A sense of solidarity which alone could have justified his action was simply not there. If there had ever been any doubt, now he knew for sure that whatever happened to him in the way of degradation, he could never be a *clochard*. In fact it was much easier to picture himself, if ostracized by his fellow-men, in the form of a stray cat running from Madame Puel's broom.

As a stray cat, all bones and fur, he would be sympathetic to himself, whereas for himself as a *clochard* he would feel an ungovernable antipathy. Yet where was the difference? If a *clochard* had fleas, a cat had fleas. The stink of human urine was not any worse than the stink of cat pee. And as for a *clochard* becoming a permanent charge if you gave them money or fed them (which some of the kids at the American Centre alleged), the same could be said with more probability of an animal, which, once you fed it, was fairly certain to return. Finally, the nervous fear that human presence was inspiring in him had no rational basis: the danger of bodily attack was infinitely less than the danger of being scratched or bitten by a crazed beast.

Yet somehow she had him on the defensive, as if being himself was a form of hypocrisy. He was bracing himself against a latent aggression he sensed in her wild dirty hair and general foulness. He sorted out his thoughts. The menace was not to his person but to his sovereignty in the little kingdom he had constructed – his nest of Borromini angels, plants, books, *espresso* pot, student lamp, the drawing he was making, from nature, of a leaf. It was not these things, as *things*, these bits of organic and inorganic materials, towards which he felt protective. If a kitten or a puppy destroyed them, he would be reconciled to the havoc, since the animal was part of Mother Nature – his and Kant's respected friend. However a puppy in your room acted, you could brush your teeth and put on your pyjamas.

If this *clocharde* seemed more alien to him than any brute creature, it was just *because* she shared with him, supposedly, a moral faculty that animals did not have, and this moral faculty in man was a regulatory instinct that kept him in balance with the natural things of the world, which were good without putting out any effort. But it was hard to believe that there was any such universal moral faculty when you had a proof to the contrary a few feet away from you. If it was not the *clocharde*'s choice that she had got into this grisly state, then there was no freedom of the will, and if it *was* her choice, of which tonight he felt convinced, then the will's objects were not the same for everybody. Either way, everything he cared about fell to pieces. As for the great Know-yourself, after tonight, he would rather not. It was no use pretending that there was common humanity in *him* when all he could think of in the midst of his philosophizing was how many minutes still had to pass before dawn would come to his rescue.

Some time before dawn came, in fact, he fell asleep. When he woke, it was already light out; the improvised couch across the room was empty. There was a trail of urine going towards the door, which was partly open. She had stolen his outside brass doorknob, of all things, and he wondered how she had managed it. Did she carry tools? Otherwise his possessions were intact.

Fate had more in store for him. There was the news in the morning papers awaiting him in the kiosk at the Madeleine as he slogged to it through a downpour. All across the front page of the *Herald Tribune* in giant black letters: US PLANES BOMB NORTH VIETNAM BASE. So it had happened, but he refused to believe it yet; he had to see it in the New York *Times*. But the *Times* international edition was sold out, and he took the *Figaro*. 49 AVIONS US (*ayant décollés de trois porte-avions*) BOMBARDENT DES INSTALLATIONS AU NORD DU 17e PARALLELE. JOHNSON AUX FAMILLES AMERICAINES: 'ORDRE DE REGAGNER LES ETATS-UNIS'. It was in *The Times* of London too. There was no escaping it, any more than he could have eluded the *clocharde* once he found her in his path.

On top of everything, the dentist found a cavity. 'Blue Monday,' he said waggishly in his Berlitz English. When Peter got out of the chair, Silly was waiting for him. He had been reading the papers that Peter left and he looked pale. 'It's bad,' he agreed. 'But maybe it's just a one-shot thing. They say it's a reprisal.' Peter shook his head. 'Why would Johnson order American families home then? Your "poker game"!' 'Well, yes. Johnson betrayed us.' 'Our country! And we're part of it. I said I'd kill myself if we did this and I'm still alive.'

'Let's go to the zoo,' urged Silly. 'It helps usually'. 'O.K.' They decided to visit the menagerie at the Jardin des Plantes.

'We'll see my bear,' said Silly. 'That will cheer you up. He's such a nice neat bear. He rakes the leaves in his den.'

In preference to the Métro they took a bus. After last night, Peter could not stand any more confinement. He sat with his chin slumped on his chest while Silly tried to make conversation. 'That poor guy Benjy, remember? He willed me his PX card.' 'You mean he's dead?' 'No, no. That was only the expression he used. But now probably he's had it. We'll send regular troops; what do you think?' 'Yes.' 'But you and I don't have too much to worry about.' 'Why?' 'On account of our French, don't you see? Because we can speak French, they won't send us into combat. Even if they draft students like in World War II. They'll keep us back of the front lines, in Saigon, doing liaison with the high-up Vietnamese. I added that up last summer, when Goldwater was making his pitch.' 'I won't go,' said Peter. 'But how? Unless you're a Quaker or join the Peace Corps or something?' 'I don't know but I won't, that's all.'

They watched Silly's brown bear for a while, but he was not raking any leaves. ' "*Ursus arctos Linné*",' read Peter. 'Aristotle talks about him.' For a moment this made him feel better; at least a few of the things of the world were indestructible. The bear acted sad and somnolent; his fur was a dirty brown like an old worn coat. 'Probably he wants to hibernate. But the zoo-keepers won't let him. He has to entertain the public.' 'I'll pep him up,' said Silly. He started aiming peanuts at his nose. The animal's red lower lip came out like a shoehorn, and they saw his teeth and small tongue. Silly thought of a new sport. He aimed the peanuts just outside the bars, so that the bear had to put his paw out to pull them in. 'Hey, quit that! Don't you see that sign?' DANGER in yellow capitals was posted on the bear cage. 'He can't reach me.' 'Anyway, it's cruel,' objected Peter. 'No, it isn't. It's a game. I always play with him. He loves it.'

Peter felt quite relieved when they finally left the bear's den. Though he had been wishing to die all morning, he did not want a bear to get him. In the avalanche of events descending on him, that would be excessive. He proposed that they go explore the labyrinth at the other end of the park. But it was not a real maze, which he had been hoping for; they climbed up a hill and saw an old armillary sphere and a weather-vane. It was easy to find their way out. Going back to the menagerie, they passed a curious exhibit: a cross-section of a sequoia tree, donated by the State of California, through the American Legion, to the *Anciens Combattants de France*, 1927. Standing on its side, the sequoia slice looked like a ringed target with shiny copper markers fixed to the widening rings like metal flags, noting mammoth occurrences in world history corresponding with the tree's age at the time they happened: the Birth of Christ, the Destruction of Pompeii, Charlemagne, the Landing of the Pilgrims. Peter laughed bitterly. 'They should bring this up to date. "February 7, 1965. Uncle Sam bombs small helpless nation."' 'Maybe the start of World War III,' suggested Silly. 'You saw: Kosygin is in Hanoi.' 'I don't care if it's World War III,' said Peter. He did, but that was not the point.

Silly wanted to visit the monkey house. Peter objected. 'Let's look at some of the trees and plants instead.' It struck him that the closer Nature got to the human, the uglier it could be. You could hardly find a plant that was not beautiful, even if in a strange mottled way, but there were plenty of hideous simians. He wondered if it could happen that one morning he might wake up and find that trees, plants, and flowers did not seem beautiful to him any more. That would have to be the end of ethics. It might be starting to happen now. To his horror, the botanical garden had a derelict, desolate appearance, and the rows on rows of denuded plants with their pale green identifying markers reminded him of a cemetery. 'Did you know that Linnaeus tried to get a job as a gardener?' 'Oh?' 'Nobody would hire him.'

Silly was still pleading for the monkeys. They compromised. Peter would look at exotic birds, and he would look at gorillas and baboons. At an entrance gate, they were stopped. Without realizing it, they had left the paying section when they went to see the labyrinth. So if they wanted to come back in, they would have to pay again. Silly put up an argument. If

the attendant did not let them in free, they would crawl
under the fence. To Peter's astonishment, the gatekeeper let
them pass.

They walked by a pond of aquatic birds. Peter recognized
some Common European Cormorants drying their wings on
the rocks. It was cold and dismal. Scattered about the grounds
were strange neglected little wooden huts cookie-cut with
stars and circles and looking as if some crazy Russian or Finn
had made them up out of a fairy-tale-witch housing, with a
renard famélique pacing the door yard. They came to the
swans, which were floating down a dirty stream or canal.
Some were waddling on their flipper feet across the grass.
'Hey, a black swan!' said Silly. 'Let's feed him.' Leaning
over the wire fence, he coaxed the swan to approach. They
both put peanuts on the iron fencebar and watched him
crack them in his coral-red bill. A white swan with a banded
leg came up. Silly tried to engage it in a staring match, but
the swan after a minute turned its head away and flapped its
wings rather crossly. He tossed peanuts between the two
birds to get them to compete.

Wearied of playing witness to this, Peter ate a few peanuts
himself. In his pocket, wrapped in a Kleenex, was a brioche
he had bought for breakfast and been unable to eat. He consumed part of that. He did not know much about swans, but
it seemed to him that they were becoming quarrelsome, and
he grew irritated with Silly for stirring up needless strife
among these captive creatures, now noisily bristling their
feathers. 'Leave them alone. Let's go.' But Silly was having
fun. As a counter-move, Peter tore up his brioche and
whistled to the black swan to come to him. Diverted, the
bird drew near. It slithered its neck along the ground like an
uncoiling garden hose, causing some sparrows to scatter.
Instead of throwing the crumbs, Peter held them out to see
if it would eat from his hand. ' "*Qu'ils mangent la brioche,*" ' he
said. Then he felt a sharp pain in the fleshy part of his palm,
the part bounded by his life line. The bird had struck at him
savagely. Before he could pull back, he felt another gash, in
his forearm, and a third. He heard his voice screaming '*No-*'

Reeling away from the low iron fence, he flung up his hand to protect his face. It faintly surprised him that the swan did not take wing and continue the attack. Silly supported him to a bench. Blood was trickling from his hand and staining his shirtcuff, but when he nerved himself to examine them, the gashes did not seem as deep as he expected. Silly had thought it was an artery. 'Or a vein anyway. Should I try to make a tourniquet?' 'No. It'll be O.K. But I think I'd like to go home now.' He accepted Silly's offer to take him in a taxi. They wrapped his hand and wrist up in their handkerchiefs, which were clean, thanks to the dental appointment.

Silly left him at his door and sped on to a pharmacy for Mercurochrome and Band-Aids. Fortunately, Madame Puel's door-curtains were drawn. Peter could not face her now. He did not want to answer any questions that might arise about the doorknob. When Silly appeared with supplies, they laved his wounds with a whole bottle of Mercurochrome and applied the Band-Aids. Silly wondered whether they should call Roberta. 'No.' He fixed Peter some coffee and went to a café and brought back sandwiches and hard-boiled eggs, which he insisted on paying for. He was still blaming himself. Then he remade Peter's tousled bed. 'You'd better try to sleep now.'

Peter was in a bed, which he suspected was in the American Hospital. He could not remember anything clearly about the last few days. The last he could recall was the swellings in his armpits which had convinced him, when he studied them in his mirror, that he had bubonic plague. They were just like the buboes *Boccaccio* described with pungent detail in the *Decameron*. Now he asked himself whether he was in a private room or in an isolation ward. He could not guess how he had got here or when. Had he turned himself in or had somebody brought him? He had a faint recollection of leaving class some morning in the middle of a lecture. He thought he would remember riding in an ambulance.

His bed was cranked down flat. There was nobody around now. But there had been a great many people in his room

quite recently, he believed. Doctors and nurses and, if he
was not mistaken, the Bonfantes, who had looked rather
awed. But if the Bonfantes had been here, he could not have
the plague. He felt that Silly Boy had been around too and
maybe Roberta but he was not sure. Some of his visitors must
have been imaginary. He assumed he had been delirious and
even now he could tell he had a fever. He drank some water
through a glass straw from a glass on his bedside table.

He tried to think back carefully. It seemed as if he had
fallen down on a tiled floor that might have been in a hospital
bathroom. After that, a total blackout. Reaching under the
hospital nightshirt, he explored his armpits; the buboes
appeared to be gone. Then his lucidity faded; he lost the
order of his thoughts. Somebody was taking his temperature
and feeling his pulse. But before he could ask her anything,
she went away. When he opened his eyes again, he was
pleasantly surprised to see the Delphic Sibyl. He recognized
her immediately; she was wearing that green peaked bonnet.
She must have come to tell him something, and he had the
feeling that she had tried to before, some other day. But
while he waited eagerly for her to unroll the prophetic scroll
she was holding, she began smiling on him with extreme
tenderness and was replaced by his mother, who also had a
roll of paper in her hand, which opened up into a valentine.

She bent down and kissed him. 'Well, Peter,' she said
fondly, pulling at his forelock. 'You've had quite an adventure.' That insanely cheerful sentence proved she was real –
the fair Rosamund coming out of her bower to interrupt the
Delphic Sibyl. Now he would never know what was in the
message. But at least she could tell him where he was. He
was right: it was the American Hospital. He had come in
with a bad infection; the Platt boy had brought him. It
actually was Valentine's Day; he had been here since Friday.
'But what happened?' 'They gave you penicillin, and you
went into shock. Somebody should have realized you were
allergic to penicillin.' 'Who?' Peter began to feel suspicious.
He was not aware of having any such allergy. She was covering up something. Maybe he was dying. He reflected. He

must be wrong. If he were dying, Bob would have come too. And his father would be stalking up and down, wearing a black frown and a black suit, looking for somebody to blame, preferably his mother. Sitting up, he imitated his voice: ' "Didn't you *know* the boy was allergic to penicillin?" '

'You must be feeling better, Peter. In fact that's what *babbo* said. But I don't think you ever had it. Just Aureomycin and those things. They don't give penicillin to children usually.' 'But what was the matter, that they gave it to me now? I thought I had the Black Death.' His mother gave her gay laugh. 'Swan bite, dearest. Don't you remember? You were bitten by a black swan. Just like a person in a myth.' 'Swans don't bite, Mother. They strike with their bill.' 'I prefer swan bite.' This insistence made Peter feel tired. 'They're extremely dangerous,' his mother went on. 'The doctor told me they can break an arm with one blow of their bill. You might have had a fracture too. The Platt boy says it was his fault.' 'It was. But never mind. What did I have – rabies?' 'I don't think swans are rabid, Peter. The doctor didn't mention that. A heavy infection, he said.' Peter nodded. 'Polluted water. But I washed the wounds out well with Mercurochrome. Every day.' 'So the doctor told me. You looked like a fire-engine. But you could have used a gallon of Mercurochrome, and it wouldn't have helped, he said. Mercurochrome is only good for superficial cuts, Peter.' 'Did you know that?' 'Not really.'

Peter's head was aching. She touched his forehead. 'You still have a little temperature. You'd better not talk any more. I'll sit here and read.' 'Have you been here before, Mother?' 'Yesterday, I came from the airport. You were delirious then.' 'Am I really going to be all right, Mother? Tell me the truth.' 'Absolutely, Peter. By tomorrow, your fever should be gone. But you'll be weak for a few days. On top of everything else, you fainted in the bathroom, from the penicillin, and may have had a slight concussion.' He lay back. 'Oh, God!' he cried, remembering. 'Are we still bombing those Vietnamese?' She nodded. Tears of rage rolled out of his eyes. 'I hate us.' 'They claim it's only military targets.' 'Do you believe that?' 'No.' 'Have we hit Hanoi?' She shook her head. 'So until that happens,' said Peter, 'we can feel it's all O.K., eh, Ma? They get us used to it by slowly increasing the dose. So we build up a tolerance.'

She smoothed his pillow and persuaded him to lie down. In a minute, he started up again. Everything was coming back. 'Is the State Department sending you to Poland?' He could see from her face that it was. 'You'll have to cancel.' 'Oh, Peter, you exaggerate. It's just music. Music isn't political.' 'You know better than that, Rosamund.' 'But I can't, at the last minute. If I'd known before . . . A performer can't do that.' 'You have to, Mother. Believe me.'

For a while, they did not talk. He actually dozed. Then a maid brought in his supper tray and cranked him up. 'It's your first meal,' his mother said, smiling. 'But I hear you had quite a lot of company. Finally they put a "No Visitors" sign on your door.' 'Who was here?' 'The Scott girl. She's delightful, Peter. And the Platt boy, of course. What a strange creature! I used to know his father, in New York, before I was married. In fact he was one of my suitors.'

Peter was too weary to reflect on the dynastic implications of this. If his mother had married Silly's father, who would he be? He saw that the fair Rosamund was hoping to divert him from the ukase he had issued and he did not mind being diverted, because he knew that in the end she would yield. She needed a little time for the point to sink in. What shook him was that it should have taken her nineteen-year-old son to make plain to her that there were things she could not do. And how had Bob let her get this far on the State Department tab? Peter pitied them both and his mother especially. She had no authority for him any more.

'Who else was there? Come on, keep the ball rolling, Mother.' 'I think your adviser came.' 'Did they let him in? God, I hope not.' His mother was not sure. 'Some just left their names. You seem to have made an extraordinary number of friends. You've been holding a regular levee here. Your concierge is very concerned about you, by the way. She sent you a Get Well card. Here it is.' Peter looked at the card. 'Oh? You went to my apartment?' 'I'm staying there. I hope you don't mind.' Actually Peter was glad. He could count on her anyway to water the plants. 'It's strange, your doorknob was stolen. How do you account for that, Peter? And the Platt boy didn't lock up when you left. The concierge thinks a derelict must have been sleeping in your room.'

Peter gulped. He wondered what his mother would do if the *clocharde* returned while she was there. The thought afforded him some disconsolate amusement. It would be interesting to see *her* tested. But that was unfair, since he would have left her the problem as a legacy. Moreover, to do her justice, she was the only adult in the world he would trust with the full story of that night. But today was not the moment. Instead, he decided to tell her about the visit of *la Delfica*. 'How marvellous! What a nice delirium!' She looked rather proud, as though her son had made a three-star acquaintance. 'I think you must have had several imaginary visitors. All your helpers and hinderers. Yesterday you were talking very volubly.' ' I had a few.' 'Who were the others? Tell me.' Peter shook his head. 'Oh, please, Peter!' 'No.'

He had remembered. A shivery sadness crept through him; he pulled the sheet over his head. He did not want to talk any more, 'Please go away, Mother, for a little while. Call up and cancel your ticket. I want to think.'

The visitor had been sitting quietly at the foot of his bed, waiting for Peter to wake up – a small man, scarcely five feet high, in an unbuttoned twill jacket with a white stock. It looked as if he had been there quite a while. His hair was curled in sausages and powdered – or was it a periwig? – and fastened behind with a grey bow. He was in the prime of life; around his bright vivacious eyes were crow's-feet, which showed intensive thought. Peter knew him at once, and he evidently had known Peter for a long time, though this was their first meeting. Breaking with his lifelong habit, he had come all the way from Königsberg because Peter was sick. He was making a double exception, since, Peter recalled, he always shunned sick rooms.

'When you were young, you wrote an ode to the West Wind,' Peter said, to show how lovingly he had collected every fact about him. '*Theory of Winds*,' the little man emended. 'Oh of course. How stupid! I'm sorry. The way I feel, my brain gets things a bit confused. Actually, I've never read it.' 'It doesn't matter,' said Kant. 'And you were for the French Revolution,' prompted Peter. But that was not what his mentor had come to talk about. 'I was thinking of you yesterday,' Peter went on, not letting the visitor speak in his excitement at having him here. 'I guess it was yesterday. In the Jardin des Plantes. Something our professor said you said about the beautiful things in the world proving that man is made for and fits into the world and that his perception of things agrees with the laws of his perception. It sounded better when he read it in German.' ' "*Die schönen Dinge zeigen an . . .*" *Ach, ja!*' Kant bowed his head and sighed.

'Excuse me, sir, you have something to tell me, don't you?' The tiny man moved forward on the counterpane and looked Peter keenly in the eyes, as though anxious as to how he would receive the message he had to deliver. He spoke in a low weak voice. 'God is dead,' Peter understood him to say. Peter sat up. 'I *know* that,' he protested. 'And you didn't say that anyway. Nietzsche did.' He felt put upon, as though by an impostor. Kant smiled. 'Yes, Nietzsche said that. And even when Nietzsche said it, the news was not new, and maybe not so tragic after all. Mankind can live without God.' 'I agree,' said Peter. 'I've always lived without him.' 'No, what *I* say to you is something important. You did not hear me correctly. Listen now carefully and remember.' Again he looked Peter steadily and searchingly in the eyes. 'Perhaps you have guessed it. Nature is dead, *mein Kind*.'